JOURNEY
TO
ENCHANTMENT

Also by Patricia Veryan

Practice to Deceive
Sanguinet's Crown
The Wagered Widow
The Noblest Frailty
Married Past Redemption
Feather Castles
Some Brief Folly
Nanette
Mistress of Willowvale
Love's Duet
The Lord and the Gypsy

JOURNEY TO ENCHANTMENT

by
Patricia Veryan

St. Martin's Press
New York

Design by Doris Borowsky

Library of Congress Cataloging in Publication Data
Veryan, Patricia.
Journey to enchantment.

I. Title.
PS3572.E766J6 1986 813'.54 86-3699
ISBN 0-312-44513-X

First Edition

10 9 8 7 6 5 4 3 2 1

For Jorge—
the dearest
and best of sons-in-law

PART ONE

Scotland

I

Inverness, Scotland
June, 1746

The breeze came up soon after noon, brisk and cool, to dance with the treetops and hurry the fluffy white clouds in their journey across the deep blue serenity of the sky. The sunlight kissed the waves with palest gold, sparkling against the long spread of sapphire that was Loch Ness set amid the emerald of field and hill and backed by rugged crags and hills that rose to the distant masses of the mountains. Far down the Great Glen, the solemn might of ruined Urquhart Castle jutted into the cold waters, and the mountain of Mealfuarvonie, lofty and impervious, kept watch over all. A sight, surely, to gladden the heart of any Scot; to awaken feelings of *joie de vivre* or inspire poetic thoughts on the beauties of creation.

The horse that followed the road, however, came not at a leisured pace, but at the gallop. The rider, leaning forward in the saddle, her dark blue habit billowing in the wind, the long feather in her broad-brimmed hat drawn out of curl by the speed of her progress, saw none of the rural delights, her concentration bent upon weightier matters. Having quite outdistanced her two attendant grooms, she left the hated road General Wade had built to help put down the Highlands and turned into a narrow lane leading down towards the water where the tower of a large house could be seen above a fine stand of trees. The girl rode on through sun-dappled woods to emerge onto broad, neatly scythed lawns and gain a full view of the thick-walled grey stone manor house and the structure beside it that had caused many guests to halt in astonishment: a good-sized pyramid.

The headlong approach of the horse brought a gardener to his feet. He waved and shouted a greeting. The girl waved back, but did not slow her mount until she reached the house, at the last moment pulling back on the reins so that the pretty mare snorted and danced at the foot of the steps.

A groom came running. "Whisht, Miss Prue! Will it be more trouble, then?"

Prudence MacTavish leaned to be lifted down. "Not for us, praise God," she said, a smile brightening her heart-shaped face. "Jamie MacDougall's safe away, thanks to Ligun Doone!"

The groom let out a whoop and tossed his bonnet in the air. "Long life and happiness tae the mon! He's a magician!"

Prudence grinned, took up her train with an impatient hand, and started to the steps.

The groom called, "The MacTavish isnae alone, miss."

She checked momentarily, glancing back at him, then hurried on. It would likely be old Duncan MacKie on his way home from Inverness and stopping to rail against Butcher Cumberland and his murderers. Or Sir Matthew Garry, his grey whiskers bristling with wrath because of the edict against the wearing of Highland dress.

Prudence hurried into the main hall and gave her hat and gloves to the footman who came to take them and remark with a hint of disapproval that the master was in the book room "wi' a guest." That meant someone less comfortable than family or old friends, but unwilling to go upstairs to tidy her hair or put off her riding habit, Prudence crossed to the golden mirror that hung on one wall and peered at herself.

The gallop had brought roses into her cheeks, and her powdered hair made her slightly tanned skin seem the darker by contrast. 'Blowsy!' she thought disparagingly and scanned her features without pleasure. Despite the fact that her hair was a light golden-red, she was the fortunate possessor of dark brows and lashes. With the latter she could find no fault, for they curled upward in a thick fringe about her deep blue eyes, but her brows were inclined to be peaked rather than arching, and, although well-defined, were too thick. Her cheekbones failed to please, for they were not as finely etched and dainty as she would have liked, and her nose had a slight upward tilt at the end rather than being classically straight and thin. Her mouth she had to admit was nicely curved, but rather too wide, and her chin was firm and undimpled. It was a young face, for she had just turned nineteen, and it was comely enough, as many a Scots lad had told her, but she admired the pale fragility that was the current mode, wherefore her red lips tightened, and, 'Blowsy!' she thought again.

She coaxed her ringlets into some semblance of order, tidied her habit, and turned towards the rear of the house and the book room.

It was a charming old house and, although fortified in the style of the earlier tower houses, had a quiet elegance that managed also to be welcoming and comfortable. The entrance hall was large and impressive with rich wainscoting from floor to ceiling. The portrait of a handsome young Scot in full Highland regalia hung defiantly above the great hearth on the east wall, and towards the rear of the room a fine staircase rose to the upper floors.

Prudence noted in some surprise that several valises and portmanteaux were piled neatly at the foot of the stairs, and she stared at them, wondering why her father had neglected to inform her that they were to entertain company. A smile crept into her eyes. How foolish to expect the MacTavish to follow a logical pattern. Amiable but absent-minded, he had likely decided this morning that he must tell his daughter of the imminent arrival of some friend or scientist, but long before he started down to the breakfast parlour his thoughts would have gone winging off to some dig in Egypt, or to the lecture he was to deliver at Edinburgh next month.

She would scold him, she decided, but gently. And then she would have to see if their housekeeper, the redoubtable Mrs. Cairn, must be placated.

The east hall was quiet, the sunbeams slanting peacefully through the open door of the main dining room and laying a shadowy outline of the latticed windows upon the pegged oak floors. The book room was also quiet, and Prudence went in, glad to find her father alone after all.

James MacTavish looked what he was: a gentle intellectual trapped in a savage world. He was a lean gentleman of middle height, with greying fair hair and rather myopic blue eyes, and a tendency to postpone anything that did not concern his preoccupation with archaeology. Just now he was standing behind his desk, frowning down at a letter he held, but he looked up as the door opened and smiled at his daughter. "Prudence, m'dear," he began.

"I've the most splendid news, Papa," she interrupted exuberantly. "The filthy Sassenachs were not able to drag Jamie MacDougall to his death! He's safely away, thanks to Li—" She checked, warned by her father's slight frown and the small but cautionary lift of one hand.

"We've a guest, Prue," he said in his mild voice. "Thaddeus, may I present my daughter?" He walked out from behind the desk as he spoke and, following his gaze, Prudence closed the half-opened door and discovered an elegant gentleman standing beyond it. "Prudence," went on MacTavish, "this is Lord Thaddeus Briley."

Frightened, and repenting her besetting sin of impulsiveness, Prudence sank into a curtsey. With a graceful flourish of his lace-trimmed handkerchief, his lordship bowed. As he straightened, her eyes swept him in a rapid appraisal. He looked to be about thirty-two or three. His features were even but unremarkable, his complexion light, his height average. Upon his head he wore the latest style of French wig, and a small patch graced his right cheekbone. His slender form was enclosed in a magnificently cut coat of dull gold velvet, the great cuffs and the pockets heavy with gold braid. A richly embroidered brown waistcoat, immaculate breeches of gold satin, cream-coloured stockings with golden clocks, and high-heeled brown shoes with topaz buckles completed his attire. Prudence thought, 'Good heavens! The creature is a dandy!'

Correctly interpreting the scorn in her lovely eyes, his lordship said apologetically, "I'd—er, not meant to hide from you, Mith MacTavith. I wath admiring thith oil. Your father told me you painted it." He smiled tentatively. It was a singularly charming smile, and Prudence noted belatedly that he had very fine eyes of an unusual tawny shade, but she thought, 'He is not only a dandy, but also an Englishman! And he has chosen his colours to match his eyes! Sickening!' Her smile should have deposited a film of ice upon his elegance. She said, "How do you do, sir? My apologies, Papa. I'd not meant to intrude. I shall leave you." She turned to go but, struck by a sudden terrible thought, enquired, "Does his lordship stay with us, sir?"

Her face was a betraying mirror of her emotions, and amusement came into Briley's tawny eyes. Mr. MacTavish, however, looked unwontedly stern. "That pleasure," he said, "is denied us."

Prudence stared at him, taken aback by his obvious censure over her manner towards this enemy.

His lordship vouchsafed with shy earnestness, "Brought a friend here, ma'am. But he won't be no trouble, do atthure you. Very good kind of fellow."

Prudence looked uncertainly to her father. "A—friend, Papa?"

"Yes, my dear. A friend of your brother's."

Her eyes lit up. "Ah! He'll be a Scot, then."

MacTavish glanced apologetically at Lord Briley. "Captain Delacourt is ill, I regret to say. I assure you, my lord, that he will be made comfortable here, despite"—he fixed his daughter with a grim look—"despite appearances to the contrary."

Prudence flushed, curtseyed, mumbled an incoherent apology, and fled, all too aware that, as usual, she had behaved in a gauche, ill-mannered way. Lord Briley was a dandified Englishman, but he was acquainted with her brother and her father, besides being a guest under their roof, and twice she had embarrassed him. She went disconsolately to the stairs, sighing over her clumsiness.

A wiry-looking individual a few years on the light side of forty was gathering up the last two valises. He put down his burdens when he saw Prudence approaching, and bowed respectfully. His scratch wig slipped a little, and he clapped a bony hand to straighten it.

"Good day," said Prudence pleasantly, for the servant could not help it if his master was a slimy Sassenach. "I am Miss MacTavish. Are you in the service of our guest?"

"Aye, miss," he replied in an unexpectedly deep bass voice. "A verra fine gentleman is the Captain. And me name is Lockerbie, ma'am."

The accent was broad Scots, and come to think of it, the MacTavish had not said their *guest* was English. The shadow lifted from her heart. "It is a Scottish gentleman, then! I might have known my father would not be offering a bed to a Sassenach!"

The thin shoulders drew back and the scrawny head lifted proudly. "Captain Delacourt is an Englishman, miss. And a right fine one, I'll hae ye tae know," he declared with an almost fierce defiance.

"Indeed?" said Prudence haughtily.

"Ye forget your place, ma wee mon," asserted another female voice from close at hand.

Prudence turned eagerly to the housekeeper, and the manservant stared as though transfixed. A fine figure of a woman was Mrs. Cairn, small of stature, large of spirit, her body softly rounded, her dark hair always neat and glossy, and her pleasant face set off by a pair of large grey eyes that were at the moment flashing with indignation.

"Ye will do well tae get yon great pile o' luggage cleared away frae the hallway rather than standing aboot saucing y'r betters," she went on sharply.

"It was a misunderstanding, merely," said Prudence. "I'd thought Lockerbie's gentleman a Scot."

"More's the pity he isnae," muttered the housekeeper.

Lockerbie gathered his impedimenta and made his laden way up the stairs grumbling *sotto voce* about the hospitality in this house.

With a pang of guilt Prudence said, "Poor fellow, he does look overburdened. Are there no footmen or maids to help him?"

"They're all busy." Mrs. Cairn glanced at Prudence, and her mulish expression softened. She said with a grin, "Too busy tae be spared fer aiding the likes o' that dirty turncoat, at all events. A fine thing fer a free Scot tae be fetching and carrying fer a Sassenach! And an officer o' murdering redcoats at that! Miss Prue, what in the worrruld is the MacTavish aboot?"

Had anyone else dared to question an action of her father, even so bewildering an action as this, Prudence would have fired up in immediate defence of him. She had a suspicion, however, that the pretty little widow regarded the MacTavish with a particularly fond eye, and that her father's interest was more than a little engaged in that direction, and thus she only sighed and said with regret that she understood Captain Delacourt to be a friend of Master Robert's. "Have you seen him, Carrie?"

"A glimpse only and 'twas more than enough!"

The hostility in the grey eyes was marked, so that Prudence felt obliged to point out that her father *had* invited the Captain to stay here. "We must not allow him to carry away a poor notion of Scots hospitality, must we? Besides, I understand he is ill. What ails the man?"

"Ah dinna ken," declared Mrs. Cairn, folding her arms across her ample bosom. "One can but hope that whatever 'tis, 'twill prove fatal and we'll hae one less Sassenach tae fash the wearrry worrruld!"

The robe *à la française* hanging from the open door of the clothes press was light blue, the low neckline and the front openings embroidered with white, and the underdress of white satin. It was one of James MacTavish's favourite gowns and, having selected it with a judicious eye to charming her papa at dinner that evening, Prudence clung to a chair whilst her abigail tightened the laces of her stays, then draped her wrapper about her. It was a minute or two before she recovered her breath and seated herself at her dressing table. Despite her own anxieties, her attention was not upon her own reflection, however, her blue eyes wide as they fixed upon her abigail's round, pleasant face. "He . . . fought at Prestonpans?" she echoed incredulously. "And—and still my papa allows him in our house?"

Kitty Campbell nodded, her light brown curls bobbing under the snowy mob cap. "Aye. But the MacTavish is a canny body, Miss Prue. He'll hae his reasons, for all it seems crazy."

Prudence tried to gather her thoughts. "Do you know what ails him?"

Kitty fastened a velvet bluebird amongst her mistress's high-piled curls and said after a moment's consideration that it was possibly the onset of old age.

"Foolish girl! I dinna mean the MacTavish—and he's neither old nor feeble!—I mean this Captain, whatever his name is."

"Ah. Well, his mon says as he took a piece of shell casing through his shoulder in the battle. I doot they expected him tae survive it."

Flinching a little, Prudence said, "But the Battle of Prestonpans was fought last September. Is he *still* so very ill of his wound?"

"Aye. In a verra bad way. His mon says he was improving, but wouldnae rest, and then they'd tae smuggle him away frae Prestonpans and couldnae get tae the Border, so had tae come up here. He went intae a decline, for which ye couldnae hardly blame him. 'Tis a long, horrid time the puir laddie's been through, no question."

"Poor laddie, indeed," snorted Prudence, recovering her sense of values. "Is a monster, and likely murdered scores of our fine Highlanders before he received his just deserts!" She handed Kitty her pearls and, as they were fastened about her white throat, enquired, "What like is this Sassenach?"

"Och, I've not set eyes on him, Miss Prue. But Mrs. Cairn said he wasnae all *that* great on looks—a puir puny thing, she said, and will likely die on us, for the steel pierced his lung and he's surely doomed."

Appalled, despite herself, Prudence said a rather feeble, "Oh. Well, it's none of my bread and butter, save to hope he repents his sins before he meets his God." Following which pious observation, she went down the hall to see if her aunt had been able to learn anything of their unwelcome guest.

Mrs. Hortense MacTavish was the relict of James MacTavish's younger brother, Victor. She was a pale, willowy lady with the aristocratically fine features her niece yearned to possess, white fluttery hands, and the constitution of an ox. In her youth she had been a great beauty, and several odes and one very bad sonnet had been written in her honour. The composer of the sonnet, a tragically inclined young man, had entitled his effort "Hortense, Ethereal Queen of Moonlight." James, who had been wont to play rounders with the 'Queen of Moonlight,' thought this hilarious and had for years teased his sister-in-law unmercifully about what he delighted to refer to as her robustly ethereal shade. Hortense, however, had thought it delicious and romantical, and had ever since attempted to live up (or down) to the appellation, wearing wispy dresses, insisting upon draping a length of zephyr about her hair and developing what was to prove a lasting, and often irksome, interest in matters astrological. She had not been blessed with children, a circumstance for which she chose to hold her husband responsible, ignoring the well-known fact that Victor had two sturdy sons by his mistress. Hortense had moved in with her brother-in-law when James' wife had died of blood poisoning from a blistered heel, and in her erratic fashion had done her best to mother his two energetic children. Robert had been her darling, and she had indulged herself with orgies of lamentation when he'd ridden off to join the forces of Bonnie Prince Charlie, but she was also genuinely fond of Prudence and now looked up from her desk with a welcoming smile as her niece came into her private parlour.

"My love," she said in an almost audible voice, "how charmingly you look. Never say I did not warn you."

Accustomed to both the whispering voice and trailing wisps, Prudence tripped to the bed and arranged herself on the end of it. "Warn me about what, Aunty Mac?"

With mild interest Hortense watched one of her shawls drift to the floor. "That a tall, dark, and handsome man would enter your life before the moon was at the full. You chose not to heed me. As everyone chooses not to heed me, alas. But it was written in the stars. All the signs were confirming. And you see, dearest Prue, that I was perfectly right." She removed her attention from the now motionless defector, and rested a patient smile upon her amused niece. "Laugh, then. But"—she raised her white hand in a graceful gesture of emphasis—"one of these days you all will be obliged to cease your mockery."

Prudence jumped up and ran to hug her. "Of course we do not mock you, dear one. We love you—you know that." She kissed the cheek lifted to her and went back to her perch, remarking, "But I think you are not quite right this time, you know, for you said 'tall and handsome' and from what Cairn says, our horrid intruder—"

"Prue! Your papa's guest!"

"—horrid Englishman is neither tall nor handsome."

"Cairn!" sniffed Hortense, forgetting, as she occasionally did, to be ethereal. "Much she knows of it! She is so biased she'd likely think an Englishman a goblin were he a veritable Adonis. You may believe *me,* Prudence. The laddie is both tall *and* handsome, and has the prettiest dark curls, for all they were tangled on his pillows when I saw him." She hove a tragic sigh. "So young to die, poor boy."

Curiosity getting the best of her, Prudence restrained an indignant comment. "So you've seen him. *Is* he going to die, do you think? I hope not. It would be purely wretched to have a funeral from Lakepoint."

Shocked, Hortense mourned the fact that her niece had been sweetly gentle as a bairn. "When did you become so heartless? If you could but have seen him lying there, his fine face all white and wasted and lined with suffering, yet"—she clapped a handkerchief to her lips and went on, fainter than ever—"yet smiled at me . . . so bravely."

Prudence was finding it difficult to maintain her callous air, for there could be little doubt but that her aunt was genuinely affected. She said uneasily, "Never cry, Aunty Mac. We'll contrive to coddle the creature, I've no doot, though *I'll* have none of him! Oh, all right! Never go into the boughs! I'll speak politely tae him—no matter how many he may hae foully murdered wi' his bluidy sabre!"

Hortense shuddered and said wiltingly, "How like you are to your sire, poor child. The angrier you become, the more broad is your speech."

Bristling, Prudence decided not to wait for her aunt and departed in search of her father.

She found him in the book room, as usual, dressed for dinner but poring over a tattered, leather-bound volume. He looked at her vaguely, then his eyes lit up when he saw her demurely clad in her great-skirted gown, her pearls, and her powder. Prudence cast down her eyes and, with her hands loosely clasped before her, said meekly, "I have made you angry, Papa. Indeed, I did not mean to, and am very sorry."

She expected him to put down his book and come and kiss her and say she was a naughty puss but that there was no prettier girl in all of Scotland and the Isles. Instead, there was a silence. Stealing a glance at him, she saw that he had set the book on the reference table and stood frowning down at his hand still resting on the closed volume. Dismay touched her. Was he really very angry? Over a miserable Sassenach? Astonished, she cried, "Papa? I dinna understand this business!"

He smiled suddenly and came over to her. "Of course you do not, child," he said, dropping a kiss on her temple. "Wherefore, I must explain." He led her to sit beside him on the brocaded cushions of the window seat. "We are," he said slowly, "indebted to Captain Dela-court."

Prudence watched him, her curiosity deepening by reason of the remark and his infinitesimal stumble over the name. "How?" she asked baldly.

"He was, ah, kind to your brother. Er, when they were at school."

"I suppose that means Rob was under the hatches, as usual, and—"

"And I could wish he had not taught you that shocking cant! Further, Miss Sauce, your brother was not in just that—particular kind of embarrassment. The point is not what he suffered, but that our guest came to his rescue at a—a time he needed help." Here, noting that his daughter's gaze was lowered but that her chin was rebellious, MacTavish seized the latter article and tilted it up so that her stormy eyes met his. "We are *indebted* to the gentleman," he reiterated firmly. "And he truly is a gentleman. I'd hoped you'd be away by now to your aunt in Edinburgh, but—" He broke off, then finished, "I must insist that you treat him with courtesy. And that you welcome his friends, should they come here."

She took his hand and held it in both her own. "Such as that silly wee Sassenach who came tripping and lisping here today?"

MacTavish frowned and stood. He was not a large man, nor of intimidating aspect, but when angered he was impressive. He was angered now, and realizing for the first time how deep were his feelings in this matter, Prudence gazed up at him, her heart beginning to flutter with fright.

"Lord Thaddeus Briley," said MacTavish in a voice of ice, "is, I grant you, an Englishman. He is also a very good man. That this recent folly occurred to bring down such bloodshed and grief upon our dear land is a tragedy beyond belief. I fear it is a tragedy with ramifications we Scots have yet to feel. For those of us who were not enamoured of your handsome Prince, it is a deeper tragedy. And I remind you, Prudence, that many English gentlemen fought for the Jacobite Cause and have given up their lives because of it."

She had already come to her feet and, shaken but stubborn, she countered, "Aye, sir. But our guest did not! He was a Captain in the service of that German usurper! He is one of the very men our Robbie fought, and we—"

"That will *do!*" The voice was not loud, but Prudence shrank. "I have extended the hand of hospitality to Captain Delacourt. If you, by word or deed, offend him, you besmirch the honour of our house. And that, Prudence, I will not tolerate!"

Pale and trembling, her head bowed, she was silent.

"Do you understand me?" demanded the MacTavish.

"Aye, sir," she whispered, fighting tears.

"Thank you. Tomorrow, is he well enough, I shall take you up and introduce you to our Captain. You will please to be available at two of the clock."

Dinner was not a pleasant meal that evening. The servants were as quietly efficient as ever but by their tight lips and flashing eyes conveyed their resentment of the situation. Hortense was in a reminiscent mood, and her soft voice prosed on interminably about her late husband's bosom bow, Major Flitton, who had fallen at Prestonpans. It was an unfortunate topic that did nothing to ease the tension. MacTavish maintained a politely attentive attitude and made an occasional attempt to change the subject. Not a sullen girl, Prudence was devastated by this first serious quarrel with her father and could scarcely touch her food, much less contribute her share of the conversation. She had seldom been more relieved than when the meal came to an end and her aunt led the way to the drawing room.

"Now, my love," said Hortense, as soon as the butler had served them their coffee and departed, "what is it that has you so up in the boughs? Is it the Englishman?"

"Papa said . . . that I must be polite to the wretched creature. And him lying above stairs in comfort and luxury while fine gentlemen like my dear brother and—and Jamie MacDougall fly for their lives with those damned hounds behind them, fairly slathering to haul them to the nearest firing squad!"

"Prue!" squealed Hortense, so agitated that two of her scarves slithered to the floor. "If your papa did but hear you *swear!*"

Dashing away tears with an angry hand, Prudence said, "Och, awie! He couldnae be more displeased wi' me than he is the noo! We never quarrel, Aunty Mac. Never! And now, because of this—this Englishman! Oh! I hate Captain whatever his name is! I *hate* him!"

"I warned you, child. Remember?" The widow's large hazel eyes took on the expression that Robert MacTavish had been wont irreverently to dub her 'Ophelia look.' "The stars told me," she half whispered, "that with his coming this family would be rent asunder. That our lives would be changed forever and ever. . . ."

Her ready sense of humour reviving, Prudence resisted the impulse to add 'Amen,' and instead gave a snort. "Huh! Then they were right for once! Only look at us—poor Rob an outcast; the cursed redcoats spreading death and destruction through the Highlands; the castle at Achnacarry burned doon, and the old fortress blown up—"

"The Jacobites did that," Hortense pointed out sighfully.

"Aye—and for good reason! The thing is, it's *him*"—Prudence jerked her head towards the upper floors—"and his kind we've to blame. But I'm to curtsey and simper and wish him well, lest my dearest papa never speak tae me again. I'd as soon smile at a snake!" She snatched up her aunt's fallen scarves and stretched them between her hands, scowling down at the taut fabric.

Hortense gasped, "Prue! You never would . . . !"

Her eyes dark with anger, Prudence said grittily, "Och, but 'twould do me hearrrt guid!"

Fanning herself and gazing at her niece with wide, awed eyes, Hortense murmured, "But whatever would we do wi' the poor laddie's corpse?"

The thought brought a glint of laughter into Prudence's eyes. "Take it doon tae the loch and give it tae the Monster fer his supper!"

At precisely two o'clock on the following afternoon, Prudence presented herself at her father's study door, and enquired innocently, "Will ye be wanting me to change my dress, sir?"

MacTavish ran a glance over her wind-blown, unpowdered hair, the glow the fresh air had brought to her cheeks, the dusty blue riding habit, and battled a smile. He realized that she thought she looked unattractive. "I doubt you can do better, my dear," he said gravely, and had to turn away as he saw indignation come into her betrayingly expressive face.

It was a fine thing, Prudence thought, as she accompanied her sire up the stairs, that the father you had worshipped all your days could turn on you like a viper when you least expected it.

The door of the enemy's room loomed ahead. She tightened her lips. She'd show this wretched little Sassenach how a proud Scotswoman could put him in his place. Unless, perhaps, he'd had the good manners to pass to his reward even as they came up the stairs.

Her morbid hopes were unwarranted. Lockerbie answered her father's knock, assured Mr. MacTavish that the Captain was awake and waiting eagerly to meet Miss Prudence, and bowed them into the room.

Keeping her eyes downcast, Prudence curtseyed through the introduction and heard a weak but pleasant voice murmur, "How do you do, ma'am? My apologies for intruding on you. I fancy you do not like to have a Sassenach in your home."

Her head jerked up. Her first reaction was shock. She thought, 'Why, he's only a boy!' The white, long-sleeved nightshirt and the wan face against the pillows gave an impression of defenceless youth, and pain had left its mark on the Captain. Dark shadows ringed the dusky brown eyes, and deep lines were etched between his heavy brows. His hair, almost black, had been brushed back severely, but was already starting to curl about his face, further emphasizing his pallor. A tentative smile tugged at his wide mouth, and his initial rather wistful look was replaced, as she watched, by admiration.

Geoffrey Delacourt was as surprised as was Miss MacTavish. Robbie's only comment about his sister had been that she was 'a very good sort of girl.' Now, Delacourt saw an exquisite little creature, all blue eyes, gleaming red-gold hair, and prideful arrogance. The little uptilted nose he thought charming, and the full lips very kissable. His gaze drifted lower. Gad, but she'd a shape to her, this Scots lass!

Prudence saw the gleam that came into the long, dark eyes, and pulled herself together. "I cannot but welcome whomever my father invites here, sir," she said meekly.

She meant, of course, I have no choice.' Amused, Delacourt murmured, "Thank you, ma'am. Have you been riding? You fairly radiate robust health! How I envy you!"

Prudence stiffened. 'Robust . . . ?' Could she have caught it from Aunty Mac?

A faint tremor in his voice, MacTavish said, "Aye, Prue's none of your dainty clinging-vine types."

Reeling, his daughter riposted, "Speaking of which, Captain

Delacourt, I met your friend Lord Briley yesterday. He spoke well of you."

Shocked, MacTavish darted a quick look at her, noted her heightened colour, and intervened hurriedly, "We must not tire you, my dear fellow. How do you go on today?"

The long thin hand on the coverlet lifted feebly. "Tol-lol, sir," sighed the invalid. "Not very much better than yesterday. But—I thank you."

'Tol-lol!' thought Prudence, contemptuously. "We will hope your recovery is rapid, Captain," she said with a bared-teeth smile.

'I am sure you will, you little vixen,' he thought. "Will you remember me in your prayers?" he begged, his voice noticeably weaker.

She answered truthfully, "You have been in them since I heard of your arrival here."

He raised a hand to his lips and coughed. It was a thin, painful sound, and tore Prudence's antagonism to shreds. She curtseyed again, murmured an appropriate farewell, and walked past Lockerbie as he swung the door open, quite forgetting to thank him.

II

Aside from the fact that he appeared to have a great number of friends who visited him at rather odd hours, one would hardly have known Captain Delacourt was in the house. And yet, in a subtle way, his influence was everywhere. The frigid demeanour of the servants began to melt on the second day of his occupation, and by the fourth was gone. The housemaids soon were competing for the privilege of waiting upon his rarely rung bell, and when it was believed he slept, a funereal silence descended upon the house. His man was a quiet type, not given to making friends easily, and the thaw did not appear to extend to him so that he became even more morose and silent. The housekeeper affected to be unaware of Lockerbie's existence and, on the few occasions that it was necessary for her to address him, would either talk right through him or at the wall beside him, but never rest her eyes upon what she referred to as 'his putrid visage.' The military doctor, who came every few days to check on his patient, encountered Mrs. Cairn early one breezy afternoon and was subjected to the same treatment. Himself a Scot, the rotund physician reached across the stairs as the housekeeper made to sweep past him. "Ye're a right bonnie lass," he said gruffly, "and

I'll no hold it against ye that ye've no love for the English, but if your soul matches your face, ye'll no vent y'r hatred on that boy above stairs. He's got all he can manage tae survive, ma'am."

"D'ye take me fer a heathen, Dr. Cauldside?" she replied, bristling as she lowered her eyes from the landing to glare at him. "Fer all we may need tae disinfect the premises when he's gone at last, I'll no add tae his misery." And on she marched, pausing at the landing to peer about and call in her softest voice for Señorita.

Prudence had returned from a visit to the buttery in time to overhear this little exchange. She nodded coolly to the physician and came up with the housekeeper halfway along the east hall.

"Are Captain Delacourt's friends becoming a nuisance, Carrie?" she asked, unfastening the silken scarf she had tied about her curls.

"Aye, they are that. Traipsin' in and oot at all hours. One might think the guid doctor would be more concerned for his patient than tae allow it. And a more sullen, scrrruffy lot ye'd never wish tae meet. Not a worrud out of 'em. Slink past wi' their heads doon and their tongues twixt their teeth, fer all the worruld as if they were ashamed—as well they should be, consorting wi' a redcoat! That lord chappie is one o' the few as will gie me the time o' day, and him lisping and fluttering like any dandified milksop! Señorita? Now where on airth has that wee besom taken hersel' tae? Señorita . . . ? Ye know ye're not allowed above stairs!"

Señorita, a small grey kitten, had been presented to Hortense a year ago by a Spanish gentleman visiting the MacTavish. She had been received without much enthusiasm, but had soon become the pet of the household. She was now large and independent and regarded the occupants of Lakepoint as *her* pets, and quite sure the animal would not be far away, Prudence went on to her room.

She was to drive into Inverness with her aunt that afternoon, and Kitty already had the cream silk Watteau gown laid out on the bed, with the hoops hanging from the wardrobe door. The abigail was agog with excitement, for it seemed that the military hunters had been foiled once again and Jock Cameron had slipped from their net, leaving his pursuers baffled. Beaming, Kitty watched Prudence clap her hands and dance a small jig. "Aye, I knew that'd please ye, miss!"

Prudence was rather more than merely pleased. Jock Cameron had been one of her most persistent beaux and she had been not at all offended by his declarations of undying affection, for he was a fine-looking lad with a grand physique and an amiable disposition, to say nothing of a respectable inheritance. Jock had been wounded at the Battle of Culloden and, despite a bold dash for freedom, was rumoured to be trapped near Beauty Firth with the redcoats enjoying a merry game of cat and mouse before seizing him. "'Tis a miracle," she cried gleefully. "I'd been fairly dreading tae hear he'd been shot. However did he get away?"

"Ligun Doone again, so they're saying at The Bonnie Heather. Risked his own skin tae lure the redcoats intae a wee defile, then threw weighted nets doon. By the time they'd got free, so had Jock!" She laughed as Prudence squealed with joy, and went on, "I reckon it's truth. Mr. Doone is worth four hundred pounds now, if taken alive. And two hundred if killed." Her eyes became very round. "Four hundred pounds! Losh! 'Tis a great fortune!"

Prudence sobered abruptly. "Aye, it is," she said, frowning. "A dreadful temptation for a poor man. Oh, Kitty! How awful if Doone should be betrayed, when he's done so much for our fighting men."

"And their families, miss! Certain it is that no Scot would betray him. Look at the time! We'd best get ye ready."

And so Prudence was relieved of her simple morning dress, hot water brought for her to wash, the hoops secured about her tiny middle, and the silken gown draped over them. Her hair was tidied, dainty slippers replaced her pattens, and a pearl pendant was fastened about her throat. And while all this was going forward, the two girls chattered on about the exploits of Mr. Ligun Doone.

The Battle of Culloden Moor had ended the hopes of Charles Stuart and the Jacobites to put King James on the throne. Their defeat had been crushing, but the victorious young Duke of Cumberland had sworn to stamp out rebellion in the Highlands once and for all. He had unleashed an unparalleled tide of savagery; murder, rapine, and looting were encouraged rather than prohibited, and many an English officer, horrified by the resultant blood-bath, had sold out and gone home rather than be a party to it. Women and children were not spared by the predatory soldiers, and soon even the staunch Highlanders feared to help the fugitives lest their own families pay a hideous price for their compassion. And then had come Ligun Doone—a man with a genius for devising escape routes, whose daring plots so often prevented the pursuit and slaughter of rebels that he had in short order become an infuriating thorn in the flesh of the military.

It was generally believed that his name was assumed, and there was a good deal of betting among the Scots as to his true identity. Kitty and Prudence had their own small wager, the abigail favouring one of her admirers, a large young man known as Little Willie Mayhew, and Prudence opting for Alec Carlton, a fiery, proud, and intelligent boy who would, she thought, be the very type to take such frightful chances.

Prudence was ready at last, but tongues had wagged faster than actions, and she was late when she took up her reticule and turned to be inspected. She looked, Kitty declared proudly, "complete to a shade!" and she set off, looking forward to the long-promised jaunt to Inverness, and happy because of the good news about Jock Cameron.

She was surprised to turn the corner of the hall and encounter Mrs. Cairn, standing motionless and staring blankly at Captain Delacourt's closed door.

"Did you find Señorita?" enquired Prudence.

"Oh, aye," murmured the housekeeper, absently.

"Where is the wee beastie?"

"I, er, let her bide."

"You did? Where?"

Mrs. Cairn seemed to come back to earth. "He had it," she said with a shrug.

"He . . . ? Oh, do you mean Captain Delacourt?"

"Aye. His mon heard me calling and opened the door. Señorita was . . . on the bed, and himself fast asleep, but wi' his hand"—her voice cracked a little—"cradling her against him."

Prudence peered at her, but the housekeeper kept her face turned away. "He's a Sassenach, nae dooting," she said rather defiantly. "But—but he's nae— Och, he's nae quite what I'd in me mind, forbye." And she fled.

"Huh!" uttered Prudence and marched to her aunt's room.

Hortense was ready but busied with a large and involved chart. "I cannot like what I read here," she said, shaking her head bodingly. "If the skies are clear I mean to go up to the roof tonight and check if my calculations are correct."

Her long-suffering abigail, well aware that this meant she also would essay the chilly climb, moaned faintly and went into the dressing room.

"Your calculations have likely been upset by our guest," said Prudence tartly. "From what I can gather, he's been casting some powerful spells in this house."

Mrs. Hortense stared, fascinated. "Spells? What kind of spells?"

"I wish you will tell me. The housemaids are all but fighting one another to fetch and carry from his room. I saw that black-haired baggage, Lucy, grinning like a silly moonling when she collected his luncheon tray yesterday. Which was quite unnecessary, since his man is here for the very same purpose! And now Carrie Cairn is drooping about in the hall fairly weepy-eyed because she found Señorita on his bed 'wi' his hand cradling her'! All he'll get of *my* hand will be the back of it, I can tell you!" She paused, scowling, then added in a near snarl, "And why must ye look at me as if I was a cannibal, ma'am?"

"I only thought," said Hortense, averting her shocked eyes, "that you are become something . . . harsh . . . love."

"Harsh! I am a *patriot,* Aunty Mac! And lest ye forget, yon Captain is a murdering enemy!"

"But—so young, Prue, dear. And so very weak and helpless. And . . . did ever you see such a fine young face? Such dreamy, dark eyes. . . ." Hortense sighed and smiled at her chart. "And his mouth, so tender, yet firm withal, and those black curls all—"

"Revolting!" cried Prudence, her eyes blazing with indignation. "Do you know what you are? All of you? You're nothing but weaklings! Only let him have been fat and forty, and you'd all have been hating him as you should! But because he chances to have a hands—er, to be reasonably good-looking and capitalizes on die-away airs—"

"No, Prue, how can you? I'll own 'tis very foolish of him to be English, but he is likely expiring. How can you *be* so unfeeling?"

"How can *you* so soon forget Culloden? How can you forget my dear brother, hunted and starved and exhausted when at last he made his way home! And weeping when he told us of the shame and the slaughter!"

"Oh, I do not! I do not! But we are still civilized human beings, Prue. We must not abandon all compassion. And only look how the Captain has paid for his sins, poor lad, and bears his woes so bravely."

"Compassion, is it? To my way of thinking the Sassenach has ye all fair bewitched. And as for his bravery—fustian! Was our Rob to have been struck doon by a musket ball—"

"A shell fragment," inserted Hortense, precisely.

"Was Robbie to have been hit, I'll lay you odds he'd not be lying about nine months later making weak little dainty gestures and saying with a martyred smile that he is 'just tol-lol.'" She straightened the bonnet that had become tilted by her vehemence, and repeated disgustedly, "Tol-lol, indeed! 'Tis enough tae make any good Scot cast up his accounts!" She saw her aunt's lower lip sag and swung around apprehensively as a tentative cough sounded behind her.

The parlour door stood wide. His face expressionless, Lockerbie waited, gripping the back of an invalid chair. Delacourt, his dark head leaning back against the cushions, and with a smug grey cat curled up in his lap, watched Prudence with a faint, wistful smile.

"I do beg your pardon," he said. "I'd understood that Mrs. Cairn was here and I wanted to ease her anxieties about her pet."

Prudence's breath seemed to completely elude her. She knew her face was scarlet, and wondered in a dim, anguished fashion why Fate must conspire against her in every possible way to aid this evil creature. It was useless to attempt the quelling responses that surged to her lips, and with him looking like a man en route to choose his burial plot, anything but a soft answer would probably have her sent to the stocks for inhumanity to man—if Captain Geoffrey Delacourt could be designated such! She closed her sagging jaw, strove valiantly to meet that martyred smile with a haughty glare, and was silent.

Hortense wafted up, dropping her handkerchief along the way, and trilled in fading accents that it was "so kind . . . so thoughtful." She took the yawning cat he handed up to her, and asked gently, "And how are you today, sir?"

The effort of lifting Señorita had apparently exhausted him. Back went his head to its cushion once more. "Oh," he said with a quivering smile, "tol-lol, you know."

Prudence had kept her fuming gaze on her aunt's slender back, but at this she slanted a narrowed glare at the invalid.

The Captain's dark eyes met hers. For an instant she thought to see a dance of laughter in them, but then they were sad again, and she fancied her imagination had been at work. She tightened her lips and said nothing.

With a languid wave of his frail hand, Delacourt said, "We

must not delay the ladies, Kerbie," and the manservant began to return the chair very carefully to the hall.

Holding the lazy grey cat still, Hortense turned to rest a grave look upon her niece.

"Tol-lol," mocked Prudence defiantly. "The Sassenach knows what one member of this household thinks of him, at all events!"

"Do you think they will let us through this time?" asked Hortense, drawing a shawl closer about her and peering anxiously at the road ahead.

Prudence withdrew her absent gaze from the proud sweep of the northern mountains. "I doot Papa would have let us come, did he think there would be trouble."

Hortense had her own ideas as to her erratic brother-in-law's awareness of trouble, and pointed out that the last time they had tried to visit cousin Hilda, they had been turned back. "I do pray we'll not be stopped again. I was never so frightened as when all those soldiers closed around us."

"That was a month ago. The English cannot expect to keep us all locked in our homes forever. And besides, they've such a stranglehold on us, they know we can do nothing, save—" Prudence checked, her brow puckering into a frown as the carriage slowed and she saw red uniforms approaching. "Now dinna go intae the boughs," she requested, her Scots accent more pronounced as it always was when she was irked. "They likely wish only tae find oot who we are and—"

"What?" cried Hortense, immediately alarmed. "You never mean—oh!"

Two troopers rode up, faces grim and muskets at the ready. A large Sergeant came to the side of the carriage, leaned forward, and wrenched open the door. "Who travels?" he demanded curtly.

"Myself and my aunt," Prudence replied, her nose very high. "Who asks?"

A warmer light crept into the man's cold eyes. "Never ye mind, lassie—"

"My name is *Miss* MacTavish!"

He grinned. "How'd you guess I was after a interduction, pretty girl?"

"That will do, Sergeant!" A young officer rode to join the little group and glanced into the carriage with swift appraisal. "Are you two ladies alone?"

It seemed so foolishly redundant that Prudence replied cuttingly, "Can you not see the two Highland regiments lurking under the seats?"

The Ensign's fair face flushed. Smothering a grin, the Sergeant said, "Miss MacTavish and her aunt, sir."

"Thank you, Sergeant. Perhaps we'd best have the ladies out, so we can find these—er, two regiments."

The Sergeant grinned broadly. Hortense, terrified, gave a little cry and shrank, trembling, against her niece.

Repenting her quick temper, Prudence said, "No, please do not. My aunt is alarmed, you see. My apologies if I—"

The Ensign, unhappily aware he'd been made to look foolish in front of a Sergeant who had several times attempted to teach him his business in this hostile land, interrupted coldly, "You heard me, Sergeant. I want a thorough search of that coach." He swung his horse and galloped off.

The Sergeant dismounted and let down the carriage steps. "If your royal highness will be so good as to step into the dirt with us simple folk."

Prudence turned away and said softly, "Aunty Mac, you must not let them see you are afraid. Come now."

She started to climb out. The wind sent her skirts billowing. The Sergeant bent quickly, peeped, and laughed. Clutching her skirts angrily, Prudence missed her footing. The Sergeant caught her and swung her around. With a squeal of rage she lashed out at him, catching him a good crack on one ear.

He grunted and tossed her down so that she staggered and fell to her knees. "'Twas just your kind shot down me brother from behind at Falkirk," he growled.

"If that is so, he was . . . likely running away," she gasped out, furious.

He swore and gripped her by the front of her gown, his hand thrusting into her bodice and jerking her upwards.

"I put it to you, thir," inserted a mild, very English voice, "that that ith not the way to treat a lady."

Keeping his grip on Prudence's bodice, the Sergeant turned to this new arrival.

Prudence tore at his hand, but he merely shook her a little, laughing as he eyed the Englishman. "And who might you be, little pretty?"

Lord Briley's tawny eyes, which had for a moment reflected anger, began to glow. "Be tho kind ath to remove your dirty hand from her gown," said he, more or less politely.

Grinning, the Sergeant shifted his hold, but not to withdraw it. With a shriek of rage, Prudence's long nails raked hard across that brawny wrist.

The Sergeant pulled his hand clear, then turned on Prudence, his eyes murderous, his curses blistering her ears.

"Oh, now really, fellow," protested his lordship, sighing.

Thinking back on it later, Prudence was unable to decide just how it happened. At one moment his lordship was standing beside his horse surveying the hulking symbol of military might reproachfully. At the next moment, that same military might performed three quite unexpected contortions. Firstly, it was doubled in half; secondly, it was expertly straightened out; and thirdly, it sort of squashed down upon itself until it sprawled, groaning, in the dust.

"Hey!" A trooper raised his musket.

"Heaven be praised," cried Hortense. "Bless the braw laddie!"

"Oh, splendid!" Prudence clapped her hands, her eyes alight with admiration.

"Botheration," mourned his lordship, inspecting one surprisingly muscular hand. "If I ain't broken my fingernail on the horrid lout."

"Stand clear, miss," commanded the other trooper, advancing to join his friend, his musket also levelled. "Up with your hands, whoever you are!"

"Oh, did you want to know?" enquired his lordship, turning an angelic gaze upon them. "My name ith Briley."

"What the devil's going on here?" His young face wrathful, the Ensign rode to join them. He stared in astonishment from Briley's elegance to the burly Sergeant, who was making feeble attempts to regain his feet.

"He wath pawing the lady," explained Briley.

"Says his name's Briley, sir," volunteered the second trooper.

"Well, whoever you are, damn you, you are under—" The Ensign checked, frowning. "Briley? Not Major Lord Thaddeus Briley?"

Prudence's delight fled, and fear touched her.

His lordship, his pleasant countenance reflecting a brief chagrin, bowed.

"Oh, egad!" the Ensign groaned under his breath. He saluted. "Your pardon, sir. I'd not intended that my men should—"

"I am not on active thervith, you know," interposed his lordship. "If I were"—his eyes blazed suddenly—"you'd wait a blathted long time before I'd put you in charge of any detail larger than a thentry!" He turned from the scarlet-faced Ensign to Prudence. "May I ethcort you into town, ma'am?"

"Oh, *please* do, your lordship," wailed Hortense, tears spilling down her white cheeks. "Prudence—poor darling girl—are you—?"

Prudence took her in her arms. "I am very well, dearest. Come, we shall go home." She glanced over her shoulder. "We are most beholden to you, my lord, and shall be grateful for your escort back to Lakepoint."

Thaddeus Briley's gallantry was considerable, but it did not extend to enduring a father's gratitude. Having escorted the ladies to the front steps of Lakepoint, he fled like a startled hare, his groom clattering along behind. This behaviour did nothing to diminish Prudence's new opinion of him. "Is just as a brave gentleman should behave," she told her aunt. "And I admire him the more for't."

"You are not . . . forgetting his lordship is an Englishman?" quavered poor Hortense, leaning heavily on her arm as she was ushered up the stairs.

Prudence was not forgetting that fact, nor the frighteningly revealed information that his lordship also held a commission in King George's army, but she said, "No, Aunty Mac. It galls me to stand in the debt of such a man, but—faith, I could fair have kissed the creature when he folded up yon Sergeant in sae bonnie a way!"

Hortense was deposited, weeping with the reaction, into the care of her dismayed abigail. Prudence, made of sterner stuff, went straight away in search of her father.

She found him sitting with their guest in a sheltered corner of the sunny garden, with the omnipresent Lockerbie hovering nearby. MacTavish and Delacourt, their heads close together, were engaged in what seemed a heated discussion. Lockerbie said loudly, "Good afternoon, miss," and the conversation stopped at once.

MacTavish's welcoming smile died as he stood to greet her. "Prue?" he said, scanning her face narrowly. "What is wrong, please?"

She had intended to ask for a private talk, but it occurred to her that it would not hurt Delacourt to be made aware of the conduct of his horrid men. She sat beside her father and told him as calmly as possible what had happened. When she reached the point at which the Sergeant had seized her gown, however, her voice faltered.

His face dark with rage, MacTavish snapped, "He did—*what?*"

Prudence began to wish she'd requested privacy, after all. "He took hold of—the front of—of my bodice," she said, her cheeks becoming hot.

"By the Lord Harry!" grated MacTavish.

The Captain enquired mildly, "In an offensive way, ma'am?"

"I'd damned well like to know how it could be done in an *in*offensive way," snarled MacTavish. "Go on, lass."

Prudence went on, becoming more and more embarrassed. She was trembling when she finished her recital, and she could feel her father shaking with wrath.

"That was jolly well done of old Thaddeus," observed Delacourt tranquilly.

Her cheeks still burning, Prudence rested a level stare upon him. "Aye. He's a right brave lad—for an Englishman," she said.

Fortunately, MacTavish's thoughts were elsewhere. "Pray excuse me, sir," he said, coming to his feet. "I must go into town."

Delacourt murmured, "Do you think that wise?"

Outraged, Prudence stared at the Captain's pale, calm face. Standing, she placed one hand on her father's arm. "I know ye'll not let me go wi' ye, but you'd best take some of the men, Papa."

"Oh, most decidedly not," said the placid English voice.

"What *would* you suggest?" MacTavish demanded harshly. "That I take my daughter and offer her for the sport of the rank and file?"

Prudence tossed her chin up and turned from the enemy, triumphant. She was considerably shocked when her father made no move to leave, but waited for a response.

Delacourt said, "Naturally not. But it does not do to, er,

alienate the military, you know. And perhaps there were"—he glanced apologetically at Prudence's bristling hostility—"extenuating circumstances."

"*Extenuating!*" Her blue eyes flashed outrage. "Do ye dare tae suggest I flirted wi' the mon, sir?"

"I'd not be so bold." One slim finger traced a figure eight on the arm of his chair and, watching it, he murmured, "Only, I thought that—being so provoked, you know—you might have said something to, ah, irritate him."

Bosom heaving and hands clenched, Prudence found herself strangled by wrath.

The MacTavish said, "Do I know my daughter, Captain, she gave the lout as good as he sent."

"Not quite as good, Papa," she managed, grinning at him. "But I boxed his ear fairly."

"Is that when he violated your—your bodice?"

Blushing, she said, "No, Papa. He knocked me doon."

A stifled exclamation came from Lockerbie. MacTavish swore audibly. Even Captain Tol-lol, as Prudence had dubbed him mentally, seemed horrified, and exclaimed, "Gad, but I'd thought my presence here would protect you from that sort of brutality. You mean, the fellow actually *struck* you, ma'am?"

"Well, he—" she began, then finished lamely, "he sort of dropped me, I suppose. And he said I was the type of woman had shot his brother in the back at Falkirk."

"Damned hound!" grated MacTavish.

"So I said if his brother *was* shot in the back, it was likely because he was running away!"

"Oh, dear," said the Captain with a sigh.

MacTavish looked amused. "Well, Delacourt?"

Astonished, Prudence thought, 'Why ask this dolt's opinion? What does it matter what *he* thinks?'

"In your shoes," said Delacourt judicially, "I would, of course, register a protest."

"Register . . . a . . . *protest?*" gasped Prudence. "Och! The daring of it!"

"But in a controlled and civilized fashion," he went on, disregarding this interruption.

"Is that what Englishmen do?" raged Prudence, her temper breaking its bounds. "Do they permit their ladies to be mauled in public, and have so little pride that—"

"You forget that Captain Delacourt is our guest," MacTavish interrupted.

"Guest! One might rather think him master o' this hoose, if we—" And her impassioned words faded. She caught her breath, blanching that she had been guilty of such flagrant insolence and, hanging her head, mumbled, "Oh, dear sir . . . I am—so sorry."

The soft, loathed voice purred, "It is understandable that Miss MacTavish is upset, sir. Under the circumstances."

Prudence darted a venomous glare at him. As if she wanted *him* to plead her case! His dark gaze met hers with so pious an understanding that she fairly itched to claw him.

In a gentler tone her father said, "Of course she is upset, poor wee lass. Come away, m'dear. I'll see you to your bedchamber. You must rest."

Prudence clung to his arm and accompanied him without a backward glance. As they stepped onto the path that led up to the house, Delacourt called wearily, "The man you'll want to see is Colonel Cunningham. Tread lightly, sir. He's a bit of a tiger."

Prudence sat on her bed and frowned at the polished boards. Despite her pleas, her father had ridden off with only his aging steward to side him, and two grooms following. In the old days he'd have ridden at the head of all the men he could muster (had such a situation arisen, which it had not), and the insult would have been wiped out in blood. Her frown wavered. It was a little difficult to picture the MacTavish behaving in such a way, but it was what the clan chieftains or the Lord of the Isles would do, and in a small way the MacTavish was a clan chieftain. She sighed. If her father was carried home wrapped in his cloak, it would be Delacourt who could be blamed. And it was the loathly Englishman who had almost brought about another quarrel with Papa.

The recollection of her angry words brought a blush of shame to her cheeks, but what she had said was truth. Since the Sassenach had come, it was as if he had some powerful hold over James MacTavish. She kicked off her slippers irritably and glared at the one that flew across the room and sent the hairbrush toppling off her dressing table. It was silly to contemplate the MacTavish being blackmailed, wasn't it? But how could that puling weakling have the power to order so proud a gentleman? Certain it was that Papa had been ready to go and fetch his horsewhip at one moment, and the next had asked meekly, "What would you suggest?"

She lay back across the bed, staring up at the soft billow of the silken canopy. My lord Briley had seemed a gentle, likeable person. And my lord Briley was now become *Major* Lord Briley! She closed her eyes, shivering. She had tried to warn Papa; she had told him it was all a plot and that Delacourt had been put here to entrap them. And Papa had uttered an exasperated exclamation, then kissed her and said he would not scold her after what she had endured today, "But—what a pother you cause with your dramatics, child." Child! A fine thing that the MacTavish would pay heed to the word of a foreigner, an enemy! and laugh to scorn the warnings of his own flesh and blood. . . .

She awoke from a crazy dream in which Delacourt had hurled a tiger from the top of the staircase. The creature's snarls still echoed in her ears, in fact. Unless . . . ? She tilted her head, listening. Someone was weeping!

She clambered from the bed and hurried to the parlour door. Kitty was huddled on the sofa, sobbing. Prudence ran to sit beside her. "What is it? Kitty—never say my papa—"

"No, miss," mumbled the abigail, drying her tears with her apron. "The MacTavish came home an hour since and . . . and—oh! 'Tis—" She burst into tears again. "'Tis . . . my Bill!"

So Little Willie was become 'my Bill.' Prudence said slowly, "I knew he admired you, but I thought you'd sent him about his business."

"Aye. Sent him off . . . with a flea in his ear. On—on account o' him not warning me he meant to go with Prince Charlie. And . . . and worrying m'self sick ever since. Wondering was he alive or . . ." She sobbed.

Prudence whispered, "Then—you've had word?"

"M'brother says as Bill's being hunted doon and—he's hurt and half starved. Poor wee laddie! Last m'brother saw, he was away up Castle Crag, running fer his life and a half-dozen troopers after him, wi' dogs. *Dogs!* Och—me poor Bill! They likely have him the noo, and—and will drag him off tae be shot!" She rocked back and forth, covering her face. "Oh, miss! If I did but know how, I'd get worrd tae Ligun Doone. He'd help, I know it!"

Aghast, Prudence slipped an arm about her shaking shoulders. "Is there a way to reach Mr. Doone that you know of?"

Scattering teardrops, Kitty shook her head. "Would that I did. The only mon I know that had words wi' him was Master Robbie. If only—"

"*What?*" Prudence's clasp tightened spasmodically. "My *brother?*"

"Aye." Kitty blinked swollen eyes at her. "'Twas Ligun Doone got Master Robbie clear. Did ye not know of it?"

"I did not!" Astounded by this intelligence, and puzzled that it had been kept from her, Prudence muttered, "So 'tis Mr. Doone I've to thank for dear Rob's life!" She jumped up. "Now try not to worry so, Kitty. If Rob was helped by Mr. Doone, then you may be sure the MacTavish knows of it. I'll seek him oot at once."

Kitty's gratitude was profuse. She wiped her eyes and stood

also. "Ye canna go doonstairs like that, miss. 'Tis nigh dinner time and his lordship invited, so Mrs. Cairn told me, tae bide wi' us a day or two."

Tonight, Prudence chose to wear one of her new gowns. Styled in the English mode, with the wide, flattened pannier skirts that were becoming popular nowadays, the material was of blue lawn, with white embroidered flowers edging the tiers, and an underdress of pale blue silk. The neckline, demurely edged with lace, was moderately low, but set off her rich little figure admirably. She selected a sapphire pendant and hung small diamond and sapphire drops from her ears, while Kitty adorned her piled curls with a bow of wide blue velvet.

Armed for the fray, Prudence took up her fan and went downstairs.

III

The entrance hall was empty, but as she descended the final flight of stairs, Prudence could hear the murmur of male voices. A footman imparted the information that the gentlemen were gathered in the gold saloon. She had feared they might have selected the red saloon or the book room, neither of which chambers would show off her blue gown to its best advantage. The gold saloon would, she thought, do very nicely.

Her entrance was satisfactory, for there was a moment's silence when she arrived. She paused, startled by two facts. The first was that Captain Delacourt was present; and the second, that an army officer stood by the empty hearth, chatting with her father and Lord Briley. Her eyes held on the stranger. A Colonel. A well-built man, in his early forties, she guessed, with a neat wig and jutting black brows. His complexion was sallow, his eyes black and keen, his nose a sharp hook over a small, tight mouth. She had an impression of intelligence and menace, and her heart beat a little faster when she thought of the questions she meant to ask her father.

"How very pretty you look, my dear," said MacTavish, coming to lead her in to the room. "I'd not expected you would join us after your shattering experience."

"For which I have come to offer the humblest of apologies," said the officer, bringing his heels sharply together and bowing in a brisk, Germanic fashion.

"Colonel Cunningham, allow me to present my daughter, Miss Prudence MacTavish."

The Colonel bowed over Prudence's hand, but kept those sharp dark eyes on her face even as he did so.

This was the man Delacourt had referred to as 'a bit of a tiger.' She believed that for once he had spoken truly, and she fluttered her lashes and tried to look simpering and stupid.

The Colonel uttered the appropriate phrases and professed himself to have been "utterly aghast to learn of such an atrocity. I can only plead that every army has its share of animals, ma'am. Sometimes the best intentioned of officers cannot control 'em. But that *you* should have been victimized after we spread the word that you were giving sanctuary to one of our men, and that the people of Lakepoint were to be left alone, is unforgiveable. I do assure you that the man who used you so brutally will long repent his lapse."

Her irritation over the suggestion that all Scots were fair game except those sheltering English officers was lost in her unease at the tight set of his thin lips. She said, "Never say he has lost his stripes."

"He lost three, ma'am. And gained three hundred."

She gave a gasp, one hand flying to her throat. "Oh—no! I never meant— That is, he was crude and vulgar, but— Oh! My heavens!"

The Colonel laughed in a thin bray that added to her distress. "Give it not another thought, dear lady. He's survived worse, I do assure you. We know how to punish, even as we know how to reward, and I'll not have our friends abused. Don't you agree, my lord?"

Feeling a veritable murderess, Prudence's distressed eyes

turned to the side. Briley bowed with easy grace and responded suitably, but it was not upon his elegance that her gaze held. Geoffrey Delacourt was clad in formal evening dress. His thick hair was powdered and tied back with a dull red riband. A half-moon patch adorned his right cheekbone, snowy Mechlin lace was at throat and wrists, and the dark red velvet coat, richly embroidered with silver, accentuated his pale, delicately molded features. All this she noted absently, for it was the expression in his eyes that was of prime importance. A look of sympathetic understanding so heartfelt that it was as though he had put a comforting arm about her. He bowed slightly in his invalid chair, and smiled at her. She thought with a shock, 'Heavens, but he's a fine handsome creature!' and had to drag her scattered wits back together so as to respond to something Briley had said, whatever it might be. His lordship was watching her curiously. She curtseyed and said quickly, "I shall never forget what you did for me today, my lord."

Her remark must not have been too out of place because he merely looked embarrassed and said, colouring up, that he was glad to have come along at a useful moment.

Prudence went with her father to occupy the white brocade sofa.

"Dare we hope that your aunt means to join us?" asked the Colonel.

"I rather doubt it, sir. She was very frightened this afternoon."

"Disgraceful business," he said, drawing a chair closer to her. "With your permission, MacTavish, I shall call again, so as to make my apologies to the lady."

As it chanced, this was not necessary. Hortense soon drifted into the room with a swish of lavender taffeta and a trail of scarves. She quailed at the sight of the scarlet uniform, and her response to the Colonel's gallantries was a faint and disjointed jumble that brought a quirk to the side of Delacourt's mouth and a twinkle to his lordship's tawny eyes.

At dinner Prudence sat opposite her father at one end of the table, with Lord Briley to her right hand and the Colonel on her left. She was thus able to chat with those gentlemen and keep an eye on the rest of the occupants of the charming old wainscoted room. Hortense appeared to have recovered her nerves and was conversing politely with her brother and the Colonel, who was obviously exerting every effort to be pleasant. Despite herself, Prudence's eyes strayed often to the quiet elegance of the young man at her father's left hand. Delacourt spoke seldom, and his voice was becoming noticeably less audible. He picked at his food, and Prudence was relieved when her father leaned to speak to him with low-voiced solicitude, then beckoned to the waiting Lockerbie.

Delacourt seemed to be painfully embarrassed and apologized for "spoiling this delightful meal in so foolish a way." His smile quivered; he looked drawn and tired as Lockerbie backed the chair away from the table, and his small farewell wave ended with a droop of his hand in a gesture so pathetic that Prudence's momentary sympathy evaporated into contempt.

Hortense looked distressed, however, and the Colonel said that the invalid did not appear to be much improved. "Nine months since he was hit," he observed. "One would think he'd either have recovered by this time, or—" He checked abruptly.

MacTavish shook his head. "It was most unfortunate the Clandons were unable to get him to the Border, but at that time the clans were up, and English officers were hunted—quite the reverse of our present—er—"

"Tragedy?" The Colonel accepted a cheese tart and said breezily, "In view of that tragedy, I must say I think it exceeding kind of you and your ladies to have taken one of our fellows into your home. I' faith, 'tis little short of extraordinary."

His smile was bland, but Prudence felt a pang of fear. This beastly Sassenach suspected that they had ulterior motives, that was very plain. She said, "My father repays a debt, sir. Captain Delacourt chances to be a very good friend of my brother, you see." Far from appearing pleased by this timely explanation, MacTavish frowned, and her heart sank.

"Is that so?" said the Colonel. "Is your brother about, ma'am? I'd very much like to meet him."

Her blood seemed to congeal. She sought frantically for something convincing to say and was immeasurably relieved when MacTavish said that his heir was in Devon, visiting his great-aunt.

"Very fond of Devon," imparted his lordship, adding inconsequently, "Know it well."

The Colonel touched his napkin to his lips. "One gathers you are also familiar with this part of the country, my lord. Do you spend a deal of time up here?"

"No, thir. I am here only to ethcort a lady to her grandmama."

"Oh, of course. Lady Ericson's granddaughter, I think. The, er, same girl whose family shielded Delacourt after Prestonpans, no?"

"Yeth, matter of fact. I'd gone there to look for the grave of a friend who fell in the battle. Mithter Clandon wath pointed out ath a man who'd helped theveral of our wounded. We became acquainted and he mentioned that hith daughter wath to have come up here to her grandmama, but that he could not undertake the journey. After all he'd done for our people"—he gave a deprecatory shrug,—"it theemed only a—er, fair."

"Quite so," said Cunningham approvingly. "Jolly good of you, just the same. Came up by ship, I understand. Only safe way, with the country in its present state, but must have been beastly tiresome."

"I think it wouldn't be quite the thing for me to admit that, Colonel," said Briley with a twinkle. "I'll own to not caring for water travel, though. Much prefer to ride. Which remindth me, you drive a fine team, thir. Very like to a pair Jack Longley tooled around Hyde Park a year or tho back."

"They are the very same," exclaimed Cunningham, his eyes lighting up with enthusiasm. "Bought 'em off him when he lost everything on 'Change. By Gad, but you've an eye, my lord! That mare you ride is no breakdown, either!"

Briley laughed and launched proudly into the bloodlines of his mare.

Prudence could breathe again, for horse talk was a sure way to please the gentlemen. The rest of the meal passed off without incident, but when her aunt stood to withdraw, Prudence asked to be excused, admitting that she was rather tired this evening.

The gentlemen were all on their feet, of course, and were unanimous in urging her to rest.

She caught her father's eye and said, "I am not too tired for you to come in and say good night as you always do, dear sir."

The Colonel and Lord Briley smiled at this evidence of family affection, but James MacTavish was surprised by it. He was devoted to his children, but not so devoted as to make a nightly pilgrimage along two long halls and up two flights of stairs so as to say his good nights. He gave no sign of anything untoward, however, and assured Prudence that he would be up within thirty minutes.

He was as good as his word. Prudence had just settled into her bed when he scratched on the door. She dismissed the nervous Kitty, then stretched out a hand to her father as he sat on the side of the bed. Clasping it, he asked, "What is all this about, miss? You know I should not leave my guests."

"I know, I know. But, Papa, I *had* to speak to you. For Kitty's sake."

He frowned. "Kitty? Oh, your abigail. Surely it can wait for—"

"No, sir, for she is in a dreadful state. Her beau was out with Prince Charles and now they're hunting him to his death. You'll recall Bill, Papa? They called him Little Willie."

"Hmmnn, yes. Mayhew. They're hard after the boy, and he's wounded, though ye'd best not tell your woman that unhappy fact."

"She already knows, sir. And she says—Papa, is it truth that Ligun Doone helped our Rob to escape?"

MacTavish started. "Now where did she hear that?"

"I don't know. But *is* it truth?"

He hesitated, looking dismayed. "I cannot answer, Prue."

"So you gave your word. I understand, and I'll not ask you to tell me aught of it, for I'd sooner die than endanger such a gallant gentleman."

"Easily said, my dear."

Anxious, she searched his face. "Do you mean because of my wretched temper?"

"We'll be charitable and call it spirit, rather, but 'tis a dangerous trait when one plays a game of life and death."

She admitted sadly, "It is my besetting sin. I said something foolish at dinner, did I not? I saw that I'd vexed you when we were speaking of Robbie, but that beastly Cunningham looked so sly, as if we'd a secret reason for allowing Captain Delacourt to stay here. I thought if he knew that Rob had cried friends with the Captain—" Her father still looked stern, and she said, "And I really dinna ken what's sae bad aboot having said it, Papa."

He hesitated, then answered slowly, "I'd not mentioned Rob for fear Cunningham would at once begin to be curious as to his whereabouts."

Remorseful, Prudence gripped her hands together. "And I had to do exactly as you feared and set the Colonel's brainbox to working! Oh, Papa!"

He patted her dainty lace-trimmed cap. "Never mind. What's done is done, lass, and I believe we shall survive your unruly tongue. Thanks to Lord Briley. How fortunate was his horse blathering."

"Yes, but"—she clutched his cravat—"Papa, you should have *seen* him this afternoon. He was not at all the dandy. In fact, sir, he frightens me! I think he is here to watch us."

MacTavish looked at her frowningly. "Why?"

"Because the Ensign called him Major Lord Briley! *Major*, Papa! And he pretends to be such a milksop."

"For goodness' sake, Prudence! He'd not be the first dandy ever to don a uniform, or to revert to type when his fighting days were done. Only look at Delacourt. He's scarcely a military type, either."

"No, but he's so ill one cannot imagine how he might have been in his prime, and there are inconsistencies about the Captain also, sir, that—"

"Child," he said impatiently, "I vow you're beside yourself! I wonder you don't suspect the butler. After all, Sidley is English. You must not allow yourself to jump at every shadow."

He tried to get up, but his daughter tightened her grip determinedly and he sat down again, perforce.

"Papa, *please* listen to me! For a moment this afternoon, Lord Thaddeus looked every inch a Major. I could see the Ensign was terrified, and spoke to him with such respect! Now, why would he primp and posture and act the fool as he does, unless it is to deceive us?" Lowering her voice, she whispered, "Papa, I am sure it is a plot to entrap us! Perhaps they are after Robbie. Does he mean to come home?"

"Heavens above!" MacTavish disentangled her grip from his laces. "D'ye take your brother for a caper-wit?"

"No, sir. But, well, now there's this business with Little Willie. Papa, can you get word to Ligun Doone?"

"Even could I, he cannot help every hunted rebel. Oh, never look so glum. If Doone comes nigh to Mayhew and learns of his plight I fancy he'll render whatever aid he may. Perchance he already has done so." He stood, wondering in an irked way whether he'd ever have time to get to the notes for his lecture. "You've had a wearying day, Prue. Go to sleep. And you might try remembering Mr. Doone in your prayers."

"I do, Papa. They say he is one of the bravest gentlemen in all Scotland, but I fancy he walks on thin ice every day of his life and can use all the prayers sent up for him."

"I'm very sure of it. Now get to sleep, and do not be lying there worrying about nonsense."

Prudence sighed, blew out her candle, and lay down. At once her thoughts turned to Delacourt. She closed her eyes and concentrated on sleep. He had looked very pale and tired this evening, but she did not believe for a moment that he was expiring. He enjoyed the part of the long-suffering invalid, was all. And could there be anything more reprehensible? Oh, pox on the man! She tossed onto her right side. What a widgeon, to be fretting about the Southron when she'd forgotten to have a word with God in behalf of an heroic Scot. Her feet were cold. Perhaps the Lord would forgive if she spoke to Him from the warmth of her bed, instead of upon her knees, as she should. "Dear Lord, will Ye no accept my apologies for addressing Ye in this lazy way? 'Tis in the matter of Mr. Ligun Doone . . ."

Prudence awoke with the dawn. She lay in her warm cocoon for a few minutes. Worrying. And it would only get worse if she stayed there. She got out of bed and went to the window. The sky was a blushing soft coral wherein floated a few fluffy clouds. Perfect weather for a ride—if she dared.

Half an hour later, having washed in the frigid water of her pitcher and dressed herself, she crept along the hall. The house was hushed, but in the stables the grooms were busily at work, and in no time her favourite dapple grey was saddled and ready. She guided the big horse across the park, skirting the woods and taking the path that led eventually to General Wade's Road. She had told the anxious grooms that she would not leave the estate, but there was a mystery about this early morning that lured her on, and after all, the redcoats would not dare harm her again after what had befallen their coarse Sergeant. She rode on. The birds were twittering now, but no other sound disturbed the still air. The waters of the great loch were smooth as glass, the roseate heavens reflecting in that mirror. A gull came cawing in from the east to swoop low over the water and settle down, leaving a long wake behind him. Prudence kicked her heels home, and the grey leapt eagerly into a gallop.

She followed the shore for a while, then turned southwards, climbing into the hills until the wild beauty of the Highlands was all about her: lonely vales, tree-clad slopes, rushing, clear burns, rugged crags, and the air so pure that far to the north she could glimpse Ben Wyvis lifting mighty shoulders against the opalescent skies.

Prudence was alert for any sign of other riders, but she saw no one until she came upon a shepherd guiding his small flock to a new pasture, the sheep hurrying and bleating to the urging of the dogs. She stopped and spoke to the man briefly, but he was a taciturn individual and eyed her with marked suspicion so that she soon left him and turned for home.

The sun was higher now, the sky a deep, clear blue. With luck, thought Prudence, she would reach home before the MacTavish arose. Assuredly, if her luck was out, she would be subjected to a severe scold for having ventured out alone. She'd done so because of a pressing need to get into more rarefied air; to try to sort out the problems that distressed her. She'd done little of sorting, but the peace of the high places had soothed her, and she did not want to go home yet. She reined in her grey as she came to a promontory that presented a fine view of Loch Ness and the surrounding countryside. She smiled proudly as she viewed the majestic panorama. And then she caught sight of a horseman far below, riding very fast and superbly. She watched him admiringly as he turned uphill, but then she reined back, alarmed, for he seemed to be coming straight for her.

About half a mile downhill from her, he halted his mount and turned back to scan the view, even as she had done. She strained her eyes, trying to identify him. A slim man, tall, and wearing a moderate wig and a tricorne. He had a good pair of shoulders and an easy swing in the saddle as his magnificent black sidled restlessly. Even as she watched, another man appeared as if from the face of the crag; a stocky individual, clad in shabby clothes and a scratch wig. The rider dismounted and they gripped hands.

Prudence caught her breath with excitement. There must be a hidden cave there, in which case the stocky fellow was likely a fugitive. If the rider had come to help him in broad daylight, it was daring that approached the level of foolhardiness. She could see them clearly—others might do so. Yet now came a third man, and she gasped because he wore the red uniform of an English officer.

A dog barked. A big collie raced up the slope, tail waving. The horseman bent to stroke the dog and take something from his collar. A note, Prudence surmised. The others stepped closer. A moment later, one gave him a leg up into the saddle. He waved and rode off, disappearing in seconds amongst the cut-up ridges and gullies. Prudence's gaze had followed him, and when she looked back the others had vanished again, only the collie remaining in sight, bounding down the slope from whence it had come.

If the men she had seen were fugitives, the rider had come to give them news or money. On the other hand, sad though it was, there were Scots who were traitors to their Prince, or who had never followed him. Perhaps she had witnessed a gathering of bounty hunters pooling information on some poor hunted rebel. The English officer could very well be a deserter. She remembered the shifty-eyed shepherd and the suspicion he had evidenced, and fear touched her. Suddenly, these loved and familiar crags were menacing, the peaceful silence a deadly hush. Oh, *why* must she always be rushing into situations that seemed simple and straightforward, but suddenly became— Not very far away a branch snapped. The grey danced, his head turned towards the sound.

Heart in her mouth, Prudence drove home her heels and urged him in the opposite direction. They went down the slope at reckless speed. Twice the grey skidded, and Prudence thought he must fall, but somehow they survived that mad scramble. She thought she heard a shout, which added to her fright. She applied the whip sharply to the horse's flank. It was not a familiar sensation and he sprang into a powerful gallop, the countryside blurring past as though he had acquired the wings of Pegasus.

Not until she was on MacTavish lands did Prudence slow their pace. She leaned forward, patting the grey's foam-streaked neck and murmuring gently to him. After a few moments she trotted him sedately across the field and into the grove. She had come home by way of a wide westerly loop to avoid any who might have lain in wait for her, and she was returning much later than she had hoped. When she reached the stableyard, however, the only person in evidence was the last man she expected to see.

Captain Delacourt watched from his invalid chair as the grooms rubbed down a magnificent black mare. He turned a surprised face as Prudence rode in. She also was surprised. He looked weary, but his face was flushed and perspiration beaded his upper lip and his temples.

Allowing Haggerty to lift her down, she murmured her polite good mornings to the Captain and went over to the mare. The horse she had seen from the hilltop had been a fine black. It was silly to think this was the same animal, and yet the mare had obviously been ridden. She said idly, "Lord Briley was up betimes, Haggerty."

"Aye, miss."

"I'd no idea he meant to ride. We could have gone out together."

"Mmmnn."

"Has he been back very long?"

"I dinna ken."

She gave it up and turned her attention to the Captain. He was peering through the yard gate. She asked, "Are you expecting someone, sir?"

"Eh? Oh, I was wondering where your groom can have got to, Miss MacTavish."

His eyes were bland and innocent.

Hers became wary. "Which one?"

"I fear I have not learned their names. I meant whichever one accompanied you."

She thought, 'That's what I thought you meant, wretched spy,' and she said with a gentle smile, "I prefer to ride unaccompanied, Captain."

"Good gracious." He leaned back in his chair as though overcome. "You *are* a bold one, ma'am!"

Prudence drew herself up to the last fraction of her insignificant height. "Sir?"

"Oh, dear." The wistfully expiring look was brought to bear. "Have I offended again? It merely seemed—ah, not very—er, wise to venture into those dreadfully wild-looking mountains alone."

Her lip curled. "It would be very unwise for you to do so, I own. Especially since you seem to be feverish this morning."

"Egad! Do I?" One white hand trembled up to feel his brow. "Alas, I think you are right! I should not have come out to see the horses, I suppose. But I do rather miss being able to go for a little trot, you know. If only—"

"What the devil . . . !" Lord Thaddeus, booted and spurred, marched into the yard, his stride a far cry from his customary mincing gait. He went straight to his mare, not noticing Prudence, who had drifted back into the shade cast by the open stable door. "By God, Geoff!" he exclaimed, swinging around to glare at his friend. "Did you have the infernal—"

Delacourt waved a languid hand. "No language, if you please, Thad. We've a lady present."

Briley jerked his head in the direction indicated, and looked comically guilty. "Oh, by Jove! Your pardon, Mith MacTavith. I wath provoked to find Geoff down here. Never will obey hith doctor."

"Most unwise," said Prudence. "And you see what has come of it, my lord. Poor Captain Delacourt has taxed himself into a fevered condition."

His lordship levelled a searching look at the invalid. "Idiot," he said pithily.

"No, how can you be so harsh," scolded Prudence. "It is but natural for the Captain to desire a—er, little trot. You can understand that, my lord, when you yourself had such a nice gallop this morning."

He adjusted his impeccable cravat. "Had I known you were out riding, ma'am," he said, "I'd have begged leave to accompany you. Will you conthole me by telling me why there ith a jolly great pyramid in your garden?"

'Oh, neatly done,' thought Prudence. "My father is an archaeologist. While he was working in Egypt a few years ago, he was able to prevent the looting of a pyramid, and the government was so grateful they built a replica of it for him. I doubt anything ever pleased him as much, and it is become quite a point of interest for the area, as you may well imagine."

Briley's personal opinion was that it was an eyesore for an object so foreign to the environment to be dumped on the shore of a Scottish loch, but he said courteously that it was 'very interesting.' "Dashed good size," he said. "About half the original, ma'am?"

"I think it's more like one-twentieth the actual size," she replied. "But very true as to detail."

Delacourt chuckled. "Even to the treasure in the burial chamber?"

"Oh, yes," she said with unshaken aplomb. "We found gold in the chamber, and a mummy."

Awed, Briley stammered, "Jupiter! A—a real live one?"

"No, you dolt." Delacourt grinned. "A real dead one! May I be so crass as to ask if there was a deal of gold, Miss MacTavish?"

She returned sweetly, "I don't mind your being crass, sir. There were two golden amulets. My father keeps them in a display case in his study, and if you are interested in Egyptology I know he will be most pleased to show you both the pyramid and his other artifacts. Now, if you will excuse me, gentlemen." She left them, and walked over to the house.

The maids were bustling about, and the smells of breakfast

drifted enticingly from the kitchens. There was no sign of her father, but Prudence had quite forgotten her fear of encountering him. Deep in thought, she went slowly up the stairs. From the remarks Briley had made on his first visit here, and to the Colonel last evening, he had met Delacourt only when he arrived at Castle Court with Lady Ericson's granddaughter. And yet Prudence had somehow gained an impression of a deep and long-established attachment. Only an old friend, she thought, would have the right to say in such a proprietory way, "Idiot!" as Briley had done just now.

Then again, the black mare had certainly been ridden, and it appeared that Briley held Delacourt responsible. Could Delacourt really have been the rider she'd seen? Very troubled, she paused on the landing, and shook her head at nothing in particular. That he was exaggerating his illness she had no doubt and had attributed it to a reluctance to rejoin his regiment. But if he was capable of riding so well, and was concealing that fact, then he was up to more mischief than a simple evasion of active service. She remembered the several times of late that she had woken in the night thinking to have heard riders outside. Twice she'd run to the window and seen nothing, but now she wondered if Delacourt was creeping out under cover of darkness. It would explain the fact that he so often appeared to be very tired, and slept the day away. It fitted neatly enough. And there could be but one logical reason for an officer to feign incapacity, be billeted in the home of an enemy family, and creep out secretly. Geoffrey Delacourt *was* a spy. He had been placed here by that horrid Colonel so as to watch them. The English probably suspected the MacTavish of being linked to Ligun Doone! By now halfway up the second flight, Prudence's hand flew to her throat as she had a sudden mental picture of her father standing before a wall in his shirt-sleeves, his wrists bound behind him, his proud head high-held, facing twelve redcoats with muskets aimed. She shrank, trembling, against the stairs, sickened by the very thought of it. Whatever could she *do?* There was no least use trying to warn the MacTavish, he would only chide her again. He was completely taken in. But she could not simply sit back and wait for them all to be arrested. She stared blankly at one of her aunt's scarves lying in a bright puddle of sunshine on the next stair. Taking it up, her lips tightened. She would watch the treacherous Sassenach. Like a hawk, she would watch him! But he must not know she suspected. He must be lulled into a false sense of security. He would make a slip, then, and she would pounce—like a snake! She mulled that over for a minute. No, not like a snake, exactly. But certainly she would pounce! She hastened to her room, planning her next move, but experiencing also a quite unaccountable sense of hurt and betrayal.

The Captain's venture out of doors appeared to have exhausted him, and he kept to his room for the rest of the morning. A breeze came up in the afternoon and blew in grey clouds to shut out the sun. Lord Briley, who had been closeted with Delacourt, joined Hortense and Prudence for a late luncheon, and afterwards accompanied the ladies to the music room, where Hortense played the harpsichord and Prudence sang some of the beautiful airs and folk-songs of her land. MacTavish, who had been obliged to attend to some pressing matter with his steward, returned to them and they all joined in singing "Women Are Angels, Wooing," Briley raising a fine clear baritone voice that compensated for the lisp. They parted in perfect amity at three o'clock, to rest before changing for dinner.

Leaving the music room on Briley's arm, Prudence saw Lockerbie wheeling his master along the corridor towards them. "Ah, Captain," she said. "How glad I am to see you up and about. I was quite alarmed by your high colour this morning. You are feeling better, I trust?"

He smiled wanly at her. "To say truth, dear ma'am, I fear you were perfectly right. I tax my strength by being up at all, but I felt I must come and thank you, Mr. MacTavish, for all your kind efforts in my behalf."

"My very great pleasure, my dear fellow," said MacTavish gravely.

Prudence murmured, "Kind . . . efforts?"

"Your papa," explained the Captain, "was so kind as to have me moved to two ground-floor rooms. It was so—so very wearying you know to be hauled up and down the stairs. I am most—" He paused, coughing, and waved his hand in a helpless fashion.

MacTavish slipped one hand onto his shoulder. "Say no more, I beg you. And pray do not attempt to come to the dining room tonight. No, 'tis no trouble to my staff to bring you your tray. You can join us tomorrow."

"I hope so," the Captain asserted forlornly. "Indeed, I hope so."

Lockerbie wheeled his drooping charge away, and the rest of the party dispersed to their various chambers.

Prudence went into her parlour and sat by the window, staring unseeingly into the drizzling afternoon. So the cunning Captain had already thrust a spoke into her wheel! With his bedchamber now two flights below hers it would be much more difficult to keep watch on his activities. She thought angrily, 'And that much easier for him to pass his spy reports on to his soldiers!' She wrung her hands. If Delacourt *was* a spy he doubtless planned to send them all to a terrible death. Well, he'd not succeed, the cruel beast! Somehow, no matter *what* the cost, she would outwit him!

IV

"The green muslin?" said Kitty, shocked. "But—'tis oot o' style, miss! People will think I dinna ken how tae dress my lady."

Prudence took down the slightly faded muslin gown and eyed it with approval. It should blend in nicely. "Have I a green bonnet? But—no. On second thought—a scarf, a green scarf for my hair will be better. And—no powder, Kitty."

"Losh, but ye'll look a fright! And the Captain's cousin coming tae visit him s'afternoon."

Reinforcements, no doubt! "Why was I not told? From whence comes this cousin?"

"I didnae hear," replied Kitty. It had not escaped her that her young mistress had been extreme preoccupied of late with Captain Delacourt, for all she tried to appear indifferent to the handsome invalid. After Lord Briley left yesterday afternoon, Miss Prue had announced her intention to devote herself to the Captain's entertainment and had sat in the book room reading Shakespeare to him until he'd fallen fast asleep. Miss Prue had seemed rather vexed when the poor laddie began to snore so loudly, but when he'd woken and apologized in so meek a way, she had wheeled his chair tae his room with her own hands so that he might rest. When Colonel Cunningham had dropped in for tea, Miss Prue had scarcely spoke of anything but the Captain and of how she admired his brave acceptance of his suffering. Though, mused Kitty, to her own way of thinking, Captain Delacourt was bonnie enough, but a wee bit of a mama's boy when it came tae spunk.

She turned from rummaging through the chest of drawers. "I canna find a scarf of green, miss. There's this blue one, but—"

"Never mind. I shall borrow one from my aunt. She's sure to have one."

Hortense was reading a letter and in a great state of agitation. "'Tis your poor Aunt Geraldine," she cried. "You'll remember her friend, Mrs. Andover? Gone! And only think—the stars told me that death was close to us this week!"

"Not very close, surely. I've never met the poor lady, have you? How came she to go to her reward?"

Hortense turned a closely written page so as to read the crossed lines. "Her doctor—MacPherson, a good man—said she'd been so unwise as to eat a quantity of gooseberries when the moon was at the full and the fruit fermenting!"

"Goodness!" said Prudence, uncertainly. "Is that dreadful?"

"It must be. Oh, dear! If the world is not full of pitfalls for the unwary!"

"All sorts of pitfalls," muttered Prudence, contemplating the villainy of English Captains. "Aunty Mac, do your stars have anything to say that would affect us—directly, I mean?"

Gratified by this interest in her favourite subject, Hortense tossed her sister-in-law's letter aside. "Indeed they do! Prue, my love, I've no wish to frighten you, but—oh, a dreadful menace is coming upon us!"

'The cousin,' thought Prudence grimly. 'Well, at all events, I'm prepared for him!' "Do you know when this menace will afflict us?"

"Very soon, I should say." Her aunt sighed. "And in a strange garment," she added dramatically.

"Strange . . . *what?*"

Hortense said defensively, "My charts say that a man wearing outlandish attire will come seeking the death—the *death,*

Prue!—of a resident of Lakepoint." She tucked in her chin, her eyes wide and tragic.

Prudence battled the impulse to laugh. "How dreadful. I hope your stars have erred this time. May I please borrow a green scarf?"

Hortense regarded her niece gloomily and acknowledged, if only to herself, that although a dear and pretty creature, Prudence was a widgeon. Green, she pointed out, was unlucky. This did not daunt her niece, and the end of it was that Hortense rang for her maid, who was able to unearth a charming zephyr shawl which, when loosely draped about Prudence's bright curls, looked so enchanting that Hortense forgave her and declared staunchly that nothing so lovely could possibly be unlucky.

Armed with this assurance, Prudence tripped downstairs and went into the kitchen to purloin a basket and some pruning scissors. She was rather taken aback to find Captain Delacourt chatting with the kitchen staff in the large sunny room. She checked, hoping to hear what he was prying out of the servants, but their startled faces betrayed her, and his dark head turned, his martyred smile dawning at once.

"How charmingly you look, Miss MacTavish. Outward bound, are you? Alas, had I but the strength to accompany you."

She told him she meant to undertake nothing of a taxing nature. "Just a little stroll before luncheon, Captain. Perhaps Lockerbie could bring you along."

"Had you come seeking me, then? How very thoughtful."

She put up her brows. "But why ever should I seek you in the kitchen? It is surely the last place I'd have expected to find a guest."

Again, for a split second she thought to glimpse that glinting dance of amusement in the dark eyes, but then the thick curling lashes swept down and he was saying that the chef had very obligingly volunteered to show him how the morning bannocks had been prepared. "Such a sure hand has your wonderful *maître de la cuisine.* It is a recipe I am very anxious to give my own cook." He sighed and added despondently, "If I am ever so fortunate as to return to England."

Prudence thought, 'Oh, you wicked liar!' She glanced at the servants, but they were looking so innocently pleased by the words of praise that she could not think they had been saying anything they shouldn't. She excused herself, collected her gardening articles, and exited by the side door.

The morning was warm and full of the scents of summer. Señorita was chasing a grasshopper in the kitchen garden, her whiskers ferocious. Oblivious to the havoc the cat was creating among the young lettuce plants, Prudence strolled around to the side of the house, frowning a little. She would have to instruct Mrs. Cairn to warn the servants. Geoffrey Delacourt had altogether too much easy charm, and although they were good, loyal people, there was no telling what he might worm out of them.

The cutting beds were located beyond the rose gardens, and here phlox and lupins, iris and daisies and cornflowers bloomed in colourful array. Prudence cut a nice bouquet and embellished it with some sprigs of apple blossom before turning back towards the house.

Captain Delacourt's ground-floor suite had been formed by allocating him two connecting ante-rooms located at the rear of the house, next to the MacTavish's study. Prudence turned her idle steps in that direction, trusting her choice of gown would render her inconspicuous against the verdant background. Several stone benches were set around the lawns, one of which was fortuitously placed just below the terrace not far from the Captain's windows which, due to the warmth of the day, were wide open. Prudence sat down and waited, hoping she had managed to reach this point unobserved.

All was quiet and peaceful. Birds chirped and flirted in the oak trees that stood one on each side of the terrace. A butterfly hovered over a low-hanging branch of the gold-laden acacia in the centre of the lawn. Prudence smiled nostalgically at the tree. Years ago, though it seemed only yesterday, she and Robbie had been used to climb into its branches to keep watch on

Papa when they were engaged in some particularly desperate enterprise. Often, their wickedness would consist of smuggling bon-bons or jam tarts outside on some glorious sunny afternoon when they were supposed to be in their rooms struggling with the studies Miss Grover had set them before luncheon. They'd had a clear view of Papa's study from the acacia and— Prudence tensed with a gasp of excitement. Captain Clever might have played right into her hands, for although she was years older now, she was not so decrepit she could not climb that tree again. And she would borrow Robbie's glass from his room. She chuckled gleefully, then listened intently as she heard a door close and Lockerbie's voice raised in a scolding way, the words not quite distinguishable.

"Oh, hush, man," said the Captain, his voice clearer, as though he had wheeled his chair close to the window. "It was a waste, at all events. They either know nothing, or will say nothing."

There was a pause, Prudence straining her ears for the least murmur.

Lockerbie said quite distinctly, "There's Miss MacTavish's girl—Kitty something or other. Frae what I hear, he was sweet on her."

"Was he, now? Splendid, Kerbie! You're a better spy than I am, be damned if you ain't! We can work through her, then. You must—"

Dimly, Prudence had heard the sound of a carriage coming up the drive. Now Lockerbie interrupted sharply. "Somebody's coming, sir!"

There was the sound of a door being wrenched open, and another voice, an Englishman's voice, husky with emotion. "Master Geoffrey!"

"Cole!" Delacourt sounded overjoyed and there were the unmistakeable sounds of an affectionate reunion.

"We thought—we thought as you was . . . dead, sir!"

"You old rascal! How did you sniff me out?"

"Mr. de Villars told me. I came at once, of course, but—oh,

sir! It's a dangerous game you're playing here. If they unmask you, it doesn't bear thinking of!"

"Then do not think on it. Just remember, Cole, I'm known as Geoffrey Delacourt up here—you must not forget. Kerbie, you'd best close those windows. Jove, but I'm glad to see you, Cole! How does my sister—"

The windows were closed and the rest of the question was lost. Prudence blinked at the acacia tree through a blur of tears. Not until that moment did she realize how desperately she'd been hoping her suspicions were groundless. Not until now had she understood that she also had been on the brink of succumbing to that little glint of laughter in a pair of dark eyes, or to the gentleness in his smile that had caressed her a time or two. Succumbing to the wiles of a spy. A man who dwelt in their home while gathering evidence against them, plotting to use sweet, trusting Kitty, who admired him so, as a tool to trap the man she loved and haul him off to be executed. "Oh!" she whispered, rubbing fiercely at her tearful eyes. "What a muckle great doddipoll ye are, Prue MacTavish! Faith, but Robbie would—would laugh himself intae a . . . spasm!"

Smothering a sob, she took up her flowers and walked quickly back to the house. She ran up the stairs to her brother's room, having given the flowers to Sidley, and sought for the spy-glass. Typical of Robbie, his press was a shambles, and the drawers of the two large chests little better, but at last she unearthed the telescoping glass, buried under a welter of old letters in his desk drawer. She dusted the lens, drew out the sections, and trained the glass on the acacia tree. She could even see the bees that darted amongst the blooms! Triumphant, she telescoped the sections and slipped the glass into her pocket. With this, she might see something so damning that Papa would fairly *have* to believe her!

Since Mr. MacTavish had gone to Inverness to confer with a fellow scholar, and Hortense was off to meet with the Astrological Circle at the home of her dearest friend, no formal luncheon was served that day, a buffet having been set up in the breakfast parlour to accommodate Prudence and Captain Delacourt whenever it should suit them to take themselves in search of food. Prudence did not see the Captain, however, and made a light meal of fruit, some lemonade, and a piece of sponge cake. By the time she had finished there was still no sign of him and she hurried into the garden once more.

All nature seemed to be drowsing that sultry afternoon. Down by the rose arbour a gardener knelt weeding, his back to the house, and another man was scything the lawn near the west wing and the music room. Prudence wandered past the acacia tree and, when she was fairly sure it shielded her from any chance of the Captain spotting her from his windows, she turned about and wandered back again. She glanced over her shoulder. The toiling gardener had not seen her. Like a flash, she darted in amongst the leafy bower of the branches.

It was cooler in here, and the air was heavy with the fragrance of the blossoms. The old bench that had been built around the trunk was still there, a forgotten bonus that made her initial climb much easier. Even so, she felt slightly apprehensive as she looked up. The first branch seemed very far. She wondered if the trunk had grown since she was a schoolroom miss, and decided that was very likely. She reached up tentatively. She could clasp the branch and it felt sturdy enough, but how to get up there? Fortunately her gown had no hoops and she had worn only four petticoats, so she should not be too encumbered. She glanced around nervously, then pulled up her skirts and stuck her left foot into the cleft remaining from a sawn-off limb. That must be the answer, of course! This had been the branch she and Robbie had used as a first step! She tightened her lips and determined that she would just have to get along with what was left of it.

Gripping the upper branch tightly, she pushed up with her right foot and shot into the air. Her head made violent contact with another slyly lurking limb. She squeaked with pain and almost lost her grip, but somehow managed to haul herself up and straddle the branch. She rocked precariously, her head hurting and an ominous tearing sound alarming her. Intensely aggravated, she discovered that she was perspiring, her hair was all knocked down, and she was most uncomfortable. Worse, it was all for naught! Instead of facing the house she was facing the tree trunk, which was ridiculous! She growled out one of Robbie's choice oaths. She might be hind end foremost, but at least she was up and it should be a simple matter to turn around. Clinging to the branch above her head, and with a great struggle, she succeeded in bringing her right leg over the branch she was straddling, but there were more tearing sounds. Oh, if *only* ladies could wear breeches! It dawned on her, then, that she must resemble a berserk gorilla, and the thought so amused that she began to giggle. She controlled herself and at length was able to turn about on the branch so that now she sat beside the trunk, facing the house. Provided she clung very tightly to the trunk with her right arm, she could fish Robbie's glass from her pocket and see whether she could get a clear view of Delacourt's room.

Contrarily, her skirts had completely reversed themselves. Not only was she sitting on the front of her gown, but the twisted-around back portion only reached to her knees. Heaven forfend anyone should discover her in such an unladylike state! She panicked momentarily, and had to remind herself grimly that it was all for Scotland, her Papa, and Little Willie Mayhew. Wriggling, she tugged and fought to straighten her gown. It was a heating and lengthy process, but at last she worked the pocket around to where she could reach the glass. She was panting when she extracted it and, balancing gingerly, devoted both hands to pulling out the three sections. She gripped the glass securely with her left hand and, again wrapping her right arm around the tree trunk, levelled the glass. *Voilà!* She could see right inside the Captain's windows, now open again. The room appeared to be empty, but she could see the foot of the bed, and he might now be having a nap, maintaining his pose of a weak invalid. Likely, he had not been wounded at all, and the entire tale concocted only so as to pull the wool over her trusting father's eyes!

She had no sooner arrived at this conclusion than she heard a man humming. Her heart gave a frightened leap. He was very close by. But it was likely the gardener, who would soon pass and go on to the house, or the outdoor servants' quarters. She waited, scarcely daring to breathe, for a glimpse of the musically inclined gardener. What a long time it was taking him to come into sight. Fretting, her heart gave another bounce as the hum became a song, sung in a deep, cultured, and melodious voice:

"Man may escape from rope and gun;
Nay, some have outlived the doctor's pill:
Who takes a woman must be undone,
That basilisk is sure to kill!
Sure to kill! Sure *to kill!*
The fly that sips treacle is lost in the sweets,
So he that tastes woman . . . woman . . . woman,
He that tastes woman—ruin meets!"

Prudence gritted her teeth. It was *him,* of course! And how like Fate to bring him to this very spot, at this of all moments, to warble his revolting little song!

Lockerbie's voice, chuckling. "That's a right good song, sir. Faith, but I've not heard ye sing in a muckle long time."

"Not had the breath for't, alas. In fact, I'm . . . not at all sure but what I've . . . used more than I had."

"Are ye all right, sir? Will I be running for your medicine?"

"Thank you. But do not bring it for a little while, please. It's grand to be away from beds and stuffy rooms for a bit."

Prudence groaned inwardly and prayed the wretch would go away.

"I dinna like leaving ye oot here, sir," said the faithful Lockerbie.

"Why, you can come and collect me in half an hour, Kerbie. Toddle off, now, there's a good fellow."

Lockerbie grumbled to himself, but (to Prudence's stark horror) trudged off towards the west wing, probably to cadge a tankard of ale from the kitchen maids.

The humming started again. That same odious song, with a

word sung softly here and there, indicating the spy had regained his wind a trifle. 'Thirty minutes!' she thought, anguished. 'I canna bear thirty minutes o' this noise!'

One single moment later, she would have gladly settled for thirty minutes of the Captain's singing, for, craning her neck to see him, she came eye to eye with a bee.

The widespread belief that if one remained still a bee would lose interest was, she soon perceived, another old wives' tale. She scarcely breathed, but the bee, fascinated, hovered before her eyes. Desperate, she hissed, "Go away! Shoo!"

The bee buzzed a little louder and showed a marked inclination to sit on the end of her nose. She jerked her head back in alarm, grasped the end of Hortense's scarf, and flapped it. This was an error. The buzz became aggressively loud, and the bee began to whip about, apparently calling in comrades, because two more wearing the same uniform swelled the ranks. With a squeal of fright, Prudence came down the tree much faster than she had gone up. She clung to her branch as she lowered herself, giving a louder squeal as a sharp pang above her elbow warned that she had been stung.

"Good gracious me!" The Captain had manoeuvred himself within the screen of the branches and was standing, clinging to his chair, an astounded expression on his face as he gazed up at her. "Whatever," he gasped, "are you doing?"

"Exercising my fingernails!" she snapped, groping vainly with her right foot for the cleft branch, and hideously aware she must look a perfect fright. "Will you please to move? I am being stung to death, and you stand like a lump, staring!"

"Poor girl!" He clambered gingerly onto the bench and reached upwards. "Only let go, and I will try to catch you."

"For heaven's sake! If—if you could just put my foot in the cleft branch, I can manage by myself."

There was a short pause during which she heard muffled sounds indicative of effort—or mirth—or both. Her arms were aching fiercely when he said sadly, "Alas . . . I cannot seem to reach it, ma'am. Do trust yourself to me. I will . . . do my poor best. I promise you."

She hesitated. If he really had been badly hurt at Prestonpans, she might cause him to suffer another setback, though why that should matter was beyond her ken. And he was probably perfectly well. Certainly well enough to have managed that spirited mare on Wednesday morning. A bee made a practice zoom at her. With a yelp, she let go.

Strong arms received and held her. Dusky eyes scanned her with a mixture of concern and amusement. The amusement eased into admiration, and his grip tightened. Prudence felt half crushed, a condition that for a moment of insanity she was willing to endure indefinitely. But then Delacourt lowered her to the ground, stepped down himself, and groped his way to his chair.

"What very odd habits . . . you Scots have," he said breathlessly.

Ignoring him, Prudence attempted to inspect her arm. The attack had been from the rear and she could not discern the site.

"Dear me," sighed the rescuer. "You have been stung, haven't you? You are very brave, ma'am, but that must come out at once."

It hurt quite nastily, but she said an austere, "It can wait until I get back to the house, thank you."

"Oh, no. Every second counts if you are not to develop *apiology acutus.*" Prudence stared at him suspiciously, and he went on with bland assurance, "I am very adept in such matters, for my sister made a habit of getting herself stung. I had to suck out the stingers very promptly for her or she became quite ill. I remember she was once stung on the—" He checked. "Well, never mind. Come now, I shan't hurt you."

His countenance was grave, but his eyes and the twitch of his lips made Prudence decide to leave him at once. She was deterred when she noticed that he was quite pale. She moved closer saying uncertainly, "Are you all right? It must have been most taxing for you to catch me. I mean—I know I'm not a wispy lass."

"No," he agreed absently, inspecting the back of her arm.

"What?" she demanded, stiffening.

"Oh—I mean, it was no bother. Besides"—he touched her arm gently—"I admire fine healthy young women."

Affronted, Prudence snorted, "Well!" and strove to pull away.

"No, no. You must not move, for I've a good grip on it. Bend down, if you please."

She thought, 'A good *grip* on it'? But for some reason that she would have been quite unable to explain, she obeyed him.

"Put back your arm a little. Ah—that's better."

She felt his lips on her skin, and a devastating shiver went through her.

After a moment he said, "Perhaps you should kneel. I can't quite get it and your arm is becoming very inflamed."

Prudence's knees were so weak that it was no handicap to sink onto them.

Delacourt bent forward. His arm slipped about her waist, and she felt the velvet touch of his mouth again. Presently, he said, "There—it's all done now." She turned to him. "If you . . . will . . ." he mumbled, and sagged weakly.

With a startled cry, she reached up to support him, but he came from the chair in a limp tumble and she clung to him, his head pillowed against her bosom.

"Oh, my heavens! Captain! Are you all right?"

His eyes still closed, he murmured dazedly, "Quite all right, dearest Mama . . ." and kissed his soft pillow lingeringly.

"Oo-oh!" cried Prudence, sputtering with indignation. "Wake up!" She tried to push his head away, but it was heavily resistant.

He sighed and blinked up at her. "What's . . . to do?"

"Aye! What indeed?" she said, her face flaming. "You kissed me—" And she broke off, her hand moving to the afflicted area.

"I would not dream of doing so improper a thing," he declared primly. "Why am I sitting under this tree? Did I go off in one of my swoons?"

She fixed him with a hard look. "You fell out of your chair. You were helping with my stinger."

"With your what?"

"I was stung," she said haughtily. "By a bee. As you very well know."

He put one hand to his brow. His hand shook. Indeed, all of him seemed to shake. "The last thing I recollect," he said, his voice muffled, "is catching you when you jumped down from your exercises. What with—er, one thing and another, I am quite overcome. Would you be so kind as to help me—back into my chair?"

Warily, she helped him. "I'll hae ye tae know ye dinna fool me, Captain Delacourt," she told him.

"Fool you? Dear ma'am, I confess I find you inexplicable. I did but offer you a helping hand, whereby I am now exhausted."

She stepped back while he gazed up at her soulfully. "I think you are very sly," she announced.

He sighed. "I trust you will not hesitate to call upon me the next time you require first aid. You see, I do not hold a grudge."

Her determination not to laugh at such schoolboy innocence was almost overborne. The Captain lowered his eyes meekly, then seemed struck to stone. Following his gaze, Prudence gave a gasp. Her gown had suffered several small tears during her adventure, and her pocket had evidently become caught on a branch, considerably to its detriment. The object she had carried there had fallen forward. Robbie's spy-glass was quite visible. Trying to think of something sensible to say, she was speechless. Delacourt looked up, his face frighteningly bleak for an instant. Then he smiled. "I am sincerely flattered, ma'am," he murmured.

She could have sunk. "Dinna be flattering ye'sel', sir! I carried yon glass purely tae—tae watch the birds."

"You are sure it was not—the bees? Or perhaps both?"

She gave an outraged gasp, but before she could retaliate, a quiver beside his mouth caught her attention and then his eyes were sparkling at her and so undermining her common sense that when he enquired if he might borrow the offending spyglass, she thrust it at him resistlessly. At once irked by such silly weakness, she began to push the chair from beneath the tree.

The Captain trained the glass on the drivepath, and Prudence saw that a coach was bowling along towards the house.

"My cousin is arrived," he said, closing the glass and returning it to her by holding it over his shoulder. "How very fatiguing. I really do not know if I have sufficient strength to receive visitors. Not after all this excitement."

Prudence glared at the back of his head. It would be interesting, she thought, to see by what name this newcomer addressed the rascally Captain.

By the time she had wheeled the chair back to the house, Captain Delacourt's cousin had been welcomed and was ensconced with Hortense. The invalid, having apparently revived to an extent, professed a weary resignation to "doing the pretty" and entreated Prudence to take him to the drawing room.

The cousin was not at all what Prudence had expected, being a petite girl of about her own age, with unpowdered ringlets the colour of ripe corn, big brown eyes, and a buoyant, happy manner. She uttered a shriek when she saw Delacourt, and flew up to embrace him while inundating him with questions as to his welfare. The Captain appeared singularly unreluctant after all, coming to his feet in quite a sprightly way, and returning his cousin's embraces with gusto. He lost no time in making the two girls known to one another, and Prudence begrudgingly admitted to herself that Miss Elizabeth Clandon was a very pretty girl, with a way of spreading her hands to emphasize her remarks which was charming. She spoke with a Scots accent—an odd fact, if she was related to the Captain. She was also, Prudence became aware, staring, with a twinkle in her eyes that was indeed reminiscent of her kinsman.

"My wee pet," cried Hortense, who had been eyeing her niece in horror. "Have you suffered an accident?"

Prudence had been so upset by the Captain's disgraceful behaviour and then the arrival of his relative that she had quite forgotten her own appearance. She became the focus of all eyes and wished the floor might open and swallow her. Putting up a hand to her tumbled curls, she stammered, "I—er, fell."

"From a tree," explained the Captain, with helpful and revolting honesty.

Hortense gave a little squawk.

"But I caught her," he added, sinking down into his chair again.

"You never did!" His cousin gave him a shocked look. "For goodness' sake, Geoffrey! One might think you'd learn—"

"She was not very high up," he said hurriedly. "Exercising, y'know."

"Ex . . . er-cising . . . ?" breathed Hortense, her eyes goggling. "In a tree? In *public?*"

Very red in the face, Prudence said, "I had not thought it to be public, Aunty Mac."

"That is perfectly true," Delacourt said supportively. "She was hiding there, ma'am."

She glared at him. "Not very successfully."

"It was fatiguing," he admitted, sighing and putting back his head. "But when a lady screams, what is a gentleman to do?"

Hortense, mesmerized by her niece's expression, took warning. "Exactly so, Captain Geoffrey," she babbled. "So you, ah, have Scots blood, do you?"

"Oh, yes," Miss Clandon said brightly. "The Montgomerys were—" She checked suddenly. Her cousin was starting to nod and had not glanced at her, but his hand, Prudence noted, was hidden by the sweep of Miss Clandon's skirts and he could very easily have given her garment a warning tug. "That is to say," the girl continued, "Geoffrey's mama's people were originally from Edinburgh."

"Why, how very nice," said Hortense. "Captain, you never mentioned— Oh, he has dropped asleep, poor boy."

Miss Clandon bent over her cousin, then said, smiling, "He looks so much better than the last time I saw him. This Highland air must agree with him."

Prudence's memory gave a jolt. She said, "Clandon! I remember now. Lord Briley told us it was the Clandons who rescued the Captain after he was wounded."

"Why, then, you must be the girl his lordship escorted up here to Castle Court," exclaimed Hortense. "How silly of me not to put two and two together, but for some reason I had thought he referred to a little girl—a child, I mean."

Miss Clandon, who had begun to look worried, said quickly that it was all very proper. "Some friends of my father were sailing on the same vessel, and the lady saw to it that everything was, er, as it should be."

Prudence smiled sweetly. Hortense again rushed into the breach. "Oh, well, of course, we never thought— That is to say, his lordship is so, er, I wonder if I should not have one of the servants take poor Captain Delacourt to his room now. I expect you have things to talk about, Miss Clandon, but—"

"Oh, I'll just run along wi' Geoffrey," said the girl blithely. "We're more like brother and sister, you know, and never ones to stand on ceremony. Unless you object, ma'am? He has a parlour, you were telling me, but if you think it not convenable . . . ?"

Hortense, inwardly reeling, said she thought it would be quite proper since Miss Clandon was so attached to her cousin. So long as her abigail went with her, of course. Miss Clandon curtseyed to the ladies and thanked them demurely for having taken such excellent care of "dear Geoffrey." A footman came in answer to the bell, and the invalid, Miss Clandon tripping along beside the chair, was wheeled gently from the room.

"Her *abigail?*" said Prudence as the door closed behind them. "Why would she bring her maid, I wonder?"

"Well, dear, since she's to stay overnight, at least, I expect Lady—"

"Papa did not tell me Miss Clandon was coming, nor that she would overnight with us!" Scowling, Prudence sat beside her aunt and muttered, "I wonder what kind of tale they fobbed him off with."

Hortense, whose sensibilities were not yet recovered, said

feebly, "She does seem rather fast, I must admit. But if they grew up together . . ."

"You surely did not believe that twaddle, ma'am? I doot there's a worrud o' truth in the whole dish! And if Mr. Clandon—if there *is* any such person—had friends coming up on the ship, why would he entreat Lord Thaddeus to escort his daughter?"

"W-well, I— They might have— Prudence, you never think that girl is— Oh, I *cannot* believe his lordship would have brought his lightskirt to this house, or that the Captain would perpetuate the—"

"The lies?" Prudence said baldly. "Aunty Mac, that man is an English spy sent here to try and trap Little Willie Mayhew and likely Ligun Doone as well!"

Hortense whitened and gave a faint shriek. "Oh, never say so! Are you sure? It does not seem— *He* does not look— He is so very—"

"Evil! A liar and a rare villain, and a very dangerous man. I fancy that dandy, Lord Thaddeus Briley, is in cahoots with him, which is a pity because I'll own I like the gentleman."

"Well, so do I," said Hortense. "And, really, dear, I cannot believe . . . Heaven help us if it is truth!"

"Aye. But I decided to do a wee bit helping on my own. I was up in the acacia tree, using Robbie's spy-glass to peep into Delacourt's room, when the wretch caught me."

"Yes, so he said. But, Prue, however did you manage to climb up in your petticoats?"

"Well, I did," said Prudence. "It was difficult, I'll admit, and horrid coming down, but then I was stung, and that wicked Englishman was so bold as to—" Flustered, she broke off, her face flaming again.

"To—what?" asked Hortense, hopefully.

"Tae kiss me. F-fair on me bosom," divulged Prudence, stammering.

Scarves flew in all directions as Hortense sprang to her feet. "The wicked rascal! Oh—you're making it all up! He never did. How *could* he?"

"By pretending to swoon, and taking advantage when I stooped tae aid him. Laugh then, Aunty Mac. But the mon's a viper, I warn ye!"

Hortense's funny bone had been tickled, however, and she went off into whoops while Prudence's warnings and dire prophecies were to no avail until, infuriated, she stormed, "For why would ye think I *say* all this? D'ye really think I'd be sae daft as tae make it all up, then?"

Wiping her eyes with one of her wisps, Hortense said, still chuckling, "Oh, my love, do you think me blind? I've seen the looks that pass between you. Prue, dear little Prue, be honest with yourself. You have fallen under the Captain's spell no less than the rest of us. Perchance a good deal more. And because you feel shame for that tender emotion, you fight it with all your strength and seek to impugn him only to allay your own conscience. Dearest, will you not—"

"Now may the guid Lord *deliver* us," snarled Prudence and, for once losing all patience with this loved but infuriating lady, she rushed from the room and ran, raging, up the stairs.

"They're all daft," she advised the door of her bedchamber as she slammed it shut. For some perverse reason, Kitty's words returned to shock her into a moment of immobility. '. . . he'll likely die on us, for the steel pierced his lung . . .' Recovering, she snorted, "Haggis feathers! The mon's no more dying than am I! He wasnae too ill tae hold me tight and . . ." And again, memory was her undoing. Once more she could see his pale, ardent face, the dizzying tenderness in those too beautiful dark eyes. She threw her hands to suddenly hot cheeks. "No, you don't! Ye'll no make *me* one o' your victims!"

"Are ye no feeling verra well, Miss Prue?" Kitty hurried in from the parlour, anxiety written large on her comely features.

"Thank goodness you're here. The very person I must warn. Oh, I do *pray* you've said nothing of Little Willie to Captain Delacourt?"

"Of course not, miss." The abigail grinned cheerily. "Nor was there the need tae speak o' the business, thank the good Lord!"

"What? Have you had news, then?"

"From Willie's brother, miss. He's safe away! Can ye credit it? He was hiding, but the troopers were coming for them. Willie wouldnae believe it until Ligun Doone hisself came tae warn them aw, and somehow spirited 'em away. Och, but I'm that joyful, I could weep!"

"Ligun Doone," whispered Prudence. "Ye'll no send *his* brave head tae the block, evil brute!"

Transfixed, Kitty whimpered, "Miss! How could ye think sae horrid a thing o' me?"

"Not you. Captain Delacourt."

"Captain . . . but—he's a helpless invalid, and can scarce leave his chair but what he falls doon."

"Stuff! He was well enough to ride oot on Lord Briley's black mare on Wednesday!"

Kitty stared, then burst into laughter. "Och, awie, I thought fer a minute ye meant it! As if the puir wee lad could—"

"*Go,*" snarled Prudence, her teeth gnashing as she flung a dramatically dismissing hand in the general direction of the window.

"Where, miss?" asked Kitty, looking, bewildered, to the open casement.

"I do not *care! Go!* You silly, muling little besom! Get ye gone before I *strangle* you!"

Kitty fled.

V

Prudence's flashes of temper were never of long duration, and when Kitty crept in cautiously an hour later, she was hugged and her forgiveness begged. While the abigail readied her for the evening, however, Prudence was unwontedly quiet. Kitty smiled dreamily, attributing Miss Prue's erratic behaviour to the pangs of love. She would have been shocked had she known her young mistress had wrenched her concentration from the abandoned behaviour of a certain blond hussy, and was now reviewing the first skirmishes in a grim if undeclared war.

Her attempt to place Geoffrey Delacourt under surveillance by way of the acacia tree could only, thought Prudence, be relegated to the status of unmitigated disaster. There were other methods, however. A touch more chancy, but not to be ruled out because of that fact.

Womanlike, her first step in the new campaign was to make herself as attractive as possible. (Which had nothing whatsoever to do with the fact that Miss Clandon had brought several bandboxes and a large portmanteau with her!) Prudence spent some considerable time making her selection and at length chose a gown of cream brocade, threaded with pink and worn over flattened panniers that were so wide she almost had to turn sideways when going through a doorway. She asked that Kitty be especially creative in dressing and powdering her hair, and was most pleased with the result. Her curls were drawn back from her face, piled high on her head, and held in place by pearl clasps. Little tendrils swooped beside her ears, and a pair of simple pearl earrings added just the right touch of elegance. She wore no other jewels, allowing her flawless skin and the soft swell of her breasts to speak for themselves. Kitty handed her a delicate fan with carven ivory sticks and she was off to collect her aunt.

Hortense looked very well in a *robe battante* of sea-green taffeta worn over hoops rounded in the English style. Her thick auburn locks were only lightly sprinkled with silver, and tonight she did not wear powder but had a Spanish comb placed atop her high coiffure, the comb being a gift from the same gentleman who had presented her with Señorita. A fine veil of black lace was draped over the comb, and Prudence brought blushes to her aunt's cheeks by remarking upon what a very handsome woman she was and asking how long she meant to keep Sir Matthew Garry and Mr. MacKie waiting before she favoured one of them with her hand. The truth was that although both gentlemen enjoyed flirting with the lady, neither had actually offered, nor was Hortense sure that she would like to exchange her placidly ordered life so as to take on the responsibilities that went with marriage. Nonetheless, she was pleased, and returned the compliment by exclaiming over her niece's tiny waistline. "Good gracious, Prue. However shall you eat anything?" she asked.

"I doubt I can," Prudence admitted. "But I believe Lord Briley is to join us tonight, and I want to look my best."

Incredulous, Hortense asked, "Have you a *tendre* for the young man? La, but I never thought you would aspire to a title. Least of all an English title."

Prudence laughed, not at the idea of becoming a nobleman's bride, but because that notion was so far from her actual intent.

Miss Clandon was not ready when they stopped to call for her. The girl's hair was charmingly dressed and already powdered, but she clutched a wrapper around her and mourned that her maid was still repairing a flounce on her gown that had been torn when it was carried from the coach. She refused their offer to wait, saying with her sunny smile that she would feel guilty did she delay them and if they permitted, she would find her way downstairs in a very short time.

MacTavish was alone in the gold saloon, reading. Lord Briley had not yet put in an appearance and although Captain Delacourt meant to join them, he intended to rest until just before dinner as this time he was determined to last through the meal. MacTavish complimented the ladies upon their looks and poured them each a glass of ratafia. They were engaged in a low-voiced discussion regarding the escape of Little Willie Mayhew when the stiffly formal English butler startled them by announcing "Colonel Archibald Cunningham."

The Colonel came into the room with many professions of regret for disturbing their evening. He made his bow to the ladies and said that there were some "funny fellas" hanging about the town, and since he'd had business this way, he had stopped to warn them. "Shouldn't wonder if they're bounty hunters," he said, accepting the glass of wine offered by his host. "Beastly lot. They can smell a rebel, and there's been one sighted nearby. Might be wise for you ladies to have an armed escort when you drive out."

"For protection against the fugitive or the bounty hunters?" asked Prudence, opening her eyes in a blue, innocent stare and fluttering her fan.

"Both, ma'am," he replied without a second's hesitation. "The rebel is like to show little mercy if he finds you've an English officer billeted here, and the bounty hunters, being several steps below your average animal, know of no such word as mercy."

Hortense uttered a nervous exclamation, and the Colonel

went on to point out that Lakepoint was "devilish isolated" and to offer to post a guard about the estate.

"Heaven forfend!" exclaimed MacTavish. "I can envision few things less appetizing than to dwell in the midst of an armed camp!"

"And I can envision nothing worse than for my presence to cause these good people distress," drawled Delacourt from the door.

Prudence glanced around quickly. Lockerbie was wheeling the chair into the room. The Captain wore a coat of bottle-green velvet trimmed with paler green embroidery down the front openings and on the cuffs of the great sleeves. His dark hair was unpowdered and tied back with a green riband. He bowed gracefully to her, kissed her aunt's hand, and shook hands with his superior officer.

"Faith, but you look better each time I see you," said the Colonel heartily. "You'll be rejoining your regiment at any day, I'll wager."

"My fondest wish," said the Captain with a sad smile. "Alas, my doctor continues to throw a rub in the way."

"As well he might," interjected Hortense, throwing an indignant look at Cunningham. "'Tis to be hoped you do not mean the Captain to go on patrol in his wheelchair, sir!"

The Colonel blinked; the Captain grinned behind his hand; and Prudence stared in astonishment at her frail aunt, suddenly become a bristling fury.

"I beg leave to tell you, sir," went on the irked lady, "that *I* could better advise the Captain when he might safely return to his military duties." She turned to the delighted Delacourt and asked in a very different voice, "Only let me have your sign, sir."

He stared blankly. "My—sign?"

MacTavish said with a furtive grin, "My sister means when is your birthday, Captain."

"Oh. August the fifth, Mrs. Hortense."

She said ecstatically, "A Leo! I *knew* it! We shall have a nice cose when you feel well enough, and I will make a chart for you. The stars will tell us when you can return to active duty."

"Ma'am," said the Colonel, "if I thought the stars could be relied upon, be dashed if I wouldn't appoint you consultant at my headquarters. You could look into the skies and work out your charts, and unearth me this traitorous dog called Ligun Doone!"

There was a breathless hush. MacTavish, standing by the hearth, continued to swirl his wine gently in his glass, his face expressionless. His sister-in-law looked frightened. Prudence, her little face an accurate mirror of her emotions, flushed, her eyes flaming with rage.

Watching her thoughtfully, the Captain murmured, "Have you learned nothing of the pest, sir? I'd fancied he'd be taken and sent to the block weeks since."

"Is—is that what you would . . . do, if you caught him?" quavered Hortense.

"He would be hanged till he was almost dead, ma'am," replied Cunningham with deliberate clarity, "then taken down and revived. His limbs would be severed one by one, his entrails cut out, and lastly, he would be beheaded." His keen eyes raked the room. "Which fate should displease none here, for we are all loyal subjects of the Crown, I feel sure."

"You may be very sure I owe no allegiance to the Stuarts," said MacTavish, and added tartly, "Nor, sir, do I appreciate having my ladies upset by a recital of the horrors of a traitor's death."

"I feel sure Colonel Cunningham had no intent to—" Delacourt began.

"Thank you, Captain, but Mr. MacTavish is quite correct." The Colonel, who had seated himself in the chair next to Prudence, came to his feet and bowed to the silent women. "My apologies, *mesdames.* I've been too long in the barracks room, I fear. I shall take my hasty tongue from your home, sir." He went over to pick up the whip and gloves he'd put on the credenza.

Feeling sick and shaken, Prudence drew a breath of relief. It was checked as she intercepted a swift exchange of glances between her father and Delacourt. MacTavish hesitated. The Captain's eyes were stern. To Prudence's horror, her father, albeit with obvious reluctance, called, "No, no, Colonel. I hope we are not so nice as to send you off with dinner almost upon the board. Please join us."

Cunningham hesitated. "You are very kind, but—I should not, you know. Already some unsavoury fellows have been observed lurking about the vicinity of your estate, and—"

"I thay now, Colonel! I take a dim view of that remark!" Thaddeus Briley came mincing in, quizzing glass upraised and a magnified and resentful eye fixed on the officer. A general laugh went up, easing the tensions of the moment. Briley, a vision in black and silver, an elaborate French peruke upon his head, advanced across the highly polished floor with a click of high red heels, still aggrievedly surveying the Colonel through his glass. "I may be unthavoury," he admitted, "but I do not lurk, thir!"

"I hope I have not kept you waiting," called a soft voice tentatively.

As MacTavish hastened to escort the Captain's cousin into the room, Prudence stared at her without delight. Miss Clandon wore a billowing *robe à la française* of white damask, caught up here and there with tiny bows of gold cord, and opening at the front to reveal a white satin underdress embroidered at the lower edge with a single golden rose. Her powdered hair was dressed high and interwoven with a golden fillet, and she looked a creature from a fairy tale, all gold-and-white daintiness.

MacTavish led her through the introductions. The Colonel bowed over her hand, his eyes frankly admiring. Lord Thaddeus, his own bow the epitome of grace, smiled, and Prudence almost thought he winked at the lovely Elizabeth.

"By Jove, sir," said the Colonel heartily, "I believe I *will* accept your kind invitation to dine." He beamed at the three ladies. "Dashed if you ain't the sly rogue, Delacourt, contriving to be billeted out here with all these beautiful creatures. Which reminds me, MacTavish, I've a replacement in today from England. Thinks he may have met your son down there. You did say he was visiting in Dorset, did you not?"

Very aware that Delacourt's eyes were fixed upon her absent-minded scholar of a father, Prudence saw MacTavish's brows pucker in confusion. She interjected swiftly, "Papa, your memory is playing you tricks, I do believe. My brother is visiting in Devonshire, Colonel."

"You're right, by Jupiter!" said Cunningham with a snap of his fingers. "My memory is no better than yours, my dear MacTavish!"

Providentially, Sidley appeared to advise that dinner was served, and they wandered down the hall to the dining room, his lordship squiring Hortense, the Colonel happily partnering Miss Clandon, and Prudence walking between her father and the Captain's invalid chair.

The chef had produced an excellent meal and although Prudence was tense and watchful, everything seemed to go along smoothly. The Colonel was clearly captivated by Miss Clandon, who flirted with him prettily; despite his lisp, Lord Thaddeus was a witty and amusing conversationalist and soon had Hortense giggling at his tales. Due to the uneven number of diners and the fact that Hortense was afraid of Colonel Cunningham, Prudence found herself with the Colonel to her left and Delacourt to her right. Her already depressed spirits were not enlivened by this arrangement, but she succeeded in behaving as though she had not a care in the world and responded politely to the Colonel's occasional remarks. Captain Delacourt had little to say, but several times she glanced up to find his eyes on her.

They were well into the second remove when Delacourt, in the midst of a casual comment regarding the beauty of the famous loch, suddenly gave an unmistakeable grimace of pain.

The Colonel enquired, *sotto voce*, "Are you all right, my dear chap?"

"Oh, tol-erable," Delacourt answered, with a sidelong glance at Prudence. "Thank you, sir. Nothing serious."

"Pray do not hesitate to retire if you would be more comfortable," said Prudence solicitously. "We shall quite understand."

"I am very sure you would, Miss MacTavish," he replied enigmatically. "You are kindness itself."

She scanned his face with suspicion, for she was very sure that he knew she suspected him. "There is, alas, too little of kindness in the world," she said.

"I'll agree with that, ma'am," the Colonel put in, his nasal voice ringing down the table. "One can but hope that now the recent tragic conflict is over, we'll enjoy a time of peace and Christian tolerance."

"Is that what the Duke of Cumberland is about?" said Hortense. "Faith, but I'd never have guessed it."

Through the following tense hush, the Captain's muffled "Ow!" was quite audible.

Amazed by her aunt's pluck, but dreading the consequences, Prudence glanced at him sharply and saw him jerk his hand from under the tablecloth.

"What the deuce have you got there, Delacourt?" asked the Colonel, not sorry for the diversion. "That's a nasty scratch on your hand."

"It's the grey cat!" exclaimed Prudence, amused. "Captain!"

Delacourt groaned. "Alas, I am betrayed."

"And should be thoroughly ashamed," scolded Hortense, smiling broadly.

"Let's see the stowaway," demanded the Colonel.

Sighing, the Captain detached the cat from his lap, and held her up. She blinked at the laughing faces, her whiskers sticking out ferociously.

"It is strictly against the house rules, Captain," said Prudence, "to feed animals at table."

"Besides which, it is suicidal," he said ruefully. "She grabbed my first offering, and the next time I put my hand down, she apparently mistook the matter and sank her claws into it." He turned the cat to face him and said, "M'dear, I fancy you are hoist by your own petard. Never bite the hand that feeds you!" He dropped her to the floor, a grinning footman held down a used plate enticingly, and Señorita, her tail sticking straight up into the air, darted from the room with him.

Amused, the Colonel asked, "What is the creature's name, ma'am?"

"Señorita," Prudence told him.

"Very Gaelic," the Captain remarked gravely.

She smiled at him with a warmth hitherto restrained, and saw puzzlement come into his eyes.

"It certainly is not a Scots name," said Cunningham. "And speaking of atypical names, what d'ye make of Ligun Doone, MacTavish? Is *it* Gaelic?"

MacTavish, who had been slicing a piece of roast beef, paused, then murmured, "I am loath to admit it, sir, but I do not know. My field, you know, is archaeology."

Cunningham nodded. "I've heard the meaning somewhere. But I cannot recollect what it is."

"I can tell you the meaning," drawled Delacourt. "Villainy personified. That rogue has confounded the rightful execution of the law at every step. But for his interference, Lord knows how many desperate renegades and murderers would have been brought to their just deserts."

"Desperate renegades, is it?" flared Prudence hotly. "Say rather brave men who were willing to die for their beliefs, as is Ligun Doone! And contrary to the Duke of Cumberland, he never kills, but merely provides escape for the poor fellows who are being hunted and persecuted and slaughtered with no trace of mercy!"

Her words seemed to hang upon a heavy silence. Aghast, she

knew that her father was frowning at her and that on every face was astonishment. She thought, 'Lord God Almighty! What have I done the noo?'

Delacourt said with a bored shrug, "The price of rebellion, ma'am, and your admired Doone no less of a traitor."

"Nor this a fit subject for the dinner table," said Cunningham benignly. "Are you fond of cats, Miss Clandon?"

The taut atmosphere eased, and Miss Clandon admitted her affection for felines and began to relate a tale of her own tabby and the various litters she had presented her family. The conversation turned to dogs. Laughter was heard again, and the meal progressed evenly.

Prudence took little part in the chatter. She was appalled by her own lack of control. Her temper had betrayed her into a major indiscretion—just as the wicked spy had planned. She dared not meet her father's stern eyes, and the balance of the meal was, for her, a misery alleviated only by the fact that she was not obliged to speak to Delacourt, who had become very silent.

Hortense stood and led the ladies from the table. Prudence heard the Captain announce his intention of withdrawing also, and the Colonel volunteer kindly to wheel him to his room.

Her mind spinning, Prudence accompanied the ladies to the rear hall, then excused herself, saying she must run upstairs for a moment. She walked sedately to the back stairs, lifted her panniers, and ran as quickly as she could manage to the first landing, flying along the corridor and frightening a housemaid who leapt from her path with a shocked squeal. Prudence raced to the main stairwell and tiptoed along, listening. She could hear the quiet murmur of male voices and she knelt beside a large aspidistra plant, straining her ears. After a moment, peering through the leaves, she saw shadows coming along the downstairs hall, then Cunningham's voice, low but irked.

". . . damned ill-timed, I can tell you. Here I've been doing all I might to convince these people I'm not the black-hearted villain they fancy me, and you've to go get 'em all stirred up again!"

The wheelchair came into view, Cunningham pushing it slowly towards the north hall.

"I thought it went rather well, sir," said Delacourt. "There was no pretence. The MacTavish girl's shrewish temper could have been controlled were it vital, I do not doubt."

"I wonder. With that red poll she likely couldn't practice deception if she tried."

Prudence pressed her hand to her mouth, struck by the truth of those unkind words.

"She's honest to a fault," said Delacourt, chuckling. "And has a right generous portion of Scots pride, among other things."

"I'll own that. But you've seen no trace of complicity here? No evidence of that thrice-damned Doone?"

"It's early days, sir. But I do think—"

A footman appeared and the conversation ceased abruptly. The Colonel turned the chair into the north hall, and Prudence got to her feet and walked with lagging steps back the way she had come.

She had her proof now. Why her father had become suspect, she did not know. Certainly, he had not been flatly betrayed, or they would all be in prison at this very moment, where Geoffrey Delacourt plotted to put them. They must be suspicious of the MacTavish, and waited, very likely, for him to lead them to Ligun Doone. At least, she could ensure that so stark a tragedy never happened. Heavy-hearted, she trod down the rear stairs. As soon as all was quiet she would go to her papa's bedchamber and tell him what she had heard. This time, he *must* believe her!

VI

Prudence waited in her room for two hours before she at last heard Lord Briley's luxurious carriage rumble down the drivepath, escorted by two troopers and doubtless with the Colonel inside with his lordship. She got out of the chair, for she'd not dared relax in bed lest she fall asleep, and stretched wearily. Walking to the door, she put her ear to the panel and listened. She heard the bolts of the front doors being shot, and a window was closed somewhere, none too gently. Still she waited. The stairs creaked. A line of light awoke briefly beneath her door, accompanied by the sound of soft footsteps. That would be the MacTavish going to his room, but she had no wish for any to see her going to her father's chamber at this hour of the night—or morning, more like—and she waited another twenty minutes or so before she at last crept into the hall.

It was very still now, the gentle quiet of a house wherein all are asleep. Prudence closed her door softly and stood motionless in the hall, waiting for her eyes to become accustomed to this deeper gloom. Gradually, from across the landing and stairwell she could detect the brighter square of the window on the west side. She turned right and crept towards her father's bed-chamber, which overlooked the terrace at the back of the house. Her scratch at the door went unanswered. She tapped gently. Still no response. Greatly daring, she lifted the iron latch, opened the door a crack, and stuck in her head.

"Papa?" she called softly. "Are you awake, sir?"

Silence.

She bit her lip, but even if Papa slept he must be awakened, so she trod resolutely inside.

The great bed with its tall posts and battlement-trimmed canopy loomed before her. Treading closer she could discern no sign of occupancy, yet she was sure Papa had come upstairs. Besides, had he not retired the candles would still be lit and the bed turned down and ready. She narrowed her eyes against the gloom and saw the coverlet move a little. She put out her hand and recoiled with a scream as a dark shape sprang at her.

An enquiring trill sounded.

"Señorita!" Prudence put one hand to her rapidly pounding heart. "You wee scamp! Does the MacTavish find ye on his bed 'tis yourself will be in a braw pickle, whatever!"

Purring grittily, the unrepentant cat rubbed against her skirts. Taking her up and stroking her, Prudence reasoned that her father must have been wakeful as he often was after an evening's company, and had likely gone downstairs again to select a book and perhaps enjoy a glass of port in peaceful solitude. She started off in search of him, but decided it would be as well to send the grey cat about her business first. The great oak tree spread its branches very close to Papa's corner windows and although it was a long way from the ground, Señorita often hunted high up in the tree. Prudence opened the casement, leaned out to set the cat securely on the branch, and watched her pick her way daintily towards the trunk with not the least appearance of unease.

From below came a faint scuffling sound. Prudence peered downwards, gave a gasp, and drew back. Someone was creeping across the terrace! Every furtive movement of the dim-seen crouched figure spoke of underhandedness. Further, whoever it was could very well be bound for Delacourt's room! She thought, 'I have him! If I can but catch him wi' his conspirator,

I'll prove his treachery to the MacTavish, beyond all doubting!' She started to the door, trying to feel triumphant. Her eyes fell on the small gun cabinet in the corner of the room. The ragtag English soldiery had broken into several estates after Culloden, and the ensuing rape and pillage had caused the MacTavish to set weapons close to hand, always loaded and ready. It was very possible that Delacourt would seek to silence her. Perhaps permanently. He might appear pale and feeble, but she'd several times fancied to glimpse a touch of steel in those dark eyes and would put nothing past the villain.

Thus it was that a few minutes later she crept along the downstairs corridor, the bell-mouthed blunderbuss heavy in her hands as she approached the Captain's door. It would not do, she decided, to attempt the room he slept in. Better if she crept in through the chamber that now served him as a parlour. And the safest way to enter that room would be from the side door. Accordingly, she went to the music room, slipped inside, and tiptoed across to the connecting door. Almost at once she heard soft, urgent voices. Her pulse racing, she inched the latch up and eased the door open.

The room was without benefit of a lighted candle, but Prudence's eyes had become accustomed to the darkness and she saw that Captain Delacourt, fully clad, was half in, half out of the window, assisting another man to climb inside.

"Quiet," he hissed, as a spur jingled. "We must not wake the house."

"Och, but ye've already done that," cried Prudence, levelling her blunderbuss.

Delacourt swore and jerked around. His accomplice, a large individual, gasped a startled, "Oh, God!"

Delacourt started forward. "Miss Prudence, is it? Give you my compliments, ma'am. You've caught us fairly."

"And will pull this trigger do either of ye take another step!"

The moonlight revealed sufficient for Delacourt to see that her little chin was resolutely set and the finger curling around that deadly trigger was too inexperienced to be tested. "Call your father," he suggested. "He'll—"

"Do whatever you say? Is that what ye think? Well, you've the wrong o' it this time, Captain Crafty. I've sufficient evidence that Papa will believe me at last." She raised her voice and shouted at the top of her lungs, "Papa! Come quick! *Papa!*"

The intruder beside Delacourt gave a wail and jumped for the window.

"Dinna move!" shrilled Prudence, raising the blunderbuss in trembling hands. "One shot frae this will serve both of ye villains!"

"Have a care, for God's sake," growled Delacourt. His eyes slid past her. "Take the gun—quick, before she kills somebody!"

"I'll no fall for that old trick," she sneered, the heavy gun wavering.

"Heaven help us! What are you about, Prue?"

"Papa!" Her stretched nerves quivering, she cried, "Thank the Lord you've come. Ye wouldnae believe me aboot this lying murderer. Ye *must* believe the—"

"Put down the gun, child!"

She turned a dismayed face. "Wh-what?"

Delacourt sprang forward and smacked the yawning barrel aside, even as her finger tightened involuntarily. There was a deafening explosion. Delacourt and his accomplice both went down, a chunk of plaster fell from the wall, and smoke filled the room.

"Oh . . . dear, oh, dear," whimpered Prudence, as her sire tore the blunderbuss from her resistless hands.

MacTavish cried a frantic, "Geoff! Are ye hurt, lad?"

His voice shaken, Delacourt declared he was all right. "Will . . . ?"

There was no response. Clambering to his feet, Delacourt said, "I'll see to him, sir. You're going to have to do some explaining. I hear your people coming."

MacTavish balanced the gun against the wall and strode to the hall door. "Prudence," he flung over his shoulder, "see if you can help Captain Delacourt."

Shaking like a leaf, her mind numbed, Prudence crept forward. The Captain knelt beside his motionless friend and she shrank, sickened as she saw the dark wetness that was blood.

"Bring a candle, quickly," he demanded. "And some clean neckcloths from my chest. *Move,* girl!"

Convinced she was having a nightmare, Prudence tottered to the adjoining room. A chest of drawers had been brought down and placed against the far wall. She snatched up one of the candelabra, appropriated several neckcloths, and took them to Delacourt, then ran back to pour some water from the pitcher and carry the washbowl to him.

Distantly, she could hear her father reassuring the servants, probably telling them he had discharged the gun by accident. She knelt beside Delacourt staring with wide horrified eyes at the ugly wound above his unconscious friend's knee. "D-did I . . . do that?" she quavered.

"Scarcely," he snapped, "since his wound was already bandaged. He hurt it when he jumped clear of your broadside." He glanced at her, his dark eyes angry and lacking all trace of their customary languor. "Egad," he said with an ugly sneer, "you're never going to faint, I hope. I thought you had more backbone. Wet one of these and give it here."

With shaking hands she obeyed him, and he bathed the wound as gently as any woman might have done.

"I'll g-go and get some b-basilicum powder . . ." she said through chattering teeth.

"You'll do better to close the curtains."

She did so, keeping her eyes averted from the wounded man.

MacTavish came back. "Luckily, Miss Clandon was not disturbed," he said, lighting several more candles.

"Not so lucky," Delacourt muttered, making a pad from a clean neckcloth. "Elizabeth's a fine nurse, as I can testify, bless her. Tear one of those for me, will you, sir? That fall broke the wound open."

MacTavish obliged and thrust the strips at the busy Captain. Prudence shrank back and sat, shivering, on a gilded chair. The wounded man moaned faintly. MacTavish said, "Brandy, Prue.

There's some in the decanter in the music room. Here, I'll help lift him for you, Geoffrey."

Prudence flew to do his bidding, her knees seeming a little steadier as she returned. Her father had his arm around the victim's shoulders and was steadying his head against his own knee. Offering the half-filled glass, Prudence gave a gasp of shock. "Little . . . *Willie?* But—but—I thought—"

Delacourt waved away the glass. "Never mind. He's gone off again. Better this way, poor fellow. If you'll give me a hand with him, sir, we'll get him onto the bed."

"Devil we will." MacTavish bent to help Delacourt to his feet. "Here—" He took the glass from Prudence and thrust it at the Captain. "You'll be the better for some of this. Prue, you're a strong lass. If I take Willie's shoulders, can you manage his legs?"

"Aye," mumbled Prudence, bending. "Say when, Papa."

"On the count of three. One, two . . ." On the third count, they both lifted. Willie Mayhew was big, and a dead weight. MacTavish was slight and fine-boned. Prudence strove valiantly, but she staggered. Delacourt set the glass down and leapt to help, and between the three of them they got the unconscious man into the bedroom and laid him down.

Delacourt went back into his parlour and returned with the glass of brandy.

Prudence pulled a blanket over Mayhew. "I'm sorrier than I can say, Papa," she murmured. "But had ye not kept everything from me, I'd not have been such a marplot."

Delacourt sat in an armchair and leaned back. "I told you, sir."

"Aye, you did that. But you've seen how excitable the lass is." MacTavish turned to his daughter. "You'll have guessed it, I fancy."

"You're helping our lads get clear." She nodded. "I'm very proud of you, Papa." Tremulously, she smiled at him, then returned her gaze to the Captain, who now sipped his brandy and watched her over the edge of the glass. "I cannot pretend to understand your involvement, Captain. You fought against us, I think?"

"I did. But I do not care for his Grace of Cumberland's way of dealing with defeated enemies. May I know why you are weeping?"

She turned away, her heart twisting. "I feel so ashamed. But . . . oh, if *only* you'd seen fit tae—tae trust me, Papa!"

MacTavish said slowly, "Yes, I can understand how you feel. But for your own protection, m'dear, it seemed—"

"My protection!" She spun to face him, tears spilling down her cheeks. "You speak of *my* protection, when this—this *Sassenach* risks his life for our men! If they catch him it will go much harder on him than on us. He's an officer in King George's service!"

"He's a sight more than that, lass," said MacTavish, dryly.

"Sir." The Captain frowned. "There's no call to—"

"It's past mending, Geoff. She's right. She'd as well know the whole." MacTavish turned to his tearful daughter. "It is my very great pride, my Prue, to present to you Captain Geoffrey—"

She said with a shaky smile, "May I guess? Is it Montgomery?"

"Close." He stood and bowed. "Geoffrey Montgomery Delavale, at your service."

MacTavish went on, "Who is also known to every Scot frae here tae the Border as Mr. Ligun Doone!"

Prudence's jaw sagged. She stared, disbelieving, at the amused twinkle in the eyes of this man she had endowed with every imaginable evil. "*You?*" she gulped in a little croak of a voice. "*You* . . . are—*Ligun Doone?*"

He said apologetically, "Sorry, ma'am. Your people have enlarged my few successes to such a degree I must only be a disappointment to you."

Prudence's knees gave out and she plumped weakly onto the bed. "But . . . but . . ."

Delacourt said, "No time for explanations now, Miss MacTavish. May I ask, though, how you rumbled me?"

She fought to pull her reeling senses together. "I heard you talking with Colonel Cunningham this evening. I was listening on the stairs. I thought—I was *sure* I could make Papa believe how—how dangerous you were to us."

"He's well aware of that," said Delacourt, with a grim look at his host.

"Yes, but, Papa, is this why you were so anxious I should go doon tae Edinburgh?"

"Yes. We're not playing parlour games here, Prue. I'd be a poor father did I not seek to protect you from peril. Geoff—what's become of your man?"

"If I know old Kerbie, he'll not come in until he's scouted the grounds. He's the world's original fusspot. What we've to do, and quickly, is get your misnamed friend to cover."

Prudence glanced at Little Willie, who appeared to have dropped off to sleep. "I heard he was safely away," she said.

"We got him out of one frying pan, and into another, sad to say." His smile flashed at her. "I think you saw us from the point last week."

"Yes. I was not sure, but later I suspected you'd been the one to ride Lord Briley's mare."

MacTavish interjected with fierce anger, "You were *alone* on the point?"

"And came down like a thunderbolt to hear my fellows tell of it," said Delacourt. "You're a bruising rider, Miss MacTavish."

She felt ridiculously pleased and knew her cheeks were reddening.

"Perhaps," said MacTavish darkly. "But it was foolish beyond permission. We'll have no more of that, Prue. We've got all we can handle."

"Yes, sir," she said meekly. "And now I can help. No—never look so cross, Papa. I'm in this, do ye not see it? Only tell me what you mean to do with poor Willie?"

"Hide him," said Delacourt. "Just so soon as Kerbie returns. He gave the troopers the slip a few miles back, but they'll likely be searching all the homes hereabouts." He smiled faintly. "I fancy he'll have to join your other hidden guests, sir."

MacTavish met his daughter's curious stare. "We've two other lads in the second room of our pyramid," he explained.

She clapped her hands delightedly. "Right under the Colonel's nose? Have they been there long, sir?"

"Upwards of a week."

Delacourt said, "The problem is less one of a hiding place than of an escape. But the patrols have become so numerous and so damned suspicious that between them and the bounty hunters . . ." He frowned. "The price of our successes, alas."

Watching him, marvelling that this ill-looking young man could be so fearless, Prudence said, "My own wicked suspicions told me you merely feigned illness. Is the truth of the matter perhaps that you are not quite recovered of your wound?"

At once, he grinned at her. "I play the self-indulgent invalid well enough to have infuriated you, ma'am. If you but knew how the sparks shot from your eyes when I said I was tol-lol."

She laughed. "Aye. I fancied you the kind to enjoy your infirmities. And I think you have not answered me, sir."

"You'll get no straight answers from him," put in MacTavish. "So I'll tell you that he's not doing so well but that he'd be doing a sight better did he not try to do so much."

"And there," chuckled Delacourt, "is your straight answer."

Prudence was mulling over that 'straight answer' when she made her way up the stairs a short while later. There were so many questions she longed to ask, so many decisions to be made, so much planning to do, but not tonight. The Captain had begun to look very tired. She was afraid his desperate leap to avoid the charge from her blunderbuss, on top of all his other activity, had taxed his strength, and although his manner was now very different from the languid martyrdom he had earlier affected, she was plagued by the notion that his health was not as good as he'd implied.

She had hoped to be able to have a cose with her father, but the MacTavish had sent her off to bed, announcing his intention to retire just as soon as Lockerbie came in and helped them get Little Willie to the secret room in the pyramid.

Three wounded men would be sharing that tiny chamber. They must be spirited away as soon as possible. Delacourt had said he had a plan for the fugitives, but how he could hope to elude Cunningham's patrols handicapped by casualties, she could not guess. Still, Ligun Doone would contrive, of that she had little doubt. Despite his modest claim of a few successes, she knew that many rebels had been shepherded to safety thanks to his intervention.

She went to her room with her heart singing; a very different girl to the heartsick creature who had left it.

She slept late the next morning, and awoke to find Kitty opening the bedcurtains and a cup of breakfast chocolate tantalizing her with its rich aroma. For a second she lay staring up at her trusting abigail, dismayed because Little Willie was now in the pyramid and she dared not tell the girl of it. Somehow, she dissembled, accepting her tray and bending her concentration upon the letters that had been brought in from the Receiving Office in Inverness. One of these was a long-awaited letter from her dearest friend who had married an army officer and gone off to the Americas with him, and another was from her favourite cousin in Perth. And both were unimportant compared to the excitement that flooded her being. She longed to jump from her bed and run to the MacTavish to demand he tell her all he knew of the gallant Ligun Doone. But even with Kitty, she dared seem no different than was usual, and she sent the girl off to press one of her most becoming gowns, a summery thing of white muslin sprigged with blue and worn over many petticoats.

She was gazing dreamily at the sunny morning, her letters still unread, when a scratch at the door announced the arrival of a guest whose existence she had quite forgotten.

Miss Clandon, it seemed, never looked anything but lovely. Her pale green silk cap was edged with rich lace, and the curls framing her piquant little face gleamed a rich gold in the early morning light. Her wrapper was of pale green taffeta and lace, and a nightgown of the same colour swirled about her dainty slippers. Running to the bed, she held out both hands in so warmly impulsive a gesture that Prudence could do nothing but clasp them.

"You are one of us!" exclaimed Miss Clandon with low-voiced exuberance. "Och, but I couldnae be more pleased! Geoffrey but now told me of it."

So she had already visited her cousin's room. And in her nightrail! Prudence interposed, "Is he all right?" An anxious look came into the big brown eyes and she added hastily, "He, er, fell last evening. Did he not tell you?"

"He did not! He knew very well I would scold him, for he will not rest!"

Clearly, she had misinterpreted the cause of the Captain's fall, but Prudence did not pursue the matter, asking instead if Miss Clandon had grown up near to her cousin.

"Oh, no." Miss Clandon appropriated one of Prudence's morning biscuits and then perched on the bed. "We are not related at all. 'Tis just the tale we put aboot to make things"—she giggled conspiratorially—"more respectable."

The MacTavish's notions of propriety in a lady were very high, and Prudence was inwardly shocked. But, after all, the man lived on the edge of death every hour of every day. Why should he be criticized for keeping a mistress? "Then you help him in his rescue work?" she asked gently. "Would you tell me how it began?"

"It began the other way round—with a vengeance, Miss MacTavish. My uncle's estate is near Prestonpans. He's a kindly gentleman and very set against war. He cares for neither the Stuarts nor the House of Hanover, and was appalled when the fighting came so near to us. The English were soundly beaten, and fled in most dreadful disorder. They were killing the wounded where they lay." Her eyes took on a haunted look, and her voice sank. "It was unco' ghastly! My uncle and my cousins could stand no more, and went out to try to help. Three young officers they brought in, and all sore wounded. Geoffrey was one. He'd a hole low on his shoulder you could put your hand in. . . . We thought only to make their last moments less terrible than to have their throats cut in the mud. The next day, one of them died. Poor lad, he was but fourteen. The second boy began to improve. But each time Geoffrey came around, he'd be fairly distracted to find he still lived, and he'd beg my uncle to put him oot, lest we were slain for sheltering him." She shook her head. "And him, breathing oot blood with every word!"

Her throat so tight as to make speech difficult, Prudence faltered, "But you nursed him back to health."

"I fancy we did, though it was a long road, and many the time I thought him gone. We were thinking we'd won our battle at Christmastime. The other boy we'd taken in was a bonnie wee lad named Abel. He'd been quite well for some time and was eager to get home. We tried to tell him there was no chance he'd get through, for the clans were hunting any English survivors. Abel loved us, but he'd no listen and slipped away, determined to spend Christmas with his family. He was almost taken, of course, and fled back to us, with a group of Jacobites hot after him."

"Heavens! Did you all have to run for your lives?"

"Not quite, but we had to get our two Southrons away. Quick! Geoffrey was fair beside himself, dreading he'd be found—and you can guess how it would have gone for us, had that happened."

"Indeed I can. I was told you tried to get him to the Border, but it was impossible."

"Aye. Aboot as impossible for an Englishman to get through then, as it would be for a Jacobite to get through today. It's full circle we've come. At any road, however they tried, they were hounded north again. Abel managed to slip through, but Abel was well, and their desperate flight had sent Geoff into a relapse. He and Lockerbie know a deal aboot being hunted, I can tell ye, and have some braw tales o' their escapes. Lockerbie has been with my family since he was a bairn, and luckily he recollected I've a grandmama living near Inverness."

"Lady Ericson."

"Yes. A grand old lady. Lockerbie brought Geoff to her, and she gave him sanctuary and took a great liking to him."

"I see. That must have been just before Culloden?"

"In March. By the time they reached Castle Court, Geoffrey had gone right doon again and was too ill to do more than lie abed. He'd every intention of contacting the military and explaining the mix-up with the names— You knew aboot that?"

"I know his real name, now, but not how the mistake occurred."

"Ah. Well, there was a laddie in Geoff's regiment named Geoffrey Delacourt. He was killed, poor fellow, but we did not learn for many weeks that it was Dela*vale* who had been reported killed, and Dela*court* missing."

"But how terrible for his family. They must have believed him slain."

"Well, they did, of course. Geoff is deeply attached to his sister, and asked me to write and tell her of the mistake. I did, but it was months before we could get it down to England, and from what we heard later, she never received the letter." She looked angry and stopped speaking, and Prudence waited a little while, then prompted, "But—how is it that Colonel Cunningham still thinks he is Captain Delacourt?"

"Because by the time Geoff was well enough to write to him, we had suffered Culloden. Cumberland went on his hideous rampage. Your brother was hunted to my grandmama's grounds. Rob and Geoffrey had been at school together, as you know, and when Geoff learned how our lads were being slaughtered, he was furious. He began to scheme a way to get Rob to safety. Did you know he's a wicked forger? And my grandmama's dresser is a most skilled lady. Between the three of them, they provided Robbie with papers, a sailor's uniform, and a passage to France. It all worked, sweetly, neatly. The word spread. More rebels came. Geoffrey went, as ye might say, into business. When they begged his name, he invented his alias, and verra soon was known tae all our people."

"Yes, indeed he is! But—why did he not tell the Colonel his true name?"

Miss Clandon gave a slow smile. "Because he is the type of man he is. I doot he ever spares a thought for himself."

Watching her, Prudence said quietly, "You make him sound a paragon."

Miss Clandon laughed. "Och, he'd fairly hate that! No—he has his faults. Not the least of which is that he's insanely reckless at times. But he'll do anything to protect his family. He knew that if he was caught aiding the rebels, his estate would be forfeit and his sister left penniless, so he allowed the Colonel to go on believing him to be Delacourt, who was alone in the world, with no wife or children, and his only brother a soldier in India."

Prudence said, frowning a little, "I could see that, right enough. But with a man like Cunningham, it would be best, I think, if the Captain went home as soon as may be. He's done more than his share."

"So says my grandmama. She's a proud lady, wi' the tartan in her blood, y'ken, but Geoff quickly won her heart, and she began to fret for his sake. She asked your papa to take him in, so he'd not be under Cunningham's nose. And since Geoffrey had helped your brother . . ."

"There was not much Papa could do but say yes." Prudence nodded. "Even so—Captain Delacourt should go home."

"He means to. But he's a fine group working with him the noo, and always someone else comes who needs his help. So he stays. And—besides . . ." Again, she did not finish the sentence, but sat staring at the biscuit in her hand.

Prudence waited, then said, "Well, I think it all superb. Where does Lord Briley fit into the plans? Or does he fit in at all?"

"He's in it up to his aristocratic neck. He works with several other English gentlemen to help those who manage to get to the Southland. And what a fine lad, for all his posing and that finicking lisp. I was that glad to meet him."

"He told us he went to Prestonpans looking for a friend's grave. Is that so?"

"Yes. But mostly he was trying to find out what had happened to Geoffrey. He needed an introduction to my grandmama, and since I'd reason to come up also, we travelled together."

"By ship," said Prudence. "Miss Clandon, would it not be the easiest way for our fugitives to escape—to take ship?"

"Of a surety! And the curst redcoats know it and watch every cove and inlet. And the English men-o'-war prowl the coastline. A sad number of our lads have been killed trying to escape by that route. Their next best chance is to run north into the mountains. But the redcoats guard the passes, so that along with the English gentlemen who were out with Prince Charles, their one last hope is to attempt the Border. Right good sport the troopers have wi' 'em! Sometimes, they're hunted clear to the south coast before they're pounced on and dragged back to be shot—the poor exhausted souls!"

"How savage!" said Prudence, clenching her fists in rage. "How damnable they are, these English!"

"True." Miss Clandon sighed. "And is it not contrary that one of the grandest gentlemen I've ever had the honour to know is English? And—sad I am to own it—one of our braw Scots lads was kicking him and aboot to bayonet him when my uncle knocked him doon fer his cruelty and carried Geoffrey from the field."

Prudence smiled at her. "You are very right, of course. Which just goes to show how silly war is, when there's good and bad on both sides, and little to be gained but suffering." She put out her hand. "Thank you so much for coming to talk with me. I hope you mean to stay a long time."

"I cannot, alas. I've work to do for my grandmama. At least"—she smiled mischievously—"I'll have a right bonnie escort."

"Lord Thaddeus?"

"Yes. He's to come at noon, so I must hurry and make myself ready."

Prudence got out of bed, and they embraced rather shyly, each girl sensing there was much yet to be learned of the other and wondering if they would have the opportunity to get to know one another.

After Miss Clandon had gone, Prudence glanced at the ormolu clock on the mantel. Half-past nine. She must see her father as soon as may be, but he was often out on the estate at this hour. She donned her grey riding habit, therefore, told Kitty to brush out her hair and tie it back without setting it into ringlets or applying powder, and announced her intention to ride and then take breakfast later. It was difficult to meet the girl's innocent eyes, knowing that her beau lay wounded in the pyramid, but Kitty was too ingenuous; it would be impossible for her to behave normally if she was aware of the truth. Already, Prudence thought worriedly, there must be so many who knew Ligun Doone's appearance, if not his actual identity. And such a terribly high price on his head! She dismissed the abigail and walked along the hall to the small chamber that served her as a workroom. Here on one side were placed her sewing materials, a table she used for cutting patterns, and a comfortable chair. Across the room were the tools of her other hobby—an easel, palette, sketching pads, paints—and the stacked fruits of her labours. She took up the most recent of these, placed it on the easel and scanned it, a little flush coming into her cheeks.

She had sketched Delacourt the day after her encounter with the bees, and had started the work in anger. Gradually, however, it had changed to a pose she had chanced upon by accident. She had come upon him in the flower gardens, and he had been gazing at the blooms with a rapt expression, quite unaware of her presence. She had abandoned the work in disgust when she became aware it was more flattering than she'd intended, and had not glanced at it since. Viewing it now, with different eyes, she marvelled at the strength of character she had been unable to erase from that fine young face. Her blush deepened. She set the sketch quickly among the others, taking care to put it further back amongst them, and went downstairs.

Reaching the main hall, she hesitated, glancing towards the back of the house, but Delacourt was doubtless still sleeping. The butler, immaculate and expressionless, approached and imparted in his cultured voice that "the master is gone out, miss." Not surprised, Prudence thanked him. And she thought as she turned down the side hall that Sidley was not only the coldest creature she'd ever encountered, but that he was so extremely English. Papa had hired the man five years since for the very quality of disdainful efficiency that was so admired, but none of them had ever been able to know him. She wondered, with a pang of unease, if since the Rising he reported to Colonel Cunningham. Faith, but there was a deal to fash a girl this morning!

Contrary to her assumption that he was still abed, Delacourt, fully dressed save for his coat, had ventured onto the terrace. He perched on the low wall, gazed across the wide panorama, drew in a deep breath, and winced. His eyes turned to and held on the acacia tree, until he sensed that he was no longer alone. He glanced up quickly and found Lockerbie watching him. He grinned and winked at the sombre-faced man.

Undeceived, Lockerbie said, "Yon hole in yer chest is fretting ye."

Delacourt shrugged. "I took a small tumble last night."

"What—sae soon?" The words were out before he could stop them. Lockerbie bit his lip, repentant.

"Don't worry so. It wasn't one of my famous swoons. I'm going on very much better, don't you think?"

"Aye," lied the Scot staunchly. "If—if ye'd just give over, sir. Small wonder ye tire sae quick. Ye push yersel'—always, ye push yersel'."

Delacourt stood and looked at him steadily. With a wry smile he said, "Needs must, when the Devil drives."

VII

It was a brilliant morning; the kind of springtime perfection that comes along occasionally as if to reassure mankind that all is indeed well with the world. Prudence forgot about war and death and peril for a while and rode joyously through the cool peace of the countryside, her gaze drinking in verdant slope and darkling wood and the two great billowy cloud ships that hung motionless against the dark blue ceiling of the heavens. It was so still, so silent that the pure notes of a meadowlark's song etched themselves crisply, almost tangibly, against the hush. She had no intention of climbing into the hills this time, but she turned her mount towards higher ground where she might get a better view of Lakepoint and the far-reaching sheen of the loch. She skirted a copse of birches and jumped the mare across the small ravine the burn had made, then gave a frightened cry as a shot rang out very close at hand. The mare shied and danced about, snorting her fear. Prudence reined her in, stroking her neck and talking softly to her, her own heart hammering as she watched the man who rode from amongst the trees astride a tall bay horse.

"My dear lady," said Colonel Cunningham, pulling up beside

her, "I do trust I did not startle you. I fancied myself quite alone up here today."

His smile was kind, his manner contrite, and his hard black eyes needle-sharp. Seldom afraid, Prudence was frightened now and prayed she might do nothing, say nothing, to endanger their valiant invalid. "You startled both my horse and myself, sir," she said calmly. "Is this an escape from your military duties? Or were you shooting at more of our unhappy rebels?"

He brandished a sleek hunting gun. "No, no. Just after a grouse. Saw some fat ones when I was down here yesterday, so came back to see if I could please my cook by bagging a couple."

She did not point out that there were many fat grouse between here and Inverness, but said, "I fancy your game bag is full already."

He had no game bag at all, belatedly aware of which he searched her face narrowly. She looked innocent and not very bright, this pretty Scots lass, but he had learned long ago that one does not judge a book by its cover. "Lost it en route," he said. "Had it tied to the pommel and it must have fallen." He restored the gun to its scabbard and went on, "I let this old fellow stretch his legs in a gallop, which probably brought about my loss. Gad, but it's a beautiful day. Would you prefer I go away and not spoil it?"

It was all said in the same friendly, conversational tone, and Prudence started. "My apologies, Colonel. I must have behaved most rudely last evening to leave you with such an impression."

"Not at all. You were most gracious." He dismounted, lifted her down, and they walked along together, leading the horses. "But an army of occupation cannot expect to be popular. And you must be irked by the presence of one of my officers in your home."

"My father is not a man to shirk his obligations, sir," she said carefully. "But I'd be telling lies did I say it was a welcome development insofar as I am concerned."

He laughed. "An honest woman! What a relief. You've no

idea of the insincere things a man in my position is obliged to listen to. I can readily appreciate your father's situation."

"Because of the 'insincere things' Captain Delacourt says?" she asked, her nerves growing tighter every moment.

His brows lifted at this immediate taking up of the gauntlet. "Do you find him so?"

"I find him as seldom as may be, Colonel."

He nodded sympathetically. "And probably imagine he was billeted upon you in order to spy."

She could not restrain a gasp. "Heavens! What would he be spying on? We are not Jacobites; my papa does not hold with the business. If you put the Captain at Lakepoint to—"

"But, my dear, I did not put him there," he said soothingly. "In fact, I was not aware he was up here at all until he sent his man to apprise me of that fact. Nine months late."

Her heart leaping about, Prudence said, "He's no been wi' us for nine months, sir! Nor is he likely to be!"

"No. Poor fellow. I'm afraid you're right." He sighed. "What a very bad time of it he has had. Dragged from pillar to post . . . to find safe haven at last in the home of his school friend's family. Despite their dislike of us. It would appear to reinforce the old adage that ties forged at Oxford hold fast unto the grave."

Another warning bell rang in Prudence's mind. If it was an old adage, which she doubted, it was one she'd not heard. She thought, 'Dear God! Did Captain Delacourt say Oxford?' And not daring to risk it, she pointed out, "If our guest told you he met my brother at Oxford, Colonel, his memory is no better than my papa's. Robbie was at Cambridge."

"By Gad, but you're correct! I vow my mind is deteriorating. It must be the rarefied air. Speaking of which—I do trust you have no thought to climb into the higher hills again, dear ma'am. Should you not have a groom to accompany you?"

How smooth he was. How slimy! What did he mean, 'again'? Had he known of her climb the other day? If so, he—or his men—must have seen the Captain and Willie! And if that was the case, he was playing cat and mouse, as the military loved to do. He was after Ligun Doone and knew he was at Lakepoint! She felt sick, her throat almost closing with panic. But this menace beside her was waiting, his mild gaze ready to detect any terror—which heaven knows she was riddled with! With all her might she fought for calm. "Now you sound like my father," she said, smiling at him sweetly and praying she was not as pale as she felt. "I seldom go into the hills any more. But sometimes I simply long to be alone."

She prayed he would take the hint, but he answered, "You'll not be alone for long do you venture into those crags, Miss MacTavish." He slanted a grim glance at the jagged peaks to the south. "They fairly swarm with ragtag soldiery who'd as soon cut your lovely throat as look at you!"

Bristling, she exclaimed, "I doubt that! They are Scots, sir!"

He bowed. "*Touché.* But you would do well to remember that not all Scots are gentlemen, any more than all Englishmen are monsters."

"I had not thought that of all Englishmen," she said, aware that it was too late to take back her unfortunate outburst.

"And that properly drives me to the ropes!" Amusement softened his eyes unexpectedly. "As well it should. I see it does not do to fence with you, ma'am. May I assist you to mount?"

He cupped his hands for her boot, and when he had tossed her into the saddle, saluted her smartly, and stepped back. Prudence remained staring down at him. He had said she'd fenced with him. She'd tried, but she doubted she was clever enough to fool this man. It was hopeless to try to be careful and diplomatic. Nonetheless, for Captain Delacourt's sake, she bent and put out her hand. "It's a thankless task you have, sir," she said with her most glowing smile. "I dinna envy you it."

He looked surprised, and took her hand firmly. "Thank you. Lovely creatures like yourself make my task more palatable."

But as she started away, he called, "Be very careful, Miss MacTavish."

"I tell you, the man suspects!" Still clad in her riding habit, Prudence gripped her hands tightly as she sat in the gold saloon with her father, Miss Clandon, and Delacourt. "That last silken little remark of his had me shivering all the way home."

Miss Clandon nodded thoughtfully. "He's a shrewd one all right. I'm thinking ye shouldnae dally up here any longer, Geoff. Somebody else can carry the cypher, if it does come doon tae that. Certainly, you're in no case—"

"He was likely only testing Miss MacTavish," Delacourt interpolated, with a warning look. "I've no reason to suppose he mistrusts me. After all, everyone imagines Ligun Doone to be a Scot."

"Aye, they do," MacTavish agreed. "But 'twas a fool boy's trick to choose such a name."

"Thumbing his nose at 'em," said Miss Clandon, regarding the Captain with exasperated affection.

Taking one puzzle at a time, Prudence asked, "What cypher?"

Miss Clandon looked dismayed. "Oh, dear! I thought you'd told her."

Troubled, MacTavish asked, "Delacourt?"

"No!" The Captain's dark brows met in a frown. "The less your daughter knows, sir, the safer she'll be."

"They dinna hang us by degrees," said Miss Clandon dryly. "And she already knows enough to hang."

"Never even think that!" gasped Delacourt, horrified.

Prudence intervened hotly, "What dreadful rubbish! You've been a godsend to our people, Captain. My father and I would be ingrates indeed were we unwilling to be at risk for your sake!"

He stared at her for a moment, then looked away. "I think you do not know what you risk, ma'am."

"How jolly it would be," drawled another English voice from

the doorway, "to walk in and find you all chatting about a new poem, or the weather, or thomething dull and normal."

Delacourt swung his chair around. "Thad! You're late, you bounder!"

His lordship entered, paid his respects to them all, and protested his innocence. "My wig, y'know," he said, smoothing that perfection. "Took my man forever." He glanced at Prudence's amused face. "Am I to gather we have a new recruit, dear boy?"

"Unhappily so," said Delacourt, frowning.

"And one who is overwhelmed by the bravery of two Englishmen in behalf of our poor rebels, my lord," Prudence declared.

His lordship acquired a hunted look. "P-pray do not refine upon it, ma'am. I plain did not like the oddth. Not a fair fight. Are you ready, Mith Clandon?"

"Yes. Is there anything else, Geoff?"

He leaned forward. "Tell me again, if you will, Elizabeth."

"I am to discover if the men who were lurking about Castle Court are gone now. I must tell Grandmama that Colonel Cunningham has had word a Jacobite was taken near Tullynessie. And that"—her voice shredded a little and she clasped her hands—"that you dinnae think it could be J-Johnny Robertson, but—but that he is being put to the question because the redcoats think he was carrying a part of the cypher."

Prudence cringed. The cypher again. And God help the poor lad—whomever he may be! She glanced at his lordship, hearing him mutter a curse under his breath.

"If that ith the cathe, then they don't yet have it."

Delacourt nodded. "And let us pray it is not Robertson they've caught. But—if it is, he likely destroyed his cypher, and we'll have to send off another. Remind Lady Ericson, Elizabeth. And don't forget. I think we must send out two of the list, just to be on the safe side."

Miss Clandon repeated the message, and he wheeled his

chair to take her hand and press it to his lips. "Very good. Now be off with you, madcap. And—God guard you both."

Mincing past, Briley paused by the wheelchair, tugged his friend's head around by the hair, and scanned him judicially. "Too wan, by half. Get into the fresh air, dear boy. Have a long walk. Do you good." He glanced slyly at Prudence, slapped his friend on the back, and was off, the clicking of his high heels on the stone floors echoing after him.

Prudence guided the invalid chair along the path that led through the shrubbery, and halted in the shade of a weeping willow tree that bowed beside the goldfish pond. "This is nice," she said tentatively.

"That would be better, I think." The Captain indicated the centre of the flower gardens where four paths came together spokelike to form an open area wherein curving stone benches offered rest amid the blossoms.

"But there is no shade for you," she demurred.

"True, but you brought your sunshade. We can huddle under it together," he said, sending a whimsical grin over his shoulder.

Prudence said, "I think we shall have the tree."

"No, if you please." He added quietly, "In the centre we can be sure we are not overheard, ma'am. Trees on this estate have a way of being most unexpectedly occupied."

She gave a trill of laughter. "How wretched of you to remind me."

"And how excellent of you to illustrate how easily one can become careless. I sent Kerbie to investigate, and he confirmed that it is very easy to see right into my windows with a glass. A nasty error on my part."

"You made a more serious one," she told him, turning the chair onto the narrow path through the flowerbeds.

"I did? Pray tell me."

"There is a bench below the level of the terrace. If you look, you will see it is directly in line with your windows."

He turned his dark head, and Prudence noted how thick was his hair, and how it strove to curl even though Lockerbie had tied it back so severely. He said, "It is a sufficient distance that a conversation in the room could not be overheard—is that what you imply?"

"Yes. And you are mistaken. I sat there and heard you telling Lockerbie what a good spy he was."

"Oh, Lord!" gasped the Captain, looking up at her, dismayed.

"And I heard your groom arrive from England, and— Good gracious! I've not seen him since!"

He said gravely, "He knew too much." He drew a finger across his throat. "Let that be a lesson to you, Madam Eavesdropper!"

His reward was a repetition of her rich little gurgle of mirth, and he divulged that Cole was caring for the men in the pyramid. "But please tell me how you heard us. We all kept our voices low, as I recall."

"'Tis some trick of the echo. Robbie and I used it occasionally to spy on our father."

"Wretched brats. I can picture Rob being so graceless, but I'd not have thought it of you, ma'am."

Seating herself on one of the benches, she admitted with a sigh, "Alas, I am very graceless at times. And when I was a child—oh, dreadful! It was Rob's doing, of course. He was my idol and allowed me to tag along after him."

He leaned forward, elbows on the arms of his chair, watching the sunshine wake her hair to a bright coppery glow and bring a golden sheen to the curve of her cheek. Smilingly, he said, "If I know aught of brothers and sisters, what you mean is that he bullied you into sharing his scrapes."

"No, no. I fear that was not the way of it, for I was a natural tomboy. Indeed"—she gazed out at the magnificent sweep of the loch—"'twas my idea aboot the Monster . . ."

"Monster?"

"Aye. We'd heard poor Aunty Mac conversing with Papa in his study, you see, while we were sitting on yon bench." She saw his dark brows lift, and went on hurriedly, "You're thinking us horrid, but truly—we seldom listened. This time, Aunty was boring on at Papa aboot her stars and the Monster, which we found delicious beyond belief."

"Never say your Monster was in Mrs. Hortense's stars? I've noticed she takes it all very seriously. Do you, Miss MacTavish?"

She hesitated. "I know astrology is not as highly thought of as it once was. But there must be *something* to it, surely? After all, many great monarchs and politicians ordered their lives according to the advice of their astrologers, and—"

"And forced their subjects to wear iron collars, and burned witches, and—"

"And I'll no have ye laughing at her, sir!" The delightful twinkle lit her eyes, although she pretended severity. He sobered and said with commendable meekness that he was very sorry and had the greatest liking and respect for Mrs. MacTavish. "But—do tell me, what was the connection between the lady's stars and your Monster? Do you mean the legendary Nessie?"

"I do, that. The Loch Ness Monster." She frowned at the quirk that tugged at his lips and said, "I suppose you think it all a hum."

"No, indeed, ma'am. I'd not dream of making so improper an observation."

He looked so prim and proper that she could not but laugh. "You have quite a way with words, Captain."

Delacourt watched the merry curve of her lips and forgot all words.

Aware of his absorption, she blushed and went on quickly, "As I was saying before you gave me such a cruel setdown . . ."

He groaned and put a hand over his eyes.

Smiling, Prudence went on, "Aunty Mac told Papa the Monster was going to come oot onto the land and would eat us all up for breakfast on the following Sunday."

He lowered his hand to stare at her. "You're making it up! She *meant* it?"

"Her stars meant it, sir. Papa laughed so hard, and we laughed, too. Poor Aunty Mac was upset and began to cry, but Papa could not stop laughing. So I got the idea for the Monster to help my aunty." She sighed. "Lud, what a flummery! Er, I mean—what an uproar that caused."

"Do tell me," he murmured, fascinated by the twinkle of mischief in her blue eyes.

"You should know that Robbie and I had for some time been building a boat. We'd had to be very secretive aboot it, for Papa did not like us to go out alone on the loch. Storms can come up suddenly, you know. The water is terribly cold, and it is bottomless in parts. We'd been doing our dark deeds in an abandoned old shed behind the stables. I'll show you, if you wish. 'Tis none so far."

"Your boat is still there, then? Jove, *yes,* I'd like to see it!"

"We'd not quite finished it when we overheard Aunty and Papa that day. I suppose it just kept growing because we were so enthused about it. But it was a wee bit odd as to shape, and 'twas that gave me the notion that with a little extra work we could make it into a grand Monster."

He laughed. "What a rascal! Did you?"

"Aye. We got two of Robbie's friends to help us hurry up. Och, it was a bonnie time we had. We made scales and a grand great head, and we varnished and painted—you'd no believe how lifelike the beastie looked when we were done."

"I can scarce wait to see it. Is it still intact?"

"More or less. A bit mildewed with age, I'd think. But I must say it didn't look near so convincing in the old shed as it did once we got it into the water."

"How did you manage that?"

"There were four of us, and we used a wheelbarrow in front and at the rear, but"—she chuckled at the recollection—"the silly thing toppled when we were going through the flower gardens, and flattened a fine stand of phlox the gardeners had set out but the day before."

"I fancy you heard about that. How did you mean to make your Monster swim? Surely, oars would have ruined the effect?"

"The boys thought of that, and we made great 'legs' and tied them on with ropes, then stuck the oars underneath." She giggled uncontrollably. "Had ye but *seen* it! The oddest motion you could conceive, but one doesn't expect a Monster to be graceful."

"No, of course. Do go on."

"We'd picked a time very early in the morning, as you may guess. The boys were afraid we'd made it so heavy it would sink, but it rode on the surface quite nicely. We all crept inside to test the oars. The boys decided then that I was too little and that if we capsized I'd freeze solid before they could tow me to shore, so I was made to get out. Oh, but I was cross and railed at them bitterly until they began to row, and then—oh . . . Captain!" Prudence had to pause, to wipe tears from her eyes. "I was so glad I was on the shore, for an odder sight you never saw. I laughed until I fell down and rolled aboot! They—they didnae row very well together, so a leg would go up and sort of—hang i' the air, and then splash doon, and then up would go another and the poor Monster . . . reeled and staggered aboot on the loch!" She broke into helpless laughter at the memory, and Delacourt, drawn into her mirth, laughed with her.

"What a sight it must have been! But how did they come to grief? You said something about terrible consequences."

"Oh . . . dear," moaned Prudence, catching her breath. "Aye—they came to grief all right. The plan had been to stay close inshore and beach our Monster when Papa or Aunty Mac chanced to catch a glimpse of it, so as to prove it really did mean to come oot onto the land. But—what with the boys' uneven rowing, and their not being able to see very well, they headed into the middle of the lake instead. Well, Captain, if ye think the Monster was effective at close range, you should've seen him at a distance! Our worst fault—the fact that the rear was not level wi' the front and sort of sagged—proved the most valuable asset, for it looked exactly as though the Monster had reared up his head and shoulders and the rest of him was still under water. Faith, 'twas enough tae put the fear o'God intae a Highland heart! And just at that time, out comes my papa from the house, running at a speed I never saw him equal in his life, and Aunty Mac and all the servants streaming along behind, and everyone waving their arms and shouting. Oh, but it was a sight to behold!"

"Yes, but did they come safely to shore?"

"Very soon, for the boys realized where they were at last, and managed to turn the beastie. Only, just then . . . poor Aunty Mac saw where we had dropped the boat into the flowerbed and . . . and she said . . ." She was overcome again and had to pause while Delacourt, grinning broadly, waited for the end of her story. "She said," went on Prudence, regaining her aplomb, "that the Monster had walked through our flowers looking for us. And she cried, 'He was *this* close to the house! And now he's coming back to *eat us up!*' And down she went in a faint, poor lady."

"Oh, dear. So that was the terrible consequence! Your father must have been enraged when the truth came out."

Drying her eyes again, Prudence sighed. "He was that. And raked the boys down properly. Although Rob was grieved already, for he is very fond of Aunty Mac, and had meant only to help her with her stars, not scare the poor lady into a decline."

"It sounds as though no real harm was done, and what a grand memory for you all." Watching her expressive face, he said, "You must have had a wonderful childhood here." He glanced around at the great loch, the powerful thrust of the mountains, the wild, cut-up hills, and thought how different it was, how untamed and lonely compared to his gentle English countryside.

"We could not have had a better one," she replied. "And what of you, Captain? Were you as fortunate?"

"Yes, I thank God. My sister and I spent most of our early years with my father at our country home in Oxfordshire."

"Not at all like our scenery, I know."

"Do you? Have you been to England, then?"

"I was in London when I was twelve. We've relations there."

She looked amused, and he asked carefully, "Did you find it pleasing?"

"I found it incredible. I really couldn't believe it. So many people, so much noise and confusion, so much excitement. I was too young, of course, to go to balls or to Court, but I used to dream of a London come-out." Her smile went a little awry. "Too late now."

"Why?"

Startled, she said, "I can well imagine how I'd be received! A Scots lady—one of those barbarians who sought to overthrow your King!"

"Oh, no. It is far more likely you'd be received with admiration. Very many English were in sympathy with your Prince's Cause, even if they did not openly support it."

"The cautious way," she said with a curl of the lip. "But you fought for what you believed. Were you in the army before the Rising?"

"No. I joined because— Oh, many reasons I'd best not go into are we to become friends." She met his smile and returned it, and he went on, "Besides which, my life at home had become—unbearable."

He looked stern. Prudence asked, "Did you lose your home?"

"After a fashion I suppose we did. My father died with very little warning."

"But—you were the heir, no?"

"Yes, but—well, Papa had always considered me a frippery fellow. Not without justification, sad to say." She was staring at him with such incredulity that a faint flush of pleasure tinged his thin face. "Thank you for that silent vote of confidence," he said warmly. "But I fear it is misplaced. I really was a wild, irresponsible chap. Only look at how I came galloping up here to fight, with never a thought for my poor sister, left with those two—" He checked, his eyes bleak and his mouth a thin, hard line.

"Had you to cope with an executor?" she asked sympathetically. "How very annoying for you."

"It was indeed. My uncle is a greedy, unprincipled nipcheese, and his wife—very beautiful, but— I should not speak ill of a lady, but between them, they enraged me to the point that I knew I must get away, or I'd say or do something beyond forgiveness. And whatever else, family is—family."

She nodded, admiring him the more for that loyalty. "Aye. And we've all some dirty dishes among our relations, alas. But what became of your sister?"

His mouth tightened. "What indeed?" he muttered. "My groom tells me she ran away with one of the men I sent to deliver part of—" He checked. "With a rebel I sent there for sanctuary."

"Oh, my! And do you know that they are safe?"

"Would to heaven I did. But I know Penny, and I know the man—the very best kind of fellow. I've no fear for her dishonour, only . . ." He was silent, staring blindly at one hand tightly gripping the arm of his chair.

"Only—he was a Jacobite?"

He nodded. "If they should take her . . . if she is charged with treason—"

Prudence's hand closed over his. "Do not! Oh, do not torment yourself so."

"Do you not see?" His hand turned to clasp hers. "It would be my fault. I *sent* Chandler there."

She leaned closer, still holding his hand. "You sought to save the life of a brave gentleman. You wrong your sister, I am sure, if you fancy she would have had you do otherwise. Besides—he is an Englishman. He will likely blend in and not be noticed."

"He was hunted all the way down," he muttered broodingly. "He's no ordinary Jacobite."

"He's—he's never one of the couriers?"

Delacourt put back his head and regarded her steadily. "So you do know of them. How much?"

"Very little. I was tiptoeing into the drawing room with a surprise birthday gift for Sir Matthew Garry, a few weeks ago. And he said, 'Johnny is a courier, God help him, but he does not carry the list.' They saw me then, and said no more. Nor did I ask, for I sensed it was private. Indeed, I had completely forgot about it until you spoke of it again this morning."

"I see. Elizabeth is right then, and you must be told the whole. But first, may I see your Monster?"

She was nothing loath, for she hoped that the sight of their childhood endeavour might drive the sombre look from his eyes. And so she wheeled the chair around to the back of the house, skirting the stables and the barn until they came to a slope with at the foot a rundown old shed. And here Prudence was thwarted; the paved path ended and the continuation was merely a track filled with loose pebbles. "Oh, well," she said, halting. "When you are better, perhaps."

"Fustian!" He threw the blanket from across his knees. "You know I am able to walk."

She glanced around apprehensively. "If someone should see . . ."

"You can support me. See—I shall lean on you, pathetically."

He did this so well that she was obliged to put her arm about his waist.

With the soft silk of her hair tickling his cheek, and the clean fragrance of her in his nostrils, he murmured, "How very kind you are, Miss Prue."

Disturbingly aware of his nearness, and recalling the glow in the face of a lovely Scots lass, she said, "So I am. But do not be preparing to collapse and tell me you are 'tol-lol,' for I'm not *that* kindly disposed towards you, sir."

He chuckled. "It had crossed my mind, I'll own." His eyes twinkled into her startled ones. "Now you cannot blame a poor lonely Sassenach when he is faced with so beautiful a spirit of *joie de vivre* as Miss Prudence MacTavish."

He was pale and ill-looking, and his long ordeal had written lines into his face, but Prudence thought him the most attractive man she'd ever seen, and the shed seemed to fade as she looked up at him. With a faint sense of self-preservation she drew back.

He ushered her inside. "I hope you will not feel compromised to be in here alone with me."

Even as she drifted nearer to him she said weakly, "The last time I was alone with you, you were—very naughty. In fact, you kissed my . . ."

He stroked the afflicted area with one gentle fingertip. "This?"

"Aye," she whispered.

"Are you sure? Was it . . . like . . ." He repeated the offence. "This?"

Dizzied and short of breath, she closed her eyes. "Not quite . . . that naughty."

"Oh? Could it have been more like . . . this . . . ?"

Her head swayed back. His arm was about her. His lips found hers with fiery urgency. She soared into a dim delight, and he kissed her lips, her soft cheek, her brows, her closed eyelids.

"My lovely little rebel," he whispered tenderly. "My pure fearless warrior maid."

His lips were awakening sensations she had never before known. She became suddenly far from fearless and, opening her eyes, scanned the dark face bent above her. His eyes were soft as night and held an expression that drove away every emotion save one. Her arms went around his neck. He bent and kissed the tip of her nose, the side of her mouth, the lobe of her ear. Drifting and warm and ecstatic, she felt a tremor go through him. As from far, far away she heard him mutter, "What a scurvy trick!" His hands were on her shoulders, gently moving her away. He said lightly, "A little more of this, m'dear, and I shall properly abuse your father's hospitality."

She bumped down to earth. He was watching her, his eyes faintly amused, his hands still holding her.

"Oh!" she gasped. "Whatever—are you about?"

"A small token of my esteem." He smiled. "Nothing more than—" He checked. His eyes encountered other eyes. Enormous, staring eyes, and a great scaly, ungainly head. "My . . . Lord . . . !" he exclaimed softly.

"Your . . . esteem?" quavered Prudence.

He did not seem to hear. "So this is your Monster!" Intrigued, he left her and wandered closer to the great hulk the children had constructed out of pieces of wood and scraps of tarpaulin and leather, and whatever they could lay their inventive hands upon.

He was completely absorbed. He had forgotten her. But watching his tall figure, the proud carriage of his head, Prudence knew painfully that she had given her hitherto untouched heart at last. To an Englishman who likely thought her an ungraceful, countrified, half-wild Scots girl; a man accustomed to mincing, elegant misses, with soft, drawling English voices and haughtily raised eyebrows. She thought, 'He will soon go away and I shall never see him again. I must do everything in my power to help him. I must not let him know that he has my heart. And I must be ready to say goodbye.'

Delacourt had walked around the bench and now stood opposite her, gazing with awed eyes at their creation. "How on earth," he muttered, "did you manage it?"

She forced herself to speak as casually as he did. "We had a favourite gardener who did a lot of it. And I made the eyes, and—"

"*You* did? But you said you were just a little girl."

"I was. But I've always had a knack for drawing and the like." She thought of the sketch she had made of him, and went on hurriedly, "And I painted his 'scales' but the boys made them. He's a wee bit faded and tattered the noo. Only look." She rattled one ungainly 'leg,' then jumped back as it fell off and landed with a crash at her feet.

Delacourt sprang to her side. "Are you all right? Did you hurt yourself?"

"No, but I hurt him, poor old Monster. I'm amazed he has lasted so well. All these years. We must have a good roof on—" She checked, peering at him. "What is it? I am all right, truly."

"For a minute, I thought—" He put a hand over hers, resting on his arm. "Prue, I'm a dreadful fellow. Can you forgive me? I had no right."

"I should have stopped you," she said with a rather too bright smile. "We shall just forget it ever happened, shall we?"

He looked down at her gravely. "I am grateful you're aware you could have stopped me, ma'am."

They were both silent on the way back to the house. Delacourt was lost in thought, and Prudence heard Elizabeth Clandon's voice again; '. . . he has his faults,' and she knew it was very true. Geoffrey Delacourt, or Delavale, or Ligun Doone, was a brave, fearless gentleman, but he was not a very honourable one. Any gentleman worthy of the name would consider himself bound to offer for an unwed lady he had kissed, especially in the way the Captain had kissed her. But it was very plain that he had no intention of doing so. She thought, trying to be objective, 'Why should he? I did not protest, and nobody saw, nobody knows.' But she knew that in honour he was no less bound; that in a like situation Robbie would have felt committed.

She stifled a sigh and guided the wheelchair through the flower gardens.

VIII

On Friday evenings when the weather was fine, Sir Matthew Garry rode the four miles from Garry House to Lakepoint and, without fail, within the hour, Duncan MacKie's enormous old coach rumbled up the drivepath. On this pleasant evening, they were waiting in the drawing room when Prudence entered, her gown of gold silk swishing about her, and she surveyed them fondly as they came to greet her and escort her into the room.

MacKie, short and stout, his cheeks like little red apples, his neatly curled wig set rather crookedly upon his head, winked his merry blue eyes and told her that she was the prettiest creature he'd seen on this, or any other day, may he be boiled if it was a lie! Sir Matthew, square of face and form, his brows beetling fiercely, growled that Duncan MacKie had ever been a squire of dames, and only seconds ago had made the very same remark to Mrs. Cairn.

Prudence laughed at them, told them they were a pair of wicked rascals, and allowed Sir Matthew to usher her to a chair, while MacKie padded over to pour her a glass of ratafia and enquire in a casual way if Mrs. Hortense was to join them this evening.

"Yes, she is, sir," confirmed Prudence, amused, as she accepted the glass he brought her.

"And is she—er, sound, ma'am?" barked Sir Matthew. "Sound of—ah, wind? Bright-eyed and full of spirit, as ever?"

"Ye make the lady sound a horse, Matt," protested MacKie. "What he means, Prue, is—we hope yer lady aunt is in good health."

Since the lady in question arrived at that point, her swains were able to judge for themselves. She looked very well indeed wearing a gown of black lace over dull red satin. Her mantilla was extremely high and rather dangerously poised, but the lace veil that was draped over it framed her delicate features very fetchingly—or so thought Prudence.

Predictably, the rivals hastened to escort their goddess to the sofa. This being Sir Matthew's week, he sat beside her, while Mr. MacKie resignedly occupied the wing chair, having first edged it as close to the sofa as he could contrive.

Glowering at MacKie, Sir Matthew enquired if Hortense intended to take a hand at the cards later.

"And for why should she not?" demanded MacKie. "Does it escape ye, mon, that Mrs. Hortense has played whist wi' us on fine Fridays any time these ten years?"

"We have a guest tonight," said Hortense. "Perchance he may be willing to take a hand."

Neither of the gentlemen remarked upon the presence of the guest, nor enquired as to his identity. When Delacourt was wheeled in just before the dinner gong was sounded, Prudence watched narrowly, and thought it singular that whilst the Englishman was not greeted with the affectionate admiration that might have been logical had they known the truth of his activities, nor was he the object of the enquiries that would have been perfectly natural had he been a complete stranger.

The conversation at table ran along easily enough. Hortense was comfortable with her two suitors, and she had become so fond of their ailing guest that in her eyes he was almost one of the family. As always, MacTavish was the perfect host. Prudence sensed that Delacourt was uneasy and, noting that his glance flickered often to the tall clock in the corner of the room, she guessed his thoughts were with Elizabeth.

Troubled because he was troubled, she accompanied Hortense to the drawing room and went at once to the windows. The moon was high and bright, making the loch into a sweep of silver and lighting the heavens to a deep clear blue. There should be little difficulty in travelling tonight, but there were countless reasons why Lord Briley might have been detained. She walked over to the sofa, lost in thought.

"You sense it, too, don't you, love?" said Hortense. "It closes in. Inevitable. Inescapable." She frowned. "And I had so wanted to get that new lavender gown finished." She tilted her head, the great Spanish comb sliding precariously. "My goodness me! Here they come, so soon. I hope there was no disagreement."

Prudence was equally surprised as the gentlemen hurried into the room, Lockerbie guiding the wheelchair. Delacourt looked grave. "Troopers," he said succinctly, meeting Prudence's questioning glance.

MacTavish added, "Quickly, ladies."

The card table was already set up, and Sir Matthew sprang to take up the cards and deal them out. Hortense, always nervous around redcoats, did not find anything to wonder at in the fact that the others behaved in a rather odd way, and she took the chair MacKie pulled out for her without hesitation.

When Colonel Cunningham strode into the room some two minutes later, he came upon a tranquil scene: the three older gentlemen and Mrs. MacTavish intent upon a game of whist, and Miss Prudence MacTavish seated nearby at her tambour frame while Captain Delacourt sorted out her tangled embroidery silks.

Looking up as the Colonel entered, unannounced, MacTavish rose, his lifting brows betraying surprise, but with a hand courteously outstretched. "I give you good evening, Colonel. Do you—" He stopped.

Lord Briley came in, looking stern, and with a pale Miss

Clandon on his arm. "Thome rabble hove a brick at my carriage," he lisped, his gaze steady on Delacourt. "Frightened Mith Clandon, I'm afraid. The Colonel wath good enough to ethcourt uth."

Prudence hastened to put her arm about Elizabeth. "How dreadful! Do you care to come upstairs and rest? We shall have a tray brought to you."

Miss Clandon admitted she was rather shaken, and indeed she looked it, a haunted expression in her big eyes. Ushering her into the hall, Prudence was annoyed to see half a dozen troopers standing about and one brazenly inspecting the gold saloon. She made no comment beyond a frigid stare, and not until the door to Miss Clandon's bedchamber was safely closed did she whisper urgently, "Whatever is it? Are you all right?"

"Yes, yes. But—oh, lud! I've bad news for Geoffrey. And that wretch Cunningham suspects something. You were right!"

This confirmation of her fears was dismaying. Prudence went over to tug at the bellrope. "What you need is a nice cup of tea. Poor girl, you're upset, and small wonder."

At the same moment, Colonel Cunningham, his back to the drawing room fireplace, and a glass of Madeira in his hand, was saying much the same thing. "Small wonder the lady was distraught. I'd hoped we had put down the troublemakers for a while, but"—he shrugged—"only let that rabble-rouser, Doone, make a move and they're all stirred up again."

Sir Matthew stared at him without pleasure. "Is Doone hereaboots? I'd heard naught of't."

"He is." Cunningham took a mouthful of wine. "We'd a traitor in our grasp, practically, but Doone whisked him away. How he managed it, I've not the remotest notion. The rebel was trapped in a farm-house. My men are ready to swear not a soul went in or left that had not been accounted for. Yet when they searched the place—no sign of him."

"Likely a secret room," said MacTavish. "These old places, you know, have many a priest's hole or hidden chamber, dating back to the days of Cromwell."

Cunningham said silkily, "Not this one. We tore it down, room by room."

A muffled snort came from Sir Matthew, and MacKie glowered in tight-lipped silence.

Delacourt yawned. "Perhaps the fellow was actually never there, sir."

"He was there all right." The Colonel put his glass on the mantelpiece. "Like all crusaders, Doone's a braggart and has a sign to let us know we've been duped." He took a tablet from his pocket and drew a large capital 'D' with inside it the letter 'L.' "We usually find one of these chalked up after one of his jaunts."

Sir Matthew said grittily, "And ye found one on the wee croft?"

"We did. And in a cave in the hills to which we were subsequently decoyed. Ah—you find that amusing? Well, I assure you, sir, I do not. This Ligun Doone may be a fine folk hero for the Jacobites, but he ferments trouble for both sides. Only let word of him be breathed in an area we've managed to subdue, and all the locals are stirred up and ready to risk life and home to shield rebels they'd not have dared aid before. He is a pest, sir! And a pest I mean to put an end to!"

Hortense, who had crossed to the quiet Delacourt, said kindly, "The poor boy's fallen asleep." She beckoned Lockerbie, and he came to take the handles of the chair and wheel it out.

Cunningham thanked MacTavish, but refused an offer of refreshments. Neither did he leave, but chatted idly with the group, his questions as mild as his eyes were sharp. In a few minutes he had deduced that both MacKie and Garry were probably sympathetic to the Jacobite Cause, and were also enamoured of Mrs. Hortense, a condition he thought rather pathetic. He judged them a pair of feeble old dodderers, all huff and no puff, and abruptly excused himself to stamp along the hall to Delacourt's door.

He did not knock, and the Captain, who had been looking worriedly at a small piece of parchment that Briley had slipped into his hand when greeting him, was barely in time to tuck it into the side of his chair before the Colonel stalked in and slammed the door behind him.

"What is the Clandon woman doing up here?" he demanded without preamble.

"She nursed me when I was hit," Delacourt replied calmly. "She was most kind, and—"

"Egad, Captain, I hope you did not rouse false expectations in the lass."

Delacourt was seized by a not unfamiliar urge to ram his fist into that smirk. He lowered his eyes, but when he looked up he was smiling. "I hope I did not, sir. But she's a handsome girl, and I fancy Thad Briley would not be averse to—er, taking her off my hands."

Cunningham chuckled. "Young reprobate. Is that the way you treat your own cousin?"

So this was what he was fishing for. Delacourt said, "I dare swear you were not gulled by that rasper, sir. Elizabeth is no kin of mine. It answered the purpose after Prestonpans, so we held to it. Thanks to her, I was brought up here when they couldn't get me to the Border."

"So you said. To her grandmama. That would have been in the new year, when the Jacobites had sniffed you out down south."

"Yes, sir. It was risky for them, and you may guess I am deeply indebted to Miss Clandon and the old lady, both."

"Hum. And now the girl is here to visit her grandmama. And—to see you, eh?"

"Yes, sir. Though I doubt MacTavish would allow her to stay here did he think that she and I, er . . ."

The Colonel gave a bark of man-to-man laughter. "I'm damned sure he would not. He speaks softly, but 'pon my word, he is a strait-laced old martinet. What I want to know, Delacourt, is where in the devil is that son of his? If I thought the boy was out with Charles Stuart . . . ! What d'you make of it?"

"If he was a rebel, sir, I've heard no breath of it. And I've been bending every effort to win over the servants."

"Play on their sympathies, do you? Excellent. Keep me informed. Cauldside will be out periodically to look at you, and you can send word by him. As for the rest of the family, the aunt's mad, but harmless enough, I fancy. What of the daughter? A spirited little piece, and ripe—eh?" He thought to detect a sudden flash in the eyes of the invalid and went on slyly, "What a luscious shape to her! I'd not blame you for a little dalliance in that quarter. Wouldn't mind a roll in the hay with her, myself."

A muscle twitched in Delacourt's cheek. He said without expression, "She's a rare little beauty, I'll own, but I fear I'm not up to a duel with claymores, which is what I fancy it would take to roll her in the hay. Have you learned aught of Doone's whereabouts, sir? If he tarries here, I'll warrant you have him before the month is out."

Cunningham's face hardened. "By God, but I will!" He brandished his riding crop at Delacourt. "He's getting too cocksure by half, but he's taken on the wrong man this time. Fiend seize him, he's good for my promotion, if nothing else."

With false eagerness, Delacourt leaned forward. "Are you assured of that, sir? Have you spoke with Cumberland?"

"I have. And his Grace promised that the day I bring about the lopping of that bastard's head, I'll be a General!" He frowned, and muttered, "He's nearby, I *know* it. If I can just manoeuvre him within my grasp."

Delacourt regarded him admiringly, then wheeled his chair closer and put out his hand. "Some day, Colonel, I shall brag of having shaken your hand."

Flattered, the Colonel grinned and returned the handclasp. "Perhaps you will, my dear fellow. Perhaps you will."

Busied with turning down the bed, Lockerbie smiled at the coverlet.

Miss Clandon would say nothing to Prudence of the news she brought, save to murmur in a distracted way that poor Geoffrey must be beside himself, having to wait to hear what she had to tell him.

"While he does so," Prudence begged, "could you please tell me about the cypher? I fancy it has to do with the treasure Prince Charles gathered, but I'd heard it was too late, and he could not get the gold to Europe to hire more men and arms." She paled at the thought that struck her. "Oh, heavens! Never say they mean to do so now?"

"Our Cause is lost, alas. And enough good men have died for't. No, the treasure—and it is not all gold, Miss MacTavish, but jewels and plate, and even artworks, I heard—all of it, has been hid at several locations."

"But if we cannot use it, why not return it to the donors?"

"A gigantic task, but it is what they hope to do. For the meanwhile it must lie concealed until the proper disposition can be made. So many who were Jacobite sympathizers, or whose menfolk were known Jacobites, have been stripped of homes and land. Some are starving. If we can restore their belongings, it may make the difference twixt life and death for them."

"Poor creatures! Oh, the suffering that has come out of all this. But if the treasure is safely hidden, I—"

"Well, there is the trouble, you see," Elizabeth interrupted wearily. "The council, those who gathered and guard the treasure, fear the locations are not as secure as they would wish. They've chosen a permanent hiding place, and all the treasure is to be gathered up and conveyed there. The problem is to get word to those who now store it, so that they know what to do and to whom it is to be finally entrusted. A tricky business, you may guess."

"Faith," whispered Prudence, her eyes wide. "How will they dare send such a message? Every renegade and bounty hunter in the three kingdoms would be after it! To say nothing of the soldiers!"

"Aye! Would they not! So the message is coded in four stanzas of a poem. Each stanza contains one word of the cypher.

When all the stanzas reach a certain man in England, he will decipher them and arrange for the treasure to be collected and taken to its new home."

"England! Why *England?*"

"Because it is already there. Oh, never look so astonished, dear ma'am. When they couldnae run the blockade from here, it was sent south in hopes of getting it to Europe from English ports. Things became desperate suddenly, and it had to be hidden fast."

"Whisht! What a bumble broth! And how shall they know to make proper distribution—if all goes well? There— Oh! Never say *that* is the list Captain Delacourt mentioned?"

"Aye. At first it was made only so that Prince Charlie could properly acknowledge the donations. Later, it was kept for a record so that restitution could be made. One o' the couriers carries it. And now Geoffrey risks sending out another copy, for fear the first is lost."

"My God! I'd not be the men carrying *those* papers!"

"'Tis a fearsome responsibility, I grant. If the list falls into English hands, everyone named will be executed, you may be— Listen!"

Together, they ran to the window and peeped out. The troopers were clattering along the drivepath. Relieved, the two girls hurried down to the drawing room. Upset by Cunningham's visit, Hortense had retired, but MacTavish, Sir Matthew, and Mr. MacKie were still there, attending to Lord Briley, who stood with his back to the hearth, speaking in a low, urgent voice. He glanced up as the girls entered, and the other gentlemen came to their feet. Prudence went at once to sit beside her father. Briley drew up a chair for Miss Clandon, and she occupied it, asking, "Did you give Geoffrey the cypher, my lord?"

"I did, but had no opportunity to talk to him, unfortunately."

Lockerbie came back, wheeling the invalid chair. Looking stern, Delacourt said, "They're away, but I've sent Cole to keep an eye out, just in case."

Prudence's suspicion that Sir Matthew and Mr. MacKie were

aware of the plotting at Lakepoint was confirmed when MacKie asked, "How do the lads in the pyramid go on?"

Delacourt replied, "A deal better than they did in that damp cave." He slanted a glance at Prudence. "I take it you've told them, Mr. MacTavish, that your daughter has joined us?" And a corner of his mind registered the fact that their new recruit managed to look enchanting, even with worry plainly writ on her face.

"Much against my better judgement," MacTavish confirmed wryly.

"I'll not let you down, gentlemen," said Prudence.

Sir Matthew gave her a troubled look and murmured that they'd not a wee bit of concern on that count.

"I think you all know that Miss Clandon went to see her grandmother, Lady Ericson," Delacourt went on briskly. "You've returned Johnny's cypher to me, Elizabeth. I take it the news is bad."

"Very bad indeed," said Miss Clandon with a sigh. "Our—second courier was intercepted near Tullynessie, and—"

"Tullynessie!" exclaimed MacKie, taken aback. "Did ye send him that route, Captain?"

"No, sir. But I know from bitter experience that the route a man starts with up here can be far from the route he's obliged to follow. Was John taken, Elizabeth?"

Her mouth trembled. She answered falteringly, "Taken and shot. But he managed to give the cypher to a shepherd, and he led the redcoats away." She bowed her head for an instant and when she looked up, her eyes were bright with the sheen of tears. "Johnny Robertson was—was executed at Perth on the morning of the tenth." On a sob, she gulped, "That . . . fine wee lad!"

Delacourt shrank in his chair. "My God!"

The MacTavish murmured, "May the Good Lord rest him."

Prudence had not known the hapless fugitive, but it was obvious that Delacourt had, for his shoulders slumped and he covered his eyes for a moment. "Cumberland!" he gritted, as though it had been an oath. "What disgrace and dishonour he visits upon our England!" Nobody spoke, and after a pause he went on with forced calm, "So the shepherd carried the cypher to Lady Ericson, did he? It was well done. And she is a most gallant lady. I only wish she'd be done with this desperate business."

Miss Clandon smiled faintly. "She says the same of you."

"I know." He gave her a rueful glance and sat straighter. "Mr. MacTavish, can you get word to Johnny's people?" MacTavish indicating that he could do so, Delacourt went on, "Robertson was a right gallant gentleman, and he'd not thank us for sitting here mourning him instead of attending to business. My friends, it seems we've a cypher to be delivered, and no courier."

"Devil take you, Geoff," exclaimed Briley, viewing Delacourt through his haughtily upheld quizzing glass, "if you can meth about in a Jacobite frolic, you might have the goodneth to allow me to play!"

"I'll hae ye to know, my lord," snorted Sir Matthew, "that there are Scotsmen here, willing and able!"

"And Scotswomen," put in Prudence, her face flushed, her eyes glowing with excitement. "*I* could carry your cypher, Captain!"

MacTavish glared at her, started to speak, but subsided. Delacourt leaned back, elbow on chair arm and chin in hand, and regarded them in turn. "Sir Matthew, your courage does you credit, but I am very sure Cunningham would never allow you to take ship without you had an excellent reason. And if we fabricated one, you would be searched from head to toe and like as not escorted and watched like a hawk thereafter." He kindly refrained from pointing out that it would be a difficult journey by land in these perilous times, and that Sir Matthew was plagued by gout. The older man's irked protests ceased when Delacourt lifted an authoritative hand and went on, "No, sir. I thank you, but it will not do. The same would apply to you, Mr. MacKie. And as for you, Miss MacTavish"—his eyes softened as they rested upon the girl's radiant eagerness—"can you really suppose I would repay your father's kind hospitality by—"

"What in the name o' our sainted Queen Mary has that tae do wi' it?" she stormed, jumping up and glaring at him. "I'm a Scot, sir! And you're a Sassenach! And—"

"And he is also Ligun Doone," interjected her father, quietly reproachful.

Her bubble burst. She mumbled, "Oh . . . aye," and, blushing, sat down again.

MacKie chuckled. "We seem to hae but one volunteer left."

They all looked at his lordship, and he stood and bowed extravagantly.

With slow reluctance, Delacourt said, "Thad, this is not your fight."

"No more ith it yourth, dear boy."

"I made it mine because Cumberland's damned butchery sickened me. I am involved with this confounded treasure only because many innocent families may starve without their belongings are returned to them, and because it galls me to think of some greedy bounty hunters—or dragoons—living in luxury at their expense."

"No need to hog all the glory for yourthelf, Geoff. I think I have not been completely idle on the other thide of the border."

"No, indeed. And fought in Holland right valiantly," Delacourt agreed warmly. "In fact, I could tell—"

With grim menace, Briley interrupted. "But will not, do you ever hope to thee England again!"

Amused, Prudence saw his grim theatrics replaced by consternation, his pleasant features becoming very red as he shot a dismayed look at Miss Clandon. That young lady, noted Prudence curiously, was glaring at him as though she might cheerfully have strangled him.

Sir Matthew laughed. "I'll nae deny I think it grand o' ye tae volunteer fer such a chancy business, Lord Thaddeus."

"Well, gentlemen," asked Delacourt, "are you all willing to entrust our vital cypher to this thimblewit?"

"A little more from you, my lad," warned Briley, "and I will forget you are an invalid."

Despite the banter, a sudden gravity fell upon them. They all knew that Briley risked a horrible death, and that because of his rank there was no power in the land could save him if he was caught with the cypher. The ayes were uttered with reluctance, and as each man voted he stood and crossed to shake Briley's hand, a procedure that left the shy peer scarlet with embarrassment.

"Very well," said Delacourt, refraining from adding to his friend's panic by gripping his hand. "Now for our other problem: We've to devise a means for getting our wounded out of the pyramid. It's a splendid hiding place for a week or so, but the poor devils are cramped and stifling, and the sooner we get them away, the better. Any notions?"

"I'd gladly take them wi' me in my carriage," said MacKie, "but they'd be no more safely hid at my hoose than where they are. Besides which, I'll admit I've a groom I'd nae trust wi' a silver coin, much less wi' six hundred pound!"

Prudence gave a shocked gasp.

Interested, Delacourt said, "No, has my worth increased again? Gad, but Cunningham did not tell me."

"Had ye no twisted his tail by gripping his hand," growled Lockerbie from his post by the door, "he might've found the time tae."

Sir Matthew enquired, "What's all this?"

"Nothing, nothing," said Delacourt hastily. "Now we must—"

"Something, something!" Lockerbie interposed with the assurance of a trusted retainer. "Yon nasty Colonel said he'd soon lop Ligun Doone's head could he but bring him in his grasp. And what must Captain Reckless do, but go and shake his hand and tell him he'd live tae brag on't!"

A shout of laughter went up, but Prudence frowned, vexed by such heroics.

Briley, grinning broadly, said, "And you call *me* thimblewit!"

"We're no closer to a solution," Delacourt said with a smile. "I've a plan we might attempt, but it's so chancy I'd as soon not try it unless nothing better offers. Thad, when do you mean to return home?"

"I ethcort Mith Clandon to her father next week. I might be able to move the date up, if there ith a boat thailing."

Delacourt shook his head. "That won't do. For Elizabeth to journey all this way to see her grandmama and then turn about in only a few days must cause comment. And were you to go back without her would excite even more attention. We shall have to wait."

"Dare we?" asked Sir Matthew, anxiously. "The other couriers were away weeks since, and—God willing—are likely close to their destinations already."

"If I am not becalmed, heaven forfend, I'm like to make jolly near ath good time," lisped Briley. "Quicker by water, y'know, thir."

Mr. MacKie, who feared water travel, shuddered. "Sooner yourself than I, my lord," he said. "I prefer a good fast team or a good fast horse!"

"The Highlands are not for an Englishman," Delacourt pointed out. "Some clans are still up, and even a Scot is as liable to be slain by an enemy clansman as not."

"How true," sighed MacTavish. "Our poor bonnie land, ever torn by these cruel clan wars."

"It's little short o' a miracle ye came through safe yourself, lad," remarked Sir Matthew.

"None of my doing, sir." Delacourt indicated the silent Lockerbie, who dozed in a chair at the rear of the room. "That gentleman, his many—nay, innumerable relations—and their combined knowledge of your beautiful mountains brought me safe here."

"For which there's many a Scot will call doon blessings on his head," said MacKie with feeling.

The immediate chorus of "Ayes" brought a flush to Delacourt's thin face and also roused Lockerbie, who took out his timepiece, rose, and announced determinedly that it was past time for his master to be abed. The girls also said their good nights, MacTavish accompanying them to the stairs and handing each her candle. Prudence went with Miss Clandon to her door, and they parted, their friendship a little more firmly established, each to climb gratefully between the sheets as soon as possible, and then to lie there, unable to sleep, though for somewhat different causes. Elizabeth's ruminations had to do with two gentlemen: one a loved and lost young Scottish fighter, the other an Englishman with tawny eyes that seemed ever to hold a smile. Prudence lay staring blindly at the silken bedcurtains, her thoughts turning back to the afternoon of this crowded day, to the old shed behind the stables and Geoffrey Delacourt's long sensitive fingers caressing her. She shivered to the recollection of his lips upon her mouth, her eyelids, her bosom. How *ever* could she have been so vulgar as to allow it? Perhaps, because this was a time of war, which always, so she'd heard, imparted an air of urgency; a clearer awareness, maybe, of the transience of life—and love. She might not even *be* in love. Not really. It would be very well if it faded away. Quietly. Delacourt seemed uninclined to offer for her. And even if he should, she had no wish to leave her beloved land. Certainly, he would never consider moving up here. 'What a muddle,' she thought. And, sighing, saw his grave eyes and the smile that would so unexpectedly creep into them. She sighed again. Yearningly.

'You, Prudence MacTavish,' she thought sternly, 'have become enchanted by a foreigner. That's what it is. It willnae last, so dinna fash yersel'. 'Tis just an . . . enchantment. . . .'

Smiling, she drifted into sleep.

IX

Life at Lakepoint settled into an outwardly quiet pattern. James MacTavish, who promised to bend his every faculty to come up with a scheme to smuggle their fugitives aboard some ship, had postponed that task so as to concentrate on researching his forthcoming talk in Edinburgh. With the best will in the world for his persecuted countrymen, he was a scientist first, and a patriot and plotter variously second and third. It was because of his absent-minded response to a remark of his sister-in-law that Hortense became suspicious and was of necessity admitted to their traitorous circle. Discovering that there were wounded men in the pyramid, she contrived to wander unobtrusively to that structure at least once a day, smuggling food, fruit, and medical supplies under the hoops of her voluminous skirts, and coming away with aching heart and tearful eyes because the fugitives endured their sufferings with such fortitude.

Lord Briley remained at Lakepoint, to the delight of Hortense, because he was fascinated by her astrological prowess and spent long hours listening to her explain the celestial bodies and marvelling at her expertise, until Miss Clandon, who had returned to her grandmother's castle, arrived—this daily visit occasioning some remark among the servants, and awakening conflicting emotions in Prudence's troubled heart. She was becoming very fond of the forthright, golden-haired girl, and she was more and more drawn to Lord Briley's bashful whimsicality. It was pleasant to think that Miss Clandon was developing a *tendre* for the young peer—unless that possibility would create more havoc with Captain Delacourt. She discovered, however, that nobility was not for her, and more and more her inclination was to wish that the friendship between the nobleman and the girl he so obviously admired would blossom into lasting devotion.

The weather, meanwhile, continued unusually fine. In the afternoons Prudence wheeled Delacourt outside and took him for leisurely strolls around the estate. Sometimes, Mrs. Cairn would pack them a hamper and Delacourt would balance it on his knees until they arrived at a suitable site, when they would picnic and talk in perfect harmony amid the quiet peace of the countryside.

As they grew to know one another better, they chatted on many subjects: Delacourt learned of her devotion to her brother, and listened with amusement to the tales of their childhood escapades. He was quick to realize that she had led a surprisingly sheltered life, and he noticed how avidly she hung upon his words when he spoke of London and the Polite World. He regaled her by the hour with descriptions of fashions, manners, balls, and parties (to most of which he had not gone). Her rapt attention was his reward, and he began to envy the fortunate man who would introduce her to such delights. Occasionally he would grow silent and withdrawn after such an interlude, and Prudence, guessing him to be tired, would betray no awareness of his shift of mood, but sing softly to herself as she puttered with the plates of food, or went off to collect flowers. Delacourt found her surprisingly knowledgeable on the subjects of music and art. Politics they mutually avoided, but he told her, rather shyly at first, of his passion for gardening. They shared enthusiasms for horses, dogs, and cats, although his interests were more catholic in this last regard than were hers, for he had a deep-rooted reverence for all living creatures and could watch a spider with as much interest as a kitten, whereas she withdrew, shuddering, from the eight-legged creatures. This aspect of his nature puzzled her, and she asked him once how he could bear to have fought in the war, when he would protest if she squashed an ant that encroached upon their luncheon. He answered with his slow smile that he had fought because he believed Prince Charles would be wrong for England, and seeing her swift frown, added whimsically, "No—do not eat me, I beg! I promise you there was no wanton killing by my men, and in my only large battle we were quite hopelessly defeated, you know."

She shrank inwardly, reminded that it was during that battle he had been so badly wounded, and trying not to picture how it must have been for him. She concentrated upon stringing together the daisies she'd picked. "And yet," she murmured, "loving England as much as you do, you now turn against her."

He was silent for so long that she glanced up, thinking he had dropped off to sleep as he sometimes did during their outings. He was staring with frowning eyes at a hovering butterfly. "Do you think me a traitor?" he asked slowly. "I have wondered if I am. But I do not fight against my countrymen. I merely try to outwit Butcher Cumberland."

"The men who do his murdering are English, forbye."

"Yes. And I fancy many of them despise what they do, yet dare not disobey."

Her lip curled. She said with scorn, "A typical wail of humanity. Men cry out against the horrors of war, against cruelty and killing, yet they go on making war just the same!"

"Not all men dislike warfare, Miss Prue. To some it is a way of life. Others are biddable and accept it as their inheritance. I suppose, for every thinking individual, it is a decision based on moral ethics. If you believe in something with all your heart and it is threatened, you should be willing to fight to defend it.

If it is not worth that effort, then you must be prepared to give it up."

"But it should not happen in that way! Men should sit down and *talk* aboot their differences. Nations should be willing to reach solutions across tables instead of slaughtering all their young men and ruining one another to achieve their aims. It is not always the wisest or the best who are the strongest, and—" She broke off, laughing at herself. "Only listen to me making speeches!" She thought, 'He looks tired,' and said, "Sir, I have thought to hear men coming late at night. Do they?"

His nights had been busy this week, and he was very tired indeed, but he only said, "Why, they cannot pop in and out during the hours of daylight, you know."

"Jacobites?"

He nodded.

"Are there many of them? How do they know where to find you?"

"There are quite a number, poor fellows. And the word is carried from one to another."

Afraid for him, she murmured, "You must go constantly in fear of betrayal."

"Oh, no. I think not. Most of them in fact would dread my capture, for if I were put to the question, I might place them in jeopardy."

If he were put to the question. Tortured is what he meant. Her hands on the daisies trembled. Long fingers closed over hers. He was leaning down, looking at her in the way she remembered from the old shed but that she had not glimpsed since, and her heart began to beat frenziedly.

"Prudence," he said, his voice low and husky, "do you know how very beautiful you are?"

She sat motionless, scarcely breathing, waiting for him to leave the chair and kiss her as he had done before; longing for his arms about her, for the touch of his lips on hers. He came closer and, reaching out, touched her cheek. He drew back abruptly. She was seized by disappointment and dimly heard him saying something about the need for a solution to the problem of the men who still languished in the pyramid. Somehow gathering her scattered wits, she said threadily, "I still do not see why they must come to you. You say you have many brave gentlemen who help you. Cannot one of them take command?"

He answered hesitantly, "Yes, of course. Only . . . the men trust me, Miss Prue. They say they feel safe with me. It's only foolish superstition, but—well, they seem to think I am their good luck. I've had a few successes, so—"

"A few! Sir, how many rebels *have* you slipped through Cumberland's lines?"

"Why, I'm not really sure. Upwards of—fifty, I suppose."

"Oh, how splendid! Over fifty lives—fifty families spared heartbreak!"

Watching her, his face flushed. He looked away, saying gruffly, "Do not look at me in that way. Can you not see that—I'm trying very hard, but . . ." The words ceased. He left the chair and walked quickly away, pausing at the edge of the shade cast by the tree, gazing out at the distant scene, but seeing it not at all.

Prudence followed. "Captain Delacourt? What is it?"

He spun around. His eyes were strained and she cried, "Oh, dear sir! I know these are desperate times, but—"

He gripped her shoulders strongly, and said in a harsh voice, "But you do *not* know, little Highland lass. It is all pointless. You know I must go away and— There is so little time."

Her lips felt cold and stiff. She said, "Yes, of course. I am silly. Shall we go back to the house?"

He returned to the chair without a word, put back his head, and soon went to sleep. Prudence left the picnic hamper for the servants to bring. She pushed the chair as smoothly as she was able, her heart heavy. It was very plain that the Captain was attracted to her, but he either wanted Miss Clandon more or was betrothed to an English lady. That last thought came as a staggering shock. How stupid that she had not considered the possibility before. Had he guessed that she had a *tendre* for him?

She felt shamed and embarrassed and as soon as she reached the house surrendered the chair to a waiting Lockerbie and walked hurriedly to the stairs.

And did not know that, obedient to the commanding lift of one thin hand, Lockerbie halted and stood patiently while a pair of dark eyes watched until Miss MacTavish disappeared from sight.

"Sir," said Little Willie Mayhew, propping himself on one elbow, his drawn face reflecting anxiety, "we dinna like biding here. We ken well that the whole countryside's swarming wi' redcoats, and we're no wishful tae bring doom on the MacTavish and his kin. Nor y'sel', neither."

The hidden room in the pyramid was a crowded place with three cots practically touching, two candles providing the only illumination, and the air that entered by way of cunningly concealed vents hot and barely adequate.

Delacourt, seated on the foot of Mayhew's cot, gently cuffed the big man's toes and said with a cheerful grin that he had no wish for such a grisly happenstance. "Now what's this I hear about Cunningham's troopers having a look at this place last night?"

"'Tis true, sir," said Jock Campbell, his bandaged right foot protruding from beneath the sheet on his cot. "It was warm, ye'll recall, and we'd taken a chance and opened the door a mite."

"Damned near didn't get it shut in time," croaked Ensign Harry Stephens, an English Jacobite aged eighteen, and the only officer among the fugitives. "We could hear 'em through the vents, Captain. They were as curious as they could stare, and I heard one of the perishers say that this would make a good hiding place for any rebs who were skulking about."

Up went Delacourt's dark brows. "Did you, now? Anything else?"

"Lord! Ain't it enough, sir? They'll tell that bloody Cunningham and he'll come and tear this pyramid apart like he did the MacKenzies' cottage."

"Our stalwart Colonel already knows about this pyramid, and I believe MacTavish was at pains to show him the hidden room. There are two, you know, but only one is public knowledge." He thought, 'I hope,' and added, "I know this is not a prime posting house, but we've plans to get you on your way very soon."

"Sir," interjected Campbell, looking appalled, "I trust ye ken how much we're beholden tae ye. 'Tis no that we're ungrateful—Gawd knows we'd all be dead was it not fer ye'sel'."

Delacourt smiled but he was uneasily aware that none of these poor fellows was in any condition to travel. Willie had that ugly wound in his knee; Campbell's ankle was shattered; and young Stephens, with the longest journey to safety, had a musket ball through his side that had broken two ribs. "If I could arrange it," he muttered, "you'd all stay where you are for at least a month. But I've a notion our time is limited."

Stephens gasped, "Never say the house is watched, sir? If that's the case we should all leave at once, and not delay another minute!"

"I don't believe it is watched. Yet. MacTavish is highly regarded throughout the world because of his contributions to archaeology. He has been honoured by several foreign governments. You may be sure that any accusations against him will have to be well substantiated, if only because of his worldwide reputation."

"Ye mean," said Jock Campbell, "they may hae their suspicions, but they'll be needing proof. And we're it, eh, sir?"

"Exactly. So, my regrets, lads, but you're all going to be arrested." Dismay came into their eyes, and he added with a grin, "By me."

"Whisht," breathed Willie, much relieved.

"What'll ye do wi' us, Captain?" asked Campbell.

"In your condition, run you through a corner of hell, I'm afraid. You're to be conveyed by wagon to Fort Augustus—or at least to a few miles northwest of the place. I've men to meet us there with horses and you'll be taken to Glenrae, where I understand your family can offer sanctuary, Mayhew."

"Aye, sir. For me and all of us. And right glad they'll be tae help."

"Splendid. As for you, Ensign, as soon as you're fit to go on from Glenrae there's a fishing boat and a guide to take you over to France if you wish."

"Thank you, sir. God send amnesty is granted soon," said the Ensign.

Campbell, who had been watching Delacourt frowningly, said, "Sir, ye said *ye* was tae be the one tae arrest us?"

"Correct. I've the uniform, you see, and papers if we're stopped."

The three men exchanged sober glances. Willie said, "Ye're never meaning tae ride all that way yersel'?"

"Oh, I shall do, never fear." They did not look much relieved, and he smiled wryly. "Unless you've another English officer handy who can fit into my uniform."

"Ye've many friends, sir," Campbell argued. "There must be some English Jacobites among 'em."

"Three. One's short and fat. Another's about the size of Willie, and the third took a musket ball through his leg when we relieved the troopers of Jamie MacDougall."

The Ensign pursed his lips. "What about the gentleman who's been staying here, sir? Lord Briley."

"Oh, he'd be more than willing. In fact, he'll likely flay me alive when he discovers I've not given him a chance at this, but the fact is, the poor fellow lisps. If you should encounter a patrol, as you very likely will do, his lordship would be too easy to identify to Colonel Cunningham." The Ensign started a further protest, but Delacourt stopped it with a lift of his hand.

"Enough, gentlemen, enough! I appreciate your concern, but I shall be suitably disguised, I assure you. We shall go on very well, I've no doubt." He stood. "Now, we shall attempt this on Sunday morning, so prepare yourselves."

Their grateful thanks followed him to the door. He stepped cautiously into the night, and stood motionless for a moment, waiting for his eyes to adjust to the darkness. When he could detect no movement or the slightest sound, he slipped into the shrubs where he had concealed his wheelchair, retrieved it, sat down, and sighed wearily. He fairly ached with tiredness, and his wound, which had been less troublesome these past few days, was causing him the old nagging pain that was like a wire band tightening around his lung. He coughed involuntarily, winced, and peered about, holding his breath. Again, he seemed to have escaped detection, and he manoeuvred the chair through the grounds to the long temporary ramp MacTavish had caused to be put up alongside the door that opened into the west side of the house.

Sidley worried him. But if he was wrong, if his uneasiness about the butler was unjustified, he was putting those poor devils through this ordeal needlessly soon. Although it was not really needless at all events—not with MacTavish and Hortense and Prudence always at risk. Nothing must happen to those good people, however willing they were to take the chance. An image of Prudence's vital little face came into his mind's eye. No. He dared not delay any longer!

The rear hall was dark and deserted, the house quiet, its inhabitants long since sleeping. He pulled on the wheels, guiding the chair silently along to the room that served him as a parlour. Cautiously, he lifted the latch. Lockerbie was not waiting to censure him for having gone out alone; a candle burned on the table as he had left it, but the room was empty. Delacourt closed the door, climbed from the chair, and started towards the bedchamber.

He had very little warning: a sudden beading of chill, clammy sweat on his face, a numbing dizziness, a complete loss of all awareness of colour. He knew he was going down and in that same instant saw a man come from the bedchamber. With his last gleam of consciousness he recognized the narrow face, shocked out of its customary imperturbability. He thought a fading, 'Sidley . . .'

"Sir, please try to take a little. Oh, God! *Sir!* Please!"

With a tremendous effort Delacourt whispered, "Did you call . . . for help?"

"No, sir. Thank the Lord you're better! Try and sip a little of the brandy."

"Do not lift me, please. I'll be—all right if you just . . . let me lie here for a minute." He could feel the man trembling and thought remotely, 'I must have put the fear of God into him.' The sick weakness began to fade, but the sharp pangs still racked him. If he could just manage to breathe very lightly for a minute or two . . .

At length Sidley whispered, "Will I lift your head a little now, Captain? So you can have the brandy?"

Delacourt nodded, and the butler slipped an arm under his shoulders and held a glass to his lips. He sipped cautiously, dreading that he might cough again. The powerful spirit blazed through him. He held his breath and was able to fight off the cough, and in a moment felt warmed and stronger. "Thank you," he managed, "for not rousing the house."

"If I can help you to your bed, sir, I'll go and find your servant."

Delacourt said with a twinkle, "Lord, no! He'd fuss me to death. Why don't you just wheel my chair over and get me into it. In a little while you can help me to bed, if you'd not object."

"Object, sir! Of course not." The butler peered into that pale but dauntless grin. Lord, but the man looked like death! "Are you sure you're ready, Captain? You went down like a stone."

"Dreadful habit. Probably scared you out of your wits, eh? Yes, I'm going along better now. Just bring the chair if you will."

Sidley snatched a cushion from the sofa and put it behind the invalid's head, then got up and wheeled the chair closer. Delacourt sagged dizzily when he first managed to get to his feet, but after he'd been placed in the chair he seemed to revive and in a few minutes the terrifying pallor began to ease a little. Sidley gave him the brandy glass, and the next healthy swallow was not followed by that betraying moment of taut immobility.

"I really think," ventured Sidley, "that I should fetch your man."

"If you do, I imagine the first thing he'll want to know is what you were doing in my room."

How odd, thought the butler, that the dark eyes that a moment ago had seemed so dazed and helpless, now glinted rather unpleasantly. He folded his hands. "I was looking for you, sir."

Delacourt took another sip of the brandy and regarded him with one eyebrow raised in a silent, ironic questioning.

"I know it sounds peculiar—to come at this hour. But I *had* to talk to you, sir." A pucker disturbed Sidley's forehead. "I'd not expected to find you gone out, Captain. When I couldn't make you hear my knock, I was afraid you might have come over queer."

"So you came in. I see. Since I was hit, I suffer these silly fainting fits occasionally." Delacourt added untruthfully, "I can feel them coming on, and sometimes, to be out in the fresh air works wonders."

"Even so, you should have rung for your man, first. Suppose you'd fallen from your chair, sir?" Sidley bent closer and whispered, "And—with what's going on in this house . . . !"

'Oh, Lord!' thought Delacourt. He watched the butler inscrutably. "I cannot imagine to what you refer."

Sidley glanced around. "Might I be permitted to sit down, Captain?"

"Of course. My apologies. Now, was it because of what you suppose to be, er, 'going on' that you came knocking on my door at dead of night?"

Sidley pulled over a straight-backed chair and disposed himself neatly upon it. "I just didn't know what to do, sir. And you, being an army officer, I thought could advise me."

"I'll try. Spit it out, man."

That brusque adjuration relieved Sidley. This might be a very sick gentleman, but he had the assurance of the officer, all right. He lowered his voice and said, "I think there's rebels being sheltered here, Captain Delacourt. Sad I am to have to say such a dreadful thing, for Mr. MacTavish has been good to me, and I have nothing but respect for him and his family."

Delacourt's heart sank. "Good God! Are you sure? I've seen nothing."

"They're very sly about it, naturally enough. But I reckon that's why you was offered to stay here. Mr. MacTavish said you being young Master Robert's friend, it was the least he could do. But I think you're being used, sir. They know Colonel Cunningham won't have this house searched if you vouch for them."

"I cannot believe it! By God, Sidley, if you're just making a mountain out of a molehill—"

"I'm doing no such thing, Captain!" His pale grey eyes glowing with zeal, Sidley declared, "I told you I like Mr. MacTavish, and I meant it. But, God, how I *hate* these dirty Jacobites! My boy was in the army." The blazing look faded. Watching him, Delacourt thought inconsequently that save for the pockmarks that scarred his face, the butler was a fine figure of a man: tall, with a good pair of shoulders, and with light brown hair, to judge from the shade of his brows. Probably in the neighbourhood of forty-three, and with only the beginnings of a paunch. Sidley said with ineffable sorrow, "Such a good boy, sir. He worked hard at his lessons. His one dream was to serve his country. My wife and I scrimped and saved to buy him a cornetcy; that's why I took this position and left my wife in England. Our son's first station was Scotland. He was so proud." He turned away and finished huskily, "He was . . . only nineteen."

Delacourt climbed from his chair and rested a hand upon the

bowed shoulder. "My poor chap," he said in his gentlest voice, "I am so very sorry. Was it at Prestonpans?"

"Culloden, sir. My—my wife suffered some sort of seizure when she got the word. The shock, they think. He was all we had, you see. Just the one boy."

Delacourt tightened his grip for a moment, then returned to his chair. "I wonder that Mr. MacTavish did not mention it to me."

"I never told them. I just said my wife had been taken ill and—and they gave me time off to go to her. I meant to tell them. But Mrs. Sidley has to have constant care. Her sister's with her, but there's doctor's bills and medicines, and a woman who comes in and helps every day. It all costs money, sir. It's hard to get an English butler to come all the way up here, and Mr. MacTavish pays me well. But their boy ran off to England instead of fighting for his Prince. If they knew about my son, it might make them feel uncomfortable. And if rich folk get uncomfortable with a servant, he's gone before you can wink your eye!"

Little wonder he hated the Jacobites, poor fellow, thought Delacourt, and asked, "Will you tell me what you have seen here?"

Sidley took a deep breath and brought his emotions under control. "I've heard a lot of comings and goings—mostly in the wee hours of the morning, sir. And I've seen food disappear like it was half a dozen guests we had here, instead of only yourself and your servants."

"We've had Miss Clandon and Lord Briley, don't forget."

"No, no, sir! Much more than that. And what would Lord Briley want with rolls of lint and bandages?"

"Jupiter! You've seen these things carried upstairs?"

"Not upstairs, sir. I don't know where. It's all done at night. I've stayed up a time or two, but whenever I peep out, I don't see anything. And I have to be careful. Mrs. Cairn is fairly crazed for the master, and she watches us like a hawk. I fancy my life wouldn't be worth much if they knew I suspect." He bent closer, his voice again dropping to little more than a whisper. "I saw muddy footsteps across the terrace early one morning when I looked out of my window. I couldn't tell which room they went to, but it looked as if someone had climbed in a downstairs window, sir! I dressed as quick as I could, but by the time I came down they were gone. Gone as if they'd never been!" He pursed his lips and stared at the young Captain solemnly.

Delacourt thought, 'That was a close one!' "You are quite sure?" he asked. "It couldn't have been a trick of the light?"

"No, sir! I've been thinking what to do, and—since you know Colonel Cunningham, I decided to go to him."

Delacourt gazed at the zealous features for a moment, then turned his chair away. He said slowly, "I wish you were a trifle less observant, Sidley."

He heard the hiss of indrawn breath and the sound of Sidley coming to his feet.

In a voice of suppressed excitement, the butler said, "I knew it! I thought you wasn't very excited about what I told you, sir. So it's all a plan, is it? The Colonel knows."

Delacourt faced him again. "You have it. You're a jolly shrewd fellow, I must say." He saw the sallow skin flush with pleasure, and went on, "You can help us. The thing is—we're after bigger fish than MacTavish."

"Bigger . . . ? Oh! Strike me dumb! You mean that filth—Ligun Doone?"

Delacourt looked down and murmured, "I did not say that, you'll mind."

"Very true, sir. By the powers, but this is grand! So you were *put* here, were you, Captain? And MacTavish thinks it was all his idea! He thinks he's using you, whereas all the time you're laying a trap for the real traitor."

"Hum," said Delacourt. "I suppose you might say that. I would prefer, however—Colonel Cunningham would much prefer—that you said nothing. Tell me whatever you see, but you'll have to be devilish cautious about it, and obey any orders

I give you, without question. If you don't think you can handle that, Sidley, I'm afraid we shall have to send you off. We cannot let anything spoil this."

"Lord, no, sir! Oh, if only I could tell my wife!"

Delacourt gave a small smile. "I fancy she'll be glad when Doone hangs."

"I don't know, sir. Women are funny, you know. But—for me, it's like the answer to a prayer! When Doone is hacked up and his head stuck on Tower Gate, my boy will be avenged! Praise God! Oh, I'll obey you, sir. Whatever you say. How shall I get word to you? Through your servant?"

"Yes. Lockerbie's to be trusted. He has no fondness for the Stuarts. If I need you, he'll slip a note to you, and if you have news for me you can get word to him."

"Yes, sir." Sidley moved to the door but turned before opening it, his eyes very bright. "You cannot know how much this means to me, Captain Delacourt. I only wish one thing—that mine could be the hand that holds the axe!" He grinned rather horribly, then said a startled, "Oh, I am sorry, sir! I was so carried away, I forgot. If you're ready, I'll prepare you for the night."

Delacourt thanked him, but said he was much restored and could manage until Lockerbie returned from his 'stroll.' It was foolish, perhaps, but he did not relish being put into his nightshirt by a man who yearned to hack him to pieces.

"The MacTavish says that Captain Delacourt has a scheme whereby they will be safely away this week-end," said Hortense, carefully unravelling a misplaced stitch in her embroidery. "This French knot is being tiresome. I vow the man is a marvel to so constantly conflummerate— Oh, dear, oh, dear!"

Seated beside her in a shady spot of the shrubbery, and thinking that her aunt's 'marvel' had seemed to avoid her these past two days, Prudence glanced up at the change in tone. Colonel Cunningham, followed by two troopers, was marching briskly towards them. Her heart gave a skip. She said in a low voice, "We must be very careful, dear. He's a terribly dangerous creature." She watched her nervous aunt anxiously, but with lives at stake Hortense resorted to an unsuspected reserve of strength. She might be a little pale, but the hand she extended did not tremble and she said quite calmly, "Good morning, Colonel. How energetic you are. I vow this muggy weather quite enervates me."

"I am not allowed to be enervated, ma'am," he responded, bowing over her hand. "Ain't in the King's Regulations, you know, and besides, this Doone fella keeps us busy enough. He was seen in the hills yesterday. You'd do well to have a care, ladies. With Captain Delacourt here, you would be judged an enemy of all rebels and there's no telling to what vengeance he and his cutthroats might resort."

Prudence blinked at him. "Good gracious! Does he lead a band of ruffians?"

"He has men everywhere, Miss MacTavish. And everywhere *he* is our troubles increase. I've come for a word with your father. Is he about?"

Hortense folded her embroidery and restored it to her work bag. "I believe he intended to take the Captain for a little drive. The poor boy looked so pulled this morning, it will likely do him good. We shall go and find Cairn, for I am very sure she will know when they mean to return. Do you come in, dear?"

Prudence said she would remain in the garden for a while, and her aunt went off with the Colonel stamping along beside her. The troopers looked at one another as if they contemplated the necessity of standing guard over the young lady, then followed their officer.

Taking up her crayon, Prudence next proceeded to sit and stare blankly at her sketch pad, wallowing in a sense of ill usage and resenting the vagaries of Fate. She heard wheels on the drivepath and thought that her papa would not be delighted to find Cunningham awaiting him. However, the voices she soon heard negated that conclusion. Lord Briley and Miss Clandon strolled onto the terrace, chatting merrily. They looked so carefree and happy together. It was more and more apparent that his lordship found the lady desirable. His intentions, however, could not be honourable, for her birth and background, although good, could not make her an eligible consort for one of his high rank. Yet, mused Prudence, Miss Clandon was fond of him. There, see how her hand was extended to him in that prettily impulsive way. Lord Briley halted at once, took up that small hand, and kissed it lingeringly. Miss Clandon laughed at him, swayed closer, then moved capriciously away.

Inexplicably irritated, Prudence drew her chair farther into the shadows of the apple tree. She had no wish to talk with them. His lordship was pleasant but disloyal to pursue his friend's mistress. And Miss Clandon was unfaithful to the man who needed her so badly. And considering that man was Ligun Doone—faith, but there was no condoning it! These bitter animadversions, so contrary to her usual sunny nature, made her feel miserable and ashamed. She watched the pair wander slowly across the verdant turf, his lordship resplendent in beige velvet, and Miss Clandon's pale yellow gown swaying provocatively. A pretty picture they made. She took up her crayon and began to sketch with swift, sure strokes.

"Oh, look, my lord! There is Miss MacTavish."

Prudence glanced up. They were almost upon her. She smiled and waved, and when they came to her with warm answering smiles, she felt repentant for her harsh judgements and said, "How nice that you have come. I hope you stay with us this time, Miss Clandon."

"Yes, thank you." Miss Clandon curtseyed demurely. "Your father has been so kind as to invite me for the whole weekend."

His lordship asked, "What ith old Geoff up to? Your butler told me he ith gone out with your father."

"Just a drive, I believe, sir. But my aunt tells me the Captain has formulated a plan to get our wounded safely away."

"I believe he hath, but I doubt he will be content with it."

"Of course not," said Miss Clandon, smiling. "Geoffrey is never satisfied, and yet his schemes always work."

"He is a very clever gentleman," said Prudence.

"Or tho outrageouth that no one ith prepared for hith daring," Briley qualified. "He taketh too many rithkth. I will be very glad when he ith comfortably in England again." He scowled. "Whenever that may be."

Prudence said, "He told me he does not expect to be here for long, so—"

"When did he say that?" demanded Miss Clandon sharply.

"Good God!" exclaimed Briley, his glance having turned to the house. "What the devil ith *he* doing here again?"

Colonel Cunningham and his small escort were returning across the lawns.

Prudence groaned softly. Miss Clandon trilled a delighted laugh and seized the sketch pad. "Only look, Thaddeus! Miss MacTavish has made the loveliest drawing of us!"

Briley turned at once. "Well done, m'dear," he murmured.

Prudence was slightly taken aback at this familiarity until she realized that he referred not to her artistic skill but to Miss Clandon's acting.

"I thay," he lisped, taking the pad and scanning the sketch admiringly, "you are very talented, ma'am," and in a soft murmur, "Why *ith* he here?"

"To see my papa—he says," she whispered, and added in a louder tone, "Flatterer! Should you like me to paint it for you?"

Miss Clandon said eagerly, "Would you? Oh, yes, please. It would be such a lovely memory." Briley glanced at her swiftly. She raised her voice and called, "Colonel! Only see how talented is our dear Miss MacTavish."

Cunningham joined them, bowed to Miss Clandon, shook his lordship's hand, apparently disturbing that gentleman's ruffles, and admired the sketch with much enthusiasm. "By

Jupiter, but you're skilful, ma'am! How cleverly you have caught their expressions: his lordship so merry, and Miss Clandon a touch melancholic."

Taken off-stride, Miss Clandon stammered, "Melancholic? Oh, do I seem so?"

They all peered at the sketch. It had not occurred to Prudence at the time, but it was truth; there was a sadness in the smile she had depicted. She thought, 'Good heavens! I drew it and did not realize, but he saw it at once. How very astute he is!' She said, "What an eye you have, Colonel."

He was pleased and said expansively that he was an admirer of art. "And I believe I know good work when I encounter it. I would be most grateful, Miss MacTavish, did you allow me to see some more of your drawings. Would that be intrusive?"

He was trying to be pleasant to the natives, of course, she thought cynically, and probably had no more interest in art than the man in the moon. Still she could not help but be flattered as she led the way back to the house, and thence to the first-floor chamber known as 'Miss Prue's Workroom.'

X

Delacourt said earnestly, "I tell you, sir, Thad bears very little resemblance to the featherhead he portrays. He's a truly splendid fellow. He fought in Holland and won himself a magnificent reputation. Did you know?"

"My daughter said he was a Major." MacTavish reined the team to a walk. "Sold out, did he?"

"Invalided out, sir. Came through the battles unscathed, but took a nasty one from a sniper after Dettingen and they thought he was finished." His smile was without mirth as he said, "Happily, he was able to confound his doctors."

MacTavish frowned, and for a moment there was silence. Then he said, "I take it he shall leave us very soon."

"Early on Sunday morning. But not for England, alas."

"What? But—I thought—in view of this damnable butler of mine—"

"*Because* of your damnable butler. Don't you see, sir? I'd intended to be the escorting officer of our rebels myself, but—"

MacTavish gawked at him. "*You?* You're mad!"

Delacourt made an impatient, dismissing gesture. "I've gone over it all a hundred times. I am their best hope. Their only hope, perhaps. We can dress my Scots as troopers, but should they encounter a patrol the officer will certainly have to talk, and he *must* be English."

"Then *I'll* be the officer!" Dismayed by his own impulsiveness, MacTavish paled, and went on with markedly less vehemence, "I, ah, think my English is as good as your own."

"Oh, certainly, sir. To a Scot. But let an Englishman listen to you for two minutes, and he'd have you! There's no imitating us, alas. At least—not without concentrated study. There is a slight burr to your 'r's when you're annoyed." He smiled faintly. "Your daughter has similar lapses."

MacTavish uttered a short bark of laughter. "Oh, Prudence becomes pure Scots when she's irked, I grant you. But—be sensible, man! When you ride out at night you return properly knocked up. How d'ye propose to stay in the saddle for twenty-five miles?"

"By having Lockerbie come after me with a chaise. I managed to get up into the hills when Willie Mayhew would trust no other." With a trace of temperament he said, "Dammitall, they could glue me to the saddle, if necessary! I *know* I could have done it."

MacTavish thought, 'The spirit is willing.' And he asked with regret, "Did you *know* that you could walk across your room on Thursday night? You'll own you are subject to such attacks. What if you were to suffer one whilst you spoke with a patrol?"

"Oh, it could be accounted for, somehow. Only"—Delacourt scowled darkly—"now it will not serve, blast it!"

"Because of Sidley. By God, the fellow's a threat to you! To us all! Get rid of him!"

"Easy said, sir. But you would not pull the trigger, I doubt. No more would I. That poor devil's had about all any man should have to endure. I've convinced him I'm at Lakepoint as Cunningham's spy, and he's willing—eager—to obey any orders I give him. It occurred to me, therefore . . ." He paused, then went on with a wry grin, "Well, as I said, the officer must be an Englishman."

MacTavish stared, then gave a hoot of mirth. "Why, you rogue! Remind me never to incur your displeasure! I vow you'd have me shipped off to some African mountaintop!"

"Dreadful, isn't it? Poor fellow. But I mean to instruct my men that he is to be treated kindly, and I shall see to it that his wife is funded until all this is done with and he is restored to her."

MacTavish looked at him in a bewildered fashion. "I pay him well enough, Delacourt, and I'll be damned if I can see why you fret so. He's a treacherous hound and has been spying on us; only too eager to hand us all over to Cunningham's tender mercies." Delacourt set his jaw but said nothing, and MacTavish went on, "Would you have my daughter's head adorn Tower Gate?"

Delacourt blanched. "Lord Almighty! Never think such a ghastly thing!"

"It is not beyond the bounds of possibility, sad to say. Now, how d'ye mean to convince him? Surely he'll think one of Cunningham's officers should take the rebels in charge?"

"Yes, of course. But I've told him he'll be masquerading as a Jacobite masquerading as an English officer in charge of prisoners, but in reality knowing he'll be met by other Jacobites along the route who mean to bring the wounded men to safety."

MacTavish laughed. "And for why would he be doing so cockaleery a thing, when he might simply report them to our cunning Colonel?"

"Why, to learn more of Ligun Doone and his reprehensible henchmen, of course. After which, the cavalry will gallop to his rescue, and all the rebels be hauled off and shot."

"Well, that, we pray, will not happen. Even so, he'll learn a good deal. I think I am not a bloodthirsty man, but . . . if Sidley should escape! The names he could name! The faces he would describe!"

"He'll not escape, sir. But just to be on the safe side, I'm sending Thad Briley along. As Sidley's Sergeant."

The thought of Major Lord Thaddeus Briley posing as a Sergeant, while the butler enacted the role of Captain, reduced the MacTavish to such hilarity that it became necessary for him to mop at his eyes. He gasped out, "Would that I might be there to see it! I—I trust you'll instruct his lordship not to open that dainty mouth of his. He'd have small chance of uttering a sentence with no sibilants, and if Cunningham hears that among a troop of English soldiers was one who carried himself like an aristocrat and spoke with a lisp, he'll no be in doubt for long!"

Delacourt sighed. "True. Lord, but I wish I could go instead of old Thad."

MacTavish sobered and laid a hand on the younger man's arm. "No, lad. Your plan is much better as it is. This way, you've an excuse for Sidley taking your place, and we'll be well rid o' the pest. Besides, I'd not be concerned about his lordship. He seems a resourceful enough fellow."

"I'm not concerned about Thad's courage, sir. He's the very best sort of man. The thing is I need him to carry our curst cypher to England. If anything should go wrong . . ." And with a sudden flare of frustration, he raged, "Oh, *damn* this everlasting—" He broke off, a hand to his lips as he coughed, ducked his head, and coughed again, his following breath coming in shallow, painful gasps.

MacTavish halted the team and watched sombrely.

After a few minutes, Delacourt straightened and lay back against the squabs, eyes closed and face waxy and streaked with sweat. He looked up then, met MacTavish's compassionate gaze, and smiled with wry amusement. "I fancy that put me in my place. You can . . . drive on now, sir. I'm better."

MacTavish regarded him in tight-lipped silence, then slapped the reins on the backs of the team, and the carriage lurched forward once more. "Let this be the last of it," he muttered.

Delacourt said, "I'd be easier if we'd a better plan. Have you come up with anything, sir?"

Guiltily aware that his efforts had been bent on his own

work, MacTavish said feebly, "Yes. Get rid of Sidley and let the men rest in my pyramid until they're stronger."

"You speak of months. I've a feeling our time is short, even without your butler."

"Have you, now? A premonition? Well, my sister would agree. Her confounded stars are warning us from hell to breakfast. Oh, grin, then; I apprehend you think it madness. I can only say she's been at this jiggery-pokery for years and never quite so agitated by what she 'reads' for us, as she is now."

"I wish to heavens Mrs. Hortense's stars could tell her if Cunningham knows of the cypher."

"Heaven forfend! He'd stop at nothing to get his hands on it. Ye canna doot that!"

"I canna doot that," Delacourt confirmed with a twinkle, and as MacTavish chuckled, went on, "To business, sir. Here is how it will go. My fellows will bring the uniforms tomorrow night, and Sidley, Thad, and those who are to be 'troopers' will escort the wagon away before dawn on Sunday. If all goes well, Thad will return here by Tuesday at the latest, pick up the cypher, and take it to its destination in England."

"It sounds simple. But what if all does not go well?"

Delacourt shrugged. "I shall have to spin a new web, sir."

Saturday was warm and hazy, the sky a whitish blue and the dampness in the air bringing lethargy. The day passed quietly enough, although for several residents of Lakepoint, coming events cast shadows that strained nerves to an almost unbearable pitch.

The evening was mild, and after dinner the terrace doors were opened to admit the cool air while MacTavish and Delacourt settled down to hear Hortense play a sonata for them on the fine harpsichord in the drawing room. Prudence took her place to turn the pages for her aunt. Hortense played quite well, even if her pace did not always match the notations indicated by Mr. Handel and, encouraged by the applause that greeted her first effort, she launched into a minuet.

Thaddeus Briley, seated at the rear of the room, shifted restlessly in his chair. He was not averse to opera, provided the chorus was pleasing to the eyes, but musicales bored him. Besides, he was to be off in the wee hours of the morning, and he could think of more interesting ways to spend these last moments at Lakepoint. With the bewitching Miss Clandon, for example. He glanced to the side. A vision in pink and ecru lace, with a small bunch of pink roses nestling amongst her high-dressed and powdered curls, his admired lady sat with her billowing skirts gracefully disposed on a cream brocade loveseat. She did not return his glance, but the corners of her pretty mouth twitched, and he knew she was aware that he watched her. He coughed softly.

Miss Clandon's fan came into play. From behind it she slanted an amused look at him, and he jerked his head towards the door, one imploring hand laid over his heart.

The fan lowered. Her lips formed the words "For shame!" But she was also conscious that he went into danger very soon, and she came to her feet and slipped quietly into the hall.

A few moments later his lordship found her in the front garden. She fluttered her fan at him. "You are very wicked, my lord."

Typical of him, he had required a maid to bring her shawl and he now draped it about her shoulders. "If it be wicked to adore tho beautiful a creation ath your lovely thelf . . ." he murmured.

She leaned in his arm, looking up at him, but as he bent to kiss her the fan swept between them. "Rascal," she chided. "Have you no sense of the proprieties?"

"On the boat coming up here—" he began.

"Never mind about that! And besides, it was very wrong of me. I'd not have you think me a fast girl, sir."

He offered his arm, she laid her mittened fingers on it, and they walked slowly through the scented sweetness of the night. "I think you are everything that ith pure and fair," he said with unusual gravity. "I think I have never been tho happy ath when I am with you."

She laughed rather unsteadily. "Flatterer! You make me sound perfection and I am not, you know."

He said whimsically, "You *would* be perfection—had you only another name. If I call you Mith Clandon, I am doomed. If I call you Elithabeth—no better. A man who lithpth hath to find a lady named Jane or Amelia. You can have no notion what a trial it ith to attempt to be romantical when you cannot even properly pronounth the name of the girl you adore." He gave an exaggerated sigh, and his lace-trimmed handkerchief fluttered in a despairing gesture.

She halted and faced him. "And do you, then—adore me, my lord?"

The laughter left his eyes. "You know I do."

"Thank you. And—you may call me Beth."

Exultant, he cried, "Wonderful! My problem ith no more!" He took her hand and pressed a kiss into the warm palm.

Miss Clandon's eyes, watching the downbent head, were soft with tenderness. She murmured, "I have not a great number of gentlemen who profess to adore me. I pray you will bring this one safely back to me, Thaddeus."

"If I do," he replied, suddenly very grave, "I will have to enquire for the right to call on your papa."

Even now she had not really thought he had marriage in mind. She gave a gasp, sudden tears filled her eyes, and she walked a few quick little paces away from him. He came up to stand behind her and grip her shoulders. "Beth, my very dear girl. . . . I am a frippery fellow and I lithp horribly, I know, but—"

"Frippery!" Wrenching around, she cried indignantly, "You came all the way to Prestonpans to give your friend what aid you might! You journeyed with me on that horrid boat into what you—being a poor Sassenach and not knowing beauty when you see it—likely regard as a desolation! I know that you have helped our fugitives in England, and you are going to risk your life tomorrow—and you call yourself *frippery?*"

"I am really a very great hero, now that you remind me of it," he acknowledged. "Wherefore, you cannot give me a nay, ma'am." He saw her eyes cloud and she shook her head and started to respond. Frightened, he put a hand over her lips. "No, no. You cannot deny it ith *de rigueur* that when the hero goeth charging into battle, hith lady ith obliged to thend him off with hope in hith heart." And abruptly abandoning frivolity, he asked wistfully, "Have you no hope to give me, my beautiful Beth?"

She thought, 'How dear he is. How gentle and kind, and strong. The very epitome of a gentleman.' And with tears beading her lashes, she said in a husky little voice, "None—I am afraid."

Some time later, beating his own craven retreat, Delacourt wheeled his chair along the terrace towards the glow of a cigarillo and the man who sat on the balustrade, gazing across the moonlit lawns. "Well, Thad," he said, "what luck, old fellow?"

The rather drooping figure straightened. Briley answered, "The lady hath a deal of brainth. Turned me down. Flat."

Delacourt, who had known what the verdict would be, said a sympathetic, "Oh, bad luck. My condolences. But, this is scarce a normal atmosphere. Can you only persuade her parent to bring her to visit you in Wiltshire, perhaps if she saw you in your natural surroundings—"

"You mean"—Briley faced him squarely—"were I to bribe her with the glorieth of Dunthter Court—" He swore and jerked his head away. "Little wonder Beth would not have me, eh? A man who cannot even pronounth hith own name!"

"What stuff! Elizabeth is not the girl to be put off because you lisp."

"Or—becauth you do not?"

Delacourt left the chair and put one hand on Briley's broad

shoulder. Before he could speak, his lordship shrugged away and stood with his back turned. "That wath dethpicable. My apologieth, Geoff. I know there ith only liking between you. I'm behaving like a whining cur. . . ." He turned again, the familiar grin on his lips, but his eyes veiled. "It'th my damned title, you thee. Properly put her off. And her love for her own land." His voice shredded a little. He went on hurriedly, "I think you are in little better cathe—eh?"

Delacourt stared blankly for an instant, then returned to his chair. "Oh, no," he said breezily. "The little Prudence is a lovely lass, but we merely enjoy a summer dalliance." He saw his friend's eyes whip to his face with a rather shocked expression and added with a lift of the brows, "Had you thought it a serious attachment? Silly gudgeon. We should not suit, you know. Besides, I fancy both our hearts are—er, engaged elsewhere."

Lord Briley grasped the handles of the chair and pushed it across the terrace. "I do not recall your having a *tendre* for any of the London ladieth," he murmured.

"Ah, but I do not tell you all my secrets."

"All! Damn you, Geoff! I think you tell me *none* at all."

Delacourt laughed.

When the doors had closed behind them, all was quiet in the garden. The moon slid slowly up the western sky; a soft night wind rustled the treetops and whispered through the shrubbery. After a while, the music that drifted pleasantly from the windows ceased; the ground-floor lights winked out, one by one, and the glow of candles being carried up the stairs could be seen. Amber brightened the windows of the first, and then the second floor. There was the click of locks turning. Two more candles ascended to the third floor.

Time passed. The second-floor lamps and candelabra were extinguished, the two glowing windows on the third floor were darkened, and the great house was silent.

It had been agreed by the conspirators that only those directly involved would leave their rooms that eventful night, so as not to excite the suspicions of the servants. James MacTavish was amused by this, and said that if he knew his staff they were likely quite aware of what was going forward. Nonetheless, every effort was made to present an appearance of normality, and anyone dwelling at Lakepoint and unaware of the treasonable activities would have supposed all inside to be peacefully sleeping. In point of fact, very few had gone to bed. Windows were open and ears straining for the first sounds of approaching riders. Elizabeth Clandon waited, weeping softly and saying some extra-fervent prayers in behalf of a young man with tawny eyes, freckles, and a lisp. Hortense sat up in bed, hugging her knees, and worrying over what her stars had imparted about one occupant of the household. Prudence knelt gazing at a sketchbook spread on the window seat of her bedchamber, the book opened to a page whereon the soft moonlight illumined the likeness of a dark young man with a thin, fine-boned face and a proud tilt to his chin.

In his converted bedchamber, the heavy draperies drawn to conceal the candlelight, that same young man sat in his wheelchair and watched an excited butler don his uniform. My lord Briley lounged on the bed, offering unhelpful but amusing suggestions that helped Sidley control his tight-strung nerves.

Out at the stables, Lockerbie and Cole argued the politics of the Jacobites and King George while they packed food and supplies into a wagon that had been driven over from the home farm earlier in the day.

Prudence closed the sketchbook, sighing, and gazed out at the night. She thus was the first to catch a glimpse of the approaching riders. She tensed, frowned in bewilderment, and stood up, then knelt on the cushions, counting, "Eight . . . ten . . . twelve . . ." Her heart began to hammer. She jumped down and, staying for neither dressing gown nor slippers, raced madly along the hall and sped like a wraith down the stairs.

Reaching the ground floor she ran to the Captain's door and threw it wide.

Sidley had already gone to the stables, fortunately, but Delacourt flung around in his wheelchair, a frown of irritation drawing his brows into a dark bar above his nose. "What the devil . . . ?"

Briley, who had been lounging on the bed, sprang to his feet, his face becoming very red and his eyes very round as he took in Prudence's nightdress and bare feet.

She came quickly into the room, closed the door, and gasped a breathless, "Captain Delacourt, from which direction are your people coming? East?"

"No!" He leaned forward in his chair, narrowed eyes watching her intently. "What have you seen, ma'am?"

"Riders," she gasped. "Fifteen or twenty. Two by two."

He drove a fist into his palm, groaning an exasperated, "Dammitall!"

"Good Lord above," exclaimed Briley. "Now the cat ith in with the chickth and no mithtake. What the devil d'ye mean to do?"

XI

'Cunningham!' thought Delacourt, ragefully. 'Cunningham!' He said to Prudence, "Bless you, brave girl." A corner of his mind stored the picture she presented, with her long, glowing hair all about her, and that delightful nightdress billowing about her shapeliness. "Run and get your spy-glass as quickly as you can and take it to your father. He'll be able to confirm whether they're our people or Cunningham's." Prudence fled, and he turned to Briley. "Thad, Sidley must not see the troopers, if that's what they are."

"And you think they are, eh, my tulip?"

Delacourt grinned his appreciation of that cool drawl. "Yes. He's probably still supervising poor old Kerbie and my groom. Get out there and tell him bounty hunters are coming and will spoil the whole scheme do they rumble us. Send him up to his room— No, wait! He'll be able to see them from up there. Hell! Send him—ah, I have it! There's an old shed behind the stables. Tell him to hide there for a bit. Then warn the fellows in the pyramid, and send Kerbie here, on the double!" Briley sprinted to the door. Delacourt called, "Oh, and tell Cole to saddle up a fast horse."

Briley nodded and was gone.

Delacourt leaned back his head, his thoughts racing. The 'escort' he'd sent for would be arriving at any moment. They were already late. They must be warned, or they'd ride into a trap. God! Had Cunningham rumbled their plan? His hands gripped the arms of the chair as he battled the frustration of being unable to do more than just sit there and scheme.

The door opened. James MacTavish hurried in wearing a bright plaid dressing gown, his thinning hair rumpled and untidy. Delacourt asked, "Troopers?" and the older man nodded. "Are they coming here, d'you think?"

"If they are, at this hour o' the night, we're betrayed, lad."

The door burst open again and Lockerbie ran in looking grim. "What aboot that wagon, sir? 'Twill give us away, surely, if—"

"Never mind that now. Kerbie, we must warn Dermott and MacWilliams or they'll ride into an ambush. I wish to God I didn't have to ask you, but—"

Lockerbie grinned and interrupted, "What am I tae tell 'em, sir?"

"To lie low until we know what's to do. Hurry! Then get back here. Fast. But don't come in if it looks like trouble." Lockerbie opened the door again. Delacourt called, "Have a care, friend. I don't know how I'd go on without you."

Lockerbie stood looking at him for a brief, meaningful instant, then left, passing Briley, who came in and reported, "They're coming on. Not in any hurry that I could tell, Geoff."

"Maybe it's simply a troop out after some poor devil. What about Sidley?"

"All right and tight. I told him the whole thing would depend on him, and he took on the look of old Thaint George." He chuckled. "Thpeaking of dragonth, you might have warned me, you fiend. We made good thpeed through the yard, but when we opened the door of that old shed, poor Thidley gave out a yell, and I had to clap my hand over hith mouth. Damn near frightened me to death, I'll admit, and the chap about fainted! What the devil *ith* that confounded creation?"

MacTavish laughed. "The Monster! Egad, I'd forgot aboot him!"

Prudence came in, wearing a simple, full-skirted beige muslin gown. "The troopers have spread out all along the top o' the slope above the hoose," she said. "They're watching us—nae doot o' it!"

Delacourt's lips gripped together.

Whitening, MacTavish said sharply, "Then they mean to stay here! Why? Ye dinna fancy your precious butler got word ta Cunningham?"

"No, I don't think so, sir." Delacourt thought it more likely that someone had claimed the reward on his own head, but he said only, "Whatever happens, we must make our move before dawn."

Briley said ironically, "With that moon, my tulip, it might ath well be dawn now."

Cole slipped inside and leaned back as he closed the door. Turning to him, Delacourt said, "You're not in this, Cole. Get yourself back to England."

"I'll do that, sir. When you come." The cadaverous features settled into a scowl. Cole added, "I'll not pretend I'm in sympathy with any of this, but for your sake, Master Geoffrey, if there's aught I can do . . ."

"There is. If you'll be good enough to take the spy-glass upstairs and let us know of any movements of the troopers."

Cole took the glass and went off, and those remaining sat down and were silent, each one striving to come at a solution.

Briley was first to speak. "Better delay, dear old boy."

MacTavish nodded, but Delacourt shook his head. "If Cunningham has sent troopers here to spy on us, this may be our last chance to get the men clear."

"It is possible the redcoats are come to protect us," MacTavish reasoned. "Cunningham warned we might be subject to reprisals because of your presence, Delacourt. I could ride out and demand to know what they're doing, and mayhap that would create sufficient of a diversion for the wagon to slip away."

Delacourt considered that for only a second. "Even if it worked, sir, the wagon cannot move rapidly—or silently. It would be shielded by the trees for only a short distance and then would be clearly visible. If possible, we must draw their attention northeast—away from the route our men will take."

"What we need," Briley said thoughtfully, "ith a large Merlin-type diverthion."

Delacourt stared at him. "Yes, by God! And I think we've just the thing, if we can pull it off!" He turned to Prudence, laughter glinting in his dark eyes. "Do not you agree, Miss MacTavish?"

For an instant she did not comprehend, then she gasped, "The Monster! Oh, it would be splendid! But, Papa, it has been lying in the shed for years, do you fancy it is seaworthy?"

MacTavish pursed his lips. "Aye, I do. 'Twas a well-made boat, and yon shed is watertight, I know, for we'd a man hidden there for a while during that last bad storm and he wasnae wet by so much as a drop."

"Wonderful," exclaimed Delacourt. "Now—can we get it launched without being seen?"

"Yes," Prudence answered eagerly. "The shed canna be seen from the hoose or the slope, because o' the stables and the trees. If we use the wheelbarrows and take the Monster doon through the copse, we can launch him in the little cove and be well oot intae the loch before the troopers see."

"No need for wheelbarrowth, ma'am," put in Briley diffidently. "We'll have your father and Cole and me, and"—he glanced at Delacourt—"and *not* you, dear boy, tho do not be arguing."

"No, but it's a solid contraption, Thad. I think we must wait until Lockerbie returns. If our chaps are not coming there will be no need to resort to all this. He can help you carry the Monster to the lake if necessary. But if we do go, I reserve the right to be a rower. That I *can* do."

"For Lord's sake," groaned MacTavish. "And what if they start shooting and sink our Monster? Are ye strong enough to swim to shore? Have ye the slightest idea o' how cold that water is?"

Delacourt's jaw set. He said stubbornly, "I shall manage."

"You must not go, Papa," said Prudence. "If there should be shooting once the Monster is seen, it would look very odd if you did not appear to enquire as to the cause. Cole can help me row."

"*You!*" Flushed with anger, Delacourt snapped, "The devil! I'll not have *you* a target for every musket on the hill!"

Briley looked at him sharply.

Warmed by this proprietary and protective stand, Prudence argued, "No, really, Captain. I can swim like a fish, and I know just where we can hide the Monster once we've drawn the troopers off. Even if Lockerbie and Cole were to row, they'd be able to see nothing. One person has to stand up so as to look through the jaws and direct the rowers. Besides, I am a Scot and have done nothing to help our fugitives. You *must* let me do this! Papa, tell him I can!"

MacTavish looked from glowing girl to glowering man, and said with slow reluctance, "My daughter knows every nook and cranny o' the loch. If aught goes wrong, the others would have a sight better chance with her to guide them."

"Sir," Delacourt snarled, "you cannot have thought that if those troopers catch sight of the monster, as we hope they will, they'll go wild! Every man jack of 'em will be charging after it, shooting like maniacs. I beg you—"

Cole burst in. "They've all dismounted and are sitting about, Captain."

"Together?"

"No, sir. All strung out, like. And all facing this way. But I can see pipes lit, and I'd say they've settled down for the night."

Delacourt turned to his host. "Sir, what time will the moon go down?"

"It's likely to be riding high long after the sun is up, I'm afraid."

Prudence said, "I shall go and get my cloak."

"No!" raged Delacourt.

Lockerbie stuck his head around the door. "Your escort's come, sir," he announced, panting. "I've got 'em safe hid doon by the big pine tree, and I've warned 'em aboot yon butler and y'r plan fer him. They're safe, so long as the redcoats dinna start nosing aboot."

Delacourt swore under his breath.

With a last look at him, Prudence ran from the room.

Lockerbie climbed to his feet, brushed dirt from his breeches, and said, "She seems so sound as any bell, Captain. If there's a hole anywhere I canna find it."

"Very well." Delacourt's worried gaze was on Prudence, standing quietly in the dusty old shed. Her gown was not encumbered by hoops, but he muttered, "If you've to swim for it, Miss Prudence, those skirts could drag you under."

"In that event, sir, I shall abandon modesty—and my skirts. They're quite easily discarded."

"In water? I doubt it. Better you should discard 'em now."

She blushed. "No, sir. I shall if I must. But not until I must."

Delacourt knew he was delaying them, his fear for the girl's safety reducing him to a craven. "As you will," he said harshly. "I fancy we're ready, gentlemen."

Prudence wheeled his chair outside, and he held the door wide as MacTavish, Briley, Lockerbie, and Cole staggered out bearing their difficult burden. The wounded men were already in the wagon and horses between the poles. 'Captain' Sidley, trembling with nervousness, stood close by, holding his horse. He gestured as they approached, and Delacourt asked that Prudence go on ahead with the boat bearers while he spoke with the butler.

"Are you all right?" he asked.

"A trifle nervy, sir," Sidley murmured. "Never worry. I won't let you down."

It was fascinating, thought Delacourt, what a difference a uniform could make. The butler had always had his aloof dignity, but now there was a resolute set to his chin, a glint of determination in his eyes. Delacourt felt a pang of guilt. He consoled himself with the knowledge that he had already handed Mrs. Cairn the letter that would ensure Mrs. Sidley was cared for until her husband's return. "I am very sure you will do your possible," he said gravely. "You know what you are to do?"

"Yes, sir. When we come up with the other men they will have uniforms for themselves and his lordship. We will go off as quickly as possible until we are out of sight of the bounty hunters, then they will change clothes." He glanced from the retreating Monster to the slope along which he had earlier glimpsed the glow of a cigar or a pipe, here and there. "There seem an unconscionable lot of 'em, and they're likely desperate rogues. If the Monster doesn't draw them off, are you sure you and Mr. MacTavish will be able to repel them should they attack?"

"Oh, quite sure. They'll likely be too busy shooting at the decoy to have any shot left for us. Good luck to you, my dear chap. And remember, keep your eyes and ears open; pick up anything you hear said of Doone, and get back here as soon as you can. I'm eager to go home."

"Yes. You are, er, quite sure Cunningham's people will be keeping an eye on things, sir?"

"I am quite sure that you will not be harmed," said Delacourt, hoping that the night was sufficiently dark to hide his red face.

Sidley put out his hand. "Thank you. I am proud to do what I can, sir. It—it has been a great honour."

Squirming, Delacourt shook hands and watched the butler mount up. He had already said his farewells to the wounded men, and now he left the chair and walked to where the Monster was in the process of being pulled into the water.

MacTavish and Lockerbie held the strange vessel steady, and Cole crawled in through the impromptu door that had been fashioned so long ago by inexpert hands. The Monster tilted, its wooden 'arms' splashing at the surface.

Prudence went to kiss her father and receive his blessing. Silently, she turned to Delacourt. He came to her and she gave him her hand. He bent and pressed a kiss upon it. "Well, you've made your choice," he said coolly. "In with you, m'dear. And God bless and keep you safe."

She thought with a sharp pang that they might never see each other again. If this venture failed—even if it succeeded—she might return to find that he had been arrested. She longed with all her heart to throw her arms about him, but the code of polite behaviour forbade so pushing a display and she turned instead towards the boat. Delacourt was not upset by this parting, evidently. But then he was accustomed to danger. Her eyes blurred; vaguely aware of her papa's murmured encouragement, she crouched, squeezed in through the little door, and made her way to the bow where, by clinging to the sides of the Monster's head, she was able to see through the great jaws. The boat rocked to Lockerbie's weight, and then Cole asked, "Ready, miss?"

"Aye," she answered, not daring to look at him and reveal her distressed face. "Row together until I tell ye otherwise. You will likely feel it strange at first, for the oars are the arms, as it were, and my brother said it was hard going."

Lockerbie was silent. She had sensed from the start that he feared the loch, and she knew how overwhelming such a dread could be. He had conquered it, evidently, which she thought admirable. "You do not care overmuch for the water, do you, Mr. Lockerbie?" she remarked.

He grunted in an embarrassed way, and then the Monster

began to move unevenly and with considerable splashing into the open water of the loch. "You're a brave man," she said, and thought, 'Lord, I hope so, for we'll need a brave man when the troopers spot us, I fancy.' For the first time it occurred to her that in case of an emergency it would be difficult to get out of the enclosed boat. Pushing such a horrifying picture from her mind, she directed them. "We must veer to the right a wee bit, so when I give you the word, Cole, you must row alone. Now!"

With slow and grotesque gait, the Monster moved northwards.

"I never said as 'ow it wasn't big," said Sergeant Hobson argumentatively. "All I said was, it's like the rest o' this perishing country. Cold and empty. I don't like it. I like it better than Injer, but I don't like it. And I don't like being out 'ere sitting on the cold grass and keeping guard over I don't know who, nor fer why!"

"If I was you, Sarge," offered Trooper Jenkins, taking the pipe from between his stained teeth and poking it at his large friend, "if I was you, I say, I'd be glad as there's a nice moon tonight. Not that it's all that bright just now. But it's there. And you know what that there big lake is, Sarge? That's Loch Ness. That's what it is."

"Cor!" exclaimed the Sergeant with an extravagant gesture of amazement. "D'you all 'ear that, my coves? Jenkins knows where we is!"

Soft laughter rose from the men who flanked them, but Trooper Jenkins was undisturbed. "You may mock," said he, bodingly. "I says as you may mock. But you'd not be mocking if there wasn't no moon. 'Cause that's when that there *thing* comes out, so the cook told me."

The few murmurous side conversations died sudden deaths and there was a tense hush.

"Wotcha mean—thing?" demanded the Sergeant. "You don't never believe all that jaw about the great serpent wot lives in that there puddle? Cor lumme! You're easy took in, ain'tcha, Jenkins? You reckon as we're all gonna be chewed up by a overgrown serpent?" He gave a soft hoot of laughter in which several diplomatic cronies joined. "You wanta watch these Scotchmen wi' their naked knees. Say anything they will, just ter—" He glanced at his companion and was shocked. Trooper Jenkins had fought beside him in India and also at the Battle of Culloden Moor. Despite his teasing, he knew the man was no coward. But now, Trooper Jenkins' pipe had fallen unheeded from between his suddenly lax jaws, and his eyes stood out like hard-boiled eggs from his greenish face. "Fred?" said the Sergeant sharply. "You sick?"

"Arrr . . ." quoth the intrepid Jenkins. "Oooo . . ." With which, he slid fluidly to the turf and lay still.

"Wot the—" began the Sergeant, dismayed.

A shrill scream shattered the silence. "Quiet, you damn dogsbody!" snarled Hobson, whirling about. He perceived then that he was the only one (save for poor Jenkins) not standing, and he clambered up as his valiant fighting men began to collect in a tight group. "See 'ere—" he howled. But then he himself saw, and his words were cut off as by an invisible knife.

A horrid sight had appeared on the hitherto serene surface of the loch: a great, dragonlike creature, with ungainly legs that tore at the water, and a huge head that rocked back and forth, searching quite obviously for prey.

"Gawd!" shrieked Trooper French, retreating. "It's coming this way!"

"To . . . to . . . arms!" whispered the Sergeant, who had faced a murderous Scots charge without a tremor.

Corporal Corbett groped for his musket and raised it with shaking hands. In that instant, the monstrous head seemed to look straight at him. His knees turned to jelly, but he fired. Unfortunately, the ball took one of the horses across the rump, and the stricken beast reared with a scream and began to kick out in pain and fright. In seconds, the staked horses, who had been grazing quietly, were transformed into a seething, squealing, panicked mass.

"Hold 'em!" shouted Trooper Church, in vain.

Recovering his nerve and his musket, not necessarily in that order, the Sergeant roared, "Come on, lads! Let's get this 'ere fish!"

A couple of troopers, less adventurously inclined than their fellows, began to spring in pursuit (or so they later declared) of the vanishing horses. The rest of the men, gripping their weapons in sweating hands, uttered a feeble huzzah or two, and staggered after their leader.

"Don't shoot till it's close enough," Hobson howled, slithering down the bank a minute later. "By gum, but it's a big 'un, and you can only see the 'ead and shoulders. It's going straight for Inverness!"

"Likely hungry," offered a youthful and considerably frightened recruit.

Inside the 'hungry big 'un,' Delacourt's arms were already trembling with fatigue and he could feel sweat coursing down his face. They'd only been rowing for a few minutes, but one would think the soldiers must have seen. . . . A distant scream rang out and was followed by the sound of a shot. Cole stopped rowing, and Prudence gave a gasp. Delacourt's head jerked up hopefully. "What's happening?"

Prudence, who had been straining her eyes through the Monster's bobbing jaws, gave a cry of shock at the sound of his voice, and swung around.

"Captain Delacourt! Oh, my God!"

"Prayers later, ma'am. What's going on?"

Obedient to that sharp, authoritative voice, she forced her head around. She might have known he'd come. Stubborn, idiotic creature! But contrarily, her fears diminished and her heart began to sing because he was here. "There seems to be a terrible lot of shouting and thrashing aboot," she reported, and with a sudden gurgle, "Faith! I think they shot one o' their own cattle!"

Phlegmatic as ever, Cole asked, "Why would they do that?"

"Sacrifice to the water god," said Delacourt, amusement brightening his eyes. "Row, Cole!"

"But they've seen us, sir. They must've. Shouldn't we turn back?"

"Not on your life! We must keep 'em away from his lordship and our wounded for at least another five minutes. Head straight for 'em, Prue, lass."

She said with a little flutter of apprehension, "As you wish. Then you must row alone now, Captain. Can you?"

"'Course . . . I can!" And he did, for his mind was busied now with a delightful twist to this scheme, and laughter was welling up inside him despite the increasing pangs that stabbed through his chest.

"That's enough!"

He stopped rowing. They heard the shouts and the crashing sounds of men charging through bracken. Prudence ducked instinctively as two more shots rang out, deafening in the stillness of the country night.

Delacourt asked urgently, "How close inshore are we?"

"Aboot a—a hundred yards, I'd think." She could see the troopers coming down the bank, brandishing their weapons, led by a Sergeant who seemed, to her frightened eyes, to be ten feet tall. She began to shake and gripped her lip between her teeth lest she whimper.

"Will we turn back now, sir?" asked Cole uneasily.

"We will not! Prudence, how do we face? Towards them?"

"No. We've drifted off to their left—we're facing more towards Inverness."

"Splendid. Try and keep us thus for a minute or—"

Whoops and shouts interrupted him. "Fire!" shouted a bull-like voice.

"Down!" Delacourt grabbed Prudence unceremoniously by her skirts and pulled her downwards.

The shots sounded like a small battleground. The old boat shuddered as several balls struck home and a section of the side was smashed in over Delacourt's bowed head.

"Geoffrey!" shrilled Prudence, in a momentary lapse from proper behaviour.

"Obliging of 'em," he exclaimed inexplicably, tearing at the splintered 'scales.' "Cole, have you your tinder box?"

"Aye, sir." Cole dragged the device from his pocket and handed it over.

His thin hands working frantically, Delacourt awoke a spark and then a flame. "Hold this till it catches, Prue," he panted, thrusting the wood at her.

Wondering if he had gone mad, she cried, "Mon, ye'll fire the boat!"

The wood was tinder dry and the old paint burned merrily. She shrank away and began to cough from the smoke.

"Take my place, ma'am, if you please." Delacourt clambered into the bow, taking the burning little torch from her and holding it out before him. "Row!" he commanded. "You alone, ma'am. That's grand! Now . . ." He held his torch out through the jaws, blowing the smoke insofar as he was able. "Both together!"

Another shot rang out, the ball coming so close they heard it screech along the side. Peering through the smoke, Delacourt saw the soldiers, dead ahead. And he saw their plunging prowess come to an abrupt halt.

"Keep it up!" he cried exultantly.

"Gawd . . . !" came a strangled shriek. Several of the troopers shrank back, gawking at the fire that blazed from the mouth of the onrushing Monster.

"It's a . . . bloody damn . . . dragon!" wailed a London voice, and one would-be fisherman fled up the bank incontinently.

Delacourt's hand was beginning to scorch. He said hurriedly, "On the count of three, everyone howl as loudly as you can. One . . . two . . . *three!*"

It was, as Sergeant Hobson later relayed to his awed comrades in Inverness, "The most God-awful roar ever a man heard!" And as that roaring screech split the night, Delacourt blew with all his might, so that the flames spewed out. Of necessity then, he tossed the burning brand towards the rapidly approaching bank.

No last straw ever proved more backbreaking. Their superstitious minds already taxed to the limit, the soldiers variously shrieked, sobbed, or swore. And to a man they deserted, vying with one another as to whose legs could sprint the fastest.

Laughing till he cried, Delacourt gasped out, "Another . . . howl, my hearties!"

Triumphant, they gave it their all, the resultant banshee wail lending wings to twenty booted feet.

There was no need now to find a hiding place for the Monster, for it was very apparent that the only thing the soldiers had in mind was escape. By the time they guided their craft into the quiet cove beyond the stables the little crew was weak with mirth. A small crowd awaited them, for the confrontation between military and Monster had been clearly visible from the house and, long before it was done, every member of the staff from the ten-year-old bootblack to the mighty Mrs. Cairn had joined the family, first on the front terrace, and then on the shore.

A muted cheer rang out as the Monster wobbled to the bank, and many eager hands helped pull it onshore.

Prudence emerged, and then Cole, their smoke-grimed faces marked with tears of laughter. Glowing with pride, James MacTavish swept his daughter into his arms. Hortense kissed the back of her head and hugged them both. Kitty ran up, babbling, "Oh, Miss Prue! 'Twas my Bill you helped and I never knew! Oh, Miss Prue!" Delacourt clambered out. Miss Clandon sped to embrace him, then he was hoisted onto the shoulders of two footmen and borne in a small victory parade to the house, while Cole was thumped on the back and exclaimed over until his dour face was one great beam of delight.

They adjourned to the drawing room. The draperies were closed and candelabra lit. No one wasted a thought on the fact that three of the celebrants were black with soot, the remainder variously *en déshabillé;* that the MacTavish wore no wig, and Miss Clandon no cap. Mrs. Cairn and her maids hastened to the kitchens to return with a small feast of wine and cheese, crusty bread, and little cakes. And everyone—even the bootblack—ate, drank, and made merry.

MacTavish exclaimed happily, "I told you they all knew!"

"Aye. To a point only," qualified Mrs. Cairn, beaming fondly at him.

"I didnae," said Kitty, between tears and joy. "Och—*had* I but known!"

"If ye but knew how we laughed," Miss Clandon cried, planting another smacking kiss on Delacourt's sooty cheek. "We saw it all. Every bit!"

"'Tis little wonder the Sassenachs—I mean, the soldiers—ran," said Mrs. Cairn, raising no objection as MacTavish's arm slipped about her waist. "Losh, but yon wee boat looked sae lifelike it fairly froze me blood, I'll no deny it!"

"I thought you meant to *divert* them," said Hortense, clinging to her niece's hand. "Not attack them!"

His cheeks aching from laughter, Delacourt said, "Attack is the best means of defence, so they say. Are Briley and the lads safely off?"

"Likely halfway to the Fort by this time," said MacTavish, in flagrant exaggeration.

Kitty slipped in to seize Delacourt's hand and kiss it, despite his protests, murmuring tearful and inarticulate thanks for his efforts in behalf of her love.

Embarrassed, he disentangled himself. "Do not thank me, m'dear. Thank your mistress. What a grand piece of luck that you and your brother built our lovely Monster, Miss MacTavish."

Prudence twinkled at him, but before she could respond her father stood, glass in hand, and waved for silence. "It would be plain foolishness," he said, "to pretend ye're not all aware of the identity of the gentleman who honours us with his presence. I give you a toast, ladies and gentlemen." Everyone stood and he turned and held his glass high. "To a right gallant Englishman. Mr. Ligun Doone!"

The following roar of his assumed name was unheard by the honouree. Unutterably tired, his chin propped on one hand, Delacourt was fast asleep.

XII

Prudence awoke to a sense of discomfort and unease. She felt stiff and her arms ached. The smell of rain hung on the air, and the room lacked the brightness that spoke of a nice day. Yawning, she remembered, and gave a gasp. They had voyaged in the Monster, and the fugitives had been enabled to get safely away. It was doubtful if they had gone farther than to draw level with Urquhart Castle, for they certainly would have had to travel with caution. She threw back the bedcurtains.

Kitty was at the window, peering into a misty, grey morning. She whirled around guiltily. "Miss Prue! Oh, I'm sorry. I fancied ye were still asleep."

Prudence hurried to join her. Everything looked thoroughly soaked, and large drops fell steadily from the eaves. "How long has it been raining?"

"Mr. Cole said his lumbago woke him at aboot five." Kitty looked worried. "Och, but 'tis thankless weather fer sick men tae be oot in."

Prudence gave her a consoling hug, then hopped back into bed. "They're bonnie lads, Kitty, for all they're a wee bit mauled just now. We must be thankful they're on their way to freedom."

"Aye. That we must!" Kitty brought over the tray, and expressed the hope the chocolate was not too cold.

"It's lovely," said Prudence, sipping gratefully. "Have you heard anything of Captain Delacourt? He was so very exhausted last night."

"Mr. Cole says he slept like a log all through what was left o' the night." Kitty did not miss the worry in the girl's expressive face and went on gently, "Come now, Miss Prue—never let your egg get cold."

Prudence pushed away the little inner voice that had begun to plague her of late, and asked brightly, "What o'clock is it?"

"Nigh on one, miss."

"*One!* My heavens, I'd thought it no later than ten! Surely there must have been some commotion over our doings last night! Has anything—" And, alerted by Kitty's solemn expression, she interrupted herself to demand, "What? Tell me quickly!"

Kitty moved closer to the bed and lowered her voice. "Sir Matthew has come, and Mr. MacKie, fair agog for news o' the Monster, ye ken. And that Dr. Cauldside came wi' the Colonel."

Her heart giving a thump, Prudence echoed, "The Colonel? Oh, dear! What did he say? Is he with Captain Delacourt now?"

Kitty answered the last question first. "No, miss. The doctor is. Your papa told him the Captain seemed to have had a bad turn, and Dr. Cauldside wouldnae let the Colonel go in till he'd seen his patient."

"Good gracious! Take this tray. I must get up at once. Oh, I do wish you'd woken me."

Fifteen minutes later, after a very hurried toilette interspersed with snatches of breakfast, Prudence was almost ready. Her unpowdered hair was tied loosely behind her head with a blue velvet bow that matched her blue taffeta morning dress, and a white fichu was fastened demurely about her shoulders. Kitty was positioning a lacy cap on her curls when Elizabeth Clandon, clad in a stylish brown riding habit, hurried in, looking troubled.

Prudence sent Kitty away, and the two girls reached out to each other. "Our Colonel wasted no time," said Prudence, as Elizabeth sat beside her. "Does he suspect?"

"Who can tell? He's not so very well pleased wi' his brave men, *that* I know!"

They giggled, and Prudence allowed that she could scarce blame him for that. "Has he asked for Lord Thaddeus?"

"Aye. Your papa said what Geoffrey had suggested, that his lordship was so excited aboot the Monster he'd taken his groom and gone to track it doon." She added with a rather feeble smile, "And your aunty said that he'd likely be eaten, and we'd ne'er see the bonnie laddie again."

Prudence watched her steadily. Elizabeth's smile faltered and died.

"You like him very much, don't you?" said Prudence softly.

"Aye." Elizabeth's colour heightened, but her gaze did not waver.

"I see. I—I had thought it was the Captain you favoured."

"Geoff? Och, I love him dearly. But, in a different way." Miss Clandon frowned slightly. "Losh, Prue, ye never thought . . . ?"

Blushing, Prudence looked down. "Well—yes, I did rather. You said you had spread it aboot that—that you were his cousin, for appearance' sake. So—so I thought—perhaps—"

Elizabeth gave a ripple of laughter. "Poor wee lassie! Did ye no stop tae consider the lad was not in the very best of health for such naughty carryings on?"

"Well, er, no. Oh! What I mean is— I didn't mean to imply—"

Elizabeth reached for her hand and squeezed it. She said fondly, "I canna be angry wi' ye, but, Prue dear, we almost lost Geoff in Prestonpans. And since Christmas, he's"—she hesitated—"he's made haste backwards, you might say. He's surely not aboot tae take on a mistress."

Scarlet with embarrassment, scarcely knowing where to look, Prudence stammered, "Oh, no. I meant—well, what I meant was that from—from the way he spoke, I thought perhaps there was a—a prior commitment, or—or—" She bit her lip, gathered her courage, and blurted out, "a betrothal."

Elizabeth stood and walked over to the window. Hoping desperately to hear a denial, Prudence stood also and ordered her gown, waiting.

In a blank voice Elizabeth said, "It is not for me to say, I'm afraid."

"Of course not." Wishing the floor might swallow her, Prudence said, "I am sorry. I should not have pried. But now I shall pry about you. Are you and Briley planning to be wed?"

Elizabeth was very still. Then she turned, her head high. "Would ye be unaccountably shocked if we were?"

"Shocked? Why, no! I should be delighted for your sake. I think him a most pleasant young man, and he is as brave as he can stare." She paused, taken aback as Miss Clandon uttered a sardonic laugh.

"Well, I'm not! Can ye no feature how joyful would be his family tae see him wed a Scots lass wi' a three thousand pounds dowry, and no great name tae bring him?" She gave a prideful toss of her lovely head. "Not great tae the Sassenachs, at all events, though I'm a long way frae being ashamed o't!" Unwanted tears stung her eyes. She said with an impatient flirt of the shoulders, "Och, awie, wherefore maudle over it? 'Tis pointless. I couldnae be happy away frae my mountains and lochs." She blinked at Prudence. "No more could you."

Prudence thought sadly, 'I could be happy wherever *he* is.' And she said with more pathos than she guessed, "Oh, yes. So long as I could come home sometimes to see my family." She saw shock come into the other girl's eyes and said wistfully, "It's lovely to be able to talk with someone of my own age. I wish you were staying longer. I'm—rather short of friends, you see."

Elizabeth promptly burst into tears. Prudence jumped up, put her arms around the weeping girl, and led her to the bed, where she sat beside her, trying to comfort that grief until it had eased, then drying Elizabeth's tears and saying kindly that they would not speak of the matter again.

"But I want . . . to," gulped Elizabeth, blowing her red little nose. She sighed gustily, clutched the sodden handkerchief, and confided, "Thaddeus did offer, Prudence. And—and I refused. D'ye understand why? There's just too much against us. He's a high-born lord, wi' an ancient name and a grand position." She gave a watery and pathetic laugh. "Can ye—can ye no see little Betsy Clandon wearing velvet and ermine . . . and walking majestically beside him intae Westminster Abbey wi' . . . wi' Kings and Queens?" She shuddered violently, and bowed her head into her hands. "I would fairly curl up and *die!* I couldnae *do* it! Never, never, *never!*"

Prudence thought, aghast, 'Lord, but it's a pickle and no mistaking!' But she said staunchly, "I think you would charm all the lords and be the envy of all the ladies. Sure it is that you'd be the prettiest among 'em all." Elizabeth smiled mistily, and Prudence went on, "Now, since you've been so forthright with me, I'll be honest also, and admit that I—I have become rather—fond of Captain Delacourt."

Elizabeth wiped away a stray tear. "You mean you admire him. Faith, but we all do."

"No," said Prudence bravely. "I do not mean that."

Elizabeth stared at her. There was no smile; no joyful exclamation. She said quietly, "Has he offered, or told you that he has a *tendre* for you?"

"Not in so many words, but—"

"I see." Elizabeth stood. "We are friends, are we not? It will be so lovely. But I must run now."

And she was gone with a swish of her skirts, the door whipping shut behind her.

Stamping to a chair in Delacourt's parlour, Cunningham occupied it and said an exasperated, "Well, I fancy you saw the rout of my 'splendid' fighting men last night?"

Delacourt leaned back against the pillow Cole had put in his invalid chair, and had no need to feign weariness. "No, sir," he answered truthfully. "Some of it only. Egad, but I'd not have missed it for the world. Did you see it, sir?"

The Colonel gave him a level look. "Let me understand you, Captain. Do you say *you* actually saw this—this reptile, or whatever it is?"

"I most certainly did. I fancy half the town's at the loch this morning, eh, sir?"

"At least. Would you be so good as to describe the creature for me?"

Delacourt paused thoughtfully. "Let's see. . . . It appeared to be about—oh, I'd say about forty feet long, and—"

"By God! You *saw* that length?"

"Oh, no. But to judge by the size of the head and the upper part of it, which was all that was visible by the time I saw it, I'd think it must be that size. At the very least."

Cunningham eased himself back in his chair and, still transfixing the younger man with his unblinking stare, asked, "What colour was it?"

Into his mind's eye came a picture of those flamboyant blue and red scales, and Delacourt had to struggle to restrain a grin. "I couldn't tell, sir. It was night, you know."

"I am aware. But you saw the smoke and flame it breathed?"

"Smoke and flame? Er, no, I cannot say I did, Colonel. Nor have I heard anyone at Lakepoint speak of such a phenomenon." The corners of his mouth would not behave, and he asked, "Are you sure that your people did not mistake it? In all the, er, excitement, I mean."

Cunningham sprang up and began to pace about, biting out his words with restrained fury. "No, I am not sure, Captain! If I were to say of what I *am* sure, it would be that either my men were properly hoaxed, or that they were roaring drunk! Of all the bumbling, maggot-witted—" He snatched a decanter of wine from the side table, ground his teeth, and fumed in silence.

"I can hardly blame them, sir. A man signs up to fight the King's enemies but he doesn't bargain for a damn great sea serpent to be thrown into the—"

The Colonel, who had been glaring down at the invalid while refilling his glass, suddenly lost his grip on the dewy surface of the crystal decanter and it plummeted from his hand. "Look out!" he exclaimed, making a futile grab for it.

Delacourt's reaction was automatic, but he was tired and his outstretched hand too slow. The decanter fell heavily onto his knee. He uttered a muffled yelp and gripped the affliction as the decanter crashed to the floor.

"Gad, what a clumsy ox!" cried the Colonel remorsefully, but with his bright, hard eyes glued to the invalid's face. "I say, I'm most frightfully sorry! Are you all right?"

"Yes," whispered Delacourt. He coughed and leaned back, turning the chair slightly so that Cunningham was obliged to move to observe him.

The door opened. Prudence hurried in, taking in the situation at a glance. "Heavens!" she cried, wrinkling her nose. "The room smells like a brewery. Have ye had a wee accident, Colonel?"

"A stupid one, miss," he admitted wryly. "Dropped the decanter on poor Delacourt, as if he'd not sufficient grief."

Prudence went to bend over the victim. "Are ye hurt, sir?"

He gave her a surreptitious wink and said feebly that it was nothing at all. But he was breathing hard, she noted, and his hand trembled as he moved it from his knee to the arm of his chair.

Prudence resisted a compelling urge to wrap the decanter

about Colonel Cunningham's gentle smile, and walked over to tug on the bellrope, then open the terrace doors.

Cunningham picked up the decanter. "You don't look driven to the brink of a decline by all the excitement of the night, Miss MacTavish," he observed mildly.

"I'll not say I enjoyed the sight. Especially since the beastie frightened my poor aunt oot o' her wits. But it was not the shock I felt when first I saw it."

"Really? And did you also remark the fire shooting from the mouth of this apparition?"

Had Delacourt mentioned fire? She dared not glance his way with Cunningham's piercing stare upon her. She summoned a puzzled look. "Fire, d'ye say? Lud, sir, 'tis a sea serpent, not a dragon! Who's been trying to scare ye wi' such stuff?"

Her gaze slipped past the Colonel to Delacourt, and his approving grin told her she had said the right thing.

Cunningham bristled. "I do not scare easily, Miss MacTavish! I believe it no more than do you! May I ask how often you have seen the creature?"

"Not very frequently, sir. Oh, Forbes, we have had a small calamity. Would you please send one of the maids to clean it up for us?" She turned an innocent smile on Cunningham as the footman bowed and departed. "Speaking of calamities, sir, whatever were your men doing on the lake in the middle of the night?"

Cunningham said with stiff hauteur, "They were here for your protection, ma'am. We've observed several bounty hunters lurking around Inverness. They're a dashed rough lot, I can tell you, and with Delacourt billeted here and feelings running high against the English because of that da— that traitor Ligun Doone, I feared for your safety."

"Well, I'm sure we are very grateful, sir," she said with her sweetest smile.

Cole came into the room and frowned at Delacourt's pale face. "You're looking properly gut-foundered," he said bluntly. "Dr. Cauldside wants him to keep to his bed, Colonel."

"No, no," Delacourt protested feebly. He coughed, and said in a failing voice, "Perfectly . . . able to—"

"Yes," said Prudence, "we can see how able you are, Captain. Shall we leave him in peace, sir?"

Cunningham chewed his teeth, but the Captain did look pulled, and the girl would serve his purpose as well, perhaps better. He bowed her to the door, told Delacourt he must get a good rest, and accompanied Prudence along the hall. "Well," he said expansively, "you're rid of one of your guests, at all events. I hear Lord Briley has gone charging off in pursuit of your famous fish."

"He'll have his work cut out to hook our Nessie, sir. And if he ventures onto the loch, the tables might be turned."

"A distinct possibility. I'll own myself surprised, for his lordship did not impress me as a clever man. I must have misjudged him."

"Indeed?" said Prudence.

"I cannot quite understand how it is that Briley allegedly raced away in the direction of Inverness, yet no one coming from town towards Lakepoint seems to have encountered him." His sly glance flickered to her face, and he waited.

"Aye, that's odd, all right," she agreed, and, her eyes widening, exclaimed, "Losh, mon! Ye never fancy he has been gobbled up by yon overgrown newt?"

Repeating this conversation to Dr. Cauldside as they drove back to Inverness together, Colonel Cunningham snorted, "Overgrown newt, indeed! I'll stake my oath, doctor, that the apparition on the loch last night was not an overgrown anything—save perhaps the product of an overgrown imagination!"

The doctor pointed to the large numbers of sightseers who swarmed in such excitement about the road that progress was slowed. "Ye'd have a hard time convincing *them,*" he said.

"Fools," snorted the Colonel contemptuously. "A parcel of witless bumpkins. The thing is"—he frowned—"Delacourt is no fool and he said— Tell me honestly, Cauldside, just how ill *is* that boy?"

The doctor hesitated. "Had he not been in superb condition before he was hit, he'd be dead and buried these nine months. That he's survived this long is remarkable. But"—he pursed his lips—"something is not as it should be."

"What?"

"My name has *nine* letters, ye ken," Cauldside retaliated irritably. "Not three! When I progress tae the point I can peep inside a mon, I'll be off tae bigger and better places than Inverness, I can assure ye!"

The Colonel grunted. "I do not question your skill. Certainly, he gives the appearance of weakness. Only sometimes, I think to catch a glimpse of—" Again, he checked, then asked, "Do you know what Ligun Doone means?"

"Trouble," said the doctor with a sly grin.

"No, man. I mean literally."

"Oh. No, I dinna. Is there a meaning? I'd thought it simply a name."

Cunningham scowled at the passing countryside. "There is a meaning. I heard it somewhere, sometime. Blast it all—if I could just remember."

"Ask Jamie MacTavish, he's the scholar amongst us."

"I asked him. He claims he's not a student of archaic languages. I think even if he did know, he'd likely not tell me."

"Do ye really doot the MacTavish? We've proved nothing; Delacourt's seen nothing. And I know he's at odds wi' most o' the clans by reason o' his political beliefs."

"True. But many a non-Jacobite Scot is now helping rebels. MacTavish would not be the only one to be playing his cards close."

Cauldside eyed the Colonel somewhat askance and wondered how he himself was regarded by that cold and impersonal mind. "I fancy every mon has his own axe tae grind."

"Hmmn." Cunningham maintained a brooding silence for some minutes, breaking it at last to exclaim, "That name holds the key, I know it! I've sent a letter to Whitehall. When I receive an answer we'll very likely have another axe in our picture—one already ground to a razor sharpness!"

Hortense looked up from her charts as Miss Clandon entered her parlour, and offered a warm, if vague, smile. "Oh dear! Am I late for luncheon again?" she asked, disentangling her quill pen from the lace at her bodice.

"Not very." Elizabeth stepped closer and peered curiously at the chart. "Good gracious, ma'am, how complex it looks. 'Tis beyond my ken how you can puzzle it all oot. What does it tell you today?"

Hortense adjusted a pale pink trailing wisp, then had to snatch it away as Señorita shot from beneath the desk to leap with frantically flailing arms in pursuit of the alluring scarf. "'Tis very worrisome," sighed Hortense, watching as Elizabeth picked up the irked cat and amused it with the quill pen. "As you will see, Saturn here is in the ascendant, and Saturn I find ominous at the best of times. Now, you will note the squares and oppositions— Oh, *do* be careful! She almost had you! And yet, perhaps that would be as well. Just a *little* bit of blood, you know. For there it is."

She pointed a bony finger at a portion of her involved chart, and Elizabeth peered in anxious bewilderment. "Alas, ma'am, I am too dense. Is the blood here? At Lakepoint?"

"I cannot tell. Only that it threatens us, and that it will be today. And because of it—oh, dear, oh, dear. It is all most alarming. I never saw our future look so bleak!" She wrung her hands, raising anguished eyes to Miss Clandon's dismayed ones.

"Ouch!" cried the girl, dropping Señorita hurriedly.

"Did she get you, then?" Hortense peered at the scratch. "Ah—snagged you right well, the rascal. It bleeds very nicely." She gave a sigh of relief. "Mayhap that is it. Still, the warnings are writ ever larger. I shall have to go up tonight and have a look, to be sure."

"Up?" queried Elizabeth, wrapping her handkerchief about the scratch and entertaining a mental image of Mrs. MacTavish wafting heavenwards in a balloon.

"To the roof. You should not have risked it when her whiskers began to stick straight out in front. That's always a sure sign of impending attack. Speaking of which, how does our dear Captain go on today?"

"Better, I think. He had a good rest yesterday, and Lockerbie says he slept well. When we came back from our drive, Prudence stopped in the gardens to pick some flowers for his room."

"How kind she is, for she does not like him, really. Him being English. Of course, his lordship is, as well. Do you think he will leave for home directly he gets back here?"

Elizabeth bit her lip. She said, "He will rest for a day or two, do you not think? I mean—he won't have to leave right away, surely?"

Hortense consulted her chart, and muttered, "I pray not. Oh, I do pray not."

She was not alone in her prayer.

Lord Thaddeus ran a finger around the collar of his uniform and grumbled, "Damme if I hadn't forgot how beathtly hot a military coat can become! How far now, Dermott?"

Alec Dermott, tall and rangy in the saddle, and hating the red coat he wore, answered in broad Scots, "We've aboot ten more miles to the rendezvous point, sirrr. Will I bring ye a bit water?"

'Ten more miles!' thought Briley. "No, I thank you. But you might thee if our Captain"—he winked at Dermott—"needth a drink."

The big Scot grinned and spurred ahead. Briley reined in his mount, drew a handkerchief across his face, and waited for the wagon to draw level. "How are you, ladth?" he asked, peering in at the three who lay there.

They were haggard, unshaven, and obviously in pain, but the responses were cheery and there was little doubt their spirits were high.

"Nearly there," said Briley, as cheerfully. "In an hour or two you'll be with your own people, and—"

"Riders coming, sir," said chubby Dennis MacWilliams from the driver's seat of the wagon.

Briley jerked around. About a dozen men were galloping down the slope ahead. Men with muskets in their hands and a grim look of determination about them. "Damned ragged," he muttered, with his beloved Fifty-Second coming to mind. He spurred to join Sidley, who was looking back at him with white-faced anxiety.

"Is this them?" gasped Sidley, terrified by the thundering charge.

"One can but hope," answered Briley, coolly. "Front, man. Front! You're the offither, do not forget."

Sidley's horse plunged, and the butler clung to the pommel. "God!" he gulped.

With a thunder of hooves and a few terse shouts, the riders were upon them. Briley saw a musket swing level. "Hey!" he shouted, and his hand flashed to the pistol at his belt.

Dermott yelled, "Ligun Doone! We're frae—"

"Death tae the redcoats!" howled a rider, brandishing a sabre.

"Devil take it," groaned Briley. "Wrong lot!"

"We want 'em alive!" roared a giant of a man, launching himself at Dermott.

All was confusion then. Men shouted, horses milled and snorted, cudgels whirled, but no one fired until a musket roared shatteringly. Thrown, Sidley started to scramble up, but was flattened as two men descended on him. At the centre of a wild melee, Briley sent one attacker reeling back, and wrenched up his pistol. The Scot with the sabre swung it, and Briley's pistol was smashed from his hand. His hat and wig already lost, he ducked a whizzing fist, but a cudgel caught him solidly. He crumpled without a sound and sprawled face down and unmoving beside the unconscious butler.

A shout rang out in the Gaelic and the maelstrom quieted abruptly.

"Blast and damn ye fer a bunch o' bluidy dimwits," raved Dermott, extricating himself from the fray with his uniform torn and a red swelling along his jaw. "Did ye no hear me yell that we were frae Ligun Doone hissel'? Are ye all deef as well as daft?"

"He's telling ye the truth o' it," confirmed Little Willie, hanging over the side of the wagon. "They're helping us get clear."

Groans of mortification went up, the casualties blisteringly expressing their views of such an ill-handled ambush.

More riders were appoaching, and Little Willie muttered, "It's Angus, praise God!"

Galloping up on a sturdy little grey horse, the leader, a husky, black-haired, black-browed man, snapped, "Yon musket shot has likely raised a patrol at the verra least! I dinna ken what ye're messin' aboot at, but there's nae time fer a friendly cuppa tea. Are ye well, Alec?"

"As could be expected, Angus," answered Dermott, wiping blood from his lips. "That one"—he indicated Briley's still form—"must be taken back tae Inverness. Quick."

Angus dismounted, dropped to one knee, and turned his lordship. Briley was deathly pale save for the crimson that streamed from a deep gash in his scalp. "Who wants him?"

"Doone. And it's verra important. *Verra!*"

"My regrets tae Mr. Doone," said Angus, standing. "But wi' a broken head like that, his mon willnae be riding anywhere fer some time."

"Angus!" cried one of the casualties sharply, staring up at the slope.

Angus jerked his head around. A horseman near the summit was waving a forbidden plaid wth unmistakeable urgency. "Hell!" grunted Angus. "They're after us already! Intae the wagon wi' anyone not able tae ride!"

The man with the sabre said urgently, "We caused this, mon. We'll be away and try tae lead the redcoats off."

Angus scowled, but nodded. "We'd be obliged."

The disastrous group of riders mounted up and in seconds were galloping back the way they had come. With a wave of his arm, Angus led the remaining men and the wagon due north.

Within minutes the little glen was as quiet and peaceful as before, only a crumpled wig remaining to indicate that a British peer would be unable to return to Inverness as promised.

XIII

"I think you are very reckless," said Prudence severely, watching Delacourt quiet his mettlesome horse.

He turned a laughing face to her. "Oh, no. I must be up and about a bit, you know, or Cunningham will suspect I do not try to get better."

She was inwardly elated both by his horsemanship and by the fact that he felt well enough to attempt a ride, but, she said, "You could have chosen a calmer mount, sir."

"What? That awful old slug Cole had saddled for me? A pretty figure I would have cut whilst you galloped circles around me."

"I do not mean to gallop at all. If you wish to stay beside me, you shall have to go along very sedately."

"Yes, ma'am," he said meekly, but with a telltale quirk tugging at the corners of his mouth.

They left the stableyard and started off, by tacit agreement turning to the southwest. The afternoon was cool and windy, with clouds gathering over the mountains. Prudence thought, 'I must not let him stay out too long; it may rain.' And she wondered if this afternoon ride had been inspired by a simple desire to be with her, or whether he was worrying. Lord Thaddeus should have returned yesterday. When there had been no sign of him by this morning, Delacourt had sent Lockerbie off in search of news, and the man had not yet come back. She glanced at the Captain covertly. His hand was firm on the reins, holding in the big grey he'd chosen over Cole's shocked—but, she suspected, prideful—objections. His riding coat was dull gold and fitted him so well that she thought it must be a recent acquisition. There was a little more colour in his cheeks today, and he rode easily, his free hand resting on his thigh, his intense gaze upon General Wade's Road, his entire demeanour one of energy restrained.

He turned so abruptly that she had no chance to look away. "Glorious, isn't it?"

"I'm glad you think so." Her gaze drifted across the wide panorama of loch, the jutting might of distant Urquhart Castle, the craggy hills, and the cloud-adorned sky. "I love it dearly, but I once heard an Englishman refer to it as 'an empty, stark, and savage land.'"

"Poor fellow. I hope you gave him a good funeral."

She laughed. "No, just a goodbye. It is sad, though, that some cannot appreciate beauty if it is different from that which they know."

"And it is, after all, to be found in . . . many forms. . . ." His eyes locked with hers and were captive. The horses drifted closer so that they sat with her skirts brushing his knee. Clouds, loch, and hills faded and were forgotten, while eyes of brown held fast to eyes of blue in an embrace no less intense because it was without the touch of hands.

The grey horse snorted and danced his impatience, and the mood was broken.

Delacourt drew a steadying breath. "He wants to run, poor fellow. He likely thinks this stranger a real marplot. Come—let us indulge him."

"Certainly not," replied Prudence, gathering her reeling

senses. "A fine scold I would get from my papa if you should be set back again."

"If you are afraid I may go off into one of my stupid fainting fits—"

"I have very good reason to fear that, sir," she said, a twinkle lurking. "I was alone with you once before when you were stricken."

"Ah, yes." His glance lowered. "What a sweet awakening."

She felt her cheeks burn. "It is naughty to speak so of your wickedness."

"I shall never do so to anyone but you," he murmured. She glanced at him, startled, and he added at once, "Speak of it, I mean. Indeed it would be most ungallant, for I fancy you've many local admirers—no?"

She thought of Richard Ahearn with his mischievous green eyes and carefree ways; of dark young Billy MacKie, who'd been among the first of the local youths to pledge their allegiance to Prince Charles; of Malcolm Hendricks, at this very moment held prisoner somewhere in England, and she said sadly, "There were more—such a wee while ago."

He sobered at once. "I'm sorry." They rode on in silence for a moment, then he said angrily, "What a damnable thing that political caperings can bring about wars, separate families, and come between people who might, otherwise, be the very best of friends." His frowning gaze came around to her wistful little face. Before he could stop himself, he said, "Well, we'll not let such nonsense come between us, will we? I, er, I mean, *we* can be friends?"

She looked at him and thought, 'No, that is not what you meant at all, foolish boy.' But she said, "Of course."

"Good. Then catch me if you can!"

He was away like the wind, bowing over the pommel, guiding the big grey with an unerring hand up hill and down, with Prudence dashing in pursuit until he reined up atop a sharp hill and swung his mount, laughing breathlessly as he watched her come up.

She was windblown and her cheeks flushed, and she could not restrain an exhilarated laugh as she drew rein beside him. "That was foolish beyond permission! Are you all right?"

"Oh, yes, thank you. But"—he turned to the southwest—"thwarted, alas."

She followed his gaze. Smoke spiralled up from a distant, unseen blaze to be soon whipped away by the wind, but there was no sign of any living creature for as far as the eye could see.

Delacourt said rather grittily, "Something has gone amiss. Would that I knew what it was."

"But you have Lockerbie out. When shall he return, do you think?"

"Tonight, I hope. But if he's not come back by tomorrow morning—"

He checked, and Prudence turned in sudden alarm to the pound of onrushing hooves.

Mounted on a fine little bay mare, Cole galloped to them, his face one large scowl. "You never learn, Master Geoff!" He flung an arm in the direction of Inverness. "Is nine months of misery not enough? D'ye see that?"

"Clouds." Delacourt nodded, repentantly. "But—"

"Clouds! And rain, belike. And if you get soaked on top of the rest, we'll be burying you!"

Delacourt sagged pathetically in the saddle. "You would not rail at a poor invalid whose condition is only tol-lol, at best?"

Cole grinned reluctantly, and Prudence had to struggle to maintain a stern demeanour. "Any poor invalid who rides *ventre á terre* through the Scottish hills," she scolded, "deserves exactly what he gets."

"And this poor invalid got to ride with you, ma'am," he riposted, smiling at her in the way that made her heart jolt. "Very well, Cole. Take me to my cell. It's bread and water for me"—he glanced at Prudence, his eyes glinting—"withoot a doot!"

"Without a doot, indeed," said Prudence exasperatedly, walking with Elizabeth into the drawing room after dinner that night. "By the time we got back, he was exhausted but would not admit it, of course. I can well sympathize with you. *What* a time he must have caused you! He's as fearless as he can stare, but with not the sense of a newborn!"

Elizabeth smiled. "He frets against his weakness, which does not help his recovery, I fancy. In truth, I canna blame him. It's been a waeful long convalescence, but he's no a whiner for all he acts the part sae well."

They made themselves comfortable in the pleasant room, and Mrs. Cairn came in with her maids and the tea tray. As Prudence poured, Elizabeth asked what had become of Hortense.

"I expect she's up to the roof. You take sugar, I think?"

"Aye. Two, if ye please. Your aunt is looking at her stars, I fancy? She's been fretting over them, I know. Is she . . . very often right wi' her predictions? She told me there was—was blood near us."

Prudence's hand shook a little as she handed Elizabeth the teacup. "She is sometimes fairly near the mark, but she tends to get the details muddled. Let us hope she has done so this time." Elizabeth made no response, her eyes fixed rather blankly upon her cup, and Prudence waited, then asked gently, "Are you quite sure you will not have him?"

Elizabeth sighed. "No. I'll not have him. But—oh, I wish I wasnae sae fashed fer the laddie."

They both started as the door burst open. Her wisps flying and her mantilla at half-mast, Hortense darted into the room, scanned the occupants, gasped out something about ". . . shooting!" and was out again at unprecedented speed with

Señorita leaping after her, making mad swipes at various trailing scarves.

The two girls exchanged a shocked glance and followed.

Hortense had already flung open the dining room door. "Come quick!" she exhorted, her voice loud and clear. "It's shooting!"

The gentlemen all stood at once. Delacourt dropped one hand to the great pocket of his coat wherein reposed a small but efficient pistol. "Who is, ma'am?" he asked sharply.

"Star!" she gasped, one hand to her heaving bosom.

"By Jupiter!" Sir Matthew hurried to take her arm and beam down at her. "A shooting star, is it? Lead the way, ma'am."

"It will be gone by now," said James MacTavish. "They're only visible for a second or two, at most."

"No, no," argued Hortense, retrieving a scarf, only to find Señorita attached to the other end. "I've been watching it for at least three minutes. Oh, do please get her off, someone! It winks and winks. Most—"

"Does it, by God," muttered Delacourt under his breath, and was at the terrace doors in three swift strides and flinging them open.

Prudence ran to join him. His keen eyes flashed to the northeast, but the trees were in the way, and with a frustrated exclamation, he sprinted back into the parlour and across to the hall, the rest trailing after him and Hortense wailing pleas that he have a care. He was up the stairs, two at a time. Prudence abandoned decorum and ran also, managing to stay close behind him. "My sewing room," she cried breathlessly. He plunged into the small chamber and threw open the casement, Prudence coming up with him to peer where he peered as the others crowded in.

Señorita shot past, sprang onto the window sill, and walked daintily along it, her upheld tail drifting under Delacourt's nose. He lowered the obstruction, then cried, "There!"

They all saw the tiny, winking light.

"That's no star," said Mr. MacKie.

MacTavish asked, "Can you make it out, Geoff?"

"A moment, sir. Two. That means riders. Five. . . . They're coming from Inverness." He frowned as the light ceased. "Dammit! Cole must have been asleep not to warn me! Ah, here we go. . . ." They all counted softly. "*Six!*" Delacourt spun around. "Sir, I must leave! We all must leave!"

Hortense gave a frightened squeak.

MacTavish demanded, "What does six mean?"

"Death! And that means they've rumbled me, belike. Which would also mean you stand at risk, unless you can convince 'em you didn't know about me, which I think unlikely!" He gripped Prudence by the arms. "Stay for nothing save your cloak, ma'am. Hurry! Mrs. Hortense—Elizabeth—run! There's not a second to lose!"

Pale with fright, the ladies fled.

MacTavish asked tautly, "What should we do?"

"If Sir Matthew and Mr. MacKie will help, get your ladies to the Monster, sir. Your best hope will be to take them to the other side of the loch. If you head in the direction of the light we saw, you'll find men waiting for you."

They all started into the hall.

Sir Matthew asked worriedly, "And what o' yourself, lad?"

MacTavish gave a gasp of horror. "The cypher! My God! What aboot the cypher?"

"I have it. I shall ride west and try to come up with Lockerbie or Thad." He ran into his room and snatched for a cloak, his pistols, and a sword-belt, which he proceeded to buckle about his middle. MacTavish joined him as he was sprinting for the door again, and he said tersely, "If I'm taken, I'll destroy the cypher, somehow. You'll have to get word to Lady Ericson."

Running to keep pace with him, MacTavish groaned, "You'll no have a chance! If Jacobites see you they'll likely take you for a Sassenach and your life won't be worth—"

"If they're Highlanders, sir, I'm as safe as in St. Paul's. If they know me. And many do. Go on, man! I don't know what happened to Cole, but we've no way of guessing how long that light was warning before—"

There came a sudden commotion from below. A shot fractured the stillness of the night, and shouts and much trampling about followed.

"Out with the lights!" cried Delacourt, racing to the hall. "Prudence? Where in the deuce are you?" She was already at his side, and slipped her hand into his. "Good. Now stay close to your father," he ordered.

The front doors burst open as they crossed the hall and a mass of struggling figures surged inside. Prudence had a brief impression of shouts and cursing; of her father, running, with Carrie Cairn close at his side; and of Sir Matthew Garry flailing a pistol butt at a burly man in a frieze coat. Then the last candle was extinguished and the uproar was all about her.

A dark figure loomed up. A man roared, "Surrender, or—" She was swept aside and heard the thud of a heavy blow. The dark shape vanished, but more came. Another shot sounded deafeningly. Someone howled. All around her were struggling forms. Also around her was a firm, guiding arm. Shrinking against it, she gave a startled cry as a man caromed into them, sending her sprawling. Hard blows; cursing; a hand groping for her, dragging her up; Delacourt's voice, panting, "Run, dammit! Your papa's out. Run!"

She ran.

She was in a blustery darkness, bedlam behind her, confusion before. A deep voice shouted, "Don't let him get clear! Shoot at anything that moves!" She thought, 'Heaven help us all!' and dropped to her knees. Crawling, she heard a yell, and a dark shape zoomed past and went down with a thump. Running feet. Delacourt, hissing, "Prue? Where the deuce are you?"

"Here!" She stood, reaching out. "How did you know?"

"I could smell your perfume. This way!"

He took her hand and they sprinted for the trees.

"Hey!" came a bellow from the rear. "Halt, in the name of the King, or I fire!"

"Christ!" muttered Delacourt, and whipped Prudence ahead of him.

She heard the blast of the shot, followed by an odd little buzzing sound. Then they were in the trees. Dimly, she saw the gleam of water, bowed figures, and a great bulk that would be the Monster.

"Jolly good," panted Delacourt. "Go on, m'dear. God speed!" And he wheeled and disappeared into the night.

Prudence hesitated. There came a shattering of glass from the house, and a window burst outwards. She ran for the shore and heard MacKie urge, puffing hard, "In wi' ye . . . Mrs. Hortense. Miss Clandon—quick now!"

Echoing from inside the Monster, Sir Matthew called, "Come on! Come *on!* I'll row wi' ye, Duncan. Mac—you be guide. Did Prudence go with Delacourt? Aye, so I thought. Sit ye doon, Hortense, ye're rockin' our wee boat. Losh, but there's nae much more room. *Come on,* Duncan!"

Prudence ran up. "Mr. MacKie!" she gasped, but in that moment Duncan MacKie gave a mighty shove. The Monster, caught in an eddy, swung out onto the loch, MacKie barely managing to drag himself in through the sagging tail.

Prudence cried, "Mr. Mac—" but then heavy footsteps were running towards her. She made a dash for a clump of shrubs and tripped over a shovel one of the gardeners had left stuck in the ground. The footsteps thumped past. A man shouted, "Stop! Come back, or I'll shoot!"

She thought, 'Wretched villain! Ye'll no shoot my papa or my aunt!' Snatching up the shovel, she swung it high, and ran forward. The man was very big and in a remote way she noted that he wore a most unusual coat of variegated coloured leathers. With both hands he aimed a blunderbuss that must surely blow a great hole in the heavily laden Monster. Enraged by such infamy, Prudence brought her shovel whizzing down. The shock of the blow made her wrists tingle, and the man went down without a sound. Horrified, she dropped the shovel and stared down at him. His legs flopped feebly. With a gasp of relief she looked up again. The Monster was well out on the loch, the arms flailing at a great rate. There was no possible way for her to catch them, and Delacourt was undoubtedly gone also. She turned and ran frantically for the stables.

Even as she approached, a horse galloped straight for her. She could not see the rider but, taking a chance, screamed, "*Geoffrey!*"

Her cry was crowned by a fierce uproar from the house, but the horse saw her waving arms and shied. The man crouched low on his back steadied the animal, and Prudence called again. In a flash Delacourt had dismounted. "Prue?" he cried.

"Yes. The others are away!"

"Here!" His arms were around her. She was swept into the saddle and, taking the reins he handed her, she cried, "What about you?"

For answer he said tersely, "Head southwest down General Wade's Road."

"But—"

He slapped the horse on the rump, and the frightened animal took the bit between its teeth and bolted.

It was some moments before Prudence could do anything more than hang on and strive not to be tossed from the saddle. The wind had blown clouds over the waning moon, and the night was very dark so that she could not at first see which horse she rode. That it was a much taller animal than she was accustomed to, she knew, and gradually it was borne in upon her that she must be up on Robbie's great half-broken Braw Blue. Her frantic attempts to check his headlong flight were ignored as though she had been the merest gnat clinging to his back. Her every fear was not for herself but for Delacourt, and she pulled on the reins, shouted, and even uttered a few of her brother's wicked oaths, to no avail. Braw Blue continued to thunder along the dimly seen road. It seemed hours later, and Prudence had given up all hope of slowing the brute, when he decided to slacken his pace. She felt bruised and battered from the effort of sitting with her knee hooked over the pommel of the man's saddle; her hair had been blown about, and she was breathless from the buffets of the wind, but she gave a tentative tug at the reins and Braw Blue pranced to a halt and stood tossing his great head about as though proud of his behaviour.

Remembering some of his less appealing habits, Prudence slipped from the saddle, staggered, and gripped the reins warily. Braw Blue put up his ears and regarded her with placid meekness. He hardly seemed to be blowing. She told him a few home truths, and turned her attention to the road.

She could not see very far, but all was still with no sign of pursuit. She led the horse to some shrubs, tethered him, and walked back, her cloak blowing. Surely Delacourt had escaped? Surely his chivalry in helping her had not brought about his own capture? She closed her eyes and offered up a small prayer for his safety.

The road was still deserted when she looked at it again. The wind was growing colder. She wrapped her cloak tighter about her, sat down on the turf, and waited. Was it only an hour ago that she had been sitting in their graceful withdrawing room? How quickly her relatively ordered world had been plunged into chaos. One thing, with any luck her family and friends would cross the loch safely and be protected by Delacourt's men. She thought then of the cypher. If he had been taken and they found it on him, he would be doomed; as would many others if the cypher was broken by the soldiers. But she knew somehow that he would have found a way to destroy it. She thought with a pang, 'Even if they destroyed him!' and bowed her head, hopelessness rising up to overwhelm her.

Braw Blue stamped a hoof as he grazed; a stamp distantly echoed by other hooves. With a leap of the heart, Prudence stood. The hoofbeats grew louder; she could detect a moving shadow against the night, and then a horse and rider raced up the slope to halt beside her.

"Geoffrey?" she cried.

"Thank God!" he gasped, and came down from the saddle in a rush to lie in the road at her feet.

She gave a little cry of terror, but had the presence of mind to grab the trailing reins before she attended to the fallen man. His mount was Flaxen, one of her father's fastest horses, and she led the cream-coloured animal to tether it beside Braw Blue. She searched the saddlebags but found only an oilskin cloak. Turning her attention to the big stallion she gingerly investigated his saddlebags and was overjoyed to discover a flask and a brace of pistols. Taking the former she ran back to kneel beside Delacourt.

He lay on one side, as he had fallen. For a terrible moment, she thought he was dead, but leaning down she could feel him breathing. She pushed him on to his back, threw open his cloak, and peered with desperate anxiety for the telltale stain of blood. She could see none, and shifting her position, she managed to pull his head and shoulders onto her lap. She uncorked the flask, took a little sip of the potent brandy herself, then tried to coax some between his lips. She was unsuccessful; the brandy trickled from the edges of his mouth and he showed no sign of regaining consciousness. Praying that this was just another of his swoons, she corked the flask again and set it aside. What would she do if someone should come? Delacourt was thin and worn from his long illness, but he was a tall man and too heavy by far for her to drag over to the shelter of the bushes. She was wondering if she could tie something around him and secure it to Flaxen's saddle so as to pull him to safety when she felt his head stir.

"Prue . . . ?"

"Yes. I'm here. Are you shot?"

He sighed. "No. Are you?"

"Bruised, merely. I could not get the wretched beast to stop." She peered at him. He seemed so listless. "Are you sure you're all right?"

"Oh, yes. Thank you." He tried to get up, but sank back and said wearily, "I'm sorry, but I seem to be . . . so very tired."

She said indignantly, "Well, ye canna sleep here, mon!"

He chuckled but responded in a drowsy murmur, "I cannot think of a . . . better place."

She thought that he must be utterly exhausted and, stroking back the curls that the wind blew about his face, asked, "Have you the cypher?"

"If it is still . . . in my pocket."

She felt in his waistcoat pocket and took out a small piece of parchment. The moon had slid from behind the cloudbank some moments ago; its light was not bright, but her eyes were accustomed to the dark now and, by tilting the parchment, she was able to read the message it contained:

II

Up and down the hill and vale
Daringly the eagle flies.
I would give my soul to be
Soaring past the wind, as he.
Sorry me.
You be free.

"It's no verra grand poetry," she decided. "What does it mean?"

"New life for a great many people. Or death . . . if it falls into the wrong . . ." The words faded into silence.

Prudence folded the parchment carefully and tucked it back into his pocket, then pulled the cloak about him. There was no sound of pursuit. She thought, 'He can rest for just a minute or two.' And she sat there on the deserted road, the Englishman asleep in her arms, and the two horses munching contentedly nearby.

Her head nodded and woke her. Her legs felt numb. Delacourt was still sleeping, and she had no idea how long they had been here. She shook him gently and saw his eyes blink open. "I think we'd best go on now," she said.

"Oh, Lord!" He sat up, staring at her, and said in a brisk, sure voice, "What a silly gudgeon I am. You should have made me get up, ma'am!" He clambered to his feet, then reached down to her.

She struggled up, but stumbled. He held her arm, steadying her. "I am a fine protector! Can you manage?"

"Oh, yes," she said staunchly. "I am quite—tol-lol, you see."

She had the satisfaction of hearing him laugh, then he was guiding her to the horses. He made her walk up and down for a minute or two before she attempted to mount, and the feeling came back into her legs with an unpleasant tingling that made her flinch. She asked, "What happened when you went back to the stables?"

"A pitched battle. No—not the big fellow, Miss Prue. I've brought Flaxen for you."

She narrowed her eyes. "Oh, and you had my saddle put on her. What a nuisance that must have been for you."

He cupped his hands and she put her little slippered foot into his grasp and was thrown into the saddle. "No more of a nuisance than for you to ride in my saddle all this way on that blasted great brute." He stood smiling up at her, the moon lighting his face softly. "And you in your evening gown and dainty slippers. Thank God you do not wear one of your great hoop skirts tonight."

"Amen to that," said Prudence.

He chuckled and swung into his own saddle. Braw Blue staged a sudden and violent display of pyrotechnics. Startled, Flaxen shied and danced away. Prudence managed to retain her seat, but watched in alarm as the big grey bucked and spun and snorted fury. She heard Delacourt give an exasperated shout, and suddenly Braw Blue ceased his tantrums and stood quietly.

Irritated, Delacourt panted, "If it isn't just like Rob to choose such a nonsensical animal! Very well, Miss Prue, we can go along now, I do believe."

Go along they did and, as they rode, he told her what had transpired in the stables. It appeared that he'd had the foresight to instruct the servants on what to do in the event of just such an invasion as they'd suffered tonight. The moment the attack had begun all the females had been rushed out of the main house and had taken refuge in the buildings where dwelt the outside servants. The grooms, gardeners, lackeys, footmen, and even their formidable chef had banded together to repulse the invaders, prepared to explain later that they'd supposed they were being attacked by thieves. To a man they'd sworn to do all in their power to delay the aggressors for as long as possible. Delacourt had found a fierce battle still under way in the house, and the grooms defending the stables from a threatened seizure of the horses. By pure luck he'd come without interference to Flaxen's stall, a groom had assisted him to saddle the horse, and only as he was prepared to mount had he been accosted. Between them, he and the groom had overpowered the attacker. Delacourt had ridden down another determined assailant, and had walked the cream-coloured Thoroughbred quietly around the *mêlée* and into the night.

Reaching this point in his account, he was silent for a moment, then said, "I'm afraid we must ride on for as long as we can. Are you very tired?"

"Oh, no," she lied bravely. "It's yourself I am worrying over. Did ye take no hurt in all that brawling?"

"Very little, I assure you. I am only sorry I had to frighten you just now. I wish I could tell you I'll not commit such a folly again, but I might."

"It is not folly. You're doing splendidly. I only hope I may not hold you back."

A laugh in his voice, he responded that he hoped she didn't hold him back either, although he promised her there would not be the need.

"I am sure," said Prudence thoughtfully, "that my papa is aware of that, Captain Delacourt."

The Captain said nothing.

XIV

The clouds soon began to drift into a more solid mass. Within an hour they had obliterated the moon, and the night became so dark that Delacourt was obliged to slow their pace. In another hour it began to rain, the wind, cold now, blowing icy drops into their faces. Delacourt stopped long enough to wrap his oilskin cape around Prudence. Chilled through, she kept an anxious eye on him. At first he had ridden with the easy grace of the born horseman, but as time went along he began to droop wearily in the saddle.

When a particularly strong gust sent her hood flying, she called, "Captain, might we stop for a little while?"

He pulled back his shoulders and turned to her. "Of course." He led the way from the road and dismounted, coming quickly to help her from the saddle.

"Dare we stop?" she asked, making no attempt to restrain her teeth from chattering.

"We *shall* stop. Poor girl, you must be frozen."

He found a scraggly clump of trees, and they took shelter under the branches. It was cold and damp and smelled of rotting vegetation, but the wind did not blow with such penetrating force here, nor the rain drip so heavily. Prudence sank onto the gnarled root Delacourt found for her, and watched him obliquely. He had appeared close to collapse on the road, but now that she was showing every sign of exhaustion, he was bustling about cheerily, maintaining a steady flow of chatter about how well she had done, and how fine were the horses, and that they would come up with some of his people from Cavern Craigalder so soon as it was light.

When he had unsaddled and hobbled the horses, he stood looking down at her and muttered, "Lord, but I wish I'd something to offer you."

"You have," she told him. "I put it back in Braw Blue's saddlebags. Not that I'm by way of being a drinking woman, you understand, sir."

He brightened and knelt to rummage in the saddlebags. The flask was unearthed, unstoppered, and offered with a flourish. Prudence sipped, coughed, and pulled a face. "Ugh, but it's horrid. How can you men stand the stuff?"

"With a good deal of difficulty," he said, his grin as unseen as her grimace. "But you'll find it warms you." He sat beside her, took a healthy mouthful of the brandy, and gasped. "Hey! I see what you mean. I wonder where Lockerbie found this."

"He likely rescued it from my father's cellars. The MacTavish prides himself upon his knowledge of fine wines." She was indeed beginning to feel less chilled and when he offered her another sip she did not protest, but took a good swallow, finding it not nearly so objectionable this time.

Following her example, he pointed out that she was still shivering.

"I know." She pulled the cloak tighter around her, but it was wet and clammy.

"That won't warm you." He edged closer, and slipped his arm about her.

She sank her head against his chest. Soon the warmth that swept over her was more than satisfying.

Delacourt murmured, "I wonder what the deuce happened to ol' Cole. He was supposed to be keeping watch for any signals."

"He didn't warn you," she said, adding, "Do you think my family were able to get away?"

"I should think so. From what you told me the fellow you crowned was not likely to be able to give the alarm before your Monster was halfway across the loch. Did you see if those ruffians wore uniforms, Prue?"

She frowned. "The man I hit did not, I know. He wore the—the very oddest sort of tunic." She felt sleepy and settled her head more comfortably against him. He urged her to have another sip of the brandy, then did the same.

Watching him drowsily, she asked, "What did my mean father aboot—I—er, that is, what did my father mean about Ligun Doone?"

Delacourt, bathed in a pleasant glow, said amiably, "What about him?"

"You 'member. It was the day th' Colonel frightened me so much when I met him oot riding. And Papa said ye shouldnae hae used the name Ligun Doone, and Liz'beth said—" She hiccuped, and apologized. "Liz'beth said—"

"Yes, m'dear," he said huskily, his lips against her ear. "Wha' did Eliz'th say?"

Prudence shivered but not from the cold. "She—she said—Geoffrey!"

"Did she now? Well, proves sh' knows m'name," he chortled.

"No. I mean— Oh, never mind. Now sit up straight, do."

"Cannot," he argued, leaning against her even more closely.

"Yes, you can." She put both hands against his chest and held him back, and he let his head sag and giggled foolishly into her hand. "You've had too much of that horrid brandy," she accused.

"No such thing!" He drew back and said in a firmer voice, "Eliz'beth was talking to Ligun Doone."

"Elizabeth said that you used the name Ligun Doone to thumb your nose at Cumberland. Is it truth? What does it mean?"

He chuckled. "It's truth the gentle Duke would be very cross. Means the Long Down."

"Long Down?" she echoed, mystified. "Why should that upset the Butcher?"

"Because." He swooped suddenly to kiss the end of her nose.

"Sorry, ma'am. Fell li'l bit. Where was I? Oh, yes. It means, at least, they *say* it was one of the early names . . ." He began to laugh softly, then hilariously. "For—"

"For what? Oh, Captain, *please* do not tease!"

"That rhymes!" He kissed her ear, a little off-centredly, but improving his aim with the second attempt.

Prudence said a breathless, "Geoffrey Delacourt!"

"Wrong! Delavale! Geoffrey Dela-*vale!*"

She pulled away with an irked exclamation.

"Now y'r cross," he said owlishly. "Doan be cross."

Because of his weariness and his weakened condition the brandy had made him silly. Faith, but she'd begun to feel silly herself there for a minute or two. But at least he was not slumped and listless, or sinking into one of those terrible swoons, and what could be sweeter than his kisses? She said gently, "I'm not cross, dear sir. But—no! Geoffrey, you must behave! Now tell me, what is the Long Down said to be a name for?"

"Very bad grammar," he said, waving one long finger under her nose. "London."

"My God! If Cunningham ever learns *that!*"

"*Wouldn'* he be in a pucker!" He gave a whoop of laughter that made her clap a hand over his mouth.

She hissed, "Yes, he would, sir! And he'd know who Ligun Doone is, pucker or no!"

"Don't see that," he argued, drawing himself up in aggrieved fashion. "Lots o' Englishman in Scotland just now."

"Yes, but you've been up here for just the right length of time, and, oh, Geoffrey! What on earth possessed—"

She was pushed aside, and Delacourt leapt to his feet. She saw the gleam of a pistol in his hand, and she realized in a shocked way that, although the wind seemed to have dropped a little, the rustlings around them had been increasing.

"All right," he said in a harsh, unfamiliar voice, "come out. And tread carefully, friends, this pistol has a set-trigger."

Prudence stood and edged closer, and he reached out to sweep her behind him.

A taut second of stillness. A cautious Scots voice: "Sir . . . ? Is that yesel', Captain?"

"Kerbie!" exclaimed Delacourt.

A dark figure rushed at them. "Of all the bonnie luck!" The two men gripped hands strongly, and Lockerbie went on, "What happened, sir? We'd word there was a signal light and we came so fast as we could. Whisht, sir, but I—I was afearin' ye'd wear the hempen cravat a sight too soon, and then that fool Cole says—"

"Cole! Where is he? Cole?" Delacourt peered into the darkness, and a shrinking form materialized to edge forward reluctantly. "So here you are! Damn you. What the devil went wrong?"

Cole, head downbent, evaded the hand Delacourt held out despite his wrath and said shamefacedly, "I failed you, Master Geoff. You as I'd cut off my arm for! Failed you—"

"Oh, don't be a gudgeon. If you failed I know blasted well it was not deliberately. Lord, man, you've looked after me all my life! Had you run to the commode, or some such major emergency?"

Cole uttered a choking laugh. "I'd saw 'em coming, sir, and I run, all right, but that damn cat was right under my feet. Down I went and give my head a crack on the side of Miss Prue's table. By the time I came round, all hell had broken loose and I got downstairs just in time to see the lights go out. I had to fight my way after that. I had the idea you might try and find his lordship, so I struck out down the road on one of Mr. MacTavish's hacks and a little while ago I was challenged by some Scots. Turned out to be Lockerbie. Sir—I'm sorrier than I can say!"

Delacourt slapped him on the back and said bracingly, "Not your fault, old fellow. Luckily, Mrs. Hortense went up to the roof to look at her stars, else we all might have had rope collars, I'll own. We all got away, I think, one way or another. Now, Kerbie, what's gone amiss? Did Briley run into trouble?"

"That he did, sir. A ragtag group o' Highlanders were oot tae avenge poor Johnny Robertson, and took yon butler and his lordship fer the military before Angus and his lads could reach 'em."

Dismayed, Delacourt gasped, "Oh, Jupiter! They never killed old Thad?"

"No, sir. But one of 'em grassed him wi' a club and he didnae come to until yesterday afternoon. He's a good man and was fair detairmined tae ride oot, but every time he gets up, doon he goes again."

"Concussion, likely," muttered Delacourt. "Well, I'm glad it's no worse. How many are with you?"

"Three, Mr. Doone," came a growl of a voice from the trees. "And we're all at yer service the noo. Or whenever."

"Thank you, gentlemen. Cole, did you see who attacked us? Were they army?"

"If so they wore civilian clothes, sir. And a more rough and ready lot I never hope to see!"

Lockerbie said, "If they were bounty hunters they must know who you are, Captain."

"I'm afraid you're in the right of it. But they're not likely to share what they know with friend Cunningham and risk losing some of the reward."

Prudence ventured, "And at least they will not have all the power of the redcoats after us."

Delacourt reached for her hand and gripped it strongly. "Very true. Can we get to the cavern, d'ye think, Kerbie?"

Lockerbie sighed. "The countryside's fair alive wi' military, sir. We'll get ye there if it can be done, but it's a fair piece fer ye tae ride."

"If I fall, you must throw me across the saddle. Let us be on our way."

The horses were saddled and brought up. As they started off, Delacourt asked, "Lord, I forgot about poor Sidley. Is he safely confined?"

"Aye, sir. He took a fair ding on the nob during the little misunderstanding, but he's going along well enough, though he's not in the verra best o' spirrrits, y'ken. Angus told the lads tae let the others think he really is a Captain. Losh, but I sometimes think he believes it his own self."

"Has he seen you? Is he aware of how we used him?"

"Nae, I think not. I've kept oot o' his sight." Lockerbie gave a dry chuckle. "He'll rumble us when *ye* come, Captain!"

They went along steadily, the clip-clop of the horses' hooves beginning to lull Prudence into a doze. After a while the drizzle started again, but it was very light and the wind had dropped, which made it bearable. She glanced to Delacourt and found him watching her anxiously. He leaned to her and asked, "How do you go on, ma'am? I promise you'll be warm and dry just as soon as we can manage."

She was about to respond that she'd been wet before in her life and would do very nicely, but in the nick of time, restrained herself, and thanked him. "I shall do my best to keep up, though I'll own I am rather tired, sir."

"Stay close to me. If you start to drop asleep I'll take you up on my horse. You'll be warmer then."

She smiled into the darkness, pleased by the confidence in his voice. For a while Lockerbie and Delacourt talked in low, guarded tones, but aside from an occasional muttered remark the other men were silent. Prudence caught herself on the brink of sleep several times as the night wore on, and awoke fully in the first grey light of dawn to see Delacourt bowed forward against his horse's mane, and Cole riding very close, keeping him in the saddle. Even as she watched, he stirred and pulled himself upright. At once, she bent forward and closed her eyes.

Delacourt said softly, "She's asleep, poor little soul. Nothing must harm her, Cole. Promise me—whatever happens."

"She'll not be touched, sir, not while I draw breath. I swear it!"

The sun was coming up when they clattered into the yard of a lonely croft. Prudence was so stiff and cold she could scarcely lean to the broad-shouldered Scot who reached up to help her from the saddle. Lockerbie had his arm about a staggering Delacourt, and then the front door swung open and the crofters were running out to them. Lockerbie spoke to them briefly, and from that moment Prudence was treated as though she were royalty, these honest folk so in awe of Ligun Doone that anyone in his train was to be venerated, however great the risk they ran in sheltering him.

The gaunt little woman of the house whisked Prudence into a tiny bedroom and scurried about, providing hot water and clean towels. She was almost too tired to wash, and all but fell into bed, sound asleep the instant her head touched the pillow. Fortunately, she had always been a good horsewoman, and despite the rigours of the night, awoke to less discomfort than a more sedentary lady might have experienced. A delectable aroma enticed her. She found her clothes, dried and neatly ironed, draped over a chair at the end of the bed. She dressed hurriedly and made grateful use of a clean but mutilated comb that had been left near a small, cracked mirror propped on a battered highboy. Surveying herself ruefully, she thought it ridiculous to be wearing an evening gown before breakfast, but at least her complexion did not come out of a pot, and if her lemon silk was inappropriate in a humble croft (and even more so on the back of a horse!), it did not cover hoops, and thanks to the kindly farm wife, was not now too badly muddied or creased.

She went to the door and opened it cautiously. She looked into the small parlour that she vaguely remembered crossing last night—no, this morning! It was empty save for a man wrapped in his plaid and sleeping on the floor near the far wall. She heard a low mutter of talk and, so as not to disturb the sleeper, tiptoed across to the kitchen door.

Her hand was on the latch when the sound of her own name caused her to check.

Delacourt was saying, ". . . and assuredly the prettiest lady I ever saw. I never thought to find her like when you hauled me up here from Prestonpans, Kerbie."

"She's fond o' ye, I'm thinking."

Prudence stiffened. Lockerbie's tone had been disapproving. Her chin lifted angrily. Wretched creature! Did he fancy her beneath Delacourt's touch, perhaps? The MacTavish was equal to any man in—

"I have made a great effort to restrain my natural, er, impulses," said Delacourt.

'You *have?*' thought Prudence.

"Not always quite successfully, alas," he admitted with a sigh.

"Aye. Well—well, ye're a mon. And if ever a mon deserved a bit o' happiness in his life, 'tis yersel'."

Prudence smiled and prepared to enter, but decided she had best wait a minute lest they worry that she might have overheard this heartwarming little exchange.

"No man," said Delacourt heavily, "has the right to snatch his own happiness without consideration for the feelings of another."

Lockerbie said, "I suppose . . . ye could tell her."

"Lord, no! Besides, I'd intended to leave when Briley returned, and I had no slightest thought of ever seeing her again." He gave a sudden bitter laugh. "Once again, Fate circumvented me."

Prudence stood very still, her eyes fixed in a blank, unseeing stare at the rough wood of the door. 'Papa,' she thought, 'was right. Listeners seldom hear well of themselves.' She turned away.

"Ye mustnae gie up, Captain," said Lockerbie stoutly. "Ye're nae worse than ye were a month since."

"Liar. Oh, never fret. I can face it. But I do not delude myself. The dizziness—that damnable weakness—comes upon me more frequently."

"Aye, because ye listen tae the doctors—dammem! They're *wrong,* I tell ye! Ye'll verra likely outlive—outlive us all!"

The Scot's voice shredded, and the last word was barely audible, yet it might have been bellowed in Prudence's ears. She stood numbed with shock, unable to move. Vaguely, she was aware that Delacourt had said something, but now there was a roaring in her ears and the floor seemed to swing under her feet. She put out a hand blindly and clasped the other over her mouth, staring at the small window in horror and anguish. It wasn't true! It *could* not be true! 'No!' she thought, frenzied. '*No! No!*'

Dimly, she heard them speaking again. She covered her ears

and fled in panic back into the little bedchamber. She sat on the bed, but she was cold with shock, and shaking, and she could not be still. Standing again, she began to pace up and down, wringing her hands, fighting to control the wild jumble of thoughts that crowded her bewildered mind. So many things came back to her; so many little incidents that—despite her tearful repudiation—began to fit into place like the pieces of a living puzzle. Lockerbie's almost tender solicitude for his master; the troubled look she had seen in Dr. Cauldside's eyes from time to time; Geoffrey's frightening swoons and frequent exhaustion. She could see Elizabeth suddenly, glaring at Thaddeus Briley—it seemed so long ago—when he'd teasingly threatened Delacourt, ". . . if you ever hope to see England again. . . ." She could hear again Elizabeth saying, "He's made haste backwards. . . ." She could see her, running from the room almost, when she herself had confessed a *tendre* for the Captain. It all fit! And how could she *not* have seen? How could she have been so *dense?*

She went back to the bed and sat there, crouched over, beginning to weep helplessly. They'd told her that Geoffrey had suffered a relapse after his terrible flight north. It was apparent now that his health had gradually deteriorated instead of improving. And yet he had refused to bow to illness, very obviously. He had fought on, seeming always so full of fun and mischief. Thumbing his nose at the approaching shadow, even as he'd thumbed his nose at Cunningham. How bright and cheerful he had been in the Monster, how sure of their success, inspiring them all with his confidence. It was said that adversity brought out the best in the British; perhaps that was the way with him. She wiped away tears with the heel of her hand, remembering how he had laughed when they'd frightened Cunningham's soldiers away. How could he have *laughed*—knowing he was soon to die?

The tears came again, scaldingly. Lockerbie had said the doctors were wrong. That was it, of course. They *were* wrong! Only look at how Geoffrey had managed to stay in the saddle all these miles. She closed her mind to the recollection of his tumbling so startlingly to lie in her arms on General Wade's Road and, gritting her teeth, she whispered fiercely, "I shall stay beside him. No matter what comes, I will be with him." Her chin came up. If he had the courage to face so dreadful a threat with his head held high and a laugh on his lips, if he could exert every effort for others, knowing he himself was doomed, then she would be courageous, too.

She crossed to the cracked little mirror and poured some cold water into the washbowl. For several moments she bathed her reddened eyes, then dried them cautiously. She looked wan and haunted, so she pinched her cheeks for colour and practised a smile. They would likely only think she looked tired, which was logical enough.

She drew a steadying breath, then walked resolutely from the room, across the parlour, and into the kitchen.

"I dinna ken who they were, or whence they came, sirrr," said the footman, his eyes round and shocked as he stood amid the wreckage of the withdrawing room. "'Twas nice and peaceful one minute, and the next the hoose was fair swarming wi' fighting men."

Colonel Cunningham, a cold fury lashing him, leaned back in James MacTavish's favourite chair and ran his keen gaze around the shambles of smashed furniture and ripped draperies. "And all this took place yesterday evening?"

"Aye, sir. We've no had the time tae clear it all up."

Cunningham thought cynically, 'Probably too busy drinking your master's wines and eating his finest foods!' He asked, "Where is Sidley?"

"I dinna ken, sir."

"Where is Mrs. Cairn?"

"Gone, sir. They're all gone!"

"Gone where?"

"I dinna ken, sir."

The Colonel folded his hands and smiled the smile that caused subalterns to shiver before him. "What may your name be?"

"Abercrombie, sir."

"Will you tell me, Abercrombie, why the authorities were not notified of this—this debacle?"

Startled, the footman exclaimed, "Och, but we couldnae do that, whatever!"

"Why could you not do that?"

"The MacTavish might nae like it."

"But the MacTavish is not here."

"He'll come back, sir. Soon or late."

"I see. These—er, invaders. They wore uniforms?"

"Not the ones I saw. Forbye, it was waeful dark."

"Did you think to recognize any of them? A mannerism? A voice?"

"Nae, sir. It was waeful—"

"Dark. Yes. You may go."

The footman bowed and took himself off.

Fuming, Cunningham turned to the quiet Dr. Cauldside. "Bovine idiot! One gathers that had we not chanced to come out here for you to check Delacourt, the servants would have gone on with their discreet silence until the food ran out!"

Cauldside looked worriedly around the chaos. "It's a fine mess. What d'ye think chanced here, Colonel?"

Cunningham flung out of his chair and marched to stand staring out of the window, hands loosely clasped behind him. "I see only three possibilities. Either they were military, thieves, or bounty hunters. They were not military, of that I am assured. And the chances of thieves banding together to stage such a raid are extreme remote."

"Which leaves the bounty hunters. But who were they hunting? And what's become o' the family? Losh, mon, there's seven people we're short. D'ye take that intae account?"

"I do." Cunningham turned to face him. "Nine, if you count Garry and MacKie."

"Lord! Were they here as well?"

"So I am informed. I think I shall lose no time in riding

down to Garry House to discover if Sir Matthew returned home safe. Do you go with me?"

"If I may." The doctor stood. "I'll own I'm fair gapped by the business."

Cunningham nodded and crossed the room with his quick, decisive stride. At the door, he paused. "By the way, doctor, I think I neglected to tell you. I have received a response to my letter to Whitehall. I know now what Ligun Doone means."

"Oh, do ye?" Unimpressed, the doctor muttered, "Is it important?"

Cunningham's lip curled. "It is to me, sir. And it will doubtless prove so to the man who laughed at us when he chose it. I fancy mine will be the longest laugh!"

Luck seemed to have deserted the fugitives that day. Everywhere they turned were redcoats, so that they had to constantly double back, or waste precious time hiding. Not until late afternoon had they travelled the length of Loch Ness and turned northward, passing into rugged country very difficult of passage, with soaring crags and sharp defiles, their path often crossed by hurrying burns making their impatient way to the loch. To the constant menace of the troopers was added exhaustion, so that Delacourt was hard put to it to keep in the saddle and Prudence drooped with weariness.

Lockerbie had sent one of his men far out in the lead, and now he came galloping back, waving his arms. His name was Graham, and he was older than the others, a scrawny little man with a bitter mouth. "Redcoats," he said, joining them. "'Fore God, but they're everywhere! One might think Prince Charlie still hereaboots, 'stead o' being safe away, God bless him!"

"*Maybe* safe away!" said Lockerbie. "Captain . . . ? Och, but he's off again, puir laddie."

"No, I'm not," said Delacourt, pulling his head up. "Can we hide somewhere till dark? Could we get through then?"

Kirkpatrick, a rugged man with flaming red hair and a whimsical grin, said, "Aye—wi' a dirk at the ready."

"No!" snapped Delacourt. "My actions will bring death upon none of my countrymen! Nor upon ourselves, God willing. There's been too damned much killing!" There was a moment of uneasy silence, then Delacourt pointed to a soaring crag that threw a deep shadow over the shrubs at its base. "We may escape detection there for a space."

They rode into the sparse little trees and bushes. Delacourt made no move to dismount, and Lockerbie jumped from the saddle and half lifted his master down. Performing the same service for Prudence, young Jock Eldredge blushed fierily when she leaned wearily against him. He took off his drab, dyed plaid and spread it on the ground for her, and she sat down, leaning against the rock and stretching out with a sigh of thankfulness. Cole and Graham loosened girths and tended to the horses, and then they all gathered around, tired and hungry, nobody speaking for a little while.

Delacourt seemed to have fallen asleep, and Prudence closed her eyes, praying that all this exertion might not prove too much for him. She was startled to hear him drawl coolly, "Can any of you climb?"

Kirkpatrick answered, "I can, sir. Half mountain goat, me ma useter say."

"You'll have a good view from the top of this shade-maker," said Delacourt with his endearing smile. "D'you think you can be our lookout?"

The redhead stood, walked up and down scanning the crag, then nodded. In another minute he was making his precarious way up the rock face. Prudence held her breath, but he had spoken truly and went on easily enough until he was lost from sight.

Climbing a little way after him, Lockerbie relayed, "He's lyin' doon."

"Jolly good. Cole, keep your eyes open for troopers coming from the east."

Kirkpatrick reported the dismal news that he could see clear across the glen, and that there were several small groups of troopers who seemed to be beating the area between them and the point to the northwest that they must reach.

"Looking fer rebels, damn them," muttered Graham.

"Well, they're looking in the wrong place," said Delacourt. "Let's hope they've already searched here."

An hour later, however, it became apparent that the search was in fact moving in their direction. It was still light but Delacourt ordered the horses to be readied for a retreat. This plan was foiled when more soldiers approached from the east. They received adequate warning from Cole, but Prudence began to feel trapped and afraid. She was reassured when Delacourt patted her shoulder and winked at her, and then asked Lockerbie to discover whether there were any habitations in sight. Kirkpatrick was contacted and said there was only a tumbledown old croft some distance north, and no hope of concealment there.

Delacourt nodded thoughtfully and crept over to talk with Graham. Prudence watched curiously as Lockerbie and Eldredge joined them. The other men began to give their supply of ammunition to Graham. Delacourt also appropriated Eldredge's dull brown plaid and thrust it at the smaller man. "Here," he said. "If you run into trouble, curl up under it and try to look like a rock."

Graham chuckled, threw the plaid about him, and was off. Prudence stood beside Delacourt, watching that small figure dart from one clump of shrubs to the next. He was almost out of her range of vision when from the corner of her eye she saw two troopers riding straight for the pile of boulders he had just reached. Aghast, she wrenched her gaze back to Graham, but he was nowhere to be seen. Delacourt squeezed her hand and whispered, "He's being a rock, ma'am. Good little actor."

She strained her eyes, incredulous, but sure enough when the troopers were safely past she saw Graham materialize from among the boulders and scurry away.

The time dragged and always the sound of the beaters drew terrifyingly nearer. Prudence whispered, "What is Graham aboot? What can he hope to do all alone?"

Delacourt gave her a little-boy grin. "Wait and see."

After another few minutes Lockerbie came to them. "Kirkpatrick says Graham's away again, sir."

"Splendid. Ready the horses. Be as quiet as you can, the troopers are almost on us."

The horses were prepared for riding, the inevitable sounds drowned by the ever-increasing noise the soldiers made in their search. Prudence could hear them talking now, and soon she could distinguish the words. A young English voice, sounding almost beside her, said gaily, ". . . and I'll be in Paris before you!" Laughter followed, and her heart gave a great thump as a branch snapped at the edge of their little sanctuary.

"Look there!" a trooper shouted. "That old croft, sir. I see smoke from the chimney!"

Prudence ducked lower, Delacourt pulling her down as an officer rode up. "Damme, but you're right! So that's where the devil's lurking. Mount up, you men! I think we've got him!"

Another moment and they were off, with many whoops and shouts of excitement.

Eldredge tossed Prudence up into her saddle, but Delacourt lifted a detaining hand. Lockerbie, who had returned to his listening post, came hurrying back. "Kirkpatrick says there's still aboot ten o' the bastards left!"

"They'll leave," said Delacourt, confidently. "Wait."

On his last word a flurry of shots and a deeper boom rang out, the explosions causing Prudence to jump, and her mount to caper about nervously. More shouts, and then a thunder of hooves as the remaining troopers went at the gallop to join the fight.

"Here we go!" said Delacourt.

Kirkpatrick came down from the top of the crag in a wild scramble and sprang onto the pony Lockerbie held for him. Even as they started into the open, hoofbeats sounded behind them and Prudence jerked her head around in fright. Graham was following, another man sharing his saddle; a young man with a gaunt, bearded face, strained eyes, and a bloody bandage about one arm.

"Flushed you out, did we?" called Delacourt. "Very well

done, Graham. All right, everyone—steady now—no faster than a canter."

Hampered by that restraint, they rode over the open stretch of level ground. It was only beginning to be dusk and they were in full view of anyone who might come within a few hundred yards of them. The green glen was incredibly wide, or so thought Prudence, and the very cut-up country for which they were obviously heading seemed miles distant. Her nerves were stretched to the breaking point when Delacourt said, a triumphant ring to his voice, "Excelsior! I think we dare risk a gallop now!"

Gallop they did, every heart lifting because they were done with that nerve-racking flight. Prudence soon understood why Delacourt had risked the noisier pace, for the ground began to fall away, sloping steadily downwards until they were in a deep defile where the air was dank and cold and seemed to vibrate oddly. Again, they had to slow, the terrain very rugged, threaded by tumbling burns and with all around them great boulders, soaring crags, and plunging gorges. Always the throb in the air grew until it was a roar of sound. They came around a curve, and through the gathering gloom Prudence saw a high scarp from which a sheet of water swept out like a white curtain, arcing down to join a racing flood that sped off to the west.

Lockerbie led the way until the river narrowed, then urged his horse into the water. Following, Prudence felt Flaxen stagger to the pull of the flood. Delacourt appeared on one side of her, and Cole on the other, staying very close. One slip here would be fatal, but in this particular place the water rose no higher than their stirrups, and a moment later they were across. Still in the lead, Lockerbie rode along the climbing, rock-strewn path, his sure-footed Highland pony stepping daintily amongst the rubble. The sound of the falls was deafening, but Lockerbie went straight forward. Prudence eyed the wall of water uneasily, and as Lockerbie rode under it, Flaxen balked. Prudence kicked home her heels and the mare capitulated and followed the pony. Spray was icy against Prudence's face. She pulled her hood closer. Only darkness lay ahead, and she shrank, frightened. A hand touched her elbow. Dimly, she saw Delacourt leaning to her, a cheerful grin on his pale face. Her heart warmed. She nodded and went on, her eyes shut tight.

The sound was like a tangible thing now, pounding at her; icy, bruising blows. Flaxen stumbled and Prudence screamed, the sound wiped away by the uproar. The Thoroughbred recovered, and they were moving again. Imperceptibly, the noise diminished, and the air became less chill. Peeping between her lashes, Prudence saw that they had left the falls behind and now followed a broad, upward winding path. It was too dark for her to distinguish much, but they went on slowly, the horses' hooves clattering against the solid rock.

She glanced around and could see the outline of the following rider. Delacourt shouted in a weary but elated voice, "We've done it! We're safe now, ma'am!"

A glow appeared on the wall ahead. The path turned sharply. Lockerbie had dismounted and was leading his pony, and he vanished from sight momentarily. Then Flaxen also turned the corner and Prudence was dazzled by the flickering flames of torches blazing in heavy iron brackets, illuminating a great cavern.

Shouts and cries of greeting rang out. Shielding her eyes against the glare, Prudence saw gradually that many men were gathered here. Everywhere was the bright flash of forbidden tartan. She saw among them the red, white, green, and black of the MacGregor; the green, black, red, and blue of MacDonell of Glengarry; the Cameron red, green, and yellow; the green, black, and blue of the MacLeod with its overchecks of red and yellow; and many more, too numerous to count. Impressions crowded her mind in those first seconds: pallets and improvised mattresses of straw lining the walls, many occupied by wounded men who lay watching, or propped on an elbow in an attempt to see more; a distant whinnying of horses, and the smell of horse on the none too pleasant air; men gathering around, raising glad, unshaven faces to scan them; the red coat of an English officer, who sat disconsolately against the wall and lifted his head to reveal a narrow face, and an expression of hopelessness that turned to horror. She thought, 'Sidley! Good

Lord!' and was aghast because the imperturbable snob of a butler was reduced to this unkempt and dishevelled creature, incongruous in the English Captain's uniform.

A Highlander shouted, "Which is he? Who's our Ligun Doone?"

More eager shouts joined the first. Prudence glanced around. Delacourt, the immediate peril over, had relaxed at last, and was slumped over in the saddle. Behind him, Graham and his passenger were coming up, and beyond them, Kirkpatrick and Eldredge were escorted by several gaunt and fierce Highlanders, armed with the terrible two-edged broadswords called claymores, the long steel blades winking in the light of the torches.

Lockerbie shouted, "Here he is, lads! Let's give a yell fer him!" He waved a hand to Delacourt, and as the Highland roar rose deafeningly, the sagging Englishman fought away weakness and slid from his saddle to stand erect and summon a grin. He could see only glaring lights and the blur of many faces and was mildly surprised to hear his real name howled above the noise.

"*Delavale!*"

Like a giant among pygmies, a great Highlander clad in the MacLeod tartan shoved his way through the throng. Uneasy, Lockerbie reached out to stay him and was tossed aside. "Filthy English spy!" howled the big man.

Before Delacourt could gather his numbed senses, or his friends rally to his aid, the giant was before him. A huge fist flailed out. Swaying dizzily, Delacourt flung up a guarding arm. It was smashed aside. A sledgehammer blow sent him hurtling into a pile of wooden chests, scattering them. He was down and rolling, to lie at last, limp and motionless on the floor of this great cavern that he had been so confident would offer them sanctuary.

XV

"*Geoffrey!*" Scarcely knowing that she screamed his name, Prudence ran forward, only to be seized and held by a frowning Cameron.

The great Highlander stood over Delacourt's sprawled figure, his claymore whipping upwards preparatory to the downward sweep that would finish his helpless victim.

As fast as Prudence ran, another was before her; a thin, unkempt man wearing a rumpled red uniform, a pathetic gallantry in the charge he essayed against the young giant who shook him off as though he had been a gnat and, with one backward swipe of his fist, sent the erstwhile butler sailing back and down so that he was unconscious before he hit the floor. Doomed as his effort had been, it had delayed the murderous descent of the claymore. Even as the shouts of acclamation metamorphosed into growls of anger and dismay, Lockerbie, Eldredge, Kirkpatrick, Cole, and Graham plunged at the Highlander. It took all of them to hold him as he fought to be free.

"Fool!" raged Lockerbie. "Damn the black and stupid heart o' ye, Stuart MacLeod!"

"*He's* no Ligun Doone," bellowed the Highlander, tearing away and facing them all, claymore at the ready. "I fought him, mon tae mòn, at Prestonpans! He's a stinkin' English Captain name o' Delavale. That I found oot when the shell got him and I went through his pockets!"

"Aye," screamed Prudence, her shrill voice striking through the hubbub and creating a small well of silence. "He's Geoffrey Delavale. An English Captain who was sore wounded at Prestonpans. And he is also Ligun Doone!" She turned on the Cameron who held her. "Let me go, you great oaf!"

MacLeod stared at her, the beginnings of unease written on his strong, bronzed features. "Ye're daft, woman."

"Then ye may call me daft, too, MacLeod," shouted Lockerbie, mad with rage and grief. "If ye've killed that mon, ye've struck doon the best friend any hunted Scot ever had!"

A tall, powerfully built individual, looking to be no more than fifty, but with a shock of white hair, shoved through the bewildered throng. His brilliant dark gaze flashed from the frantically struggling girl to the grim-faced Scots who held MacLeod's might at bay to the unconscious young man at their feet. Dropping to one knee, he slid an arm under Delacourt and raised his shoulders.

Prudence sank her teeth into the wrist of the Cameron and managed to wrench free. She ran to kneel beside Delacourt. His head sagged back as he was lifted. Blood streaked from the corners of his mouth, and he looked quite dead. She clutched one unresponsive hand and pressed it to her cheek. It was warm still. Blinded by tears, she looked at the older man pleadingly. "Dinna say he's killed. Dinna say it," she begged.

"Who are ye, lassie?"

"Prudence MacTavish. Daughter of James MacTavish of Inverness. Sir, is he—"

"More to the point. Is this boy Ligun Doone?"

"Yes! Yes!"

A rumbling arose from those gathered around. A tall, shaggy-haired man, with a great black beard and flashing jet eyes, growled, "I dinna believe it! Ligun Doone's no an Englishman! He's—"

"He's an Englishman!" With the aid of a friend, Jock Campbell hobbled through the crowd. "I'm here, thanks tae his wit and courage!"

"And I!" called another man. And throughout the close-packed men came more cries of anger and confirmation, climaxed when Angus Fraser stalked from the rear of the great cavern, a bridle in one hand and curiosity on his dark face. He made his way through to the center of the throng and checked, the breath hissing through his suddenly clenched teeth. "Lord ha' mercy!" He dropped the bridle and ran to bend over the stricken man. "Doone! Great God! What happened?"

MacLeod, his face white and drawn, muttered, "I hit him."

Fraser's hand darted for the dirk at his belt, and he turned on the big man, his lips drawn back in a snarl of rage. The white-haired individual said sharply, "None of that, Angus. It was a mistake. Let's get him onto a bed."

Delacourt was lifted tenderly and borne to a crude bed, the occupant having demanded he be moved so that the Englishman might have his place.

A bowl of water and rags were brought. With Cole's help, Prudence went to work. Lockerbie disappeared to return with a glass of brandy, which she waved away. "Some water, please," she begged, and there was a rush to respond.

The white-haired man said, "You know me, Lockerbie?"

"Aye, sir. Ye're Sir Ian Crowley and were on the Prince's staff."

"Yes. I was cut off from him, and by great good luck your people found me and brought me here."

Gently folding back Delacourt's lower lip to inspect the cuts his teeth had made, Prudence asked anxiously, "And His Highness, sir? Is he safe away?"

Crowley's mouth tightened. He said curtly, "He's away to the Western Sea. But he'll be back, I've no doot. Now—what of this brave fellow? Is it true he has a mortal wound?"

Lockerbie nodded glumly. "'Tis truth. He grows ever weaker, however he fights it. And"—he slanted a murderous glare at the young giant who stood silently a short distance away, his brown curly head bowed and massive shoulders slumped—"and fight it he does, though his chances are a muckle smaller the noo—or damned well gone, more like—thanks tae the MacLeod!"

A fierce muttering went up, many heads turning in wrath to the big man, but he neither looked up nor spoke.

Sir Ian, who had been watching Delacourt narrowly, murmured, "Lassie—I think perhaps ye waste your efforts. He looks to be—"

"Don't," sobbed Prudence, distraught, "oh, dinna say it! Tae think one o' the very men he's risked his life for . . ." She sprang up, turning on MacLeod like a mad thing, the tears streaming unchecked down her cheeks. "Beast," she raged, her fists clenched. "Horrid savage! God in heaven! What is wrong wi' us? Always fighting! Always killing! If not the English, then our own folk! And now we must turn on the man who has helped more than two score of our lads escape death! Is *this* how you thank him, you wretched . . . evil brute?" Hysterical, she ran at him, her fists pounding furiously against his muscular chest. And still MacLeod did not move, or make the least attempt to defend himself or to stop her, while the company looked on in a grim silence, even Sir Ian making no move to intervene.

Prudence's fury spent itself. She bowed her face into her throbbing hands and wept, then, looking up, saw that MacLeod's head had lifted. In his face was a stark look of misery. Without a word, he drew the dirk that hung at his belt, and handed it to her, hilt foremost.

She snatched the glittering weapon and drew back her arm, fully prepared to strike. And still no one remonstrated with her.

MacLeod stood unmoving, his eyes lowered and a suspicious brightness on his lashes.

It was that brightness that stopped her; that and the echo of Delacourt's voice: ". . . there's been too damned much killing . . ." She lowered her arm, then flung the dirk at the Highlander's feet. "I'll no soil my hands," she said in a voice that rang with loathing.

A sort of rippling sigh stirred the watching men. Not taking up the dirk, MacLeod moved off towards the mouth of the cavern, only young Jock Eldredge slipping quietly after him.

Sir Ian touched Prudence's elbow, his compassionate gaze on her. He said gently, "You must be very tired, Miss MacTavish. We will contrive a private couch for you, so you can rest."

"If the Captain is dying," she answered in a dulled, despairing voice, "I'll no leave his side." And glancing to where several men bent over Sidley, she asked, "Is he dead, too?"

Graham, one of the group, called, "Just stunned, ma'am. 'Twas a brave thing he did, fer such a scrawny Sassenach."

The butler was carried back towards the rear, where the cavern, as Prudence was later to discover, branched into several other connecting chambers. Sir Ian called Fraser and went off with him in low-voiced conference. Many willing hands worked to erect a partition formed of plaids hung on strung ropes. A rough bed was fashioned, and more plaids and cloaks were offered to serve in lieu of blankets. Prudence was ushered inside, a pan of hot water was brought, and she washed as best she could. Soon, shy offerings of food were tendered: a mug of pure mountain water laced with whisky, a piece of dried fish, a hunk of dark bread, and some rather questionable cheese. Her heart was heavy because Cole told her that Delacourt had not stirred, but she was not so lost in grief that she was oblivious of the sacrifice these offerings constituted, and she thanked the ragged donors warmly. She fell asleep sitting beside the bed in the crude chair they had brought for her, and it was big Stuart MacLeod who, unknown to the exhausted girl, lifted her and laid her gently on her own makeshift bed.

The sound of low voices woke her some hours later. For an instant she was bewildered by strangeness; the mattress was excessive lumpy, she was cold, and something was tickling her cheek. She blinked at the muted light of the torches and memory rushed in. She was up in a flash and pulling back the plaid curtain. Lockerbie was bending over the pallet. Delacourt was awake, and saw her at once. A smile quivered on his lips. He tried to speak, coughed, and doubled up, jerking his head away so that she could not see his face.

Lockerbie came to her and whispered, "Belike his wound was torn by that fall. It never has healed right. Best ye go, miss. He'd no wish that ye see him like—like this."

She drew back reluctantly. Sir Ian came through the plaids that now enclosed Delacourt's small area. He had brought a flask, and urged him to try to drink. Prudence intervened hurriedly. "Not if it is spirits, sir. You are very kind, but it will make him cough, and that pains him so."

Delacourt's dark head turned on the cloak Lockerbie had rolled up for a pillow. His face shone with sweat, and there was a frantic look in his eyes. His lips were clamped shut, and he made no further effort to speak, but she could feel his suffering and she knelt to stroke the damp hair back from his forehead.

"I hae nursed my papa and my brother many's the time, Captain," she murmured, "and I will think no less o' ye do ye feel the need tae swear or to cry oot."

She took up the hand that was tight-clenched on the plaid. Briefly, his fingers relaxed, then clamped over her own so that she was hard put to it not to whimper. Delacourt closed his eyes and lay rigid, but after a moment the paroxysm appeared to ease, for his hold relaxed again. He whispered in broken little gasps, "Fought him . . . Prestonpans." Incredibly, a twinkle came into the dark eyes. "Beat him, too!" His mouth twisted, he jerked his head away again, and his grip was bruising her.

She took his other hand and held both strongly and, seeing blood creep down his chin, blinked in anguish, but said, "Do not dare to bite your lip, Geoffrey Delacourt! Trouble enough I've had, tending your cuts."

He shuddered, and peered around as though he could not see her. "I'll not have them say . . . the English . . . whine." The heavy lids drooped, the grip on her hands eased and became limp.

Terrified, she bent closer and was inexpressibly relieved to find that he was still breathing. Lockerbie leaned to her ear. "Belike he'll sleep the noo. Ye need rest yersel', miss. I'll call ye if he wakes."

She nodded, but when she made to slip her hand away, Delacourt's fingers tightened about it. She glanced up, smiling. Lockerbie smiled back, brought in some plaids, and did all he might to make her comfortable.

Prudence leaned back in the chair, thinking drearily that only two nights since, she had been in a gracious home with servants to do her bidding, and a warm bed with a soft feather mattress awaiting her. She closed her eyes, listening drowsily to the snores of the men who slept all around her, and to an occasional smothered moan from the wounded. She dozed briefly, and her fingers slid from Delacourt's grasp. He groaned in his sleep, and his hand groped about, his head beginning to toss agitatedly. Prudence was awake at once and clasped his thin fingers again, and he was quiet.

She smiled into the darkness and dismissed all thought of her feather bed.

All the next day and night she scarcely left her vigil. Delacourt kept his head turned from her, but she knew when he was conscious, for then would come the spasmodic clutch at the covers, and the breaths he drew would become spaced and shallow or, sometimes in his worst moments, a harsh, painful panting. At these times she would hold his hands, praying silently that he would not die, and he would cling to her until the attack eased. She bathed his wet face and murmured to him that it was better now and he must try to go back to sleep. He watched her then, his eyes narrowed and dulled, but not a word passed his compressed lips. Occasionally, he would cry out or moan in his sleep, but always he would jerk awake and peer anxiously to see if she had heard, and to spare his pride she would feign sleep.

Lockerbie and Cole stayed close by, providing their own care of the sick man, and bringing Prudence food, though they had given up trying to persuade her to go to her own bed. Always, beyond the plaid curtain she could see a great shadow lurking, and she knew Stuart MacLeod waited there. She sensed something of his remorse, but she could not forgive him, and she hoped bitterly that he heard when Delacourt's implacable hold on himself was broken and faint sounds of pain would escape him.

On the third day she whispered to Lockerbie that nothing had passed the invalid's lips save for a few drops of water she'd managed to coax him to swallow from time to time. "He must have nourishment," she whispered. "Only see how thin he grows. Ask if someone can make gruel."

Lockerbie thought it would be a miracle if Delacourt was able to swallow anything, or if they could prepare it in time, but he went off and came back in a quarter of an hour with a cracked bowl of broth that had, he said, been taken from a weak stew they had made of some rabbits one of the hunters had snared.

Delacourt was quiet, apparently sleeping, but one hand was fast gripped on the plaid, and Prudence was not deceived. She said softly, "I know ye're awake, sir. We are going to lift you, just a wee bit, so you can take some broth."

His eyes shot open to direct a horrified glance at her. There was a faint shake of the head but, hardening her heart, she nodded to the apprehensive Lockerbie, and he slid an arm very gently under Delacourt's shoulders. The Englishman kept his pleading gaze on Prudence, but although she suffered her own agonies, she forced herself to ignore that mute appeal. His eyes closed and his head rolled against Lockerbie's shoulder. The spoon in Prudence's hand shook. She thought, 'Dear Lord! Have I killed the brave soul?' but she said in a voice that quavered, "Geoffrey . . . please try. . . ."

The dark eyes opened. Through his misery he saw her tears. That must not be, so he tried, and managed to get down a few mouthfuls. Surprisingly, it was not as excruciating as he had expected, and he sank back into the dark depths, wanting to thank her but lacking the strength to do so.

It seemed to him then that he slept for a very long time. When he awoke, Prudence was gone and Cole sat dozing in the chair. Delacourt watched his old groom and wondered wearily how much more of this he must endure. He slept again, and once more, when he awoke, Cole was snoring softly. The pain was very bad. But different, in some odd way, and not nearly as terrible as it had been when first he had crashed into those boxes.

He was suffering another pain, however; a pain in his stomach. He thought, 'Lord, but I'm ravenous!' He contemplated waking Cole, but then he thought that there were many other wounded, and that everyone was ravenous, so he lay quietly, trying to ignore the pain and pull his thoughts together. He must have been lounging here for several days. He wondered if old Thad was about and, even as the thought struck him, saw the plaid cautiously drawn back and Angus Fraser's bearded face peering in at him.

"Angus," he whispered recklessly, and thought a surprised, 'Jupiter!' for the expected tightening of that ruthless jagged band around his lung did not materialize.

Cole gave a start and fell off the chair, and Angus hurried in, beaming. "Mon, are ye alive yet?" he enquired with a sad want of tact.

"No." Delacourt managed to grin at him. "Is . . . Briley . . . ?"

Angus slanted a glance at Cole, who knelt on the floor staring at Delacourt in total disbelief. "Master Geoff!" gulped the groom, his eyes misting. "You—you can—talk!"

"Enough to ask . . . if I might have just—a crust of . . . bread, maybe."

Cole scrambled up. One hand went out shyly to touch Delacourt's arm, then he rushed out.

"By God," Angus murmured, taking the chair and pulling it closer to the bed. "I think ye mean tae make me lose my bet, Captain."

"Sorry. Briley . . . ?"

Angus glanced cautiously to the small 'chamber' where Prudence slept. He kept his voice very low. "Ye'll be knowing that he took a right smart ding o' the sconce? Aye, well, we couldnae bring him roond fer days. Then, he was fair beside hissel tae get back tae Lakepoint. He said 'twas on account o' a promise he'd made tae ye, but I suspicion there's a lassie in the plot, forbye. At all events, nothing could hold him, and off he went wi' one o' Crowley's gillies tae guide him." Delacourt was tiring fast, but he watched anxiously as Angus shrugged and went on, "He'd a garron as sure-footed as any mountain goat, but in the high pass he tumbled oot o' the saddle. Gave his ankle a bad sprain and has lain cursing ever since."

Delacourt thought fuzzily, 'Damnation! Then Thad cannot carry the cypher,' and fell asleep again.

"Are ye awake, miss?"

Prudence was so drugged with sleep that she lay unmoving for a few seconds, her thoughts muddled and half formed. Something dark and terrible hung over her, she knew that. Something she shrank from facing. She blinked at the plaid curtains and remembered. Fear gripping her, she threw back the covers and ran to slip through the plaids, her eyes flying to the bed.

Delacourt lay with head and shoulders propped against a saddle. Sir Ian Crowley, Angus Fraser, Cole, and many others were crowding about the open 'curtains,' faces wreathed in grins. She scarcely saw them, or MacLeod who, supporting Thaddeus Briley, shrank back at the sight of her. She saw only a face, newly shaven, that showed alarmingly pale where it was not bruised; two dark eyes set in shadowed hollows that yet held a glowing look; the tug of a smile at cracked lips; the eager outreaching of one thin hand.

The hum of conversation died into a hush, as she flew to

kneel beside him. She could not see, but she felt Delacourt's touch on her cheek.

"Prudence," he said weakly.

Prudence could not say a word.

After ten long months of misery, Delacourt now began to enjoy a gradual cessation of pain. His recovery was astonishingly rapid. Throughout his illness he had maintained a dogged optimism, but in his heart he'd known he was losing the battle. Now, instead of being plagued by an ominously increasing listlessness, he rejoiced in his growing strength; the return of health was a heady delight; his spirits were restored and his buoyant enthusiasm infectious.

He was soon engaging in daily conferences with Angus Fraser and Sir Ian Crowley, as a result of which discussions a system of relay stations was set up. Two-man teams were positioned at high points in a three-mile radius of the cavern. Each team was equipped with short rations for their four-day period of duty, and also with lanterns, mirrors, and spy-glasses, the latter articles having been begged or borrowed from nearby crofters. A code for light signals was devised, very similar to that which Delacourt had initiated in the Lakepoint area. The occupants of the cavern were thus kept apprised of the proximity of redcoats. The lookouts proved remarkably effective; by the end of a week, fifteen men were enabled to slip safely through the patrols and make their way northwards to the MacKenzie country, into whose rugged fastnesses no dragoon would dare follow.

Despite the primitive conditions, these were happy days for Prudence. Delacourt was still weak, and she suspected he occasionally suffered some bad moments, but there was no doubt that he was greatly improved and she no longer had to go to sleep at night dreading what the morning might bring.

Lockerbie and Cole collected their share of whatever food

was available and for a time they all took very small portions so as to ensure that the sick man received sufficient nourishment to speed his recovery. It was evident that others went hungry for his sake, as Prudence often found pieces of bread, roots, or dried meats left on the chair in Delacourt's section of the screened area, though never were any of them able to determine who was their benefactor. As his body mended, Delacourt began to watch the portions with an eagle eye and when he realized what they had sacrificed for his sake, he was both touched and angered. He did not propose, he declared, to be the only fat man in a company of skeletons. They would survive or starve together, and if he received more food than the others of their little group, he would donate his entire meal to one of the wounded men. He made good his threat one day when he suspected (rightly) that he had been given three-quarters of a carrot for his dinner, instead of the half-carrot the others drew. After that, they dared not indulge him and their portions were arranged equally. The anonymous donations continued, however, for which Prudence could not be sorry.

She had no want of tasks to keep her occupied. The Highlanders were a resourceful lot, and a surprising number of them carried needle and thread about their persons. Since many of their garments were in rags, Prudence lost no time in offering her services as a seamstress—an art in which she was quite proficient—and was soon busily repairing ripped shirts, torn jackets, and worn stockings. She also made her rounds of the wounded at least once a day, and that alone was sufficient to keep her fully employed. Most of the men were ambulatory, but two were completely helpless, having been carried here by comrades. One, a gentle Lowlander named Matthew Rogers, had been shot through the body and had lost the use of his legs. Her efforts in his behalf seemed doomed to failure. He was a patient and uncomplaining boy of seventeen, and Prudence spent many hours sitting with him, doing what little she might to ease his suffering, and even singing the old country songs he would beg for. She chatted often with Thaddeus Briley, trying to alleviate his worries for Elizabeth. He was much changed from the debonair dandy she first had met, his pleasant face thinner and a haunted look to his tawny eyes, but his manner was as bright, his smile as ready, his humour as effervescent as ever, so that he had become quite a favourite with the men.

Inevitably, Prudence had a few favourites of her own. One of these was the young Highlander Graham had brought back from the abandoned croft. He was a shy young man named Rafe Stevenson, and rather pathetically grateful for her attention to his wounded arm. He had been able to creep into the croft, he told her, after the soldiers searched it for the first time. When Graham later arrived, he had guessed from the man's furtive approach that he was a fugitive, and had been only too delighted to learn that Ligun Doone was close by. "I knew, ma'am," he said, wincing from her ministrations, "that if I could but join up wi' Doone, I'd be safe. 'Twas fortunate, though, I still had me water canteen."

Prudence stayed her efforts and looked at him curiously. "Graham was thirsty, was he?"

He laughed. "Och, nae! We used it tae attract the troopers, accordin' tae Mr. Doone's plan. Did he no tell ye?"

"To tell you the truth, I'd forgot to ask him, but I'd wondered at the time how it was done. The troopers were shouting that they'd seen smoke, and then I heard an explosion. Had you started a fire?"

"Aye. And filled me canteen wi' powder and shot. 'Twas wood, ye ken, and just slow enough tae burn that we could get oot before the black powder went up. Bein' closed intae the canteen it made a bonnie wee bang and sent the shot flying in all directions. The troopers were properly taken in. Mr. Doone's a canny one all right. This cave was found by him, I'm told."

"Yes. When he was a fugitive himself, last year. It was Lockerbie or his relations who knew of it, I believe. Captain Delacourt has sent many of our men here since, as you can see." She glanced around the cavern. "How many are there now?"

"We're back up tae fifty, I think. More came in after the others left." He gave a rather wry grin. "Likely the first time sae many clans have gathered wi'oot a fight!"

It was all too true. The fugitives were grateful for this sanctuary, but inactivity, enforced proximity, shortness of food, discomfort of wounds, and above all, anxiety for their loved ones began to tell. Like many another before him, Delacourt found himself trying to cope with the swift flare of clan rivalry, the fierce Scots pride, the fighting spirit that centuries of warfare had built into these young warriors. Sir Ian Crowley and Angus Fraser struggled to keep the peace, but it was an uphill endeavour. Delacourt's dramatic arrival had brought a temporary cessation of bickering, and in the days after he was struck down, the fear that he might die had resulted in a drawing together of the rebels. Once he was on the mend, however, hostilities resumed. He was so venerated by the men that he had more success than had Crowley or Fraser in controlling the quarrelling. He was not a hot-tempered person, but when he was called upon for the fourth time in one day to terminate a violent squabble, his patience ran out. He signalled to Lockerbie, who was always at his side, to call a meeting. The hanging iron bar was struck softly, its gonglike summons bringing an immediate hush. Lockerbie helped Delacourt onto the makeshift table they had wrought, and every eye turned to him.

"You're a damnable pack of rabble," he told them with a grin.

Laughter rang out.

"We've been lucky with this cave up to now, but I think we should be ready for a quick evacuation—just in case. To that end, I want you to look to your gear. You've all been taking care of your own needs very well, but it would be more efficient had we a list of experts in all the trades. For instance: barbers, farriers, saddlemakers, fishermen, men who know how to make nets, especially; and many other skills. It would be helpful for those of us not familiar with the Highlands, if maps could be drawn up and routes gone over by those who know the area well. I've asked Jock Eldredge, Alec Dermott, and Thaddeus Briley to make lists of the trades each of you can master. Please divide yourselves into groups and report to these gentlemen so that we can learn how much talent we have here." He waved a dismissing hand, and MacLeod assisted him from the table.

The men began to form up as he had requested, and Sir Ian, curious, wandered over to Delacourt, who had returned to his pallet. "It's something tardy for all that, is it not?" he enquired, seating himself on the makeshift chair.

"Shakespeare said, 'All our yesterdays have lighted fools the way to dusty death.'" Delacourt looked at Sir Ian levelly. "To my mind, that is what you Scots have done." He threw up one hand, smiling as Crowley stiffened, his eyes sparking resentment. "No, do not eat me. I mean no disrespect. God knows I've never seen more courageous fighting men than you breed up here, sir."

"But . . . ?"

"But your land is cursed by this terrible divisioning—this need to separate into clans that are ruled like so many individual kingdoms."

"Well—so they are."

"Sir, that was well enough in past centuries. It will not do now. You are not Clan MacGregor, or Cameron, or MacDonell. You are Scotland!"

"And had we fought as one . . . is that what you mean?"

"From what I can gather, the quarrelling, the old festering hatreds and animosities went on even when the Rebellion was at its height. Few of your clans trust the others. Your unfortunate Prince was bedevilled by constantly differing counsel from this or that clan chieftain so that he must have been half mad to know which way to lean." Delacourt leaned forward and said intensely, "Sir, had your clans truly united for Charles Stuart instead of each feeling its own path was best, by God, you'd have marched into London with half the populace flying before you and the other half cheering you on!"

His eyes alight, the Scot said, "D'ye think so, honestly?"

"I do! We were not ready—as usual! What a' God's name induced Prince Charles to turn back from Derby, I don't pretend to know. But by the Lord Harry, you bare-kneed Scots can fight!"

Sir Ian grinned. "Aye, we can that. You've come to know us well, Delacourt. Much you say is truth. And much good can your hindsight do us now."

"Hindsight, perhaps, but we don't want the clan wars reenacted in this cavern, do we, sir? It's not Hampton Court, but it's the only safe place we have at this moment, and—" He stopped speaking as Angus came over to sit cross-legged on the floor beside Sir Ian's chair.

"Damned crafty Sassenach," he said, a grin negating the harsh words. "Ye've got 'em all busy, right enough."

"And you must keep them so, after I leave."

Sir Ian said, "You mean to go on, then?"

"I gave Lady Ericson my word, sir."

Fraser scowled. "You've done enough. Let young Stephens carry the cypher, he's English."

"And far too ill," Sir Ian said quietly. "I grant you he can hobble around our cave, but it will be weeks before he can make an extended journey."

Delacourt nodded, and pointed out that Briley was the only other Englishman in the cavern, and could not hope to win through with one leg incapacitated.

"We could send a Scot, I suppose," Crowley muttered dubiously. "It would involve a greater risk of detection, but my own accent is not too broad, is it, Delacourt?"

"No, sir. You could do it well enough, save for the fact that you were a Colonel on the Prince's staff, and I fancy many men know you."

There was a rather heavy silence. Angus, carefully straightening the pleats in his kilts, muttered, "I wish I could take the wee bit message. It seems tae much tae ask o' a mon we fought against and near killed."

Crowley asked, "Why d'ye do it, Captain? Why hazard your

life for your enemies when you might be safely and comfortably home?"

Delacourt hesitated. "Because I saw the horrors wrought by Cumberland's savages. I saw the women and chldren needlessly ravaged and slain, the homes burned, the wanton destruction and brutality. I could scarce believe English troops could do such things. I'll own I was sick. Ashamed of my countrymen—though it was Cumberland's doing and he—"

"Is a German," Crowley pounced. "The verra thing *we* fought for! You were on our side all the time and never knew it!"

His piercing eyes were full of laughter, and Delacourt smiled. "*Peccavi,* sir! *Peccavi!* I'll not fight that battle again. Suffice it to say I wanted to . . . in some small way . . ." He flushed uncomfortably and went on in a rather embarrassed fashion, "Well—to make amends, if you will."

Angus stood and clapped a hand gently onto his shoulder. "Ye've done a muckle grand job o' that, laddie."

Delacourt muttered, "And have heard myself named traitor for it."

"That's fustian!" exclaimed Sir Ian, irked. "You've performed a service to humanity merely. If that's traitorous to your country, you're well rid of't."

Delacourt's dark eyes flashed. "Never! You love these great proud mountains and raging burns, and your wide straths and glens and lochs. I love my gentle green hills and lush valleys; the great cities, the wide rivers, the drowsing villages—all the endless variety of countryside and people that is England. I am an officer in the service of my King. I had no thought to raise my hand against him. I would die sooner, but—" He stopped, flushing darkly. "My apologies to you both. You think me a properly idealistic young fool to make such a speech, I've no doubt."

Sir Ian looked at him steadily. He thought Delacourt a hotheaded but fine young fellow, with little chance of surviving the consequences of his humane impulses. But he said only, "You seek to help the one without harming the other. A chancy endeavour. Lord knows, I thank you, and wish you well—we all do." He glanced through the pushed-back plaids to where Prudence sat beside young Rogers. "You'll be taking Miss MacTavish with you, eh?"

Delacourt's gaze did not waver, but he came to his feet and said coolly, "I'd not dare leave her behind, sir."

Standing also, very well aware that he was being subtly told this interview was over, and marvelling that so young a man had such a presence, Sir Ian pointed out, "She would be safer in the north."

"Aye," said Angus. "Safer than with you, I'm thinking."

Delacourt frowned. "I've seen many a Scots lady lying ravished and slain whose men thought she would be safe. I'd not have a moment's peace."

"You are a serving English officer," said Sir Ian. "If you're caught with that cypher they'll visit the whole ghastly traitor's death on you, lad. And her."

Delacourt stared at him, then sat down again. "Lord God!" he muttered.

XVI

All day the men were busied at the various tasks set them, several working on the nets Delacourt had asked for, these being woven from unravelled plaids and any materials they could lay their hands on. One of the fugitives was a talented whittler and from scraps of wood he had fashioned a set of spillikins. That evening, Delacourt, Crowley, Prudence, and Briley played the simple game, with many problems on their minds at first, but at the end thoroughly enjoying themselves. Quite a crowd gathered to watch, and soon there was some reckless betting under way, the items wagered ranging from valuable commodities such as a more comfortable place to sleep, or a comb, to vast sums of money that none of the participants possessed. Crowley won the last game, but Briley became the richest among them, with a paper 'fortune' valued at approximately a million Scots pounds.

It had been some time since Prudence had so enjoyed herself. Many eyes were on her laughing little face and shapely figure, and when she agreed to sing for them, an expectant hush fell. She was lifted to the table so that all could see, Jock Eldredge put paper to comb to provide her 'accompaniment,' and there, with the torches flaring in their brackets and the battle-weary men gathered close about her, she sang the dear songs of memory. No man there that night was ever to forget the scene, and many a fierce heart was so wrung that tears dimmed manly eyes, and throats were choked by nostalgia. When she finished, her gaze was on Delacourt, and he, awe in his thin face, watched her, hoarding his own memories.

There was a long, taut silence. Sir Ian stood and went over to take Prudence's hand and lift it to his lips. "Thank you, dear lady," he said fervently. "You have brought a sweetly feminine touch of gentleness into our troubled lives."

The applause rang out then, so loud and so sustained that Delacourt had to caution them lest even the roar of the falls did not quite drown it. When the shouts died down, he turned to Prudence, smiling, then sobered as his gaze moved past her. He had sought out the former butler as soon as he'd been able to get about again, but Sidley had only stared in stony silence when he'd tried to thank him. Now, the man had made his way through the throng and was glaring at him, hatred plainly written in the narrow face. Delacourt said quietly, "Will you talk to me now?"

Sidley stepped closer, and the ever-watchful Lockerbie moved nearer also, one hand dropping to the dirk at his belt.

"You have many names, sir," said the butler acidly. "Montgomery, Delacourt, Delavale, Ligun Doone. Luckily, I know your real name." Without warning, he spat in Delacourt's face. "Filthy traitor," he snarled. And as he was seized and dragged, struggling, into the distant cave, he screamed, "Traitor! Filthy stinking traitor!"

Prudence gripped her hands helplessly, not knowing what to do or say.

His face very white, his eyes blank and expressionless, Delacourt wiped his cheek, then turned and strode quickly to the rear and the dark tunnel that sloped upwards through the rock and where steps had been chiselled so that one could climb to the top of the crag. The men made way for him, a few calling encouragement, but most watching in silence.

Sir Ian said softly, "Go after him, lass. He'll likely need a friend."

Prudence ran. Cole ran after her, lending a hand as she clambered up the steep, rough steps, but turning back at the summit.

She had never been up here, and she was elated by the smell of fresh air before they came to the open. When Cole left her, she was in darkness, but with the lighter glow of the sky ahead. She walked cautiously to the narrow opening in the rock and slipped through. She stood on a broad natural path and she went on, edging around the shrubs and boulders that helped conceal the entrance, emerging into a faerie world where a quarter-moon shed a gentle silvery light over the glen far below, softening the sharp contours of the wild land and making of the distant loch a great mirror.

She did not see Delacourt at first, but a powerfully built Highlander greeted her, warned her to stay back from the edge, and gestured along the path with a faint, knowing grin.

Prudence went on, staying close against the side of the crag. The path wound around, narrowing, and littered with rocks and boulders from the upthrust of granite that soared beside it. Picking her way cautiously, she saw him then, standing with one hand on a giant boulder that blocked further progress, and staring out at the loch. She bit her lip, then moved to his side.

The wild country was more clearly seen here, the burns threading like streaks of silver through deep ravines and tumbling down ragged crags to their rendezvous with the loch. To the north and east rose high peaks, black against the luminous blue-purple of the night sky. Looking that way, Prudence sighed.

Delacourt said, "I am very sure they are safe."

She turned to him, smiling. "How did you know I was here?"

"How could I not know?" He leaned back against the boulder and faced her, then touched the silk of a stray curl with one slim finger. "Prue—have you any idea of how splendid you are?"

"Why? I have done nothing. You are the one who has—"

"To thank you for your unselfish care, your endless kindness, your unfailing lack of complaint. Do you know how much your presence here has meant to these poor devils?"

"Why, I suppose—"

"To me, especially?"

Experiencing a singular difficulty in the simple business of drawing a breath, she stammered, "I—if I was able to—to help, it was only—"

He turned her chin. She looked up into eyes that were soft wells of tenderness. "Foolish child," he murmured. And kissed her.

It was a long kiss, gentle at first. But then he felt her responding to him, her soft little body pressing closer, and the longing became a flame that swept away all his resolution. He was gasping when he put her from him, and Prudence sagged weakly, convinced that her bones had melted and drained from her body.

"By . . . heaven!" he exclaimed. "Had you forgot we're on a mountain path with a clear drop to the strath, ma'am?"

She laughed unsteadily. "Ye'll mind it was no my doing, sir."

"True. Well, then"—he clasped his hands behind him—"we must be sensible. You have my humblest apologies, Miss MacTavish. I'd not the right to take advantage of you."

"Again," she said demurely.

"Yes. Oh, Prue—if you did but know how I have—er, I mean—yes."

"For a convalescent, you've a remarkable pair of arms, Captain. Faith, but I think I've one or two ribs not crushed."

Eyes gleaming, he leaned to her. "Then I will try to—" But at the last instant, with her lips a breath away, he gave a gasp and drew back. "No, by God! This is wrong, Prue."

She said with a twinkle, "Indeed but you are become something strait-laced, I think."

He grinned. "Acquit me of that! Only you've been swept into an insane existence these past three weeks. You are far from family and friends. Unprotected by your men. I'd be a sorry rogue to capitalize on your helplessness."

She watched his strong profile silhouetted against the sky. As usual, Lockerbie had brushed his hair severely back, and as usual the unruly curls were creeping into disorder again. Longing to tidy them, she murmured, "I was not far from my family in the shed when first we went to see the Monster. But you gave me a—er, I think you said 'twas a token o' your esteem."

"Good gracious, ma'am! I'd fancied you would have forgot that naughty interlude."

"I think I will never forget it."

He looked at her for a long silent moment, then turned away. "You heard what Sidley named me," he said sternly. "Others—many others—would think as he thinks."

She frowned. "Did you bring me out here to talk of Sidley?"

He smiled at her. "I did not bring you, little rascal. But I'm glad you came, because I must be away, Prue."

"Are you strong enough?" she said eagerly. "You seem much improved, I'll own, but if you mean to make for Loch nan Uamh, 'tis a long, hard journey."

In her excitement her hand had closed on his arm. He put his own hand over hers and said, "I am so much better that I feel no anxiety on that score. It is only—only hard to—say goodbye."

Stunned and disbelieving, she echoed, "Goodbye? But—but you would not abandon me here? Geoffrey, you *would* not?"

"But I must, m'dear. Briley and Angus and Sir Ian will care for you. And perchance, someday, when all this is done with—"

Her heart cried out, 'Do not leave me! Do not leave me!' But she had her full share of Scottish pride and thus said in a scratchy but controlled voice, "I see. And when do you mean to leave?"

"At dawn."

"Dawn comes early to the roof of Scotland, Captain."

"Yes." He said with less assurance, "I knew you would be angry. I—"

"I am not angry." She thought, 'My heart is breaking, is all.'

"I was going to leave and say nothing. But I could not. Prue—" His grip on her hand tightened. "You have been so good. I am very grateful."

"Thank you." He was grateful. But not so grateful as to take her with him. She pulled away and started down the path.

He knew he should let her go, but somehow he was running to catch her arm and pull her to him. With his hands on her shoulders, he said, "You know how Ligun Doone is sought—the reward on my head is—"

"There is thirty thousand pounds on Prince Charles' head," she interrupted fiercely. "Dead or alive! And no Highlander has made one move tae collect a single groat o' the filthy blood money!"

"Prince Charles is a Scot, Prue." He put up a quick hand to stifle her angry response. "No—hear me. I know your people are grateful, though in truth I did precious little. The thing is, six hundred guineas in a poor man's eyes is almost as vast a sum as thirty thousand. And a Sassenach, however well thought of, is still a Sassenach. Do you not see? The temptation would be so much greater in my case."

A small corner of her mind whispered that he spoke truly, and another voice urged, 'Don't be a fool! He doesn't want you! Don't beg!' But she could not stop herself. "Is it the gold, Captain? You were free with your kisses, but when all's said and done, I'm just a Scots lassie—not sufficiently well born, I collect for you to—to show off to your Southron friends." And because she was so bitterly grieved, she added, "I fancy your proud sister would despise me."

He lowered his hands and stood very still. "I expect," he said quietly, "you are right at that, m'dear."

Shocked, she stared at his darkly handsome countenance.

His eyes were stern now, his mouth unsmiling. With a muffled sob she turned and sped down the path towards the cavern.

Delacourt walked to the edge and looked blindly northwards. It was, after all, better this way. He sighed heavily, then tensed, staring.

From a high place not too far distant, a little light winked. . . .

Love, thought Prudence, was a horrid emotion. Before she had laid eyes on the sensitive, fine-boned face of Geoffrey Delacourt, she had been a happy girl. She sniffed, and wiped the heel of a grubby hand across her tearful eyes. Since she had met that high-in-the-instep, inflexible, cruel (adored) Sassenach, she seemed to spend more time weeping than she ever had done in her entire life. She blinked around her small 'room.' How ineffably lonely and cold it seemed now. Geoffrey, Lockerbie, and Cole were gone this hour and more. Thaddeus Briley had been very kind, comforting the sorrow she had fancied she was concealing, trying to make her laugh with droll tales of his adventures with Cumberland in Holland before he had been wounded and sent home. And, because she knew his own heart was heavy, she had appreciated his efforts the more.

It had all happened so fast. The lookouts had reported a large troop of dragoons moving in this direction. Sir Ian had said worriedly that they were likely heading for the Western Sea because Prince Charles was now widely believed to have taken that route. Once the soldiers passed, there would be little chance of getting through, for if Loch nan Uamh was their destination, the approaches would be sealed off tighter than a drum and, with Fort William a deadly menace at the head of Loch Linnhe and troops spread thick as fleas on a fox from Loch Eil to Glenfinnan, Delacourt would have no hope of escape to the south.

Three of the sturdy little Highland ponies they called garrons had been saddled; Delacourt had primed and loaded his pistols and buckled on his sword; his two servants had armed themselves to the teeth, and the other fugitives, glum and silent to see their 'luck' depart, had watched them mount up.

Delacourt had turned briefly towards Prudence. Despite the knife in her breast, she had somehow managed a smile. It had not been returned. His face expressionless, he had guided his mount on. Just before he disappeared around the bend of the tunnel, he had reined up and turned back. Sitting very straight in the saddle, he'd called, "God be with you all," then swung up his arm in salute. Angus Fraser had shouted, "Highlanders—up!" and every man capable of it had stood at stiff attention. Someone had cried, "Gie him a yell, lads!" The response had been immediate, the Scots cry rising from upwards of fifty throats. Delacourt had waved and ridden off without so much as another glance at Prudence.

She pushed back her plaids and stood. It was no use lying there with the miseries. She knew from experience that unless she got up and busied herself with something, her thoughts would churn around for hours and, however she might try to direct them into cheerful channels, the chances were that she would merely become deeper sunk in gloom. She walked to her 'curtain' and pulled the plaids aside.

Most of the men had already composed themselves to slumber, but a drowsy discussion was still under way by the fire. She recognized Angus Fraser and was starting towards him when she saw that a man lay practically at her feet. She drew back, shocked to discover that it was Stuart MacLeod, his claymore unsheathed beside him.

When he knew she had seen him he stood, moving with grace despite his size. He said nothing, standing with eyes downcast, waiting.

Prudence said haughtily, "I would prefer that you sought another resting place."

He shook his head.

"Then I shall ask Mr. Fraser to see to it."

"No use. Hissel' told me tae guard ye. I'll guard ye."

Her heartbeat quickening, she said, "Do you mean Captain Delacourt?" And when he nodded, she asked, "Why should you obey his commands when you all but killed him?"

The shaggy head ducked lower. He said, his voice muffled, "D'ye think I wouldnae ha' struck off me right hand sooner than cause him grief?" Anguished blue eyes lifted to meet her cold stare. "Lady—I'd gie him me life did he but ask."

"Why?"

He looked down again, and said slowly, "Me brother fell at Falkirk, and me father was sore wounded at Prestonpans. He's no a well man, even now. After Culloden Moor, with Butcher Cumberland's animals burning and killing, I feared fer me mother and sisters, wi' only me father tae guard 'em. I went back. I got home so quick as I could, but—" He shrugged. "It was done. Our croft—burned tae the ground and the stock shot. Even those they'd nae use fer, they slaughtered."

"And your family?"

"Gone. I didnae dare tae think what had become o' the women. I sought and sought, and at last I heard. Doone had been oot one night—which he shouldnae ha done, ye'll mind—and he'd seen a wee hoose burning and the women ravished and murdered. The soldiers, drunk, were riding towards our croft. Doone sent the man wi' him tae warn my father while he drew the redcoats off. It meant leaving hissel' wi' none fer protection, but he did it, wi' all the redcoats howling after him. His mon got tae me pa in time, and me family's safe away where they'll no be harmed. But for—but for hissel' I'd hae lost them all, y'ken. I hate all redcoats. I'd fought Delavale, or Delacourt as he calls hissel', at Prestonpans. When I saw him here . . . I thought . . ." He groaned. "God forgive me! If I'd but known, but I was sae sure he was a spy."

Prudence asked after a minute, "Does Captain Delacourt know this?"

He shook his head. "I tried tae tell him, but when he looks

at me and—and I see the bruises I put on him. . . ." He finished brokenly, "och—I canna say—a worrud."

Touched, she could not find it in her heart to continue to blame him, and said kindly, "Even so, he must know, else he'd no have asked ye to guard me. I suppose you were the one gave us the extra food." He did not answer, but his broad face flamed. In view of his great size, Prudence could only marvel at his resolution. "You must be nigh starved," she said.

He made a swift, impatient gesture. "'Twas naught. Naught! He shouldnae hae made me bide. He'll get hissel' killed, sure as sure."

Prudence said uneasily, "Lockerbie brought him all the way up here from Prestonpans, when he was very ill. He's much better now, and they've a very short way to go, by comparison. I do not see—"

"Lockerbie had tae deal wi' angry Scots, I'll no deny. But no wi' the like as follow the Captain the noo." He glowered at the little worn slipper that peeped from under Prudence's frayed gown, and muttered, "He should've let me be wi' him."

She regarded him frowningly, then bade him come into her tiny chamber and sit down. When she had seated herself on the bed, he perched on the edge of the chair with shy reluctance, twisting his bonnet nervously between his great hands.

"Who follows Captain Delacourt?" she asked. "Cunningham's men? The lookouts will warn him if that is so."

"Not Cunningham's men, lady. The Butcher's, maybe."

Her heart jumped. "You frighten me. What do you mean? Who are they?"

"I dinna ken. I tried tae tell hissel', but all he'd say was that I was tae let nothing happen tae ye." He glanced at her scared, lovely face, and muttered a bashful, "Not as I blame him fer that, whatever. But the lookouts will nae be able tae warn him once he's past these hills."

"How do you know they follow him? Why did you not tell Sir Ian or Lord Briley, if that was so?"

"I heard that there was an ugly lot hanging aboot Castle

Court, and that they'd been asking fer a dark-haired Englishman who'd been staying wi' the lady. I dinna connect an Englishman wi' Ligun Doone, and thought nae more aboot it. But one o' them was described tae me verrra close, because he wore a strange sort of tunic 'stead o' a coat. I passed him wi' several others i' the Great Glen. They dinna see me, y'ken, fer I heard 'em coming, but I'll tell ye, mistress, I'd nae care tae tangle wi' 'em!"

Her eyes wide and terrified, she whispered, "What d'ye mean? What kind of tunic? Was it of leather and like patchwork?"

"Aye! Ye've seen him, also?"

"The night our home was attacked there was a man like that in the stables. Oh! We must tell Angus and Sir Ian."

"I tried tae tell 'em," he said glumly. "But they'll no listen. They said Captain Delacourt had his mon and his groom, and that he'd get through."

She wrung her hands. If she went to Angus or Sir Ian and told them that her aunt's 'stars' had warned of the man in the leathern tunic, they'd likely think her ripe for Bedlam. She said, "Then you must go after him."

He shook his head. "I canna do that, lady. Hissel' charged me tae guard ye. I'll no break me given worrud."

"Och, ye great looby," she cried, springing up and stamping her little foot at him. "Would ye see him murdered because o' yer stupid oath?"

He blinked and stood also. "Dinna fash ye'sel'. I'm likely borrowing trouble as they said."

"You're not! I tell ye, you're *not!*" She tried to think of a way to convince him, but nothing sensible came to mind. In desperation she cried, "My aunt is very learned in—in the stars. She was warned of a man in a multi-coloured leathern tunic who brought death tae one o' our hoosehold."

The MacLeod's bronzed features paled. Behind his back, he crooked the first two fingers of his right hand. "Is—is y'r aunty a witch, mistress?"

With a mental apology to Hortense, Prudence confirmed this. "But a very kind witch, you understand," she qualified.

Logic might fail with Stuart MacLeod, but witches he understood, having been overlooked by one in his youth and having suffered the measles as a result. "Maybe I can persuade the Fraser," he muttered, turning to take up his great claymore.

"There is no need to persuade him," said Prudence. "Simply tell him you must leave. Do you know this country? Can you come up with Captain Delacourt, do you think?"

"I know it like the back o' me hand. But I canna leave ye."

"You'll not leave me. I shall travel with you."

His jaw dropped. "Ye canna be seerious? 'Tis hard country for a mon, fer all I ken every track and shortcut frae here tae Loch nan Uamh."

"Can we ride?"

"By my roads, lady, we could ride a wee bit, but there are places we'd need tae lead even a garron."

"And you have your own garron?"

"Aye. But I canna take two, ye ken."

"Go and get it saddled. There's no reason you cannot leave here if you wish to."

He said mulishly, "I'll *nae* leave ye here wi' this wild pack, when hissel' ordered me tae guard ye; and Angus wouldnae let ye go wi' me, anyway."

Clenching her small hands with frustration, she gritted, "I'm well aware. So get your things, and I'll meet you in the tunnel. They're almost all asleep. Oh, hurry, hurry! Every minute we waste may be vital!"

MacLeod shook his head determinedly. He was doomed, of course, and in the end, did as she bade him.

Prudence clung to the stirrup of the little pony and trudged on mechanically, looking only at the path beneath her feet, for long ago she had learned that to see their way was to invite paralyzing terror.

The journey had gone on endlessly, MacLeod leading the way with his long tireless stride, and the path often becoming so steep that—as was now the case—she was obliged to walk also. Her feet felt swollen to twice their size, and she could only be grateful for the brogues he had provided her. They were so much too large that she'd been able to slip her feet into them complete with slippers, but she knew that without them what was left of those dainty evening slippers would have been in rags by this time.

It had been dark when they'd left the cavern. She had drifted into the tunnel, unobserved, and MacLeod had come very soon. None had attempted to stay them. The guards at the waterfall had accepted his statement that they were going to try to get through to Moidart, where friends would shelter them, but had cautioned against soldiers who were now a scant mile or so to the east. MacLeod had set off at once, and it seemed to Prudence that he had scarcely stopped since, only once or twice leaving her in the shelter of some tree or outcropping while he clambered up to where he could search for patrols.

She had no idea of how many hours they had travelled, nor of how far they had come. The going was incredibly difficult, for MacLeod's way was dangerous and almost impossible at times, and few travellers would have attempted it. At the end of the first hour she was convinced she could take not another step, only the thought of Delacourt enabling her to go on. At last, MacLeod said she could ride again, and carefully lifted her into the saddle. She rode astride, her full skirts enabling her to do so, and she wasted not a second upon qualms for such improper behaviour. In this way she was enabled to lean forward against the garron's mane and at times to doze off. When MacLeod woke her from one of these slumbers she could have wept, but she allowed him to help her dismount and forced her poor feet to tread bravely, reminding herself that she had insisted upon coming and that, whatever else, she must not prove a hindrance to their coming up with Geoffrey. The way levelled off at last and she could ride again. She was somewhere between sleep and waking when she heard MacLeod swear and lifted her head wearily.

Where they were she did not know, but they journeyed along a high ridge and far below a croft was burning. It seemed to her that she heard a shot and then a woman screaming. She had seen many burned-out dwellings since Culloden but this was the first time she had actually seen the flames and been so close to suffering and terror and death. She felt faint with horror and threw her hands over her eyes. "God help them," she whispered.

MacLeod growled, "Amen tae that, mistress," and led the pony on.

All too soon the way became steep again. MacLeod lifted Prudence down and peered anxiously into her tired little face. "Be ye all right, mistress? We've come a far piece, but there's a'many long miles yet."

"I am . . . perfectly able to go on," she said staunchly, her voice sounding reedy and distant. "You—you must be a deal more tired than I."

"No, lady. I can carry ye, if—"

Her chin lifted. "I am a MacTavish," she said, and stepped out bravely. With that first step she almost fell, for her feet seemed so worn away that she was sure she must be treading on stumps. She forced back a sob and made herself keep trying. The first pale light of dawn, streaking the eastern skies, afforded her a glimpse of the path down the crag—so precipitous and rock-strewn a slope that her courage failed her and she dared not look again. She clung tighter to the stirrup and concentrated on one step at a time, and she thought of how proud Delacourt would be when they reached him with their warning.

"MacLeod!" she called suddenly.

The big man was at her side on the instant.

"Where are we?" she demanded.

"Look there, lady."

She turned in the direction of his pointing hand and caught her breath at the beauty of it. The skies were now a clear violet-pink. To the north loomed the rugged peaks. Closer at hand, for as far as she could see, were little ravines and towering crags threaded by the sparkle of waterfalls and the hurrying leap of rushing burns. Here and there a clear slope was gowned in the rich purple of the heather; white wraiths of mist twined lazily from high corries into the still air, and far below a great sheet of blue water spread mile upon mile to left and right of them. It was the loch that sank Prudence into despair. "Och . . ." she wailed tragically, "I had thought we'd come farther than this!"

MacLeod's bushy brows went up. "*Dia,*" he muttered under his breath, and added, "'Tis a hard taskmaster ye are and no doubting, mistress. Come awie, then. And keep yer eyes open if ye will, for we're more like tae be seen now 'tis daybreak, and we must head west, which is verra chancy."

He trotted on, following the general direction of the loch.

Prudence was silent for a while, then asked a puzzled, "Are ye no heading the wrong way, MacLeod? This leads south, surely?"

"West, mistress."

"But Loch Lochy runs southwards, I'd thought."

"Aye. Southwestwards." He glanced around at her, his blue eyes twinkling. "Only, yon's Loch Arkaig, ma'am."

Her heart gave a great leap. With a beam of joy she exclaimed, "Arkaig! Och, then we're doing verra *weell,* MacLeod!"

"Better than twenty miles we've come this night, mistress."

She clapped her hands. "How splendid! Do ye fancy we shall come up with them soon? Shall we be able to see them?"

"Not if Ligun Doone kens what he's aboot. I'm of a mind we've passed them by long since. Nae—never look sae doomstruck. Did I no tell ye I ken this country like the back o' me hand? A sight better nor the Captain and that gowk Lockerbie. All we've tae do is head fer a pass I know of, and wi' luck we'll spot 'em when they come through." He thought he sounded a fine braggart and, embarrassed, closed his lips, took the tired garron's bridle, and led on.

With her first step, Prudence slipped and came down hard, scraping the heel of her hand on the sharp gravel, and bruising her hip. MacLeod rushed back to her, and only then did she notice that he was limping. He had walked and trotted all those twenty miles, over countless rocky slopes and through hundreds of icy burns, with never a complaint, and because he was so big and strong it had failed to occur to her that he was human, too, and not above being hurt and weary. He helped her up, and she made light of her scrapes and hobbled on. She saw him watching her with a grin, and she felt ridiculously pleased that she had won the approval of this young giant whom, a few days ago, she had regarded with such abhorrence.

The sun began to come up as they struggled side by side through a ravine treacherous with shifting shale and littered with boulders from the higher slopes. Prudence was so tired she had to fight to stay awake, and she began to sing softly, every Scottish song she knew, breathless and stumbling and often improvising the words until MacLeod, chuckling, joined in. The songs faded at last, and died away, but her throbbing feet went on. She did not realize she was asleep until a hand on her shoulder woke her. She was still clutching the garron's stirrup, and her forehead was leaning against the tired beast's shoulder. MacLeod swept her up and carried her to a clump of dense shrubs that grew against the rock face. A burn tumbled noisily down the slope close by. She felt the spray of it, cold against her face as the Highlander put her down. He looked pale and exhausted, his eyes ringed with the shadows of fatigue. "We must hide the noo," he said.

"Where?"

He pulled the shrubs aside to reveal a hollow cut where there would be ample room for the two of them and the little pony to lie hidden until dusk. Aching with the need to lie down in that lovely hollowed-out teacup, she mumbled, "What about the poor garron?"

MacLeod said he would water the pony and unsaddle it, then bring it into the hollow. "He can graze frae inside," he said. "Do ye get in and lie ye doon, mistress."

"I shall. After you come." She was adamant, and with a sigh for the pigheadedness of even the best of women, MacLeod went over and stripped the pony of saddle and blanket and led it to the burn. He returned with the expectation of finding the girl asleep in the hollow, but she waited, her shoulder propped against the rock wall and her eyes glazed with weariness. When he had tethered the pony, she said, "Come wi' me," led him to the burn, and commanded, "Sit ye doon. Now dinna argue, mon! Sit ye doon!"

The broad Scots brought a grin to his face and he obeyed wonderingly. She knelt beside him and began to unlace his crude sandals. With a startled exclamation, he wrenched away. For the first time in her life, Prudence gripped a hairy male limb and hung on. Horrified, MacLeod ceased his struggles, but shrank back, peering at her with aghast eyes. "Whatever are ye aboot, lady?" he gulped.

She peeled off his tattered stockings, flinched to see his bruised and blistered feet, and exclaimed, "Oh! Ye poor wee lad!"

MacLeod was very near exhaustion, and the sight of this diminutive girl holding his great foot and calling him a 'wee lad' struck him as so hilarious that he began to chuckle. Glancing up in surprise, Prudence caught his mirth and the two of them sat there laughing—as she said later—like a pair of gormless thimblewits. Wiping tears from her eyes, she instructed him to soak his feet in the burn. He eyed the water dubiously, stuck in one toe, and gave a yelp.

"It will feel better soon," said Prudence.

"Aye—it'll be froze solid," he grumbled.

She turned her back and, commanding him not to look, removed her shoes, slippers, and stockings. Her own feet were not in much better condition than his, but when she shyly immersed them, her breath was snatched away and she whipped her feet back.

MacLeod grinned at her. “It’ll feel better soon,” he said.

XVII

Prudence awoke stiff, cold, and hungry. At some time while she slept MacLeod had spread his plaid over her and she tugged it closer about her chin and snuggled down drowsily. Loud, drunken voices raised in dissension brought her fully to awareness. A dim light filtered in through the branches of the shrubs, and MacLeod crouched by the opening, peering out.

She crept to join him. "Who is it?" she whispered.

"The men I told ye of," he responded as softly. "Anyone coming this way has tae travel through this pass. 'Tis why I thought we'd meet up wi' Mr. Doone here. They've got some Southron—poor chappie."

Her heart pounding, Prudence peeped through the foliage. And there he was, sure enough: the big lout in the strange leathern tunic that was like a rough patchwork quilt. He had a small, cruel mouth, hard eyes, and a sneering, vindictive expression. There were two others of his kind with him: big, crude-looking individuals, wearing dyed plaids so that the tartan was obliterated. All three were sprawled very close by the side of the burn, arguing mildly among themselves, and passing a flask back and forth. To one side, a youthful redcoat, his hands bound before him, was attempting to gather firewood, presumably to heat the contents of an iron pot that hung on a trivet nearby.

Prudence thought worriedly that if they meant to eat, they'd likely be here for some time. She glanced to the garron. It was asleep, head down. If the bounty hunters had horses, they were not within her range of vision, but she thought they must have, to have come all this way.

The young captive stumbled, dropping the branch he was attempting to haul to the site of his fire and, knocking over the trivet, sent the contents of the pot spilling into the dirt. A shout of rage went up from his captors. The bully in the leathern vest got to his feet and fetched the youth a buffet that sent him sprawling. He fell with head and shoulders in the burn, and the Scot laughed and put one large foot on the back of his neck, holding his head under.

Prudence gave a gasp of horror. MacLeod spun around and clapped a hand over her mouth. "There's naught we can do, mistress," he whispered. "And he's only a redcoat, forbye." She struggled angrily, but then the man with the leathern vest removed his foot and bent to haul the half-drowned boy from the water. "Get up, stupid dog's meat," he snarled, kicking his victim savagely. "Now we've tae find more food, damn yer eyes! Get and saddle the garrons."

Coughing and gulping air, the redcoat came to his knees. Prudence saw that he was very young—no more than eighteen or nineteen, she judged—his fair face cruelly marked by cuts and abrasions, but his spirit unbroken as yet, evidently, for he swore feebly at his persecutor. His reward was a kick that doubled him up, and he lay choking and helpless while Prudence shook with rage that a bound prisoner should be so ill-used.

Another man, with greying straggly hair, and a long ragged beard, now clambered to his feet and demanded testily that 'Zeke' stop beating the boy. "If ye kick his ribs in, he'll no be able tae lead us tae Loch nan Uamh," he growled, "and I dinna ken the way, nor I doot we'd get much help frae the crofters hereaboots, if they're as loyal tae Doone as yon fools we questioned last night."

The third bounty hunter, a pallid, shifty-eyed man with long twitching hands and hunched shoulders, stood and wandered out of Prudence's sight. "They'll no forget us in a hurry, Jem, lad," he jeered.

"Mur-derers!" croaked the young trooper, with valour if not wisdom. "Is that . . . how you mean to serve this . . . poor fellow you . . . seek?"

The pallid man came back to bend over him. "Doone will be lucky if we come up wi' him first—he'll die quick. If the military get their hands on him, it's the Tower, where they'll put him tae the question, fer he likely knows a deal o' that fool Stuart. And when he's nigh dead they'll stop kindly fer rope and block, wi' his head saved fer Tower Bridge! We do the laddie a favour, y'ken." He seized the boy's dishevelled fair hair, and hauled. "Up wi' ye. We'd as well get on, since ye've spoiled our dinner, ye perishin' clod."

Prudence closed her eyes and did not move until the sound of hooves and the coarse voices began to face. She peered out then. They were making their way along the ravine, the prisoner at the end of a rope, staggering after them. "Poor lad," she whispered.

MacLeod said, "Are ye able tae go on now, lady? As soon as yon fine gentlemen are clear, we can leave."

"How could they?" she asked, raising appalled eyes to his face. "They were Scots, yet they cared neither for Ligun Doone nor Prince Charles. And to so brutalize that helpless lad . . ."

MacLeod grunted. "Did ye fancy cruelty spoke only wi' an English accent, mistress? The deeds done by clan tae clan would make St. Peter weep, I reckon. Especially the bloody Campbells—black be their fall!" He went, muttering, to the garron and began to saddle up the sleepy animal.

Prudence slipped cautiously outside. To judge by the position of the sun it was mid-afternoon. There were clouds building above, and a cool wind tossed the tops of the few aspens and pines scattered along the ravine. The bounty hunters and their hapless prisoner were far off, but she stayed in the screening shrubs until they should be out of sight. Just before they turned the last bend, she saw the captive fall. There came the faint sound of a laugh and they spurred their horses so that the boy could not regain his feet and was dragged ruthlessly. Tears of rage and helplessness blurred her eyes as she crept from her hiding place and went to the burn to wash. There was no sign of MacLeod when she returned to the hollow, and she supposed he had gone off to attend to his own needs. The garron was saddled and chewing placidly on the shrubs at the entrance. Prudence put on her cloak, did her best to tidy her hair, and went outside again. She heard a pebble roll behind her and turned about, a smile ready for MacLeod. The smile died. The ravine seemed to tilt and her head spun.

Geoffrey Delacourt, leading Braw Blue, stood staring at her in speechless astonishment, Lockerbie and Cole, equally astounded, behind him.

"Geoffrey!" she cried, and flung herself into his arms. Briefly, those arms tightened about her. She heard him breathe her name, and one hand pressed her head closer against him. Then, she was pulled back.

"What the *devil* are you doing here?" His voice was harsh, his dark brows meeting in a scowl of anger.

Indignant, she wrenched away. "To bring you a message! Though much you—"

"Captain!" MacLeod scrambled down the opposite bank, his broad features alight with joy. "I hoped ye'd come up wi' us!"

Mindful of this man's initial reaction to his master, Lockerbie swung up the musket he carried and held it pointed steadily at MacLeod's middle.

Delacourt pushed the long barrel aside and strode to face MacLeod, his jaw set and grim. "*You* brought her? Damn your eyes—are ye daft? This is no country for a woman, much less a lady of quality!"

MacLeod's head sank. "I know," he mumbled. "I know, sir.

But—whisht, the lady wouldnae have it otherwise, and I *had* tae reach ye, sir."

Delacourt tossed a glare at Prudence's saintly martyrdom. "Why?"

"Because you are being followed by murdering cutthroats," Prudence put in. "Do ye not recall what Aunty Mac had to say aboot the man wearing the strange coat?"

He stared at her with stark incredulity. "Great heavens! Do you say that you came all this perilous distance because of that nonsensical—"

"He was in the stables at Lakepoint," she hurried on. "You'll recollect I told ye I'd seen him?"

"He's after ye the noo, master," said MacLeod earnestly. "I saw him also, on General Wade's Road. And he was here but a minute syne. He's following ye, sir. And two more o' his like wi' him—all mean as mad dogs."

"I've Lockerbie and Cole to side me, and I think we are not helpless! I charged you with the care of Miss MacTavish. She was safe in the cavern, and—"

"She wasnae safe, sir," said MacLeod quietly. "I didnae tell the lady, fer I'd no wish tae add tae her miseries. After ye left, the scouts reported redcoats on the move. Scores of 'em. All making straight for the wee glen. Angus Fraser had it in his mind we'd been betrayed, and was preparing tae wake the men and see if they couldnae slip away over the top o' the crag."

Delacourt gave a groan of exasperation. "Madness! One can but hope he did not yield to it! The troopers are likely moving this way because your Prince is believed to have been sighted heading for the Western Sea. I've no doubt the soldiers will pass right by the cavern and never suspect any of our people are there." He turned a fuming glance on Prudence. "Only look at the poor girl! All mud and tatters and looking as if she's been dragged through a gooseberry bush!"

"Well! Of all the ingrates!" Prudence drew herself up, seething with resentment. "We risked life and limb, struggled straight up mountains and all but fell doon t'other sides! Cut our poor feet to shreds for your sake and all you can say is—"

"Thank you," he intervened, gripping her shoulders and smiling warmly at her. "Poor little lass. I am an ingrate, indeed! But—my apologies, m'dear—I cannot dawdle about here, else we'll never come up with our quarry."

"Quarry . . . ? Did ye no hear us warn ye that you're being stalked?"

He glanced at MacLeod. "Lift the lady into my saddle, if you please." He added, "You're mistaken, ma'am. *We* follow *them*, not t'other way around."

"Follow—*them?*" she said stupidly, settling her skirts and taking the reins he handed up to her.

"Yes. And a fortunate happenstance that we did, else we'd likely have missed you. Have you a pony, MacLeod? We must hasten."

"There is not the need to follow them," said Prudence. "The MacLeod knows this country exceeding well, Captain. He can guide us safely to Loch nan Uamh, never fear."

"Since you beat us here although we'd left ahead of you, I cannot doubt that." He set one foot in the stirrup and swung up behind her. "Let's go as quietly as may be. They're half drunk, but I'd as lief they not hear us coming. Cole, do you slip out ahead and act as scout for us."

Cole nodded and urged his garron past.

"Delacourt," said Prudence, craning her neck around so as to look up at him, "do ye never listen tae what people try tae tell ye?"

He tightened his arm around her, his dark eyes twinkling into hers in a most disarming way. "Yes, m'dear. But I do not follow those animals for want of a way to Loch nan Uamh."

"The captain is at his rescuing again, mistress," said Lockerbie dryly.

Prudence gave a gasp. "*What?* Geoffrey, are ye quite daft?

These hills swarm with troopers. You must not risk your life for the sake of that poor boy."

He slapped the reins against Braw Blue's neck. "I have risked it for your people, ma'am. I will not now leave one of my own to be murdered by those carrion."

Admiring his courage, and fearing for his safety, she cried, "You would rather they murdered me, I suppose?"

"I had rather you would stay in the little cave. Perhaps that would be best, and we could come back for you—unless we all perish in this attempt."

He made as if to check the big grey, and Prudence dug her nails into his wrist. "Do not *dare!*" she hissed.

They caught sight of the bounty hunters ten minutes later. The three Scots were riding at an easy trot, quarrelling apparently, for the man called Zeke suddenly leaned over to cuff his companion and earned a furious snarl of curses in response. Their captive staggered along behind, but as the pursuing group drew near, he went down again, and struggled feebly to regain his feet.

Delacourt swore under his breath.

MacLeod murmured softly, "What d'ye wish we should do, sir?"

"We canna shoot, Captain," warned Lockerbie, eyeing the big Highlander with dislike. "Gunfire will bring redcoats—certain."

Cole, who had waited for them, said, "They've spotted a farm up ahead, sir. I think they're deciding to stop and try to find food there."

"Good. Let's tether the cattle and try to get closer."

Prudence was told severely to stay with the horses, but as the men crept away, she crept after them.

The bounty hunters had dismounted and Zeke was bending over the huddled figure of the trooper. "He's alive," he growled, "but I doot he'll gie us any jaw fer a bit."

The one they called Jem walked over to join his crony. "Best tie him."

Delacourt whispered, "They're all together. We can move now, though we'd do better with a diversion."

"You shall have one," said Prudence, and before any of them could stay her, she was running down the path in full view of the bounty hunters. "*Help!*" she screamed. "Oh—help me, please!"

They reacted as one man, crouching, ready for combat, weapons springing to their hands. Zeke levelled a musket unerringly at Prudence.

Her heart quailing, she ran on, stretching forth her hands. "Redcoats came tae our croft," she gasped. "I'm lost the noo. Will ye no help me?"

They straightened, grins appearing on three savage faces as they took in the youth and beauty of the girl who approached.

Zeke set down his musket. "Where'd ye get that pretty frock, lassie?"

"Come ye here," invited Jem. "We'll take good care o' ye."

Chuckling, but his eyes hungry, the pallid man slid his dirk back in its scabbard.

The young redcoat pulled himself to one elbow. "Run, miss," he croaked weakly. "Run before they—"

Zeke levelled him with a well-placed kick. "Quiet," he said redundantly. "We know how tae deal wi' Sassenachs, as ye can see, lass. Come here."

Prudence hesitated and, appearing uncertain, edged back against the cliff and crept along abreast of the three who watched her, gloating. "Ye—ye *are* all good Scots?" she quavered.

"Och, awie! We're awfu' good," asserted the pallid man, drawing guffaws from his companions.

They began to advance on her. From the corner of her eye she could see Delacourt and the others creeping up. The three bounty hunters were coming closer and, as if suddenly taking fright, she ran past them.

They were after her in a flash, their concerted lunge affording MacLeod, who had climbed to a point above them, the opportunity he needed. The net he had fashioned in response to Delacourt's orders soared out and down. Three would-be rapists found themselves caught in a clinging, strong, and weighted mesh. Their lustful whoops became shouts of rageful bewilderment. These were not simple fighting men, however, but hardened assassins, seasoned by countless desperate forays. Zeke's dirk flashed and the net was ripped apart, his sword seeming to leap into his other hand. His own weapon ready, Delacourt sprang to the attack, while Cole drove a fist into the snarling face of the pallid man, and Lockerbie, slight beside the bulk of the bearded Jem, fought with grim ferocity.

The pallid man staggered, recovered, and drove his club in a savage jab under Cole's ribs. Cole gasped and doubled up, the pallid man's dirk darted, and Cole fell, clutching his arm. The pallid man leapt over him to swell the attack on Delacourt. Hard-pressed, Delacourt's sword sang down Zeke's blade in a glizade that sent the bounty hunter's weapon spinning from his hand, but the pallid man sent the heavy cudgel whistling at his head and he had to jump desperately to avoid it. In the same instant, Zeke flung up his dirk and sprang at Delacourt. The descending cudgel caught him fairly on the shoulder. Screaming profanities, he reeled, the pallid man gawking at him in dismay. Simultaneously, Lockerbie was clubbed down. The triumphant Jem looked up to discover a steel blade flashing at him, a grim face beyond it. He jerked away, but Delacourt lunged to the full length of his arm and Jem howled and fell. Disengaging, Delacourt spun, knowing the pallid man was behind him. The flying cudgel that would have brained him struck home glancingly, and he was down, the glen wheeling crazily.

A Highland war cry roared out, and Stuart MacLeod, charging down the slope, cried, "Ye shouldnae ha' done that, mon!" The pallid man, his dirk upraised to plunge at Delacourt, was seized from behind, swept up, shrieking, and hurled at the advancing Zeke. They went down like ninepins, but Zeke rolled and was up again. Dizzy but persisting, Delacourt took up a rock and smashed it onto Zeke's foot. Zeke hopped and howled.

MacLeod unleashed a sledgehammer uppercut. Zeke did three fast and fancy backward toe steps and went down like a falling tree. Jem was quite *hors de combat,* but the pallid man was floundering about feebly. MacLeod silenced him with one chopping blow to the base of the neck.

Trembling, Prudence flew to kneel beside Delacourt. His temple was red and bruising, but he grinned lopsidedly at her. MacLeod came over, and Delacourt held up one hand and was hoisted to his feet. "Is the enemy . . . secure, for the . . . time being?" he asked, swaying rather uncertainly.

"Verra secure, sir," said MacLeod with a chuckle.

Delacourt turned to Prudence. "Thank you, my sturdy Amazon. Would you please see to poor Cole?"

After another anxious scan of his face, she hurried to do what she might for the groom.

Delacourt and MacLeod went to Lockerbie, who was sitting up, holding his head and swearing softly. Aside from a large lump above his ear, he did not seem badly hurt, and assured them he would be able to travel "in two shakes o' a lamb's tail." Delacourt set MacLeod to truss up the bounty hunters and bind Jem's wound, then, retrieving one of the fallen dirks, turned his attention to the young captive. The boy was sitting up looking considerably the worse for wear, but watching him jubilantly.

"Sir," he said, as Delacourt dropped to one knee beside him, "I don't know who you are, but—God bless you! I thought I was finished!"

"They have not treated you with loving kindness," Delacourt observed, sawing through the ropes that bound the boy's hands. "How were they able to detach you from your troop?"

The light went out of the young face. "I—er, well, I was alone, sir. You're English, I think?"

"Yes." Delacourt unwound the severed rope and introduced himself, omitting his rank, but adding, "We'll not be able to escort you back to your regiment, I fear." He saw the betraying rush of colour that stained the battered features, and added quietly, "If you mean to rejoin your regiment, that is."

MacLeod came up and stood watching. The boy was silent, his eyes lowered.

"May we know your name?" asked Delacourt.

The response was muffled. "Percy Nelson."

MacLeod rumbled, "Sir, are ye well? That was a woundy ding ye took fer this ungrateful whelp."

"I am not ungrateful!" The fair head lifted, the grey eyes glaring resentment. "Only I think I've seen you before, sir. At Prestonpans. And you're a Captain?"

"You're right, by Jove! What a memory."

"Why, I saw you in action, sir." He sighed, then went on in a hopeless voice, "I suppose—if I have to be arrested, I'd as soon you were the one to do it."

MacLeod gave a contemptuous snort.

Delacourt said, "A deserter, are you?"

Meeting his eyes, Nelson said wretchedly, "Not because I was afraid, if that's what you're thinking! I served through Prestonpans and that awful massacre at Culloden. I thought it was done then." His eyes slid away to stare at Prudence, who was washing her hands in a nearby rivulet. "I didn't realize," he muttered, half to himself. "I joined up to serve my country. I wasn't afraid to fight. But—God! I did not join to murder helpless women and babes. Or . . ." He closed his eyes as though to shut out images too horrible to contemplate. "My God! If I must be shot for deserting Butcher Cumberland, then shoot me now and be done with it!" He looked up at Delacourt with desperate pleading. "Go on, sir! It would be kinder than—than to send me back to disgrace and execution."

"Well, MacLeod," said Delacourt gravely, "what d'you think of that?"

"I'm nae a gert thinker, sir. Whatever ye say is enough fer me. Now and hence." His colour heightened as Delacourt darted a surprised glance at him, but he said doggedly, "Sae long as I do live, sir."

"What's all this?" said Delacourt. "Here, give me a hand up, will you?"

At once MacLeod's strong arm was hoisting him to his feet. His head ached and he was dizzied for an instant.

Watching him as she secured the knot of the makeshift bandage about Cole's arm, Prudence called, "Ye've done too much! You're not well enough to—"

"Well enough? Little lass, I am so well I scarce can believe it!" He gripped the brawny hand on his arm and said intensely, "Stuart MacLeod, if you are still remorseful because you knocked me down, pray know that wallop you gave me saved my life. No, man! I am not mad—I mean it. Truly, I do not know how to thank you."

MacLeod glanced at Prudence and stammered, "Nay, sir. I ken ye're kindly seekin' tae ease me mind, but—"

"The devil I am! It is so, I tell you. I always knew my wound was not healing properly. It became more and more of a nuisance, with the feeling that something tight and sharp was bound through my chest. My doctor had implied I would not—well, that it was only a matter of time. When I came round after you grassed me, it took a few days to realize the tightness was gone. Now, Lord, if you could but know how grand it is to feel well! To feel my strength coming back. You've given me back my health, you great looby! *Now* will you believe me?" He put out his hand and said rather unsteadily, "And allow me to thank you."

MacLeod hesitated, then shyly he took Delacourt's hand. "If 'tis as ye say, I couldnae be more grateful. But were it not for Ligun Doone, I'd ha' lost me whole family, I dinna doot. There's no way ye can be rid o' me, lest—"

"*Ligun . . . Doone . . . ?*" gasped Nelson, who had managed to get to his knees and had been watching this exchange with growing excitement. "Sir? Captain, never say *you* are Ligun Doone?"

MacLeod groaned and clapped a hand over his unguarded lips.

"Oh, dear," sighed Delacourt.

Lockerbie came up, a fierce scowl on his pale face and his

musket aimed at the young trooper. "Great loose-mouthed gowk," he snarled, glaring at MacLeod. "Now we've tae kill the lad!"

"Absolutely not!" said Delacourt sharply.

"If 'tis a matter o' the Sassenach's life or yours, sir," said MacLeod, "ye must stop and think there's the reward, y'ken."

"As if I would touch it," said Nelson, indignant. "And how could I claim it? I'm a deserter."

Worried, Prudence interjected, "You could send your kinfolks to claim it when the Captain let you go."

"Well, you may be sure I would not!" Nelson struggled to his feet only to hop painfully, and sink down again. "Sir," he said desperately, "I give you my oath! You cannot know how *glad* I am. To think Ligun Doone is English and has done so much of good. I'll *never* betray you!"

"Easy said." Cole came up to join them, his face haggard and Prudence's impromptu bandage already showing a red stain. "Your ugly friends are stirring about, sir. 'Tis past time we was on our way."

Delacourt turned to survey the vanquished. "What in the deuce are we to do with the clods?"

Nelson said, "Sir, if you'd seen what I have, you'd do the world a favour and shoot them out of hand."

The other men voiced their approval of these sentiments, but Delacourt shook his head. "Likely you're right, but I do not fancy the role of executioner. I wish to God I could hand 'em over to a military tribunal."

"One of Cumberland's appointing?" Prudence said a mocking, "Hah!"

The end of it was that Delacourt ordered Stuart MacLeod to strip the bounty hunters of all weapons and valuables, gag them, and dump them in the hollow. And with a thought to his own sore heels, he added, "And remove their shoes!"

It was dusk as they resumed their interrupted journey, MacLeod far out in front; Nelson, mounted on one of their appropriated horses, behind him; Delacourt and Prudence following; and Lockerbie and Cole bringing up the rear.

XVIII

For several miles the little band travelled in silence, every ear stretched for sounds of other riders. When it became necessary that they lead the horses, they were a sorry lot, Lockerbie's broken head causing him to become so dizzied at times that Cole, himself weakened, would have to steady him, and MacLeod more or less carrying young Nelson, whose right leg was so badly bruised he could scarcely endure to set foot to ground. Delacourt's head pounded unremittingly, but it was so trifling a discomfort compared with the misery he had now escaped that he scarcely heeded it. His main concern was for Prudence. She struggled on gamely, but with each mile the way seemed to become more difficult, and for all of them fatigue was a daunting enemy. His arm about Prudence, Delacourt glanced up at the fearsome pass they must ascend and paused, dreading to subject the girl to such a climb.

Nelson saw his face and peered upward also. "Holy Christ!" he gasped. "Sir—you're never bound for Loch nan Uamh?"

"We are. Do you know the area?"

"I know it well, and I know also that it fairly bristles with troops. They think the Young Pretender—"

"D'ye mean Prince Charles Edward Stuart?" demanded MacLeod, angrily.

"Well, of course that's who I mean! Who else could—"

"Never mind," said Delacourt. "What do they think about the Prince?"

"That he sailed for the Isles, but is coming back with another army and will land at Loch nan Uamh. Sir, if you go there, your life will not be worth a groat! If those bounty hunters knew who you were—"

"They *knew* me?" asked Delacourt, coming level with MacLeod and halting, his arm still supporting the wilting Prudence. "Do you mean they *knew* I was Ligun Doone?"

"Well, they must have, sir. I heard them speaking of 'settling the Englishman' several times, though I'd no notion then it was you they meant."

MacLeod growled, "We daren't go there, then."

Delacourt said nothing for a moment, then, "*You* could get through, though, and put Miss MacTavish on a boat, perchance?"

"I'll nae creep off alone," declared Prudence, anger returning the spark to her eyes.

"Be still," said Delacourt. "Well, MacLeod?"

"I hae me doots, sir. If the loch is swarming wi' redcoats, every ship will likely be guarded."

"And there is not the need," Nelson put in. "Captain, my aunt married a Scottish gentleman. They've a neat little croft on the coast, not ten miles from here, and my uncle—a very good sort of man—fishes the Sea of the Hebrides, and sometimes sails as far as Ireland. I spent many summers up here. I was trying to reach the croft, in fact, when the bounty hunters got me."

"Whisht," exclaimed Lockerbie, elated. "Does y'r uncle hae his own boat, laddie?"

"Yes. He and my cousins built it themselves, and a right good boat it is. Sturdy, and rigged for ocean travel."

"What a piece of luck we found you, Percy," said Delacourt. "Lead us, then."

Afterwards, Prudence could never summon a clear recollection of that last phase of their ride. She remembered that it was interminable, miserable, and yet holding a very deep and special joy because it seemed her love was reprieved and would, with God's mercy, live after all. She remembered cold and wind and a freezing drizzle; her feet slipping in the mud, or being bruised by rocks, and when she thought she could take not another step, MacLeod suggesting they might better rest for a wee bit, "for 'tis a touch rough up ahead, sir." After that, only a blur of effort through which Geoffrey's voice came to encourage and sustain her, until even that faded into darkness.

Her clear memory began with a neat little wooden bed in a small bare room with a washstand on one wall, and on the other a small press and a battered old chest of drawers. A particularly dreadful painting of a despondent-looking horse graced the space between two narrow windows, and a tall, angular woman was pulling back the skimpy curtains to reveal wind-tossed trees and stormy grey skies.

"You must be Percy's aunt," said Prudence.

The woman spun around. She had fading fair hair drawn back into so tight a bun that her eyebrows seemed stretched upwards. Her features were sharp and unattractive, and her complexion colourless, but her mouth was curved into a warm smile, and her hazel eyes beamed so welcomingly that Prudence thought her very comely indeed.

"Aye, my poor dearie," she said, hurrying to the bed. "I'm Mrs. Nutthall, and more proud than I can say to have you here, though 'tis little enough I can offer in the way of the luxuries to which yourself is accustomed. Or himself, either. So fine a gentleman, and doing very much better this morning."

Alarmed by this ominous statement, Prudence started to throw back the bedclothes, but pulled them up again as a knock sounded and MacLeod came in, with an anxious expression and a cup and saucer in one great hand and a plate of buttered bannocks in the other. "Ah, ye're awake at last, little mistress," he said, grinning at her.

She sat up, wished him a good morning, and desired to know if Captain Delacourt was all right.

"Aye," said MacLeod, handing Prudence the cup of tea.

"You must be fair clemmed, poor lass," fussed Mrs. Nutthall, taking the plate and setting it carefully on Prudence's lap. "Would ye like some jam with your bannocks? I've some I made myself."

"Oh, but you are so generous. I've no wish to run you short."

The kindly woman beamed at her and hurried out saying she'd fetch some hot water also, since the sweet lady had been too wearied to wash last night.

MacLeod came at once to the side of the bed. "I'll tell ye as quick as quick, fer the lady will be back and her tongue runs on wheels, I dinna doot. Do ye mind us getting doon frae the high places, and Cole falling tae the groond?"

"No! Heavens! Is he all right?"

"A sight pulled. I carried the poor lad, for 'twas child's play once we came tae the level, y'ken. Nelson was forespent, but led us right bravely, and the rain stopped, which was no a bad thing. When we came tae the croft the lad went in first and then his uncle ran oot, bidding us all tae come inside. The Captain was cheery, but looked nae sae very alive when we came intae the barn. I set poor Cole on the hay, and the Captain handed ye doon, but couldnae climb oot o' the saddle. I caught him when he did come doon—all of a rush. I was a muckle scared, but 'twas just exhaustion, and small wonder. We made him cosy i' the barn wi' Lockerbie and me. He never stirred until this morning, but he's oot the noo, and—"

"Out!" Prudence was sufficently relieved to sip her tea and take a hungry bite of a jamless bannock. "There are no troopers about?"

"The crofter, Mr. Nutthall, says they're thick as flies aroond the loch, and that they've come here a time or two, but wi' his lady being a Sassenach they're let be."

Prudence thought, 'So far . . .'

There was no time for more. Mrs. Nutthall bustled back in. She was a kind-hearted woman and overcome with gratitude because her beloved nephew had told them of his desertion and that Captain Delacourt and his friends had come to this sorry state in rescuing him from the bounty hunters.

"He's not a bad boy, ma'am," said the lady earnestly, spooning a generous helping of jam onto Prudence's plate, "but he's been brought up gentle-like, and if all we hear of the Duke of Cumberland is truth, I'd think less of our Percy did he *not* desert from such evil doings. He tells us you're in bad trouble because you aided him, but there's no cause to fret. My man's a good sailor and we've a fine boat will carry you all safe home, never fear. Your husband is better this morning, I'm glad to tell you, and— Whoops! Never worry, ma'am. A little jam on the eiderdown won't matter. Only look, it blends in quite nicely with the pattern. I sewed it. I'm a rare good seamstress, if I say so myself. So you married an Englishman? Well, look at us, will you—me wed to a Scot, and you and your husband turnabout. He's a fine-looking young fellow, your man, and don't you be worrying yourself about him nor your servants, either. The chap with the cut in his arm is resting still, for he was in a proper fever when they carried him, and 'tis a nasty wound, but he's going on better already. . . ."

On she went, conveying a good deal of information to Prudence and obviating the need for that damsel to do much more than nod, marvel over her sudden and unexpected 'marriage,' and eat her breakfast.

As soon as she was left alone, she washed and dressed herself. Her slippers were past redemption, but Mrs. Nutthall was able to provide a pair of serviceable pattens for her to wear, and with the addition of some thick socks, for her stockings were ruined, she was able to fit into the wooden shoes quite comfortably. Her dress had been laundered and the larger tears neatly repaired, and by the time she had brushed out her tangled curls and pulled them back so as to fall from a knot high on her head, she felt halfway human again.

She found Percy Nelson chatting with his aunt in the immaculate kitchen. Mrs. Nutthall was sewing busily on a simple gown of pale green cloth which she explained would be more fitting for a sea voyage than Prudence's silk. She would hear of no thanks and went hurrying off to find a shawl so that her guest might go outside. Percy looked thoroughly mauled, but he got to his feet and greeted Prudence with shy courtesy. His aunt returned to wrap the shawl about Prudence's shoulders, and Percy, leaning heavily on a walking cane, led the way through the parlour to the front of the croft. "My uncle has taken the Captain to see his boat, Miss MacTavish, and—"

"Mrs. Delacourt," she corrected.

He grinned. "Oh—of course. We—er, thought it best. With things being . . . as they are, you know."

"Very wise. Will your uncle take us to England, do you think?"

"I cannot tell. They have to be so careful. It will be tricky, but"—he glanced up at the stormy skies—"if the weather breaks— Oh, there they come now, miss."

Prudence left the shelter of the overhanging roof and went into the wind to meet Delacourt, who, together with a very fat middle-aged man, was walking up the slope from a stand of trees.

Delacourt looked tired, she thought, but his eyes lit up when he saw her and it was all she could do not to throw herself into his arms. She gave him her hand, and he held it for a moment, wordlessly, his eyes locked with hers, before pressing it to his lips.

Mr. Nutthall chuckled, his middle bobbing up and down as a result. "Ye're nae past yer first year o' wedlock, that's verra clear," he said genially. He bowed slightly when Delacourt introduced Prudence, her cheeks blushing because she was presented as his "dear wife."

"I've been telling yer mon we might venture it tonight, if so be the storm rolls in," Nutthall said. "It'll be right chancy sailing, but I'm nae a novice at this game. Are ye a good sailor, missus?"

Prudence had never sailed on any body of water larger than Loch Ness, which had always seemed to be water enough for anyone, but she answered confidently that she had never experienced the least discomfort in a boat, even in rough weather.

They chatted for another minute or two, and then Nutthall left them so that Prudence might be taken down to see the boat while he warned his wife to prepare supplies for a long journey.

Delacourt drew Prudence's hand through his arm. "Did you sleep well?" he asked. "You look wonderful, but perhaps I should not take you to see our man-o'-war in this cold wind."

"Never mind about me." She scanned his face. "Are you better?"

He assured her that he was feeling "splendid, thank you," and led her past the trees, moving ever downhill. They came out onto a curving headland above a sheltered cove, where a two-masted fishing vessel, with sails reefed, lay at anchor, rocking to the surge of the tide. The sea looked dark and the waves threatening and topped with foam when the wind caught them, and low-hanging clouds surged swiftly over the sullen waters. The wind carried spray and the clean smell of the sea, and sent Prudence's curls whipping about. "Oh, but it's wild-looking," she exclaimed. "What do you think, sir? Will he take us?"

Delacourt was silent for a moment. Then he said quietly, "Prue, have you thought about this? From what I've been able to gather we were attacked not by military, but by bounty hunters—likely out for my valuable head. It might well be exceeding dangerous for you to leave Scotland with me."

Her heart gave a lurch. She said, "And what if you leave me here and it turns out that the 'bounty hunters' were soldiers after all, masquerading as civilians so as to do Cumberland's work without the risk of censure? If I stay I might be hurried off to the block even—"

She was crushed close against him, and he groaned, "Do not! It is abominable to think of such a horror!"

"It is very possible," she said into his cravat.

"Unlikely. But, Prue, if I take you from home and family, where shall I safely deliver you? Is there a relative you could stay with for a time?"

Her spirits sank. She had been so sure he meant to offer. But he must not see her disappointment, so she said cheerfully, "Oh, yes. I've an aunt lives on a beautiful estate near Richmond who will be very glad of my company."

Still he hesitated, muttering, "Lord, but I wish Robbie were here to take care of you. If they know who I am, and you're caught with me . . ." He frowned, and did not finish the sentence.

A chill crept between her shoulders. "Then I shall say you kidnapped me, and that I knew naught of your wickedness."

He grinned at that. "You'd be far more like to rail at them and proclaim that I had come to realize the Jacobite Cause was the right one!" He put a hand over her parting lips and went on in a very grave manner, "Prudence, aside from all else, you heard what Nutthall said. Our best hope is to set sail during a storm, and it will be a chancy business. So many risks for you, so many dangers. I shall never forgive myself if I bring you to disaster."

She smiled into his worried eyes and set herself to allay his fears. And she thought, 'The storm will pass, and then—days and nights of sailing. Days and nights at sea, to all intents and purposes alone with him.' How wonderful it would be. To stroll the decks together; to eat luncheon and dinner together; to be free from danger and distractions. She would twine herself around his heart and so enchant him that he would have offered (and been accepted) long before they set foot in England!

Four days later, Stuart MacLeod guided Prudence's faltering steps along the deck and supported her as she gazed across the grey tumbling sea to the distant coastline. She asked in a thread of a voice, "Is it truly England? You are quite sure I am not dead?"

He smiled down at her. "Sae soon as 'tis dusk we'll have ye on solid groond again, lady."

She gave a great sigh. When they had boarded *The Maid o' Moidart* she'd thought it a fine boat, well able to withstand the rigours of any storm. They had set sail after dark, in heavy rain, with a strong wind blowing from the east, and Mr. Nutthall and his sons working frenziedly to guide the vessel clear of the cove. The fear of the water that had kept Lockerbie from venturing into the Monster had again prevailed to separate him from his beloved master. He and Delacourt had said their farewells in private, but that it had been a sad parting, Prudence was sure. Cole, although still weak, had not so much as considered being left behind, and MacLeod, ignoring all counsel to the contrary, had announced he meant to be sure that Mr. Doone came safely to his own shores.

Happily packing the necessary articles Delacourt had been able to purchase from Mrs. Nutthall, and much more comfortable in the green cloth gown that had miraculously been altered so as to fit very nicely, Prudence had been bathed in a rosy glow of happiness. It had been a surprise when the hairbrush she had put on top of the small chest had suddenly sailed past, but she had caught it with faint amusement and tucked it into a drawer. Moments later she had experienced an uneasy sensation when the floor of the cabin dropped suddenly from beneath her feet, a sensation that intensified when the little cabin tilted slowly onto its side. Within another quarter-hour she had come to the appalling realization that, firmly believing they had survived the worst of their personal nightmare, she was now entering another phase of it.

She had heard of the evils of *mal de mer,* but never had she dreamed how truly ghastly is that allegedly trite affliction. Delacourt, who had gone up on deck to give a hand with sails, ropes, and spars—or some such—had returned to find her huddled on the floor in a pitiful condition. With a cry of sympathy he had swept her up, deposited her in the bunk, and run for the basin. And, with true heroism, had not left her through that long, hideous night, while the storm mounted in fury until it was all he could do to balance himself and keep her securely in the bunk.

Longing to be comfortably dead, Prudence had found that the dawn brought no relief. For the next two days Delacourt held her much-employed bowl, bathed her clammy face, murmured encouragement, and plied her with brandy and water. Between paroxysms she moaned out thanks and apologies and begged that he leave her to expire, asking only that she not be buried at sea.

Delacourt had little respite, for MacLeod and Cole were almost as badly afflicted, and even when thunder, lightning, and torrential rain abated, the wind continued at gale force.

The third day was slightly less violent, and Mr. Nutthall, guiding *The Maid o' Moidart* before the wind with shortened sail, and struggling to repair the damage they had sustained, was able to report that they had been swept along at such a rate that by the following afternoon they would be cruising the coast of South Wales.

That evening, Prudence had been able to take some soup that MacLeod contrived to heat in the ravaged galley. She had slept then, from pure exhaustion, awakening late this morning, limp as a rag and aching in every bone from the endless retching that had so drained her strength, but without that hideous feeling of nausea. Delacourt had come early with hot water and towels and the information that as soon as she was decent she was to ring the little bell he brought her and MacLeod would be at her disposal.

Now, watching the loom of the land draw nearer, she heard a quick light step and turned to find Delacourt coming towards her, all eager solicitude.

He took the unsteady hand she held out to him, kissed it, and said, "How splendid to see you up and about again, my wan wisp. Only another hour or so, and you shall walk on 'this green and pleasant land' and not find it heave under your feet."

It was closer to two hours, however, and just after dark, before Mr. Nutthall guided *The Maid o' Moidart* into a secluded inlet some fourteen miles south of Bristol.

Their thanks were waved aside. "Nae call fer that, sir," said Nutthall, shaking hands with Delacourt. "That Percy lad's as close tae a fourth son as I'll ever get, I fancy. And a damned good lad—saving yer presence, ma'am. I owe ye a sight more than a rough journey in my wee *Maid,* let alone allowing ye tae ha' paid me so handsome. Me boy, Bruce, has the dinghy ready and will row ye ashore. God be wi' ye, sir and ma'am."

Looking strangely alien in the breeches Mrs. Nutthall had managed to procure for him, MacLeod climbed into the dinghy and Delacourt guided Prudence down into his arms. They were rowed ashore under a moonless sky, the gusty wind blowing up the waves in a way that made Prudence shrink in Delacourt's protective arm, dreading lest she become ill again. Very soon, however, Bruce Nutthall ran the dinghy onto the beach and jumped out to hold her secure while MacLeod lifted Prudence over the side and carried her onto the sand. Following, Delacourt said his farewells to young Nutthall, then reached out to the towering Scot. "God speed, Stuart. I shall never forget you, my good friend."

"I'll take guid care o' that, sir," growled MacLeod, ignoring his hand. "I said I'd bide wi' ye, and I meant it."

Delacourt gripped his arm. "Curst idiot," he said affectionately. "You belong in Scotland's glens and great mountains. You'd be miserable in England, and you know it."

"I'd nae be content away frae ye, sir. And—and the little lady. If ye make me leave, I'll just bide a wee while and follow."

Delacourt shook his head. "It is very good of you, but—there's your accent, you see, and it might mean—"

"Death tae ye? D'ye think I dinna ken that, Captain? I'll be mute."

"A fine existence! MacLeod, you great madman, do you not know to what you condemn yourself? If all goes well and I escape arrest, mine will be the tranquil life of a country gentleman. You'd fairly die of boredom."

"I've had me share o' excitement, sir. And d'ye take me fer a nincompoop? Ye're in as much danger here as ever ye were in the north. More, maybe. I'll *nae* leave ye, sir."

Delacourt groaned and clutched his hair, and MacLeod said haltingly, "Sir . . . dinna turn me off."

Prudence touched Delacourt's arm. "It is what he wants, dear sir."

He sighed. "So be it, Stuart. But I'll not hold you to it, should you change your mind."

MacLeod gave a great beaming grin. "Will I carry your wee lady, sir?"

Experiencing the odd sensation that she still rocked to the motion of the waves, Prudence said, "That would be lovely, MacLeod."

He bent and lifted her gently. They waved farewell to Bruce Nutthall and began to trudge up the beach.

With a gesture to the north, Cole said, "Bristol lies that way, sir. It would be best, I think, did we find a sheltered spot where you and the lady might rest, while MacLeod and I go to the nearest village and hire a carriage and team."

This was agreed upon, Delacourt handing Cole the money belt Sir Ian had loaned him when he had left the cavern. Strapping this about his trim middle with a little help from MacLeod, Cole glanced around the dim-seen landscape and sighed. "Lor', but it's good to be home, isn't it, sir?"

Delacourt agreed, but recalling his last sight of his own home, wondered what he might find when he came again to Highview.

PART TWO

England

XIX

Cole's hiring of a coach and four was achieved at the cost of a large bribe and exorbitant fees. The coach was shabby and the horses the best of a poor lot, but due to the state of their garments it was a major triumph that they were able to ride in a carriage at all. With Cole and MacLeod on the box, Delacourt gave instructions that they head for the Bath Road and find a hostelry for the night. Prudence dozed as the carriage jolted eastward, and Delacourt was quiet, lost in introspection. The hour was advanced when Cole turned into the yard of a small but neat hostelry and went inside to arrange accommodations. The transaction was made, but when it was seen that they had very little luggage, the host became suspicious and Delacourt was obliged to invent a tale of their having started out to attend a dinner party but one of the horses having gone lame, so delaying them that they could not hope to reach home tonight. "Especially," he added, inspired, "since my wife has been very ill and is still frail."

This brought the host's lady to investigate, and the sight of Prudence's pale face so wrought upon her that there were no more questions and they were shown to very pleasant chambers. Within ten minutes, Prudence was in bed. She slept like one dead, and awoke next morning to the delight of a stationary room with sunlight flooding through the open casements. She lay drowsing for a few minutes, reflecting gratefully on having been spared to set foot on dry land again—even if it was England. It was a pity she had missed her anticipated opportunities on *The Maid o' Moidart,* but she had today, at least, before Geoffrey could rush her off to Aunt Geraldine's great house in Richmond. She smiled faintly, wondering what that crusty old lady would say if he really did deliver to her doorstep the niece she had seen twice during her lifetime. Her most fervent prayer was that he would change his mind and ask her to become his bride. He cared for her, she was very sure, for how many gentlemen would have stayed by her while she was so horribly sick? How many gentlemen would have held the basin so heroically, or cradled her in their arms while the vessel was hurled about the surface as though kicked by some capricious giant? He loved her. Perhaps he did not realize it himself as yet, but he loved her, and somehow, soon or late, she would manoeuvre him into offering. Poor doomed soul. She smiled at the flirting window curtains, then rang for hot water.

She had enjoyed a steaming cup of hot chocolate and was getting dressed when a maid scratched at the door and delivered a large bandbox and three parcels. The bandbox contained a demure cap of white lawn, the edges ruffled and trimmed with fine lace. Also in the box were two sprays of silk flowers, one scarlet and one blue. Prudence touched them lovingly, but was amused by the realization that her gallant gentleman knew little of the ways of women if he fancied she would wear scarlet blossoms against her "red poll." She opened the parcels. One, long and flat, contained the hoops for a pannier skirt. The second held petticoats and a charming shawl of pale green silk. Eagerly opening the last package, she stared, then burst into laughter. The gown was lovely; and pink. Bless his heart, she thought, he had tried.

Half an hour later, wearing the pink gown, a dainty cap fastened over the crown of her head, and scarlet blooms nestled in her curls, Prudence adjusted the green shawl about her shoulders, and tripped along the corridor.

Delacourt awaited her in the vestibule. He looked very well in a maroon velvet coat, with snowy lace at throat and wrists, his curling hair powdered and tied back with a black riband. His dark eyes bright and eager, he hastened to take both her hands and kiss them tenderly. "You look the spirit of Spring," he told her.

"If I do, 'tis because of your thoughtfulness. Oh, Geoffrey, my very dear friend, thank you so much. My poor gown was in rags, and the dress Mrs. Nutthall made for me was badly torn when I climbed into *The Maid o' Moidart.* However did you find these pretty things?"

Delighted because he had pleased her, and because she looked almost her usual bright self again, he said blithely, "By rising at an ungodly hour and riding into Bath. I had some business to attend to there, so do not reproach yourself. Besides, it was worth every minute, just to see you so bonnie!"

She laughed at the Scots term. "And you also, sir. How fine and grand we are. I expect Cole and MacLeod are fitted out in livery."

To her surprise, he took the remark seriously. "Never be able to find it on the spur of the moment, least of all in MacLeod's size! They both have new rigs, though, and only wait till you see MacLeod. Gad, but he's impressive. If he wasn't a Scot, he'd make a dashed fine Horse Guardsman!"

"Ye'd best not tell him that, Captain Delacourt," she said, smilingly.

"No. And you'd best not name me so any more, m'dear. I am Geoffrey Delavale now, and also—" He checked, then said quietly, "Well, never mind that. Come on, little lass. You're thin as a rail after all your jauntering about the Seven Seas. It is past time I was fattening you up!"

He led her to the coffee room, where they enjoyed an excellent breakfast, to which Prudence did full justice. Delavale was pleased to see the return of her appetite, and said he feared she must think the selection poor compared to what she had been used to at Lakepoint. Sorrow came into her eyes, and he cursed himself for a fool and said remorsefully, "I am sorry, Prue. We will bend every effort to find out what happened, I do promise you."

"If they reached the other side of the Loch and your friends found them they will be safe—no?"

"Absolutely safe. So, eat up, lovely one."

"Oh, no, thank you. This huge meal was only to, er, to make up for—"

"For lost time?" he suggested with a grin.

"Horrid man! No, truly, I have to be very careful, Geoffrey. I am so short, you know. If I ate as I would like to do, by the time I am middle-aged I would be a dumpling."

He laughed and declared that he loved middle-aged dumplings. "For they are always so happy and contented. The thin ones are very often scratchy, and I do believe 'tis only because the poor dears are always half starved!"

Prudence smiled, but her thoughts still dwelt on an earlier topic. "Sir," she said mildly, "you *did* say that Highview is not a very large house?"

"True. Shall that disappoint you? I'd not meant to imply it is a cottage, exactly, but compared to some like—well, there's an estate we'll be passing this morning that is quite large, and I do assure you my home is nothing to it."

An hour later, as Cole guided the team along the rather precipitous road that hugged the slope of a hill, Prudence gazed in awe at the great red-brick mansion spread across the brow of a lower hill. "Oh, but it is magnificent! To my mind, that is *exceeding* large, Geoffrey!"

"There are larger, little lass, but certainly few lovelier. I fancy Lac Brillant, the Chandlers' place in Kent, may rival Dominer for beauty, though. If you judge the exterior large, you should see the inside. Do you notice how the wings curve back? It tends to diminish their true size. Jove, but I wish we'd the time to stop, I'd show you through. But, as it is, we're trespassing. This is an estate road."

She eyed him in alarm. "Good gracious! We'll not have the troops after us again, I hope?"

"No, no." He patted her hand, amused. "Marbury's a very good old fellow and was a bosom bow of my father."

"Marbury?" She knit her brows. "It seems I've heard the name."

"Likely you have. Thaddeus knows the Duke, and—"

"And the Duke was a very good friend of your papa?"

"Yes. You'd like him, I think, though he can be quite a tartar when he chooses." He leaned forward and pulled on the check string.

The trap opened and Cole peered down at him. "Yes, sir?"

"I don't want to go through Bath, Cole. Swing southeast at the next crossroads and take the Trowbridge road."

"Trowbridge? But I thought— Aren't we going home, Master Geoffrey?"

"Yes. But I've to make a stop, first. We'll change teams and take luncheon in Trowbridge. Oh—and, Cole, I will use my own name from now on."

Cole looked puzzled, but said only, "Yes, sir," and closed the trap again.

Prudence asked anxiously, "Do you fear patrols, Geoffrey?"

He did fear patrols, for he had no identification of any kind and in the event they were stopped things might go badly, especially with Stuart MacLeod to be accounted for. He gave no sign of this, however, slipping an arm about her and kissing the end of her little nose while telling her not to look so scared. "It has gone quietly enough up to now, has it not?"

It continued to go quietly. Delavale was determined for several reasons not to lay any further siege to Prudence's heart, and beyond keeping her hand tucked into his arm, behaved with propriety. Prudence, still rather weak, was pleased by this southwest countryside and viewed with interest the peaceful, prosperous hamlets, the tidy farms with their neatly laid out fields, the richly wooded valleys, and the emerald velvet folds of the hills. The sun shone, the birds sang, her love was beside her and, except for the worry for her family that lurked ever at the edge of her mind, she was content.

They reached Trowbridge at half-past one o'clock, and Cole pulled in to the yard of a prosperous-looking posting house named The Black Lion, that unlikely beast snarling ferociously from the gently swinging sign, more as if to frighten travellers away than welcome them to alight. Glancing at Delavale to comment upon this, Prudence surprised a frown on his face. When MacLeod, resplendent in a brown velvet coat and knee breeches, swung open the door, Delavale hesitated momentarily, then gave a somewhat resigned shrug and descended, turning back to hand Prudence out.

Ostlers were already busied with straps and buckles and Cole was dickering with them regarding the acquisition of another team. Delavale called that he had changed his mind and they would likely overnight here, and asked MacLeod to bring in the luggage.

Prudence felt a little twinge of anxiety. "Are you feeling not quite the thing, sir?"

He smiled down at her and ushered her into the vestibule of the posting house. "I feel very well, thank you, Prue, but we'd better stay here, for I—"

"Del! Why, you dashed rum touch, I thought you was dead!"

Delavale stiffened and swore under his breath, but put out his hand cordially enough. It was taken by a slim young exquisite with a round, guileless face, brown eyes, and a very large nose. He was impressively clad in an awesome wig, an elaborate buff coat trimmed with gold lace, fawn small clothes and stockings, and shoes of Morocco having amber buckles and extremely high heels. "Gad, but you look a rail," quoth this paragon of fashion. "Saw your carriage—no panels, dear boy. Are you—er"—he slanted a shrewd glance at Prudence and grinned—"travelling incognito, perchance?"

Having coped with the long nightmare of battle, illness, and the horrors of war, Delavale had quite overlooked the matter of what people down here would think of his journey with Miss MacTavish. 'My God,' he thought, aghast, 'he fancies she's my mistress!'

Prudence, waiting fumingly for him to introduce her, was shattered by his silence.

Before Delavale could recover from the shock of his own stupidity, his friend stepped into the breach. "How do, ma'am? Permit me to make m'self known t'you. I am Bertram Crisp—known to m'friends as Bertie." He swept her a low bow. "Now come on, dear old boy. Introduce me to your lovely lady, or I shall pos'tively—"

Cole came hurrying to murmur softly that there were no rooms available.

"'Course there are," exclaimed Crisp, incensed. "Host! You certainly can find suites for Lord Delavale and his party! Bestir y'self, silly creature!"

A gentleman of portly habit, who was stretched out in a corner armchair with a newspaper over his face, roused sufficiently to peer at them from under a corner of his cover, then restore it again. A wispy-looking man, poring through the pages of *The Spectator,* did not look up at all.

Prudence, much shocked, turned to find Delavale watching her apprehensively. Before she could say a word, the host ran up, beaming and rubbing his hands together. Certainly, there was room for milor'. The foolish clerk had misunderstood. If milor' would only step this way . . .

Mr. Crisp, his admiring gaze still travelling Prudence, made as if to intervene, but was suddenly engulfed by a party of vociferous friends who surged in from the tap to sweep him, protesting, away.

Her head held very high, her face red, Prudence followed the host upstairs.

Taking her elbow, Delavale said *sotto voce,* "Alas, ma'am, I'd not planned sufficiently far ahead."

"How unusual of you," she said tartly. And she thought in anguish, 'So he is a peer! And he was horrified when that silly fribble recognized him, because he did not want to be seen with me!' She was still weak, and her nerves on end, so that she had to fight the grief and hurt pride that threatened to overwhelm her.

The host swung open the door of a sunny bedchamber. "There is a connecting parlour, ma'am," he said, and looked questioningly at Delavale.

Very aware of the question, and even more mortified, Prudence swept into the bedchamber, glanced blindly about, and went on into the neat parlour.

Delavale had noted the fierce jut of her small chin, and with sinking heart knew he had made a proper mull of things. Fixing the host with an icy stare, he said, "This will do very nicely for my betrothed. I trust my room is not too far away."

The host looked relieved and said that there was a nice room just down the hall that would be made ready immediately.

"Very well," said Delavale. "I shall wait in your parlour if I may, my dear."

"By all means," said Prudence with an indifferent shrug.

Hurrying downstairs, the host crossed the vestibule just as the gentleman who had been snoozing there wandered from his corner, yawning. He was a large, florid-featured man, with small hard eyes and a lower lip that drooped petulantly. "Did I hear someone say that young Delavale has come here?" he enquired.

The host, a garrulous individual, waited to admit this was so. "And travels with his affianced bride. A rare pretty lady, if I may say so."

"Is that a fact? Egad, but his family will be overjoyed. He was given up for dead a year since. The Jacobite business, y'know."

"Good gracious me. I thought he looked rather wan. What a happy homecoming lies ahead of the poor gentleman. Well, if you will excuse me, sir, I've to find him a room, and a pickle I'm in, for it means putting off someone else, but it's more than

I dare do to fob off a earl, or whatever he is, with a small back room."

"A baron," said the portly guest absently. "And he may have my room."

Startled, the host exclaimed, "No, do you mean to leave us so soon, Mr. Beasley? I'd thought you planned to overnight. I hopes as nothing has upset you here. If I can make things right—"

"No, no, my good fellow," said Thomas Beasley with an affability that would have caused several of his acquaintances no little astonishment. "Truth is, I interrupted my journey because I was feeling out of sorts. Stomach, y'know. Feeling better now—thanks to your good food, I've no doubt. So I think I'll push on. Must be in London tomorrow."

He reiterated his delight with The Black Lion, and everything about it, and sent a maid to tell his valet to pack at once. Directing his steps stablewards, he paused and called softly, "Oh, by the bye, be a good fellow and do not mention my name to his lordship. I fancy he means to surprise us all, and I'd not wish to spoil things for him. Especially in view of his, er"—he winked, man-to-man fashion—"his betrothed."

Somewhat taken aback, the host agreed and watched Mr. Beasley saunter into the outer sunshine. So that lovely little damsel was *not* the future Lady Delavale. It would explain why there had been no crest on the door of that shabby carriage and why my lord had simply signed the register as Geoffrey Delavale and party. No wonder the girl had been so red in the face. He frowned, his honest heart troubled to have hanky-panky dealings in his house. Still, with the Quality one had to be careful. Sighing, he went into his own quarters to tell his good wife that they'd have a baron under the roof tonight. The rest of the tale could wait until milor' had taken himself and his lightskirt off. And the charges, he thought grimly, would reflect the price of sin!

Meanwhile, with a briskness foreign to his nature, Thomas Beasley crossed the yard and went into the dim fragrance of the stables. Here, some moments later, his valet found him, with ostlers scurrying to pole up a team to a luxurious travelling coach.

"I thought the maid must have made an error, sir," murmured the valet.

Taking care to keep out of sight of the inn windows, Beasley said irritably, "Did she not tell you to pack up and bring the bags down here?"

"Yes, sir. But I'd understood we was to stay here tonight, and—"

"I suppose I may change my mind," said his employer arctically. "Perhaps you would oblige me by hastening. I want to be away within ten minutes! Well, never stand there, gawking! *Move,* damn you!"

The valet ran.

Within the prescribed time, Mr. Beasley was seated in his speeding coach. At the crossroads, the direction *To London* was on the sign pointing to the east. Mr. Beasley's coachman did not turn his team to the right, however, but continued northwards on the road that led to Chippenham and, eventually, to Oxfordshire.

As soon as the host closed the parlour door, Delavale turned to Prudence. Her nose had an upward tilt, her vivid mouth drooped at the corners, her brows arched with studied nonchalance. He reached for her hand. "Little lass, I know—"

She pulled away and dropped her reticule on the sofa. "La, sir, but I believe you. Certain it is that you know more than I do! I vow, you've more identities than a bird has feathers." She sat down in a high-backed chair and arranged her draperies meticulously. "My *lord,* no less! I canna wonder ye concealed it frae me. Ye likely feared I'd be drrropping the handkerchief did I suspect ye'd a title tae be captured!"

He flushed darkly. "As if I would think so of you. And I did not conceal it from you, exactly. Elizabeth was so repulsed by Thad's title, and—"

"Really?" Despite the frigid interruption, hope had begun to burgeon in her breast. Was it possible that he'd fancied she would refuse him for fear of having to take on the duties of a baroness? Her accent less noticeable, she asked airily, "Why should it matter to me whether or not you have a title? You need be bothered wi' me no longer once you've conveyed me to my aunt's house."

She gave a gasp as she was jerked from the chair and slightly shaken. His eyes glinting with anger, he grated, "Gad, Prue, but I could throttle you when you talk so. Of course you are not a bother! And before I take you to your aunt's home I want to show you Highview, and . . ."

She was looking up at him in frightened fashion, all great eyes and shrinking femininity, and his words died away, the anger in his face replaced by a tenderness that made her heart leap. She said quaveringly, "Please—do not throttle me . . . Geoffrey."

"My darling . . ." he whispered, and pulled her into his arms.

She surrendered quite willingly to his brutality, but if she was not throttled when he raised his head at length, she was certainly breathless and considerably crushed. "Oh, Geoffrey . . . Geoffrey . . ." she murmured, lying limply in his embrace.

"My dainty Scots beauty," he responded, pressing kisses into her curls.

She stroked his sleeve lovingly. "If you take me to Highview, whatever will your family think?"

"They may think what they will, much I care!" After several more kisses, however, he added thoughtfully, "Of course, I shall have to find you a maid before we go. It would never do for you to drive up without one."

This struck her as ridiculous, in view of all their desperate journeying with no thought of maids or chaperones. She giggled, and asked, "Would your lady aunt be very shocked?"

Her cheek was nestled against his cravat, wherefore she did not see his face become set and grim. He said, "Oh, very. You will find her quite a different article to Mrs. MacTavish, or the ladies you have known."

She tensed, and a tiny frown tugged at her brows. "Shall I? I suppose they are very grand and will fancy me a proper country bumpkin."

It was said with the sure knowledge that he would immediately deny such snobbery. Geoffrey, however, with half his mind on the deadly cypher still residing in his waistcoat pocket, and the other half on his predatory relations, replied absently, "Never fear, Prue. With some proper clothes, the maid will be able to make you appear a grand lady, also."

Her eyes widened. She left his arms and wandered across the room to pause beside an occasional table and stare blindly at the feather duster some flurried housemaid had accidentally left there. "Do you really think a maid can work such a transformation?" she asked, her hands clenching.

He took out the cypher and stared down at it. He must find a better place of concealment than his pocket. "Oh, yes. If we find one who is very well trained."

Very—well—*trained?* Prudence, beginning to breathe rapidly, took up the little duster and gripped it until her knuckles whitened. Did the man fancy her unable properly to manipulate knife and fork, perhaps? "How nice it will be," she said, her white teeth flashing in a glittering smile, "when I learn to go on in a well-bred way."

He folded the cypher and put it in the back compartment of his watch, then glanced at the hour. Two o'clock almost. Time yet, if he left at once. "What? Oh, yes, very nice," he agreed disastrously.

Gritting her teeth, she went on, "To be demure and gently spoken, and mannerly—like an English lady."

"Just so," he said, tucking his watch in his pocket and crossing to her.

Prudence spun around, gripping her duster savagely, and Delavale recoiled from the fury that glared from her narrowed eyes.

"Horrid, high-in-the-instep, opinionated *Sassenach,*" she snarled. "Little wonder ye were ashamed tae introduce this savage baggage tae yer fine-feathered friend!"

"Wh-what? Prudence, I promise you—"

"Aye—that ye do! Promises and—and insincere speeches and vows of undying love that mean nae more t'ye than any commonplace!"

He paled, and his dark brows drew down. "Now just one moment, if y'please, ma'am—"

"I dinna please," she declared, stamping her tiny foot at him. "So there's nae call fer ye tae waste yer aristocratic breath on a wee bit Scots lassie wi' not a dram o' culture or refinement in her entire uncouth person!"

"What in the deuce are you so in the boughs about? If it is on account of my title—"

"Oh, pish for your silly title—much I care for't! Did ye fancy t'would bring me grovelling tae me knees in humility before your fine worship?"

Stung, Delavale stalked to stand before the infuriated girl. "If *ever* I heard such unmitigated balderdash! I think I have never puffed off my consequence to you—or anyone else for that matter." She thrust her lower lip out at him, but some of the wrath went out of her blue eyes and, his own eyes softening, he added a teasing, "Besides, from what I know of *you,* my lass, humility is not noticeable among your virtues. Courage, I'll admit, but—"

"Oooh!" snorted Prudence, inflamed again. "So I'm a bold, encroaching hussy, the noo!" She shook her duster at him as he stepped closer, thus producing a cloud of dust that caused him to move back hurriedly. "Well, ye need nae tremble, my lord Delavale! This Scots baggage"—she paused as he sneezed violently—"will nae cause ye the embarrassment o' being obliged tae introduce her vulgarity tae yer hoity-toity family!"

Snatching for his handkerchief, Delavale mopped at his eyes and growled an incensed, "You are behaving like—like"—another staggering sneeze—"a silly little girl. And for no— *Ar-roush!* No—cause. I could spank you and—" He mopped his eyes again and glared at her. "And should!"

"Do not *dare* to strike me!" She lifted her little duster again, but with less hostility, for he stood so close and dear, and he was so very cross that he was pale with it.

Delavale had no suspicion of the fact that she waited to be seized and crushed and kissed. And he ground out between his teeth, "I have never yet raised my hand against a lady, but 'fore God, you tempt me, madam!" He drew himself up to his full height and said with fine disdain, "I shall leave you to attempt to regain your composure. Good afternoon, Miss MacTavish."

Prudence sank into a deep and mocking curtsey, quite forgetting that in one gracefully extended hand she clutched a worn feather duster.

Equally blind to this ludicrous finale, Delavale swore under his breath and, sneezing, left her.

Stuart MacLeod had supposed that since he and Delavale rode alone, it would be safe for him to venture a word or two. He discovered, however, that his words fell on deaf ears, the frowning man beside him not so much refusing to respond as seeming oblivious of his presence. Their pace had been furious at first, but just as MacLeod had been about to enter a plea for the sake of the horses, Delavale drew rein and slowed to a walk for the next half-mile before starting off again at a steady canter.

Not having the remotest notion of where they were, or whither they were bound, MacLeod took in his surroundings with interest. It was a bonnie country. Puny, but bonnie. They had ridden through serene fields and farmland, by winding lanes lined with hedgerows where wild flowers scented the air with their fragrance and trees threw a grateful shade across their way. The hamlets were a joy to the eye, with sturdy thatched cottages and carefully tended gardens, the brief and often single thoroughfare almost invariably boasting an inn on which MacLeod's gaze rested longingly. But Delavale had pressed on, ever in the same grim-lipped silence, until now, in late afternoon, they were riding through open country; a place of rounded rolling hills, mightily short of trees, thought MacLeod, and dotted here and there with flocks of sheep and shepherds whose friendly waves he returned, but which Delavale ignored.

Far ahead now rose the spires and chimneys of a town. MacLeod glanced at his companion's stern face. "Sir," he said tentatively, "I'd nae interrupt yer glummery, but in aboot a minute or two, we'll ride smack intae yon troop."

The words jolted Delavale from his absorption with the extraordinary tantrums of Miss Prudence MacTavish. In the near distance he caught a glimpse of red uniforms. "Good Gad!" he exclaimed, and with a remorseful glance at the Scot, "Mac, you should have rapped your claymore over my stupid head! Into that stand of trees! Fast!"

They entered the shade of the trees and proceeded with caution. At the brow of the hill the birches petered out. Fortunately, the troopers were riding off to the south, and there were no more in sight. The experience was a warning, however. Resuming their journey, Delavale kept his wits about him, which was as well; soon, they encountered several more straggling groups of military, two on foot and the others mounted. MacLeod pointed out a halted carriage with troopers inspecting the papers of the occupants, and the two men looked at each other, unhappily aware that they carried no identification that would satisfy the redcoats.

Delavale checked their speed, and they rode with ever-increasing vigilance, skirting the ancient market town of Devizes with its great old church and the ruins of the once proud castle which Oliver Cromwell had destroyed. MacLeod suggested that they stop and rest at a cosy hedge tavern just east of the town, but Delavale shook his head and pressed on across Roundway Down, ever north and east.

The sun was setting when they came into a tiny hamlet, where a Gothic church tower rose with sturdy placidity above a little cluster of trees and cottages.

"D'ye see any uniforms?" asked Delavale, scanning the drowsing street.

"Nary a one, sir. But there's a wee tavern. D'ye mean tae wet yer whistle, I can take the horses tae yon smithy, and see them fed and rubbed doon."

"I'll go with you and make the arrangements. Do you stay with the hacks until I return, and we'll find ourselves some dinner sooner or later."

MacLeod did not relish the thought of Delavale going on alone, but his protests were overborne. Delavale was determined not to involve the Scot in the perilous business he must now undertake. He had a near rebellion on his hands when, having arranged for the care of the horses, he left the smithy beside MacLeod and demanded that in the event of trouble the big man should keep out of sight. Not until Delavale pointed out that someone must get back to Miss MacTavish and conduct her safely to her aunt's home, did MacLeod vow to do as he was instructed.

The two men looked at each other and, not daring to allow this to seem a possible farewell, said nothing. Delavale smiled and winked. MacLeod regarded him miserably, and watched as the tall, slim figure wandered off.

Farther along the street a tiny bow window offered a glimpse of bon-bons and comfits. With Prudence in mind, Delavale stooped to the narrow door and went inside. The interior was warm and fragrant, and the rather deaf elderly lady behind the counter was shyly pleased by his compliments on her neat establishment. He chatted at a shout with her, explaining that he was en route to visit a friend in Hungerford, but had never passed this way before. He was at once regaled with a listing of noteworthy attractions, and urged not to miss the earthwork where had been found many prehistoric artifacts well worth the viewing.

He listened to her with his usual courteous attention and said he would certainly plan to pay it a visit, then added idly, "It seems I heard something about a fine church nearby. It must be very old, I collect, for it is said to have a leper's window."

"Aye. Ye'll be meaning St. Peter's in Greater Shottup. A very nice old church, sir, and lies about six miles east."

"On this same road, ma'am?"

"Yes. You'll have no trouble finding it," she said, smiling at him. "Just keep yer eyes open for scarlet coats."

En route to the door, he checked. "Huntsmen?" he asked, turning back.

"Of a sort. They do say they're after the man what has the poem."

Delavale's breath seemed to freeze in his throat. "Poem . . . ?"

"Have ye not heard about it, sir? Why, there's notices up everywhere. There's a reward of a hundred pound. A *hundred pound!* Fancy that. It's for anyone laying a information 'gainst one of those poor Jacobite gentlemen. If he turns out to be the one with a poem of some kind. Did ever you hear anything so odd?"

He said with forced nonchalance, "Mayhap the Duke of Cumberland has a taste for poetry."

She said with a frown, "Perhaps so, sir. Though from all we hear his Grace has little taste for aught but cruelty. Be that as it may, if you just follow the road east, you can't miss it." Rather wistfully, she asked, "Was your honour meaning to buy something?"

He thought he should buy the whole shop, considering the service she had unknowingly rendered him, but settled for a bag of sweets, squandering a whole groat on his selection, much to her delight.

Striding back along the quiet street towards the smithy, he was frowning and dismayed. The military might not know about his rendezvous point, but they had learned about the cypher. To wonder how was pointless. There were a hundred ways they might have obtained the information, none pleasant. He and MacLeod had been six miles from death! Had he not stayed to buy those sweets. . . . His lips tightened. No possibility to deliver the cypher tonight. He must get Prudence safely to Highview Manor, and then try again.

MacLeod was waiting anxiously, and Delavale brought a comical look of dismay to the Scot's broad features when he murmured that they dare not stay to eat here. He tossed over the bag of sweets. "This will help assuage that great hunger of yours."

MacLeod was almost childishly pleased. He possessed a sweet tooth and made no complaint as he mounted up, chewing contentedly on a piece of toffee.

Delavale chose a route that avoided all frequented byways. He rode fast, eager to get back to Prudence, not noticing MacLeod's occasional attempts at conversation until the Scot thrust the bag at him and leaned over to shout, "Ye're looking proper doon in the doldrums, sir. Will ye nae try a bit? They're verra good."

Delavale grinned and took a piece. He began to unwind the twist of paper, then paused, staring down at it. Slowing, he demanded, "Give me the bag again. Are they all the same colour?"

MacLeod said uncertainly, "I dinna ken what colour they are, but they taste like—"

"Not the sweets, man! The paper wrapping."

"Ah. Why, some are red, I fancy, and there's a few whites, and one or two blues. If ye dinna care for the one ye got—"

Delavale reined up and poked about in the bag. "I'll take all the blues," he declared, stuffing them into his pocket. He unwrapped one piece, put the toffee into his mouth, then took out his watch. MacLeod drew back a little, eyeing him uneasily. Delavale extracted a small fold of parchment. "Och, awie!" groaned MacLeod, with belated comprehension. "Did ye no get loose o' yon cypher?"

"Not only did I not, but it seems the army knows about it, and have put up a reward of one hundred pounds for any Jacobite fugitive caught carrying a 'poem.'"

MacLeod voiced a string of profanity. "What d'ye mean tae do, sir?"

Delavale put the blue-wrapped cypher into the bag. "For a start, eat no more of these. Never look so glum. Here, you may have the other blue ones. If anything should happen to me, you must take the sweets to the home of Lord Boudreaux. It is in Grosvenor Square in London. Now—ride, man! The sooner we're back in Trowbridge with Miss Prue, the better I'll like it!"

His anxiety communicated itself to the Scotsman, and they rode on at reckless speed through the quiet night. They saw only one group of redcoats, torches bright as they searched a large farm wagon on a distant lane. Neither man commented, but they increased their speed.

At ten minutes past nine o'clock they paused at a decrepit hedge tavern to rest the horses and snatch a quick cold supper and a glass of ale, and half an hour later, they were back in the saddle, riding steadily westwards.

With every mile, Delavale's fears increased. What an unconscionable fool he had been! She would not have left him, surely? That fierce pride of hers would not cause her to run into danger? But Cole would guard her. She would be safe. She *must* be safe! If she was not, it would be all his fault. How could he have become so angry? But she'd been angry, too. He smiled fondly at his mount's ears. How she'd railed at him. And how gracefully she had sunk into that curtsey—with a feather duster flourished in her little hand.

"Did ye say something, sir?"

"Oh, er, no, Mac. I was just thinking of something."

MacLeod's lips curved into a grin. He could guess of what the master had been thinking to bring that silly chuckle from him. He said nothing, however, and side by side they galloped on.

Delavale was crushingly weary when at last the many chimneys of The Black Lion loomed through the trees and they turned into the still lane. His eager eyes sought the window of her chamber. No light, but it was, of course, very late. Past one o'clock, for he'd heard a churchbell toll the—

The Black Lion leapt crazily onto its side. The moon shot down the heavens. In a wild tumbling confusion, Delavale was down, his hack squealing with terror, and a triumphant howl filling his ears. Dazedly, he fought his way to his knees. A gleam of steel plunged down at him, and he flung up one arm in a feeble attempt to protect himself.

As from a distance, he heard the eldritch blast of a Highland war cry. . . .

For Prudence, the hours that followed Geoffrey's grandiose exit separated into three distinct phases. The first was commandeered by rage: a seething resentment that Geoffrey, Lord Delavale, had dared to judge a MacTavish to be so deficient in manners as to require instruction! And, even more heinous, that he had cringed from presenting so uncouth a peasant to his fine friend! Polite Society, Miss MacTavish impolitely informed a passing moth, could go and boil its collective head! She began to rehearse what she would say to my lord Delavale when he returned. This impressive speech began with a denunciation of outmoded snobbery and pretension, went on to condemn high-flown English arrogance, and, whipped by her growing passion, took in and elaborated upon Butcher Cumberland and the savage nature of the English army in general, and my lord Delavale in particular. At this point, reason crept in to remind her of Mr. Ligun Doone. Her rageful bubble collapsed.

Here began the second phase, this being a growing unease because Geoffrey (reprieved from being my lord Delavale) did not return. If he had been displeased, she thought resentfully, he had deserved it. Ligun Doone was well and good, but he was still a mere man. And she a woman. Refusing to admit that she wished to look her best when she devastated him with her speech (which would have to be edited, just a little), she rang for a maid and sent her gown to be pressed. She spent the intervening time in polishing her speech and planning her future. She would go home, of course, as soon as that could be arranged. Only she had no money to pay for her journey. She thought forlornly that she might have no home to go to, either, and two big tears slid slowly down her cheeks. Where did she belong? Her heart was in smashed, trampled pieces. She was unloved and unwanted. Her family was scattered, for she refused to believe that anything worse could have happened to them. Life, she decided, was treacherously hard. She thought, 'Och, poor wee bairn,' and a watery giggle broke the silence of the little bedchamber.

The maid returned with her gown neatly pressed. Prudence allowed the girl to help her don it, then asked that she carry a message to her betrothed.

"Lord Delavale is gone out, biss," said the maid snuffily, dabbing at her red nose.

Fright ushered Prudence into the third phase. Had Geoffrey left her? She managed to sound calm and said that my lord had indeed mentioned that he might have to leave for a short while. The maid's only comment being another sniff, Prudence was emboldened to request that Delavale's man be sent to her.

Since Cole soon scratched on her door, she was relieved of the fear that she was truly abandoned, but he told her that Master Geoffrey had left almost two hours since. His gloom was all too understandable. Whitening, Prudence gasped, "My God! The cypher!" and sat down abruptly.

"Aye," Cole confirmed. "Gone off without me, and God only knows what he might run into. He's got no papers, Miss Prue. And if he should be stopped—" Here, belatedly, he noted the girl's terror and said bracingly, "Never look so afeared, ma'am. My lord took that great bare-kneed MacLeod with him, and for all he's a new man, he's devoted, I suppose." He added grudgingly, "And he can fight, I'll say that for him. Better than I could, with one arm! Master will be back at any minute. You just wait and see."

Wait, they did. Afternoon became dusk, dusk dragged into evening, night fell, and still Delavale had not returned. He had left strict instructions with Cole, so that Prudence was obliged to attempt to eat the dinner that was brought up to her parlour at seven o'clock.

The evening was cool and the wind blustery, but she was restless after her solitary meal, and she walked in the garden, going reluctantly to her parlour soon after nine o'clock. To prepare for bed was out of the question, and she looked through some old copies of *Ladies Magazine,* turning the pages with restless, unsteady hands until at last she became so drowsy that she fell asleep in the chair.

An ear-splitting Highland war cry woke her. It was cold and dark, for the candles had guttered and the fire was almost out, but from the windows came the glow of lanterns, and a great hubbub was arising in the yard.

Prudence was across the room in a flash and running to the stairs. She knew beyond doubting who was at the heart of the uproar, and a great flood of relief swept her when she saw him being aided into the vestibule, his arm across MacLeod's broad shoulders and his dark head bowed. She came down the stairs with a flutter of draperies and pushed her way through the excited little crowd of men in nightcaps and dressing gowns. MacLeod tossed her a tense look, opened his mouth, then shut it again. He looked rumpled, and there was a cut along his jaw. Cole, wearing a garish red-and-black dressing gown and a nightcap with a long red tassel, said quickly, "It's not bad, miss. Some thieves tried to waylay the Captain and he took a spill. Just a few grazes—nothing to be in the boughs about."

Delavale lifted his head and peered at her. There was a large graze above his right eye, and his face was mud-streaked. He said thickly, "Prue . . . ? You all right?"

She clasped his hand and assured him she was perfectly well.

"Disgraceful! Disgraceful!" cried the host, flushed and distressed. "That one of my guests should have been set upon! Practically in our own yard! We'd best have the Constable in!"

Delavale threw a warning glance at Prudence and she said quickly, "No, no. It was not your blame, host, and I had sooner see my lord brought quietly to my parlour so I can tend his hurts. Can you manage the stairs, dear sir?"

To the tremendous relief of the host, his lordship mumbled an affirmative and, to the accompaniment of much shocked comment from the little crowd, was assisted above stairs and into Prudence's parlour. The host departed, saying he would have a pot of hot tea sent up as soon as may be, and MacLeod lowered Delavale onto the sofa. Prudence ran to the washstand, wet a small towel, and came back to gently remove the mud from his face. "Oh, what a nasty scrape! But how fortunate your eye was not—"

He waved the towel away and peered at her anxiously. "Prue, my dearest girl, I am so sorry. In truth, I'm the veriest fool. Can you ever forgive me?"

She sank to her knees beside him, tears gemming her lashes. "'Twas my fault, and none o' yer own. If ye knew what I've suffered, fearing you taken or—or shot. . . ." Her voice broke. Delavale tossed the towel away and gathered her into his arms.

Cole looked at MacLeod's rugged and bloody features and grinned. "Looks as if ye've caught yerself a fine ding, you wild man," he said cheerfully. "Let me see if I can help."

Mildly astonished, MacLeod followed meekly. Cole led him to the washstand, bade him sit beside it, and proceeded to bathe the gash along the Scot's jaw. "Did they follow you?" he asked.

"Nae, mon. There were four of 'em waiting us here. Beyond the yard, y'ken."

Cole's deft hands checked. "They *knew* you were coming here?" he said, aghast.

Delavale's arms were fast locked about Prudence, his aching head forgotten as, between kisses, he whispered of his adoration and heard her soft voice thrilling with emotion as she murmured her tender responses. The others in the room ceased to exist, but through the ecstatic haze, Cole's shocked question drifted to Prudence's ears. With a little cry of alarm, she drew back. It was a testimonial to all they had gone through together that she experienced no embarrassment because their tender love-making had been observed. "Did you say the men who attacked you were *waiting* here?"

MacLeod nodded grimly.

Delavale said wearily, "You have it, Prue. They were not thieves."

"My heavens! Not—not troopers?"

MacLeod stood and came over, holding the cloth to his jaw. "No, lady. Belike they were after yon cypher, Captain."

Cole groaned. "Never say you could not deliver it, sir?"

"The man I was to give it to was away," Delavale lied, watching Prudence's scared face. "Just as well, for it will give me a chance to get you safely to Highview. Lord, but I never drew an easy breath whilst I was away from you."

This intensely uttered declaration won him such a melting look that it was as much as he could do not to pull her back into his arms.

Cole asked, "Were they after the cypher, sir?"

"If they were, they're an inept crew. What d'you think, MacLeod?"

The big man frowned. "I dinna ken, sir. Only they were powerfu' eager tae snuff ye. When ye went doon, I heard one o' the heathens shout, 'Is he finished?' And aw' wi' never a look tae me, whatever."

Prudence said, "But if they only wanted the cypher, why should they care if you were dead?"

"Why, indeed," said Delavale. "Unless they were known to me, perchance, and feared I might betray them. What did bring me down, Mac? Did you see?"

"Aye. A thin rope across the lane."

"Lying slack until we came up, no doubt, and then pulled

taut. An old trick, and too damned effective. But— My God! What a dimwit I am!" He got to his feet and took the alarmed MacLeod by the hand. "Again, you have saved my life! You should have seen him, Prue, standing over me and fighting like a whole battalion, while I was useless."

Colouring up, the Scot said gruffly, "Ye were nae useless fer long, sir. Else this"—he gestured to the cut on his face—"would hae found me throat instead."

They smiled upon one another, their hands fast gripped, each knowing that the bond between them was deep and strong and would endure for a lifetime.

A scratch at the door announced the arrival of the tea tray, which was carried in by a sleepy-eyed maid who blushed rosily because she was clad in her nightrail with her hair a thick braided rope hanging down over one shoulder. There were little cakes, buttered bread, and cheese on the tray, but MacLeod, although ravenous, could scarcely drag his eyes from the buxom maid. She flashed him a shy smile as she set down the tray, and he darted over to hold open the door for her.

Delavale glanced at Cole and winked, and the groom muttered, "Great lummox!"

"Well, Mac," said Delavale, sitting down and taking the steaming cup Prudence handed him, "did you notice anything about those louts?"

"Och, I do . . ." murmured the Scot dreamily. Delavale laughed. Reddening, MacLeod said, "Er, I'm sorry, sir. But ye'll own she's a bonnie wee lassie."

"Not so wee," muttered Cole. "But the right size for you, I'd— Hey, what's that you have?"

MacLeod inspected the small package he held. "Mistress Hetty give it me the noo. 'Tis fer yersel', sir."

"Mistress Hetty, is it?" Amused, Delavale took the package and opened it. He took out a folded letter and excused himself while he read it quickly. "By Jove!" He looked up and said an enthused, "It's from Treve de Villars, the rascal. He has sent me identification papers." He read from the letter: "'. . . due to the state of unrest because of these damned Jacobites, it might be well for you to postpone your sightseeing for a day or two, and be sure to keep your papers with you. England has changed since you left, my lad, as has your ancestral mansion. You should be prepared for a surprise.'" He frowned thoughtfully. "He wrote this with an eye to the possibility of its being intercepted, that's certain." Looking up again, he met Prudence's worried glance with a smile. "These papers will serve us well, I've no doubt. Good old Treve! We're almost there, my friends! We're almost safe home!"

Highview Manor was listed in the guidebooks as a three-storey Tudor mansion set in a nice park with woods and acreage comprising approximately one square mile. It was a good-sized house, constructed of red brick with white ornamented balustrades and having some four and fifty rooms, plus numerous outbuildings. Since, however, it did not possess such lures as battlements, turrets, pagodas, moats, or any outstanding uniqueness of design, and had not even a ghost or two to recommend it, it was not much patronized by sightseers. For two hundred years the principal seat of the head of the house of Montgomery, it was perhaps a trifle less attractive now than it had been in earlier years, for the beautiful gardens that had long ago been the pride and joy of Margaret, Lady Delavale, had been torn out by the present baron, Joseph Montgomery, this particular Lord Delavale being out of sympathy with the expense of maintaining such frivolities as flowers.

On this pleasant summer afternoon a deep silence had descended upon the manor. The lawns having been neatly scythed, the three overworked gardeners were labouring in the area of the cottage that had once been occupied by the nurse of poor young Lord Geoffrey Delavale—dead these ten months and more—and his sister, Miss Penelope, who had fled England with her traitorous Jacobite husband, and whose name was not permitted to be uttered at Highview.

The lord of the manor was closeted in his study with his bosom bow, Mr. Thomas Beasley, who had arrived but an hour since, his carriage caked with mud and his horses in a fine sweat.

In the servants' hall, Mrs. King, the housekeeper, was enjoying a cup of tea with the butler. Tall and broad-shouldered was Mr. Hargrave, with a proud and graceful carriage, an ingratiating manner, and a vicious, bullying temperament which was frequently turned upon those unfortunates who served him. He was very aware that Mrs. King adored him and, although inwardly designating her a scrawny old hen, he took care to stay in her good graces, knowing that Mrs. K, as he called her, had the ear of the master, and did not hesitate to fill it to the detriment of those who earned her displeasure. An excellent understanding existed between these two rulers of the staff, and thus it was that Mr. Hargrave, with a cautious glance at the door, went on, " . . . oh, I agree with you, Mrs. K. A beautiful woman is her ladyship. And knows how to use it. But I repeat, she's been very careful since the business with that strange old gentleman, Sir George Somerville. An odd affair"—he smirked—"*if* I may use the play on words, ma'am. A *very* odd affair."

Mrs. King threw one hand to her face in mock embarrassment, but although assuring the butler he was "such a naughty boy!" followed this pleasing admonition by reminding him that the gentleman's name had been John, not George Somerville. The pucker of annoyance that disturbed the brow of the object of her regard caused her to add quickly that Mr. Hargrave was "so very right, just the same. Was there anything more"—she lowered her voice—"more *disgraceful* than the way she flung herself at that poor old fellow? I'll lay you odds she'd not have give the old man one look had Captain Arrogant Otton not been off with the master. Hardly able to keep their hands from one another, milady and that there Captain—if he *is* one."

"They think the master don't see, Mrs. K. But he suspects, I'll warrant. And one of these days. . . ."

"One of these days, Sybil," murmured Captain Roland Otton, nuzzling the warm curve of Lady Delavale's soft throat, "your estimable husband will catch us fondling. You take too many chances, m'dear."

Sybil drew back pettishly and took up the embroidery hoop that lay on the grass. "Joseph," she muttered. "Always Joseph. He grows to be such a bore. I vow, Roly, this month you've been ill has been the dullest of my life." She turned her lovely but dissatisfied brown eyes to the man who lay propped against the tree beside her. A month since, Quentin Chandler had driven his sword into Otton's chest during a desperate fight for possession of a valuable cypher and her detestable niece, Penelope. Otton had been held prisoner by Jacobite sympathizers but, two weeks after he had taken his wound, had managed to get away, and had arrived at Highview in a sorry state. Sybil had enjoyed several pleasant little dalliances with him while 'nursing' him back to health, but it seemed to her that he was not quite as ardent as he had been before Penelope had run off with her traitor. She scanned him narrowly. His pallor seemed to enhance his dark good looks, and if the cynical twist to his mouth was more marked, his black eyes were dreamy at this moment and did not hold the hard, calculating look that usually characterized them.

"I'll own it has not been the happiest period of my existence." He smiled wryly at the beauteous little lady and reached out to touch a soft ringlet that drooped upon her shoulder. "I wonder why you are always so desirable when you pout."

Her eyes lit up. Eager, she leaned to him again, taking care not to rest her weight where it might pain him. A lovely armful, my lady Sybil, with a magnificent swell of bosom that so inflamed the convalescent gentlemen he sat up, seized her in an unexpectedly strong grasp, and with a twist laid her across his knees and proceeded to kiss and caress her in a way that would have enraged her husband almost as much as it delighted her.

She was limp and panting when he sighed and leaned back against the tree trunk. "Egad, woman, but you exhaust me. If your valiant spouse saw that, he's like to regret his charity in allowing me to return after my—failure."

"Failure!" She sat up and restored her gown. "You were nigh killed by that—that rebel vermin! I'll own I was surprised, for I've seen you fence." Her eyes became remote and a little wistful. "Was Chandler very good, Roly?"

"He was lucky!" he declared, his own eyes glinting angrily. "I'd have had the bastard and that cypher were it . . . not—" His lips tightened. He checked, then said as though compelled, "Yes—may he rot! He was very good. A truly magnificent swordsman, and beat me properly, damn him. Speaking of which, your lord and master is a long time with the beastly Beasley."

My lady looked to the house uneasily. "Yes. Thomas sounded alarmed when he arrived, did you—Have a care! Here comes Joseph now!"

"Your 'broidery," he hissed, closing his eyes. "At least, Thomas does not accompany him. One fat fool at a time, eh, my lovely wanton?"

She flushed, but kept her head downbent as she murmured, "Vicious beast! If he knew how you have cuckolded him . . ."

"Then it would be your loss as well as mine own, lovely one. Which is also why you let Chandler get away—no?"

Sybil gave a gasp. Her eyes darted to the unpleasant sneer on his face and the colour drained from her cheeks.

"What the devil are you about down here?" puffed Joseph, coming up with them, his protruding dark eyes turning suspiciously from his wife to his henchman's drowsing indolence. "One might think you more recovered by now, Otton."

"You give me too much credit, sir. I am a mere mortal man, after all."

"Aye. As you demonstrated last month," said his lordship, hands on fat hips and lower lip jutting petulantly over his weak chin. A faint flush crept into Otton's pale cheeks, and his shapely mouth tightened. Joseph had scored, and pleased, he reminded, "I pay you to defend my interests. Not to fail me when most I need you."

"You have not paid me at all, of late," Otton pointed out, a note of steel in his voice.

"I do not pay for failure. Count yourself lucky you have been cared for here."

Otton's dark gaze rested upon him in a chill, unblinking stare, and Joseph, more than a little afraid of this man, went on hurriedly, "If you're capable of it, you may soon have a chance to redeem yourself."

Otton got to his feet and bowed. "You are too good. Blubbery Thomas Beasley has upset you, I see."

Unhappily reminded of his own girth, and suspecting rightly that the reminder had been deliberate, his lordship snapped, "Beasley may have staved off disaster for all of us, which is more than you have done."

Sybil put up her hand and, as her husband assisted her to her feet, asked, "What is amiss, my lord? Never say Chandler and Penelope have been taken?"

"Not my niece," muttered Joseph gloomily. "It is the other thorn in my flesh who has returned—odd rot the boy!"

My lady gave a little scream, her hand flying to her throat. "*Geoffrey?* But—but you said he would never leave Scotland alive!"

"No more he should have, damn his tricky soul! I paid a pretty price for his, er—"

"Extermination?" supplied Otton helpfully.

Joseph glared at him, but before he could respond, Sybil squeaked, "Is he *here?* Nearby? My God! My *God!* We are *ruined!*" She wrung her little hands pathetically. "Whatever shall we do? He will take back the title and the fortune, and turn us out! He never liked us. We shall be penniless!"

"Beasley had the presence of mind to set some ruffians after him," said her spouse, offering his arm and starting slowly back to the house. "Do they fail, you'll have your chance, Otton. At all events," he muttered dismally, "if worst comes to worst, the boy's not a clutchfist—he'll give us an adequate allowance, I do not doubt."

Behind him, Otton's lip curled contemptuously. "Where is he now, sir?"

"He was in Trowbridge yesterday," said his lordship over his shoulder. "Pray God he'll get no farther north!"

"Perhaps you had best send me to verify your piety, my lord."

My lord's pudgy face purpled and he spun around, eyes narrowed and venomous. "Have a care, soldier! That damned mouth of yours will run my temper too thin one of these days. There are things I could tell the authorities—"

"A two-edged sword, *Mr. Montgomery,*" Otton interposed acidly.

The implication checked Joseph's wrath, for it was true that he had a tiger by the tail. If he informed on Otton, the soldier of fortune could inform no less lethally against him—and Sybil, and Beasley. It was borne in upon Joseph, and not for the first time, that this volatile tool would someday have to be quietly and permanently silenced.

Sybil cried distractedly, "Why must you quarrel? Our way of life is at risk! We must all contrive to *protect* ourselves!"

Otton bowed with his usual grace. For a while, at least, this treacherous lump of a man was the goose that laid the golden eggs, besides which, his wife, immoral tart that she was, was an ever-willing lover, and he was quite fond of her. He said with a winning smile, "You are as usual the wise one, ma'am. And I the fool. I ask your pardon, my lord."

Mollified, Joseph grunted and walked on, his wife flashing a smile at the Captain, and Otton unobtrusively kissing his hand to her.

They entered the great house through the rear terrace and the book room. Beasley waited there, and he glowered to see Otton saunter into the room behind Joseph and Sybil. Beasley, unhappily conscious of his florid, heavy features and ungainly body, was jealous of Otton's good looks and superb physique, feared his fighting capabilities, and resented the easy arrogance with which the younger man carried himself. "Gives himself all the airs of the aristocrat," he had grumbled to Joseph, to which his friend had shrugged. "How d'ye know he ain't one?" This was unanswerable, as Otton's past was shrouded in mystery, but the uneasy suspicion that the soldier might be better born than he himself (the pampered product of a family of cits) did little to reduce Beasley's dislike of the man.

Sybil demanded, as she sank onto the sofa, "Thomas, are you *sure* it was my nephew? Joseph sent men to Scotland to—er, handle matters."

"You arranged that for me, Otton," growled Joseph. "Another of your bungles."

Otton had been expecting this attack. He said coolly, "If Geoffrey escaped the rogues I hired, he either bears a charmed life or had a great deal of help." He added with a thoughtful frown, "One must hope the help did not wear red coats."

"It was Geoffrey, I tell you," said Beasley. "Or," he amended slyly, "perhaps I should say—it was Lord Delavale."

Otton grinned behind his hand. His lordship raged, "If I lose the title, Tom, you're like to lose your head, so smirk not!"

"I have done nothing," said Beasley. "The boy did not see me, I took good care of that. Besides, he was preoccupied. Had a damned pretty lightskirt with him. He told the host she was his betrothed."

"Betrothed!" gasped Sybil. "My heavens! Suppose—suppose she's his wife!"

"Married or not, she'll be here in jig time, has she an eye to the fortune," Otton murmured.

"She'll be too busy arranging for a funeral," said Beasley. "I sent four good men, Joseph. Geoffrey's dead as a doornail this very minute!"

The door was flung open. His voice shrill with excitement, Hargrave announced, "Lord Geoffrey Delavale!"

White as death, Sybil sprang to her feet; Joseph, who had just taken a mouthful of brandy, choked and dropped his glass; Beasley gave a yelp of shock and spun to face the door; Otton's eyes narrowed and he crouched a little as one prepared for action.

Geoffrey Montgomery, sixth Baron Delavale, strode into the room, pale with anger. His eyes swept the occupants and came to rest, blazing, on his uncle. "What the devil have you done to my mother's flowerbeds?" he demanded.

"I—I—" gulped Joseph, his face like putty.

"She loved those gardens. By what right—"

"Geoffrey! Oh, my dearest boy!" With a rush and a rustle, Sybil was upon her nephew and he was wrapped in two soft arms, engulfed in a cloud of heady perfume, and his head pulled down to be kissed, all in an instant. Unnerved, he shrank back. "Aunt . . . Sybil," he muttered, with difficulty disentangling himself.

"We thought you were dead, dearest boy."

"By Gad, Geoffrey," exclaimed Joseph, coming forward belatedly, hand outstretched. "What a shock! I wonder I did not suffer a seizure!"

"Then you will know how I felt when I saw my denuded lawns," snapped Delavale, pointedly ignoring his uncle's hand.

Joseph glared at him. Thomas Beasley also glared at him. Roland Otton, observing the scene with sardonic enjoyment, folded his arms and waited.

"And while you're at it," Delavale went on, "I should like an explanation of why my sister was obliged to flee this house."

"She took up with a traitorous damned rebel," blustered Joseph.

His head high and slightly backward tilted, his drooping eyelids conveying the scorn that had always enraged his uncle, Delavale drawled, "To the contrary, sir. Penelope attempted to befriend an old friend of my father's, whom I had offered sanctuary. As head of this house, I—"

"You will, I trust," Sybil interpolated desperately, "introduce us to this charming girl."

Prudence watched from the doorway. Delavale groaned, "Oh, Gad! Did it again, didn't I?" He hurried over to take her hand, and she smiled up at him in so revealing a way that Sybil and her husband exchanged a mournful glance.

Leading her into the room, Delavale said, "This lady is Miss Prudence MacTavish. Her father was exceeding kind and hospitable whilst I was in Scotland, and entrusted her to my escort. She goes to stay with relations. Prudence, may I present my uncle, Joseph Montgomery, and my aunt, Sybil." His gaze flickered to Beasley and Otton. "And two of their friends—Beasley, and the dark chap is Roland Otton."

Prudence curtseyed, startled by the ravishing beauty of the golden-haired Sybil, and by the admiration in the velvety black eyes of the pale young Adonis Geoffrey had introduced so cuttingly. Joseph deigned a jerky bow; Beasley nodded bleakly; Otton smiled a slow, appraising smile.

"My dear!" gushed Sybil, fervently wishing Prudence had smothered in her cradle. "You cannot know how joyous an occasion is this, to have our nephew restored to us."

Prudence said with a demure smile, "I can guess, ma'am."

Delavale gave a grin. Otton turned amused eyes to Joseph and encountered a murderous look. He lifted his brows questioningly. Joseph's head tilted surreptitiously towards his nephew. Otton pursed his lips, shrugged, and nodded. He pushed his hips away from the end of the sofa and sauntered to the credenza to refill his glass.

"We—must have a—a celebration," Sybil declared, breathless but trying.

"Capital idea," said Joseph with equally forced heartiness.

"Nonsense," said Delavale.

Otton chuckled, but a quick flush of anger replaced Joseph's pallor and Delavale, wishing to spare Prudence the scene that must follow, went to tug on the bellpull.

That the news had spread was very evident, for almost before he had turned about, the door opened to admit the housekeeper, her eyes bright with curiosity. He had never liked the woman, but one was not rude to females, and therefore he said with chill politeness, "As you can see, Mrs. King, I survived in spite of"—he looked steadily at his uncle—"of everything. Miss MacTavish has had a long, tiring journey and will want to rest. Please show her to our best guest suite."

Mrs. King's eyes darted to Joseph. "Mr. Beasley's things have been put in the blue room, my lord. I—"

"Remove them. Mr. Beasley is leaving." Delavale directed a chill stare at the sputtering Beasley. "Momentarily." He took Prudence's hand and said in a very different tone, "Mrs. King will assign a maid to you on a temporary basis, ma'am. You will please to ring for any least thing you desire."

Prudence saw malevolence in Joseph's eyes and, frightened, murmured, "I would prefer to stay here with you, sir."

He smiled down at her. "Then come back so soon as you are rested and have put off your travelling clothes." And to Mrs. King he added, "Miss MacTavish's abigail is following with the rest of her luggage. Cole returned with me. The other man is called Stuart MacLeod. He is to be found a nice room in the main house. Thank you, that will be all."

Mrs. King quailed before the hauteur in his dark gaze. She felt impelled to drop a curtsey, and went out, considerably shaken, ushering Prudence before her.

Having opened the door for them, Delavale closed it and turned to face four stares: two wrathful, one anxious, and one black and sardonically impenetrable. "I would suggest you leave us, ma'am," he said.

Sybil fluttered, "I do not know why you seem so—almost *cold*, dearest Geoffrey. But—I shall stay, if you please."

"So be it." He turned frigid eyes on his uncle. "I'll have an accounting now, sir."

"What the devil do you mean by that?" Joseph struck an offended pose. "You were reported killed in action. I took over my duties as head of the family, and—"

"And proceeded to ruin the grounds, discharge the servants who have served my family for many years, and drive my sister from her home! You've an odd interpretation of your 'duties,' sir!"

His angry flush deepening, Joseph took the weak man's refuge and lost his temper. "Do not take that tone with me, you traitorous young whelp. D'ye think I don't know what you've been about in Scotland?"

"If you knew what I was doing in Scotland, you also knew I was alive, and thus had no right whatsoever to claim either the title or the fortune."

Joseph huffed and puffed and finally blustered, "We believed the report of your death for some time. Later, it—it seemed unlikely you would survive your wounds. When we learned you were involved in treasonable activities—"

"Which you could only have learned by intercepting my letters to my sister! I sent Tim Buchanan here, and now there is some doubt but that he was betrayed to his death!" Eyes narrowing with wrath, Delavale stalked forward. "*Your* doing, my noble kinsman?"

His face twitching with nervousness, Joseph drew himself up. "Have a care, sir!"

"I sent Quentin Chandler here, and I now learn that he only escaped thanks to the intervention of my dear sister."

"Chandler is a rogue and a traitor. He was involved in a plot to smuggle a cargo of Jacobite gold across England! And when poor Otton here strove to protect your sister from his lecherous advances, he was nigh killed for his pains and is but now recovered."

"What a pity," said Delavale, darting a contemptuous glance at the soldier of fortune.

"Do you doubt the veracity of your uncle's tale?" Otton waved a graceful hand. "It was a fair duel, I'll admit. But—I can show you the scar."

"If you took a wound, Captain Otton, it was more likely that *you* were attempting to run off with my sister. I recollect you had a *tendre* for her, and I'd put no villainy past you!"

Otton's dark eyes flashed and his jaw tightened, but he said nothing.

Dabbing at tears that had nothing to do with remorse, Sybil wailed, "Of what avail is all this? You come home and are gladly welcomed, but—but say all these dreadful things and threaten to put us out . . . and whatever is to—"

Beasley, who had been watching in glowering silence, interrupted rudely, "And why has he come home after all this time? I'll warrant I know! He was the one sending out the couriers. Likely he's one himself, and has a cypher concealed about his person!"

An electric silence fell. Glancing from one suddenly hungry face to the next, Delavale knew that he was in peril in his own home and from his own family. His hand dropped to his sword hilt. He said coldly, "I do not recall asking for your drivel, Beasley. As for your abode, ma'am, you—"

Joseph's hot little eyes were glowing at the thought that his nephew who brought so deadly a threat might also be the source of untold riches. "It's true, by Jupiter," he said in a half-whisper. "He *is* a courier! Only look at how he reaches for his sword. By God, but you'll hand the cypher over, Geoffrey, or—"

"Don't be a fool," said Delavale, his hand tightening about the grip of his sword. "Two of my men wait in the hall, and

Miss MacTavish is above stairs. Do you dare threaten me in my own house?"

"One does not threaten a traitor," declared Joseph, moving closer.

Delavale whipped sword from scabbard. "Stay back, or by God, I shall—"

"Do—precisely—nothing," purred Otton. A sleek pistol was held steadily in his hand, aimed straight at Delavale's heart.

"One shot," said Delavale, "and you will have everyone in the house down here."

"And almost everyone in the house is loyal to Joseph," said Beasley. "Not to you. I'll tell Hargrave to call the men."

"Do you move a step closer to that bellrope, my fat friend," said Delavale, "I shall cut you down. Never look at my uncle's paid killer. He'll not dare shoot, which he knows as well as I."

The door burst open. Delavale's back was to it, and he dared not glance from the threat that faced him.

Otton smiled. "How obliging. Do come in, Miss MacTavish."

With a dismayed gasp, Delavale spun around. He had been fooled by an old trick. Instead of Prudence, Mrs. King stood on the threshold, her goggling eyes taking in the scene.

Delavale jerked back immediately, but with a pantherish leap, Otton sent the pistol flailing at his head. Delavale swayed aside and whipped up his sword, but with courage born of desperation, Sybil snatched up a heavy candelabra and threw it with such accuracy that the sword was smashed from Delavale's hand. Otton grabbed his wrist, twisting it back; Beasley clamped a brutal grasp on his other arm. Joseph drew back his hamlike fist, his eyes glittering with triumph.

Recovering her wits, Mrs. King squealed, "*Soldiers!* There be soldiers in the house!"

XXI

Prudence thanked the timid housemaid and, clad in the hastily pressed pink silken gown, stepped into the hall. The staircase wound in a central spiral through the three storeys of the great house and, walking to the well, she looked down to the ground floor. She could see many servants milling about in the main hall, and there was a deal of flurried, low-voiced chatter, especially between the tall butler and the housekeeper. Prudence smiled faintly. They would do well to be disturbed, for from what Geoffrey had told her, they had made his poor sister miserably unhappy. She could not be easy to think of him, alone in the drawing room with Joseph and his cronies, and she trod swiftly down the stairs.

She was descending the final flight when she became aware that the servants had dispersed and that there was some kind of commotion outside. Uneasy, she slowed her steps. Mrs. King fairly shot across the hall and galloped to the drawing room. Her heart beginning to flutter, Prudence followed. She approached the door in time to hear Mrs. King's dramatic pronouncement. Once again, the cold and familiar hand of fear had her in its grip. There were no uniforms to be seen, but the housekeeper was plainly terrified. "My Gawd!" she gasped. "I don't want none of this, I don't!" and she fled back the way she had come, brushing past Prudence without a check.

Hurrying to the drawing room, Prudence closed the open door and leaned back against it, stunned. The occupants were gathered in a close unmoving group, like the figures in a charade. Geoffrey's sword was on the floor; Otton and Beasley held his arms, and Joseph Montgomery's upraised fist was menacingly clenched.

From beyond the door a loathed voice rang out. "Where is the master? No, not Montgomery. Captain Lord Delavale. I know he's here!"

Prudence shrank, the name 'Cunningham!' emblazoned on her mind.

The frozen tableau sprang to life. Otton released Delavale, picked up the fallen sword, and handed it to him. Beasley ran to sit in an armchair and snatch up a glass of wine. Sybil and Joseph hastened to occupy the sofa. Geoffrey raced to the credenza and emptied the contents of a small rumpled bag into a comfit dish. His hair was dishevelled, and he thrust a quick hand through it, which was of little help. Prudence ran to his side, and he scowled as though vexed to see her there.

"Good afternoon, Captain Delacourt."

Delavale wrenched his eyes from Prudence's bewildered little face and turned about, brows lifting in apparent surprise. "Colonel Cunningham! Jove, but you travel swiftly."

"And sadly," declared Cunningham with doubtful veracity since his hard eyes fairly blazed with triumph. "You cannot know how it grieves me to have to arrest one of my officers for desertion . . . at the very least." Since Delavale betrayed nothing more than polite interest, he thought that this was going to be more difficult than he had hoped, and said with an air of regret, "How do you do, Miss MacTavish? I am glad to find you safe, but sorry to find you in such company."

"What the deuce kind of remark is that?" demanded Joseph, affronted.

"My uncle, sir," said Delavale, his mind racing. "Mr. and

Mrs. Joseph Montgomery—Colonel Cunningham. Mr. Beasley. And this is—"

"We are acquainted." Having bowed shortly to the Montgomerys and Beasley, the Colonel turned a speculative gaze upon Otton. "Faith, but you never cease to astound me, my dear Roland. I'd fancied to have seen the end of you in Flanders, and here you are again. I wonder what you are after this time. Treasure?"

Five startled pairs of eyes shot to Otton. He smiled faintly. "Always, sir. Always. And you?"

"My treasure, alas, is dross." Cunningham's gaze returned to the dark young man who stood straight and tall beside the girl. Delavale looked proud and oddly regal, and the girl's hair gleamed like a flame around her pale face. He thought a detached, 'They make a fine couple. Pity.' And he snapped his fingers.

Delavale stood motionless as a Sergeant and a trooper marched across the room to position themselves on both sides of him. His heart sank, but as usual, at the approach of danger a tingle of excitement went through him. "Sir?" he said, managing to sound astonished. "Am I to deduce that you believe me to have deserted?"

"I wonder why I should assume such a thing," said Cunningham with a twisted smile. "Only because you used an assumed name whilst you were in Scotland?"

"I think you are provoked, Colonel, but the truth is that after I was hit I was quite incapacitated for several months. The people who rescued me on the field mistook me for poor Delacourt. I was told that was my name, and I believed it."

"They call it amnesia, I believe." Cunningham smiled. "How convenient."

It would have pleased Joseph Montgomery had his nephew been so accommodating as to die of his wounds. He would have been only mildly remorseful had Beasley's hired assassins done their job properly here in England, or Otton's men succeeded in Scotland. But for Geoffrey to be dragged to the Tower of

London, put to the question, and, eventually, condemned to a traitor's death did not suit him at all. It was not the prospect of his nephew being tortured and killed that appalled him. He had no use for either of his brother's children and was quite aware that Geoffrey disliked him. He was equally aware that the boy would make adequate—probably generous—provision for him and Sybil. If Delavale should die a traitor's death, however, his estates would be forfeit, leaving Joseph penniless. A horrid circumstance. Therefore, although he was very frightened, he now intervened, his voice louder than ever. "What the devil d'you mean, sir, by bursting in here and upsetting my dear wife? We've scarce had time to welcome m'nephew and his guest. And since when is it become a treasonable act to lose one's memory? A pretty pass we've come to, if a peer can be summarily brought to book for such nonsense! You'd as well arrest me for believing him killed!"

"Not at all, sir." A gleam lighting his cold eyes, Cunningham replied, "I have no doubt at all of your motive in doing so."

"The . . . deuce . . . !" Purpling, Joseph stood up and stepped forward.

Cunningham's voice was ice. "It is only fair to warn you, Mr. Montgomery, that if any here attempt to interfere in this matter, they will be arrested as conspirators!"

Sybil gave a whimper of terror and ran to clutch her husband's arm. The high colour draining from his face, Joseph led her to the rear of the room, temporarily, at least, out of the line of fire.

"As for you, Captain." Cunningham turned back to Delavale. "The first charge against you is desertion in time of war. The second, and major charge, is of fermenting rebellion and unrest among the Scots; of assisting numerous enemies of the State to escape apprehension, and of treasonable activities against the Crown while masquerading under the name of Ligun Doone."

At this terrible list of crimes, Prudence felt dizzied and sick. Sybil gave a shriek and sank, half fainting, against a pallid-faced Joseph. Delavale, his expression one of tolerant amusement, decided that if worst came to worst, he would try to fight his way out. Better to die quickly.

Genuinely surprised, Otton started and exclaimed, "By God! I thought Doone was a Scot!"

"He is," said Prudence, trying to speak clearly though her lips felt cold and numb. "It is a mistake, is all."

Delavale murmured, "Am I to understand, Colonel, that you suspect me of being a Scot? No, but I do assure you that I was born in this very house."

Irked by the complete lack of panic in his prey, Cunningham rasped, "I accuse you of being Ligun Doone, not of being a Scot. I will not ask you for a refutation, however. You would doubtless suffer another 'lapse of memory,' and I detest to waste time. It will go easier on you, my lord, if you confess now and hand over the cypher."

Whether it was a bluff, or whether Cunningham had certain knowledge that he carried the cypher, Delavale could not guess. He frowned as though perplexed. "Cypher? Sir, I must disappoint you. I have no cypher."

"Alas, my lord. You leave me no alternative but to have you searched."

Trembling with terror, and sure that the deadly cypher was even now residing in the comfit dish, Joseph spluttered, "Search a *peer*? 'Sblood, but the fella babbles like a halfwit. What's all this about a cypher?"

"Nothing that need concern you, Mr. Montgomery," said Cunningham. "Unless your nephew proves to have it concealed about his person, or in this house. In which case, it will be my unhappy duty to arrest you all. Well, my lord? Have you decided to be sensible and hand it over?"

"I think I am a reasonable man, sir. But if you wish to search me—or my home—I shall have to ask to see your warrant."

Cunningham's jaw set. The truth was that he had no warrant. His General had been sceptical that any English aristocrat who had been brutally handled by the Scots would subsequently so bestir himself in their behalf. Nor had he been easy as to the consequences of mistakenly arresting a peer of the realm. Eager for promotion and convinced his suspicions were justified, Cunningham had gone over his General's head and had approached his Grace the Duke of Cumberland in the matter. His Grace, infuriated by Ligun Doone's successes, had roared hearty approval. He had always applauded initiative in his officers, he said, and did Cunningham pull off his coup, he would be "suitably and gratefully rewarded." That, of course, meant the long yearned for promotion, but Cunningham was under no illusions. If things went awry, his Grace would have no part of it, and the first to be flung to the lions would be himself.

There was no hint of any of this in his demeanour, however, when he said with cold inflexibility that no warrants were needed for traitors. "Sergeant, I want Lord Delavale stripped and thoroughly searched. Leave no seam or lining of his clothing intact. We seek a quite small piece of parchment containing a poem. Otton—be so good as to escort the ladies from the room."

Delavale turned to Prudence and reached for her hand. It was cold as ice, and he squeezed it and said coolly, "My dear lady, I am indeed sorry that your arrival at Highview has been marred in this ridiculous fashion. I fear that poor Cunningham has been ill advised, but we must give him enough rope, so please do not be alarmed."

Taking her cue from him, she murmured, "But, my lord, it is so disgraceful. Do you mean to do nothing?"

"No need, ma'am. My solicitors will handle matters."

He looked so calm, so unruffled; certainly not afraid. Commencing to experience the first twinges of nerves, Cunningham's choler rose. "Very impressive," he snapped. "Captain Otton?"

Ten minutes later, grim-lipped and inwardly seething, Delavale adjusted the lace at his wrists, shrugged into the jacket the butler had brought him, and enquired, "Well, Colonel? You have torn to shreds several perfectly serviceable articles of clothing and a costly pair of boots. I have explained why I did not advise you of my true identity. I have told you how Miss MacTavish and I were abducted from Lakepoint and held for ransom, and why I have only now managed to return here. I have yet to hear one iota of evidence against me."

"You will, my lord," said the Colonel with a tight smile. "A witness is en route here who will testify as to your treachery in so damning a way you must be convicted beyond hope of reprieve. Otton, I ask you as a former officer in the service of our King, did this traitor hand anything to anyone upon arriving? Did you see him put anything away, or go to any drawer or cupboard? There is a large reward for the capture of Ligun Doone, to say nothing of the amount offered for the cypher he likely carries."

Very aware of the mercenary nature of his hired sword, and of his lack of loyalty to any but himself, Joseph stared at Otton in mute despair. Beasley, his heart leaping crazily, began to weave desperate schemes to exonerate himself from any suspicion of complicity in Joseph's activities. Delavale stood very still, prepared for the words that would spell his doom. Otton had seen him empty the toffees into the comfit dish. The man's impenetrable gaze was steady on him. He knew. A few words only, and he could collect the rewards, while the rest of them would face arrest, and his own fate— Delavale forced his mind away from that horror.

Otton said smoothly, "It is very fortunate that I am here to be your eyes and ears, Colonel. I saw Delavale enter the house. I've not left his side since. To my knowledge, he has hid nothing since he came."

A tremor shook Delavale. His hands were suddenly wet, but he dared not show relief, and said with a frown, "One can but hope you are satisfied, sir."

Cunningham's jaw was a grim jut. He scowled at the shredded garments the trooper still pawed through. Then, watching Delavale keenly, said, "Bring in the ladies, if you please, Sergeant."

Delavale tensed.

Otton murmured, "I wish I might have had better news for you, sir. Perchance you should search his saddle."

"My men have attended to that. No, I think it more likely he has passed the cypher to his lady—er, friend."

"You go too far, Cunningham," grated Delavale. "I escorted Miss MacTavish here. If I had this cypher you speak of, do you seriously think I would imperil her with it?"

Archibald Cunningham was a ruthless and ambitious individual, but he was a good officer, and he knew men. He was very sure that nothing would have induced Delavale to place a lady in jeopardy. But he was equally sure now that the girl was Delavale's Achilles' heel, and he meant to make good use of that fact. "Come in, Miss MacTavish," he called genially. "Poor lady, you have had a very sad time of it, his lordship tells me. Captured by thieves and murderers; held prisoner in a great cave! Egad, 'tis no wonder he felt safer with the poem in your possession. I will relieve you of it, ma'am."

Prudence had dreaded what she might find when allowed to return to the drawing room. She was relieved to see Geoffrey looking white and furious but unharmed, and noting also his grim look of warning, she said calmly, "That should be simple to do, Colonel, save that I do not recall his lordship ever giving me any poetry."

Otton, his eyes dancing, murmured, "I hereby volunteer to search the lady."

Prudence drew back instinctively.

Cursing, Delavale sprang at him, and the Sergeant and trooper ran to seize his arms and jerk him away. "Do you lay a hand on her," he raged, "and as God is my judge, I swear I shall—"

"You shall be imprisoned in the Tower, Captain," snapped Cunningham. "And it looks as if you mean to drag this poor lady to her death beside you." He strode closer to Delavale and, his voice rising, thundered, "Hand over the cypher now, and spare her!"

"I have not got your cypher—damn you!"

"Rank insubordination," said Otton, chidingly. "Sir, I wonder you—"

The hall door burst open. The butler said, "Colonel Cunningham. There is a man come asking for you."

"Bring him in!" His eyes bright, Cunningham said, "*Now* you will see how stupid you are to lie to me, Delavale!"

Hurrying footsteps in the hall, and every eye was fixed on the doorway. A man came up, paused on the threshold an instant, then came inside.

Prudence's dread was justified, and despair overwhelmed her.

His heart plummeting, Delavale thought an anguished, 'We have come so far. Almost, we escaped . . .' Prudence looked at him, tears trembling on her lashes. Somehow, he made his lips smile at her.

"Mr. Sidley," said Cunningham, advancing to greet the newcomer. "My dear fellow, how very good in you to come all this distance. I was never more pleased than to hear of your miraculous escape."

"Miraculous indeed," replied Sidley, his stern gaze fixed on Delavale. "I doubt you can credit, sir, how glad I was to answer your summons and come down here. Such despicable treachery must not be allowed to go unpunished."

"No more it shall, I promise you. We lack only the verification of it by a witness such as yourself. Had you any suspicion, poor fellow, of the fate that awaited you when you agreed to the scheme Captain Delavale proposed?"

"No, sir. I have a deep loathing for the Jacobites and I was willing, nay, eager, to do what I might to apprehend the traitor. But I'll own I had hoped to come safely back to Lakepoint, as the Captain—I had thought his name was Delacourt, sir—as he had said would certainly transpire."

"Aye. Instead of which, you were seized and held captive and damn near killed! I can well imagine how you must have felt when you saw the Captain arrive."

"There are no words to express it. I thought that great heathen had killed him, sir. And the next instant, he had turned his brutality on me. My head ached for days afterwards, and I was not hurt near so bad as the Captain."

Cunningham frowned a little. "How's that? You mean—some one of the rebels made a mistake?"

"Oh, I don't think I would call it that, Colonel. They hate us, you know. And in a way I cannot blame them, for had my boy lived, I know he'd not have liked to see what the Duke of Cumber—"

"Yes, well, never mind that. What I mean is, when they realized their leader was come among them, they must have been wild with joy. And you, my dear chap, must have fancied you'd succeeded beyond your wildest hopes."

Sidley shook his head rather despondently. "Oh. Well, I never saw *him*, you know."

Delavale, who had been watching the erstwhile butler narrowly, was already experiencing the first stirrings of hope. Not daring to look at Prudence, he waited tensely.

"Never *saw* him?" echoed Cunningham, glaring at Sidley. "You just said that you saw Delavale ride in."

"Oh, yes. I saw the Captain and Miss MacTavish, poor lady. But I did not see the man they call Ligun Doone. They took good care of that."

Through the following deathly hush, Cunningham became very white and then as red. "Do you say," he snarled, "do you say that the man standing before you—" He flung an arm ferociously in the general direction of Delavale. "Do you say he is *not* Ligun Doone?"

Sidley's eyes opened very wide, and his jaw dropped with what Delavale thought admirable 'astonishment.' "Captain . . . *Delacourt* . . . ?" he gasped.

"No!" roared Cunningham, savage with frustration. "Captain Lord Geoffrey Delavale!"

"Lord?" said Sidley, impressed. "I never knew you was a lord, sir."

His eyes beginning to dance, Delavale said, "Well, you see I—"

"I do not give one thin *damn* whether you knew he was a lord," Cunningham howled. "*Is* he, or is he *not*, Ligun Doone?"

"Well, of course he's not, sir," Sidley answered. "They'd scarce have tried to kill him, had he been. Very near succeeded, too. Indeed, I am most glad to see you well, my lord," he added, turning to beam at Delavale.

"It is a *conspiracy!*" Cunningham raged, his face purpling. "*Damn* your eyes, I will—"

Delavale interposed in a voice of steel. "You will be well advised to abandon this unfortunate obsession. I have the greatest respect for your rank and your abilities, Colonel, but I must warn you that if you do not cease this persecution, I shall have no choice but to lay the matter in the hands of my solicitors and lodge a formal complaint at the Horse Guards. You have invaded my home, intimidated my servants, frightened my family, destroyed my property, threatened me, and all without a vestige of proof." And for once in his life using his rank, he added sternly, "As a British peer, I am not obliged to stand still for such nonsense. My godparent, the Duke of Marbury, is expected here momentarily, and I should grieve to have his Grace disturbed by this fiasco."

It was a telling stroke. Marbury was a confidant of His Majesty, a man of tremendous wealth and power, and known to be a placid, rather bored individual who could become a terror when aroused. Torn between rage and self-preservation, the Colonel chewed his lower lip, clenched his fists, glared at Delavale, and, grasping at his last straw, said hoarsely, "You are, nonetheless, most assuredly guilty of desertion, and—"

"Ah—I had quite forgot to tell you. During my illness in the cavern I regained my memory. Therefore, as soon as we reached England, I reported to the army post at Bath, explained my absence, and advised the commanding officer that I will be selling out. Major Price-Danby was most understanding. He has forwarded my papers to Whitehall, and advised me to consider myself on medical leave until the separation can be effected."

Quivering with mortification, Cunningham gritted, "Very clever. You think to have won, but we shall see who has the last laugh, Delavale!" He turned and began to stamp out, pausing only to bow jerkily to Sybil, whose charms had done little to calm his emotions.

Always aware when a gentleman found her desirable, she cried, "Oh, poor Colonel! Such a disappointment. We must not send you off angry. Here . . ." She had been scrambling to the sofa when Cunningham arrived and thus had not seen Delavale fill the comfit dish, but noting it contained sweets, she took it up and swung with a flutter of skirts to offer it to the glowering officer.

Delavale caught his breath. Moving to the Colonel's side, he said, "Sir, I hope this need not cause ill-feeling."

Cunningham ignored him and reached for the single blue-wrapped toffee.

"I really had no . . . no intent . . ." Delavale's voice became thready.

His gaze having returned to its preoccupation with Sybil's beautiful bosom, Cunningham was staggered as Delavale lurched against them and fell headlong, dashing the bowl from Sybil's hand, the sweets scattering.

With a shriek, Prudence ran to him. "It is one of his swoons! Poor soul!"

Consternation reigned as they crowded around the stricken man, but even as Sidley asked anxiously if he should bring some brandy, Prudence noted that among the toffees littering the carpet, not one had a blue wrapper. She chafed Delavale's unresponsive (and clenched) hand. Joseph bellowed for a lackey to ride for the apothecary. Sybil, who had a morbid fear of death, shrank away moaning that her nephew looked to have expired, and only Otton, once more perched against the arm of the sofa, remained an amused and unmoved spectator.

Colonel Cunningham bowed to defeat and stamped out, toffeeless.

Highview Manor was seldom more beautiful than when bathed in the warm glow of sunset, and this afternoon was no exception. The roseate beams illumined a busy scene: A small mountain of luggage was piled on the front steps. Footmen and lackeys scurried to load the boot of the next-best carriage, and the team stamped and snorted, impatient to be gone.

Not at all eager to be gone, Sybil wept as she was handed into the coach. With a thoughtful look at Delavale, Otton swung into the saddle of his tall chestnut horse. "We shall meet again, I think," he murmured.

"Do you?" said Delavale with a marked lack of enthusiasm.

His florid face even more so in the glow of the sunset, Joseph grumbled, "A fine reward for my silence! You are properly high-handed, nephew, to kick us out. I wonder what your poor papa would think."

Delavale took him firmly by the arm and marched him out of earshot. "Let me tell you what he would think, sir—that I am a fool to allow you to leave without lodging charges against you!"

"For what, I should like to know, damme!"

"For my attempted murder. Not once—but several times."

"By *Gad,* sir! Of all the *damned* beastly lies! D'ye dare to imply—"

"No, Uncle. I do not imply. I state. We were invaded at Lakepoint by men whose one aim was to put an end to me. One of them wore a multi-coloured leathern vest. It seemed to me I had seen it before, but not until very recently did I recall where. It was here—at The Blue Boar in the village. Coincidence? Hardly. Again, when you learned I had left Scotland and was likely to arrive here uncomfortably alive, you sent out assassins to ensure you would retain the title and estates you had unlawfully appropriated."

"Why, you—you ungrateful . . . blasted young . . . ingrate!" blustered Joseph, very pale. "Much chance you have of—of proving your Canterbury tale!"

"No. Because your would-be murderers are scattered, I've no doubt. But *I* know, Uncle. And *you* know. You will be wise to settle for the consolation prize of the house in Town, and an allowance. But—know this—should my life end suddenly, for *any* reason; should Miss MacTavish be hurt or threatened in any way, my solicitors will find in their safe a written statement to be opened in such an eventuality. Also, the Duke of Marbury has a like statement. Your arrest on charges of conspiracy, attempted murder, and treason would say the least of the matter. Perhaps your past affairs would stand up well. I doubt it."

Joseph's pudgy features were the colour of pastry dough. His mouth opened, yet nothing but an inarticulate gabble came forth and he closed it again, staring at his nephew's grave face in helpless chagrin.

Delavale said regretfully, "A sad pass we have come to that I must speak so to my father's brother. Yet I do believe my sire would have been less lenient with you than I. Goodbye, Uncle Joseph. It will be better, I think, do we not meet again. I am assured you will be able to live comfortably on the allowance I shall make you. But you had best hope, sir, that *I* live to a ripe old age."

Delavale paused outside the drawing room door and, with an effort, erased the grimness from his eyes and entered cheerfully.

Prudence was seated by the empty fireplace talking with Sidley, who sprang up as he came in. Delavale went forward, his hand outstretched.

"My dear fellow! However could you have been so very magnanimous as to come to my rescue when I had served you so shabbily?"

Rather bashfully taking his lordship's hand, Sidley returned the strong grip. "Shabbily, sir? Scarcely. Oh, you had me properly gammoned, I'll admit, but I'd not been long in that wretched cave before I came to realize how much simpler it would have been for you to have me killed out of hand. And, after being with those poor devils for a while . . ." He shook his head and smiled wryly. "Nothing is ever a simple black or white, is it? When I escaped—"

"How did you manage that?" interpolated Delavale, sitting beside Prudence and waving the butler to a chair.

"We'd a great storm, sir," said Sidley. "Several of the rebels decided to try to win through to the north in the uproar, and luckily I was able to slip out amongst them, wrapped in a stolen plaid. I had some close calls, I will say, but by great good fortune I met up with a troop of dragoons and was conducted back to Inverness."

Prudence put in eagerly, "Sidley has brought me a letter, dear sir. My papa and all are safe! They returned to Lakepoint when they learned Cunningham had left, and were able to convince the authorities they had fled a band of murderous deserters who attacked the house in search of valuables. Our servants, of course, supported this, and Papa says that so long as they lead what he calls 'exemplary lives' there should be no more trouble. Oh, if you could but *know* how I am relieved!"

He smiled at her understandingly. "Of course I know, ma'am. Sidley, what about poor Briley?"

"Safe away and gone back to—I believe he said Sussex, my lord. It seems there is a very lovely lady there of whom he is most fond. I—er, believe a Countess . . ."

"Ah, yes. Lady Aynsworth. Her twin sons served in my regiment . . ." Briefly, sadness clouded his eyes. Then he said, "I am more grateful than I can say, but I wish you will believe,

Sidley, that I never entertained the notion of having you slain."

"I do believe it, sir. When I think how I behaved to you in the cave, and then to learn that far from starving, as I'd feared, my wife and sister have been very generously supported by an 'anonymous gentleman . . .'" Leaning forward, his eyes very grave, he added, "I knew who was that gentleman, my lord. Except for your kind concern for a man who was at the very least a thorn in your flesh, I might have returned to tragedy. As it is, well, when Colonel Cunningham sent a Sergeant to escort me here, I was only too glad to repay, in some small fashion, what you have done for me."

"I am more than repaid. And yet I mean to ask another favour of you. Tell me—do you mean to return to Inverness?"

Sidley looked glum. "I fancy I shall, sir. It is hard to be so far from my wife, but she seems to be making a recovery at last, and—I am most fond of Mr. MacTavish and his sister. And the—remuneration is such . . ."

"I quite understand. We had a most excellent butler while my parents were alive. I believe he has found employment elsewhere, alas. And my present butler"—Delavale's expression became bleak—"I will not tolerate." He glanced at Sidley's hopeful face and went on, "I was thinking, you see, that there is a very comfortable cottage on the grounds that might suit your family nicely. And I hope I am not a nipcheese; I shall be glad to pay half again what MacTavish was—"

Prudence cried indignantly, "Unprincipled wretch! You mean to steal my papa's fine butler away!"

He laughed and took up her hand. "No, but you must admit it would be very pleasant for Mrs. Sidley to have her husband near to her again."

"Oh, s-sir," cried the butler tremulously. "Do you mean it? If—if only it might be!"

"It was certainly my intent, but"—Delavale sighed—"I dare not provoke Miss MacTavish. She might decide to return home, and another sea voyage with her, alas, I do not think I could support."

"Evil, evil creature," said Prudence with a little trill of mirth. "*How* you do manipulate us all! Of course I shall not object, Mr. Sidley. Indeed, nothing would be more delightful than—" And she stopped, blushing and confused, because she had no right to presume so. Whatever his intentions towards her might be, my lord Delavale had said not one word that would lead her to believe he meant to make her his wife.

XXII

Reacquainted now with the spectre of unyielding propriety, Delavale moved very fast. Mrs. King and an outraged Mr. Hargrave were presented with three months' wages and dismissed. The entire staff was summoned to a meeting in the hall whereat Mr. Sidley was presented as the new butler. Cheers rang out when Delavale announced that, if at all possible, the lady who had been his father's housekeeper would be returned to the position she had left. A groom was sent off at the gallop with an urgent letter addressed to his Grace, the Duke of Marbury, at the great estate which Delavale had pointed out to Prudence the previous morning. Another groom, accompanied by Stuart MacLeod, drove a chaise to The Black Lion inn near Trowbridge, where a blushing Mistress Hetty Burnett, meeting MacLeod's admiring gaze, was overjoyed to accept an offer to become abigail to Miss Prudence MacTavish. The chef, a gloomy Frenchman, was sent for and inestimably cheered by an audience with Highview's new butler. He returned, elated, to his kitchens, and announced that he would now concoct meals suitable for one "who 'ave know how to command ze *haute cuisine!*" And last but not least, the dogs, for three years penned up behind the stables, were released to go mad with delight upon being reunited with their long-lost god.

Impressed by the crisp commands, the cool efficiency, the ease with which Geoffrey resumed the mantle of master of this great estate, Prudence was whisked on a whirlwind tour of the main rooms, told that MacLeod would return very soon with her new abigail, and fondly commanded to go upstairs and rest until dinner time.

She had no notion that she had been deserted until she made her way to the ground floor at six o'clock. Mr. Sidley was standing in the main hall, gazing as if frozen at a letter he held. Not until her second call did he look up, his expression so stunned that she knew. Her heart seemed to contract. She flew down the remaining steps. "What is it? Has my lord—"

"He has gone, miss," he said hoarsely. "He—left this . . ."

With trembling hands she took the folded sheet he held out, and broke the seal:

> Loveliest and dearest of all shipmates,
>
> I have sent for my godparent and very good friend, the Duke of Marbury. Likely he will arrive tomorrow, and in the event I should be unavoidably delayed, will know how to care for you and arrange your future.
>
> I pray that we will meet again, but in case that cannot be, the memory of your beauty, your courage, your uncomplaining endurance of your many hard knocks during our travels, will be cherished always, by—
>
> Yr. most humble admirer,
> Delavale

Cold and numb, she looked up in time to see the butler slipping another paper into his pocket. His reply to her question was evasive, and when with sudden ferocity she demanded to see it, he held it out wordlessly.

Vaguely, she was aware that his arm was about her; that he

was saying something in a very gentle voice. But the only words she could comprehend were those written on the parchment in the bold masculine hand. 'Last Will and Testament of Geoffrey John Montgomery, Baron Delavale.'

Having successfully duped Prudence, manoeuvred Stuart MacLeod out of the way, and lulled Cole into the belief he would not set forth so late in the day, Delavale, determined that no other should share his peril, rode steadily southwards. A brace of loaded pistols rested in his saddle holsters, and his long Andrea Ferrara, the favourite of his swords, was at his side.

He swung gradually to the east, as aware he was followed as though he could see the tall chestnut horse and the dark-haired man who had kept so carefully out of sight. Otton's refusal to speak out against him had been motivated, he knew very well, not by compassion but by greed. The mercenary had allowed one section of the cypher to slip through his hands and, unless Delavale misread his man, Otton had not the remotest intention of allowing Cunningham, or any other, to best him this time.

The sun was lowering in a blaze of crimson and gold when Delavale set his mare at a hump-backed bridge, spurred suddenly, and was down the other side and under the ancient structure in a flash. Scant moments later, hooves clattered above him. His lips curved to a grim smile as Otton rode down the far side, then set off at a gallop into the copse of birches ahead. Half an hour later, the sixth sense that had several times saved Delavale on the battlefield sent tiny electric fingers whispering down his spine. He slowed, heard following hoofbeats slow, and swore lustily.

Until long after the moon was up, he dodged and detoured and went in circles, but when he rode wearily into the yard of a small hedge tavern, he had no sooner been shown to a room than shouts in the yard announced a new arrival. A glance through the window revealed a tall chestnut horse and a man who staggered slightly as he dismounted. Delavale blistered the air with his reaction, and contemplated the advisability of leaving in the middle of the night. It was very likely, however, that the devious Otton had already greased someone in the fist to warn him of such a contingency. "Devil take him," muttered Delavale. "I shall have my sleep!" and he went to bed.

He was up and in the stables before dawn. The chestnut was gone, and a sleepy-eyed ostler told him the "other gent" had ridden out half an hour since. Fuming, Delavale mounted up.

And it began again. The diversions, the wide aimless detours. But Roland Otton, for all his determination, was scarcely recovered of his wound, and Delavale strove not for his own gain but for many lives. Thus it was that, after an almost ambling period during which his quarry was lost to view, Otton spurred upon hearing a suddenly accelerated pound of hooves. His chestnut burst from the stand of trees, and in the same second Otton was smashed from the saddle by an unseen and mighty hand.

With the wind knocked out of him, he lay sprawled for a minute or two, then groaned, and blinked at a pair of gleaming knee boots and a glittering blade that came from somewhere above to tickle his throat. He tried to focus his eyes and saw the blur of a much disliked face frowning down at him. "Damn you," he muttered. "You walked your hack . . . while you tied a rope across the lane . . . I collect."

Delavale smiled mirthlessly. "Tit for tat. And since you are at a disadvantage, you will tell me now, was Quentin Chandler mistreated in my home?"

Otton stared along the glitter of that long blade. "Let me sit up."

"Oh, I think not. This arrangement suits me nicely." The sword point nudged a little more firmly. "Was he?"

"He was—questioned."

"Elaborate, if you please."

Otton's lips tightened. The sword bit a trace more deeply and a small crimson stain appeared on the white cravat. "He was wounded, hauled to Highview, and was so unwise as to refuse to—er, cooperate."

Delavale cursed softly, and the sword bit deeper.

Otton's hands dug into the grass on each side of him. He gasped out, "Dammitall! The fortunes of war!"

"The fortunes of greed and savagery! But since you live by that credo, you'll not object do I claim my rights as winner of this joust."

There was grim loathing in the dark eyes above him, and as grim a purpose. Otton had long known just such a moment as this would sooner or later face him. No use, he thought, to whine now. His fingers tightened on the grass. He smiled crookedly. "If you put an end to me, Delavale, you may be at ease on one count—my family will thank you for it."

"And the world be freed of a womanizing, heartless rogue and murderer!"

Anger flashed in the black eyes. "Then, why hesitate, my lord Virtuous? Do your noble best for civilization—and be damned! Strike, man, and have done!"

Delavale drew back his steel. Otton tried to get to his knees to meet death, but he was too dizzied and sank down again. He made no sound, but his face was very white and streaked with sweat. Delavale hesitated. Whatever else, the soldier of fortune was no coward. There was no whimpering, no sobbing pleas for mercy. Braced on one elbow, Otton's black eyes met his own with a prideful defiance. Curiosity touched him. He asked, "Who are you? I mean—what is your real name?"

The thin lips twisted sardonically. "Roland Fairleigh Mathieson."

"Jupiter!" Delavale stared at him.

Otton said faintly, "*Noblesse oblige?* Are you truly Ligun Doone?"

Still stunned that this unprincipled mercenary was the scion of one of the finest families in the land, Delavale frowned. "What difference?"

"I'd like to know the worth of mine executioner . . ."

"Very well. I am. But—never try to prove it."

Otton's gaze sharpened.

Delavale stepped back and put up his sword. "I'm a fool and will no doubt regret this," he said, and went over to take up the reins of the big horse.

For the first time exhibiting panic, Otton cried, "No! Leave Rump. I—I beg you."

"I'm not that much of a fool," said Delavale, swinging into the saddle. "Besides, I need him to come up to my own mount."

Cursing him frenziedly, Otton struggled to stand.

Delavale reined around. "Rump?"

"Short for—Rumpelstiltskin."

With a curl of the lip, Delavale said, "Might have known. Gold is your god, isn't it, Otton?"

"Because he . . . stamps his feet, damn you!"

Delavale regarded him thoughtfully, then rode away.

Otton called with desperate pleading, "Let him go when you find your mare. I give you my solemn oath, I'll not follow."

"Hah!"

"Damn you! *Delavale!* God, if I but had my pistol! *Delavale!*" And in a croaking voice that was as if torn from him, "*Please*— I beg you!"

Delavale spurred and rode on. Glancing back after a moment or two, he saw Otton crawling after him, but then crumple and lie still. He drew rein, frowning at that limp, distant form. The man was a vulture. He had done his damnedest to seduce Penelope, had doubtless had a hand in tormenting poor Quentin, and had attempted his own murder with not a *soupçon* of conscience. Shrugging, Delavale rode on.

But when he came up with his mare, he turned the chestnut loose.

He was hot and tired and irked, but look as he might, he could see no sign of following riders, and at last he risked the long descent that led to the village—a busy place, for it was Market Day and the street was crowded. Wagons rumbled along, laden with fresh vegetables and dairy goods; sturdy yeomen drove promising livestock to be sold; housewives trudged along with baskets of jams and jellies; farmers drove their serviceable carts; and all was good-humoured noise and confusion.

Delavale became involved with a wagon full of crated chickens and racks of eggs. A goosegirl scolded when his mare trod too close to her flock, and he turned aside and rode to join a Sergeant of dragoons, mounted beside the road, who had been watching him narrowly.

"Jove," exclaimed Delavale with a rueful grin, "I see I chose the wrong day to ride over to Greater Shottup. One takes one's life in one's hands!"

It was unlikely, the Sergeant thought, that a guilty man would go out of his way to talk to a soldier. Therefore, he touched his brow respectfully, and said that some of these country folk were no respecters of Quality. "Which I can see as you is, sir," he added. "A fine piece o' horseflesh you got there."

Delavale agreeing with this observation, they entered into an involved and rather lengthy discussion of the merits of Arabians versus Thoroughbreds, this turning eventually to the reason for my lord Delavale having come to Greater Shottup. They parted amicably, the Sergeant directing his lordship to the ancient church and advising him that although Father Charles Albritton was a sterling young man, he was a foreigner from Little Snoring, t'other side of the New Forest, brought in temporary to substitute for the regular vicar, now indisposed.

Delavale thanked him and guided his mare through the sea of

humanity until he was safely clear of the marketplace and approaching the serenity of the church. He rode around to the side and dismounted where he could tether his horse in the shade of some trees. There was no sign of activity, nor of a leper's window. He wandered around to the front and from thence to the west side. The gardens had been sadly neglected, and a wooden archway heavily overgrown with climbing roses had sagged against a headstone. Making his way amongst the debris and around the drooping arch, he saw at last the ancient little door set in the wall at eye level so that the lepers could stand outside and watch the services. He sauntered over to investigate, then he turned and wandered about, apparently aimlessly, but his keen eyes were alert for possible watchers. Convinced at length that he was safe, he returned quickly, took the fatal piece of parchment from the cuff of his shirt, and laid it on the deep ledge just inside the leper's window.

He was closing that sad little door when he sensed rather than heard someone close behind him. His hand darted to his sword hilt. Half crouching, he whirled, his broad-bladed sword whipping out in a blur of steel. And in his heart was the aching awareness that in the moment of triumph he was lost, for steadily aimed in the hand of the man behind him was a long-barreled pistol.

Stuart MacLeod and Mistress Hetty Burnett reached Highview Manor just after dark. The big Scot's jubilance faded when he looked into the stricken eyes of Miss MacTavish. Sidley came up and murmured that the master had ridden out some four hours previously, and MacLeod's wrath was changed to dismay when he discovered that not only had he been quietly excluded from Delavale's hazardous mission but that Cole also had been given the slip.

Hetty knew nothing of what had brought this sudden sense of

disaster, but her kind heart was wrung by the tragedy in the lovely Scottish girl's blue eyes. She lost no time in mothering her new lady and doing all she might to soothe and bear her company. Prudence was pampered and cosseted and tucked into a vast and luxurious feather bed. Tearless, in a dull haze of misery, she lay staring into the darkness, convinced she would not be able to close her eyes, but just as dawn streaked the clouds with pale fingers, she fell gently asleep.

At eleven o'clock the groom returned from Dominer with word that his Grace the Duke was presently in Sussex, his exact whereabouts unknown. Prudence was not sorry. Much as she appreciated Geoffrey's efforts to provide her with respectability, she was in no mood for small talk with strangers. She occupied herself by wandering through the endless rooms of the mansion, picturing Geoffrey and his sister dwelling here, confronting a splendid portrait of him and having to run from it, so shattered she could not endure the house and fled into the grounds. Sometimes, during the less ghastly moments of their voyage aboard *The Maid o' Moidart,* he had spoken to her softly of his home. At the time, in her misery she had paid little heed to his words, but now they came back to her. Amiably accompanied by a spaniel named Flower, she sought out the old summer-house where Geoffrey and Penelope had been used to play crusades, or Roundheads and Royalists; and from there she found his most cherished secret hideaway in the wood, to which he had retreated as a very small boy when his beloved mama had been called from this life, and when other youthful sorrows had been too painful to be shared—even with Penelope.

The day dragged past, empty afternoon giving way to haunted evening and bedevilled night. Hetty stayed with her until she fell asleep in the chair and was packed off to bed, and Prudence was alone again, with her fear and her prayers.

Yet still, with another dawn there was no word: no sound of rapid hoofbeats, no cheery, laughing voice.

MacLeod was silent and sombre, but always nearby. Cole invented endless excuses to come up to the house. Sidley drifted about, never beyond call. And at last, Prudence gathered these faithful friends about her and they sat together in the gold saloon, and chatted of their ordeal shared, while the slow moments ticked away.

In the early afternoon she went outside. The skies were cloudy today, a rather chill wind stirring the trees and waking little waves on the river that wound in front of the great house.

Prudence drew her shawl closer about her and walked slowly. He had gone back to that place near Trowbridge. And he should have been home yesterday. Unless he had been seen and recognized and perhaps hounded far from his destination. He would try to get through, she knew that. No matter how deadly the risk to himself, he would try. Walking aimlessly, she found that she had been adopted by a bloodhound whose name was Grimy, and that Flower was also more or less with her. Grateful, she wondered what she would do if he was taken. If he was—the very thought made her knees quake—if he was condemned to death . . . dragged to the Tower . . . But it was really quite simple. Her life would end, for there would be no reason to go on living.

She had come, perhaps subconsciously she had meant to come, to his woodland hideaway—a small round glade where the light filtered gently through the branches, and a brook babbled and chuckled and spoke of the mysteries of life and love, for anyone with ears to hear and time to listen. She sat on the stump of a tree and wondered drearily where he was and what was happening to him. . . .

She could not have said how long it was before the dogs startled her by jerking up and racing off. Above Grimy's deep baying and Flower's frenzied yelps, Prudence thought to hear another voice. Her heart fluttering, she stood, not daring to move.

"The fly that sips treacle is lost in the sweets,
So he that tastes woman . . . woman . . . woman,
He that tastes woman—ruin meets!"

She was running long before the final word was sung in that pleasant baritone, the blessed tears coming at last, to stream down her cheeks.

He was striding down the slope, the dogs going mad as they sprang and raced around him. He stopped when he saw her and she stopped also and for an ecstatic suspended moment, they stood gazing at one another. Then, he said a firm, "Down!" The dogs dropped at once, and the pandemonium ceased.

Geoffrey held out his arms and, sobbing, Prudence flew into them, and he held her tight against his heart, his eyes closed, his cheek against her soft curls, while she clung to him in a silent rapture.

She was mildly surprised, a little while later, to find them sitting on the tree stump in the peaceful glade. This, of course, was after he *had* kissed her. Very thoroughly. Beginning with her tears, and proceeding to her brows, her cheeks, the end of her nose, and—at last—her lips.

With his arms tight around her, she sighed, and asked softly, "Is it done?"

"It is done."

"And you are free? No one follows? You are not suspect?"

"I'm free. But, dashitall, I damned near died of fright!"

Terrified anew, she pulled away and scanned his face and thus, viewing him clearly for the first time, saw that a stubble of beard darkened his chin and that his eyes were shadowed with fatigue. "What do you mean? My dear—you look—have you rid all night?"

"I was just putting the cypher in where it was to be left, and that silly fribble Charles Albritton came up behind me with a damned great pistol in his fist. I came near spitting the gudgeon, which might have been rather a nuisance, y'know, him being a priest."

Prudence gave a gasp. "Good heavens! But why had he the pistol?"

"Said he'd been expecting someone else to bring the cypher. Which he had, of course." He saw sorrow come into those great eyes, and went on quickly, "At all events, we'd a deal of business to do, which made me late, and then I must run into a great bother near Devizes with half the populace searching for some poor devil, which made me late. But—here I am."

There was more he might have told her, but if she knew he'd become involved in that same 'great bother' and that even now a fugitive was well away from the hue and cry thanks to his involvement, she would only fuss. And so he merely smiled at her.

"Then," she said, knowing him and therefore suspicious, "you *did* ride all night."

"Well, yes, as a matter of fact." A dance of mischief dawned in his tired eyes. "Tried to find your aunt's house. Well, never look so vexed, love. This is a bachelor establishment, you cannot stay here. Even was I to move out, people would be sure to think—"

She turned away and said quietly, "That I was your mistress. As Mr. Crisp did."

Bertram Crisp was a Marquis, and to hear him referred to as a 'mister' brought a chuckle to Delavale's lips.

Misinterpreting, Prudence's chin came up at once. She stood, turning her back on him. "It will not be necessary that I stay with my aunt, for I mean to return home."

"Don't be a widgeon," he said, coming up behind her to seize her shoulders and pull her against him. "I want my wife here—not four hundred miles away!"

Bliss possessed her. So he did mean marriage, after all. For a moment she had thought— But he had offered. More or less. She stepped away from him, and said demurely, "Was that a proposal, my lord?"

"Well, of course it was." He walked around to search her face rather uneasily. "What did you think? If you did but know how I have longed to tell you I wanted you to be my wife!"

"You had," she pointed out, with no indication of how her heart was singing, "many opportunities, sir, but said not one word."

"But, my darling girl, how could I? To risk your becoming attached to me when my future was so uncertain, would have been despicable."

It was very hard, but she meant to have the proper words, and so said, "You did not seem to count that risk when we were at Lakepoint."

She seemed aloof and cool. Beginning to really be afraid, he said, "No, but—I thought we were just enjoying a light flirtation, and—I thought I was— Well, I thought I'd not be pestering you for very long."

She suffered a sharp pang at this, but said resolutely, "And yet afterwards, in the cave, when you knew you were getting better, you said nothing."

"My God!" He took up her hand and held it tightly between both his own. "Prue, you cannot mean it! I had still to deliver the cypher. Anything might have gone wrong. Had you not been so ill on the ship, perhaps . . . but—"

Her head was bowed. Had his family given her a distaste of Highview? Did she suffer the same qualms as Elizabeth about being saddled with a title? "Prue?" he said anxiously. "Prue—dearest, most beloved, bravest of women. Will you not give me an answer?" Still, she said nothing. He put one slim finger beneath her chin and lifted her face, and its radiance pierced him. He whispered, "Prue, my little lass—I do so love you."

She had her words. "Oh . . . Geoffrey . . ." she said, and melted into his arms.

And, womanlike, when they had assured each other of their undying adoration, she told him that he must not feel obligated to wed her because they had travelled alone for such a long way, without a chaperone. "Not," she amended hurriedly, "unless you feel you could not live without me."

"Well, I do," he admitted, ceasing his depredations when she quieted his hand by holding it. "But—there is one thing . . ."

"What is it?" she asked, experiencing her own qualms.

"You know, light of my world, that I loved my papa very deeply, but I cannot like our firstborn to be named Hector."

Scandalized, Prudence gasped, "Geoffrey . . . Delavale!" and buried her hot face in his much violated cravat.

"Nor," he went on thoughtfully, "do I much care for the name James. And if, as I should very much like, we call him Stuart, why, there's Cole, you see. He would fairly die of jealousy."

Too shy to look at him, she murmured, "We could—could name him MacTavish, and everyone would call him Mac, which would please both Papa and the MacLeod."

"Famous!" He tilted up her face and said blandly, "And our second son can be called Hector." Adoring her for the deepening blush, he asked, his voice very tender, "And what do you have to say to that, shy eyes?"

Prudence risked a sparkling glance at him. "Oh, tol-lol," she said.